OUNTY L

THE VIOLINS OF AUTUMN

THE VIOLINS OF AUTUMN

Margaret Pemberton

This title first published in Great Britain 2006 by
SEVERN HOUSE PUBLISHERS LTD of
9–15 High Street, Sutton, Surrey SM1 1DF.
Originally published 1987 in Great Britain
under the title *Never Leave Me*.
This title first published in the USA 2006 by
SEVERN HOUSE PUBLISHERS INC of
595 Madison Avenue, New York, N.Y. 10022.

British Library Cataloguing in Publication Data

Pemberton, Margaret
    The violins of autumn
    1.   Guilt - Fiction
    2.   Love stories
    I.   Title
    823.9'14 [F]

    ISBN-13: 978-0-7278-6362-1
    ISBN-10: 0-7278-6362-2

Printed and bound in Great Britain by
MPG Books Ltd., Bodmin, Cornwall.

For Mike, as always.

THE VIOLINS OF AUTUMN

1

Spring had come early to Sainte-Marie-des-Ponts. The fierce Atlantic winds that whipped the cliff tops with such savagery a mere mile away skimmed the hollow of land in which the village sheltered.

Lisette de Valmy swung a woolen stockinged leg to the ground and, using the toe of her shoe, slowed her bicycle to a halt. Tubs of daffodils and crocuses flourished, the colors of those flowers vivid against the drab Norman stone of the slate roofed houses. The cheerful blossoms further inflamed Lisette's rage. Flowers represented normality, and normality was a thing of the past. She leaned her bicycle against the wall of the village café, thrust her hands deep into the pockets of her coat, and hurried into the building in search of Paul.

He wasn't there, nor were any of the other habitués of the café. Chairs were tipped inward against the tables, and the middle-aged proprietor, André Caldron, was desultorily polishing glasses, a wine-stained towel wrapped around his waist, his shirt sleeves rolled to the elbow.

"Where is everyone?" Lisette asked, her hands clenching until the knuckles showed white. Dear God. She had to talk to somebody. Her fury and revulsion had to have some outlet.

"Vierville," André replied tersely, putting down the glass he had been polishing and leaning across the bar toward her, his weight on his muscular arms. "The Boche rounded them all up at five this morning for work on the coastal defenses."

The delicate line of Lisette's jaw hardened. "Haven't they done enough at Vierville?" she demanded, her eyes sparkling

1

as she pulled a red beret from the back of her head, her smoke-dark hair falling free. "They've dug and tunneled and burrowed until there isn't a yard of beach that isn't mined."

"Now they are destroying the houses." André shrugged. "Not a thing fronting the sea is to remain standing."

"*Salauds!*" Lisette said expressively, and André grinned. The vocabulary of the eighteen-year-old daughter of the Comte and Comtesse de Valmy had been greatly enriched by the rigors of the Occupation.

"They'll be gone every day for a week, maybe two. If I were you, I'd stay away from the village until Paul sends you word that he needs you."

A small shiver ran down her spine. To be needed was to be asked by the village schoolmaster to take messages inland to Bayeux and Trévières—to pass through German patrols with information that, if found, would be her death warrant. She didn't know who else was in the Resistance in Sainte-Marie-des-Ponts. André, by the expression in his voice when he had spoken of Paul "needing" her, obviously suspected that she was a courier, but whether or not he was an active member of the village cell, she didn't know, nor did she want to know. The more she knew, the more she could tell the Germans if she were caught. It was better this way. Picking up the messages that Paul left for her, leaving them at prearranged tables in cafés in Bayeux and Trévières; not knowing whom they were for or who was to collect them.

"There's things happening here, too," André said, leaning closer to her, his voice dropping even though they were alone. "A large black, chauffeur-driven Horch with outriders swept through the village half an hour ago. My wife thinks it was Field Marshal Rommel on his way to Caen."

A scowl marred Lisette's lovely heart-shaped face. "It wasn't Rommel," she said bitterly, "and the car wasn't on its way to Caen."

André's heavy eyebrows rose.

"It was a Major Meyer and he was on his way to Valmy." The skin was taut across her cheekbones, and her eyes were overly bright.

André was very still, filled with sudden apprehension. "What did the major want with your father?"

"Hospitality," Lisette said, her nails digging into the wool of her beret.

2

André whistled through his teeth. Six months before, Hitler had appointed Field Marshal Rommel Inspector General of Defense in the west. Rommel's task: to render over eight hundred miles of coastline safe from invasion by the Allies. He had made La Roche-Guyon his headquarters, and the men of Normandy had been impressed into labor battalions, forced to work on erecting a giant steel and cement Atlantic wall, and to riddle the beaches with jagged triangles of steel, metal tipped stakes, and hundreds of mines.

The people of Sainte-Marie-des-Ponts had become accustomed to the presence of Germans—to Germans requisitioning farm produce, to the Gestapo and SS headquarters at Cherbourg and Caen. Now a high-ranking major had been thrust in their midst, the unwelcome guest of Comte de Valmy. Why? What new plans did the Nazis have for them?

"Have a cognac," André said, understanding all too well why Lisette was so pale.

She shook her head, lights dancing in the dark cloud of her hair as she turned to leave. "No thank you, André. If you should see Paul, tell him about the major."

"I will," André said, once more picking up a cloth and a glass. Beneath their beetling brows his eyes were thoughtful. Lisette would be in an ideal position to discover Major Meyer's reasons for taking up residence at Valmy, and pass the information on.

Lisette's hands were shaking as she wheeled her bicycle away from the wall and stepped on the pedals. Telling André about the German now living under her father's roof had done nothing to dissipate her rage. For the past four years they had been lucky. Her father had told her so many times. Nearly every house in the area had been billetted with Germans. The Lechevaliers in Vierville were allowed access only to a small part of their home; in Colleville, the Mercadors lived together in just one room while German staff officers slept in their bedrooms, relaxed in the drawing rooms, and forbade the Mercador children to play in their own garden. Valmy had been spared—until an hour ago.

Lisette crammed her beret once more onto the back of her head and began to cycle down the main street and out of the village. Every few yards she had to return a greeting as the women of Sainte-Marie-des-Ponts called out good-day to her;

3

they were going stoically about their daily chores—shopping, talking, doing their best to ignore the presence of the enemy in their streets.

Lisette returned their greetings grimly, wondering if the soldiers lounging at the street corners thought them as resigned and subservient as they seemed. If they did, they sadly underrated the tenaciousness of Norman hatred. Once the Allies invaded, everyone, from elderly Madame Pichon, who had delivered every child in the village for the past thirty years, to the eleven- and twelve-year-olds in Paul's classroom, would rise up against them.

Sentries in camouflage cloaks barred the exit from the village, and she slowed down, slipping off the saddle and holding the bicycle steady with one hand as she showed her identity card with the other. The soldier flicked it against his thumbnail without looking at it. He knew damn well who she was and was determined to know her better. The village girls were pretty, but there was something special about Lisette de Valmy. Even in coarse stockings she exuded class and breeding, and he found her hauteur deeply exciting. She was looking at him now, her chin high, her gaze contemptuous, for all the world as if she were royalty and he the scum of the earth.

"Would you like a cigarette?" he asked, moving forward and standing very close to her, her identity card still in his hand.

Lisette's hands tightened fractionally on the handlebars of her bicycle, her only reply the scorching expression in her eyes. They were beautiful eyes, tip tilted and thick lashed, the color of smoked quartz. Heat flared through his groin.. She was the kind of French girl men dreamed of, the kind German generals sported on their arm in Paris. Her silk-dark hair fell in a long, smooth wave to her shoulders, pushed away from her face on one side with a tortoiseshell comb, crowned on the other by a provocatively tilted scarlet beret.

The soldier grinned. "Come on," he said in his execrable French. "Be friendly."

Lisette's voice dripped ice. "I would rather be dead," she said, her eyes feral, "than be friends with a German."

Behind him his companion laughed and the sentry's smile vanished. Who the hell did she think she was, speaking to him

4

as if he were a peasant? Bloody French with their airs and graces. Anyone would think that *they* were the victors. "*Weggehen*," he snarled viciously, thrusting her card back at her. There would be another day—a day when his staff officer would not be so particular about the treatment meted out to the local landowning family. Then he would see if she meant what she said about preferring to be dead.

Lisette, dismissing him as below contempt, cycled over one of the low stone bridges that gave the village its name, and then on and up through high-hedged lanes and beech woods to Valmy.

She had been having breakfast with her father when the scout car had sped up Valmy's gravel drive, scattering stones and skidding to a halt before the entrance. Marie, their only remaining maid, had nervously opened the doors to the two occupants of the car and ushered them into the breakfast room. Lisette had risen to her feet behind her father, her table napkin still in her hand, her throat tight as one of the officers removed his peaked combat cap and tucked it beneath his arm, saying coolly, "From ten o'clock this morning, Valmy will be at the disposal of Major Meyer. I trust the major's presence here will not be inconveniencing, Monsieur le Comte?"

The tendons in her father's neck had tightened as he had said, "No, Lieutenant. Will Major Meyer be accompanied by his own household staff?"

The lieutenant's eyes skimmed the silver on the breakfast table, the sixteenth-century tapestries adorning the walls, the faded colors of the Aubusson carpet. The major was going to have a very comfortable billet. "You have a cook?" he asked peremptorily.

"No." When the Germans had first invaded Normandy, thousands of men and women from the towns and villages had been herded away as slave labor, and their cook and her husband had been among those who had disappeared and had not been heard of again. Lisette saw the tendons in her father's neck flex once again. "My wife does the cooking now."

"Then she can cook for Major Meyer as well." The lieutenant's pale blue eyes registered the exquisite lace tablecloth, the embroidered crest on the comte's table napkin. He knew exactly what kind of Frenchwoman the comtesse would be: freezingly elegant, possessing the effortless chic that

5

made German women seem so gauche by comparison. "And she can do his washing," he added, seeing with satisfaction a dull red stain color the comte's face and neck. *Verdamt Gott!* If he were being posted here, she would do far more than his washing!

His eyes flicked insolently from the comte to the young girl standing a foot or so behind him. She was eighteen, possibly nineteen, with an air of fragility that begged to be broken. Glossy dark hair fell to her shoulders, dipping provocatively forward toward high, perfect cheekbones. Her mouth was generous, a faint downward curve at the corners giving it a look of vulnerability and sensuality. Her jaw line was pure, and there was a tantalizing hint of willfulness about the chin. His gaze moved unhurriedly downward, noting the full, high breasts, the narrow waist, and the arousing curve of her hips beneath the serviceable tweed of her skirt. He felt his sex stir. Major Dieter Meyer would not have far to look for relaxation in his new posting.

Reluctantly, he clicked his heels, and replaced his cap. "Good-bye, Monsieur le Comte," he said smoothly, aware that the girl was looking at him with undisguised loathing and uncaring of the fact. He found it far more arousing then servile submission.

When the doors had closed behind them, Lisette asked in a strangled voice, "Couldn't we have refused? Couldn't you have protested?"

Her father's long, thin face was somber. "It would have been useless. Major Meyer will just have to be endured, Lisette. There is no other way."

She swung away from him quickly, loving him too much to want him to see the disappointment in her eyes. There *were* other ways: Paul Gilles's way. Occupation did not have to mean capitulation. But her father thought the risks too great. He had seen what had happened to the innocent when the Germans had discovered members of the Resistance in their midst, and he had no desire to see women and children led away and shot because he, Henri de Valmy, had tried to be a hero.

His family history went back over six hundred years. A de Valmy had been in Reims cathedral when Charles VII had been crowned. De Valmys had fought in the Hundred Years War; English knights under Henry V had deluged the walls of

6

the early castle with arrows from their longbows. The exuberant, flamboyant château that a de Valmy, influenced by the architecture of the Italian Renaissance, had built in the fifteen hundreds had withstood onslaught time and time again. The Nazis were only the last in a long line of marauders, and they, too, one day would be no more, he told himself. All that was needed for Valmy's survival was endurance. And patience.

Lisette skidded to a halt as the woods petered out and Valmy stood before her—its long, elegant windows catching the sunlight. Her father was wrong. It wasn't enough simply to sit back and wait. The Germans had to be fought, and she would fight them in any way she could. The driveway, flanked by linden trees, terminated in a gravel sweep before huge oak double doors, and a large, sleek black Horch was parked in front of them. Bile rose in her throat. He had come. Even now he was sitting in one of Valmy's exquisitely proportioned rooms, fouling it with his presence.

Savagely, she remounted her bicycle, swinging it away from Valmy and out toward the coast. The cliff top was off limits now, girdled with barbed wire, defiled by pillboxes and monstrous bunkers. She didn't care. She needed solitude, and ever since she had been a child, the long beach and the windswept cliffs had afforded it.

She bumped the bicycle off the path and onto rough ground thick with marram grass. The sea wind tugged at her hair, whipping it across her face, stinging her cheeks. A little over a hundred yards away, a pillbox squatted, ugly and pale. A group of soldiers huddled outside it, their backs to the wind. If they saw her, she would be forced to halt. The coast had been out of bounds for over two years. Only when the villagers were rounded up to help with the building of the defenses were they allowed access. Lisette continued to cycle defiantly. They were French cliffs, goddamn it, French beaches. If she wanted to go on them, she would. Her defiance was defeated by the six-foot-high coils of barbed wire that stretched away on either side as far as she could see. With an unladylike epithet, she ground to a halt, flinging her bicycle onto the grass and sitting down beside it, hugging her knees.

Beyond the barbed wire, the mined and despoiled land rose, its undulations culminating in a lip of chalk from which the cliffs fell steeply to the sea. Far away to the left were the silver flanks of Pointe du Hoc as it thrust its needlelike rocks out into the gray waters of the Channel and beyond, unseen, the wide estuary of the Vire. To the right, the coast curved gently around to Vierville, to St. Clair and Ste. Honourine. Few people now lived in the hamlets and villages strung out along the coast. The Germans had moved them away, ordering them from their homes as they turned the western seaboard of France into a mighty defensive wall.

Lisette stared ferociously at the barbed wire and the giant steel jaws embedded along the beach and primed with mines. Rommel was wasting his time. If the Allies invaded, they would not do so in Normandy but across the narrow neck of the Channel between Dover and Calais. Her father had carefully explained it all to her, showing on a map how easy it would be then for the Allies to push through northern France into the heart of the Ruhr.

Her eyes clouded. Her father wanted the Germans defeated as passionately as she, yet he would be appalled if he knew of her involvement with the Resistance. Screaming raucously, a seabird wheeled over her head. She watched it bleakly. If he knew of her activities, he would forbid her to leave the château. As it was, she was free to come and go as she pleased, and the Germans rarely hindered her. She was Lisette de Valmy, daughter of the local landowner, and a regular visitor to the sick and needy in Sainte-Marie-des-Ponts and the neighboring villages. Her bicycle was a regular sight along the lanes and aroused little comment.

Her hands tightened around her knees. She was lucky. The life expectancy of a courier was not much more than six months, and she had been active for eight. Eight long months of deceiving the person she loved most in the world. She sighed, hating the feeling of isolation that it gave, knowing that there was no alternative.

Despite the sunlight, the February wind was raw. Angry caps of surf beat at the cliff face, eroding it as they had done for centuries. Reluctantly, Lisette rose to her feet, her fingers stinging with cold as she gripped the handlebars of her bicycle. For the first time in her life, she did not want to return home.

Valmy lay between the cliff top and the woods, a small, turretted château of gray stone with a slate roof, a tower at its north side, and gardens that in summer were awash with roses. Perfect and exquisite, the Germans had considered it too small to serve as headquarters for the local garrison. That doubtful privilege had fallen to the Lechevaliers with their big, ugly manor house on the outskirts of Vierville.

She wheeled her bicycle over the large tufts of grass and onto the narrow road. The soldiers were still outside the pillbox, hunkered down as if they were playing cards. She looked away from them contemptuously. She loathed them. They made her flesh crawl. And now she would be in day-to-day contact with one of them: a strutting, swaggering, heel-clicking major. Hatred coursed through her veins, warming her against the chill wind. She would not speak to him and she would not look at him. In no way would she acknowledge his presence in her home.

She stopped pedaling and let the bicycle coast down the narrow road. Beech woods shelved away on her right hand side, and between the budding branches she could see the tapering spire of Sainte-Marie-des-Ponts's tiny church and the muted gray of village roofs. Since the days of the Conqueror, the village had nestled in its sheltered hollow behind the high bluff of the cliffs, overlooked and protected by Valmy. Now Valmy could protect it no longer. The enemy were not only at the gates, they were in residence.

Her mother was in the front salon, sitting at her delicately carved desk writing a letter. She raised her head when Lisette entered the room, her fine-boned face taut with strain.

"Have you met him, Maman?" Lisette asked, her heart twisting at the sight of her mother's pale face.

"Yes." Her mother put down her pen, and Lisette walked across to the fireplace where logs burned in a stone grate. For several moments neither of them spoke. Lisette rested her arm along the marble mantlepiece, staring down into the flames. Already the atmosphere at Valmy had changed. It was as if a cold wind had swept through the rooms, penetrating even the walls.

Her mother abandoned her letter. It was not important and her head ached. She rose to her feet—a tall, elegant woman with a long, straight back and narrow hips. Her beauty was bone deep. It was in the shape of her head and temples and the thin-bridged, faintly aquiline nose, but her silvered hair and cool gray eyes held none of Lisette's vibrancy. She sat down on one of the deep, chintz-covered armchairs near the fireplace, her fine-boned hands folded lightly in her lap. "He's quite young," she said unemotionally.

Lisette shrugged. She didn't care whether he was young or old. It made no difference to the fact that he existed and was an invader. The logs flared and crackled.

"What rooms have you given him?"

"Papa's rooms."

Lisette's head shot upward, her eyes revealing the shock she felt.

"Your father thought them the most suitable," her mother said, an underlying tremor in her voice.

Lisette's hand clenched on the marble. Her mother rarely gave way to emotion. Self-control was as important to her as good manners. That her cool facade showed signs of crumbling indicated how deep her detestation had been at removing her husband's clothes and possessions from the suite of rooms that had been his and his father's before him, and preparing them for Major Meyer.

"God, how I wish the Allies would come!" Lisette said passionately, kicking at one of the logs with the toe of her shoe, sending sparks shooting up the chimney.

Her mother gave a quick, darting look toward the door. "Be careful, *chérie!* It is no longer safe to say such things!"

At the throb of panic in her mother's voice, Lisette was filled with remorse. She was making things worse for her, not better. She moved across to her, dropping to her knees at the side of her chair, taking hold of her hands.

"I'm sorry, Maman. I'll try to curb my tongue, but it's hard. I have so much hatred in me that I can hardly breathe."

The comtesse looked at her sadly. Her daughter was young, beautiful, well bred. She should have been enjoying life: attending parties and dances, visiting Paris and the Riviera, receiving the attention of eligible young men. It should have been love that was catching at her heart, not hate. She sighed, wondering how many more years of their lives the war would eat into—years that, for Lisette, could never be recaptured. "Perhaps he will not be with us for long," she said, but her voice held little conviction.

Lisette stared into the fire, her eyes thoughtful. "I wonder why he is here," she said slowly. "I wonder what is so special about him."

Her mother shrugged a slender shoulder. "He is a German. What more do we need to know?"

Lisette did not answer. Her reply would have caused distress. She knew that some people would like very much to know why Major Meyer had been posted to Valmy—people like Paul Gilles and his friends, people like herself. It was yet another occasion when her thoughts could not be shared. "I'll make some tea," she said, rising to her feet and wondering how long it would be before she could arrange a meeting with Paul. She knew already what he would wish her to do.

Dinner that evening was unusually quiet. Neither of her parents seemed disposed to talk. It was as if the unseen presence of Major Meyer was weighing tangibly on them. Marie served them *omelette aux fines herbes,* her heavy face somber, her mouth pulled into a disapproving line as she set the plates on the table. Henri de Valmy saw her expression and suppressed a sigh of irritation. She had been a young girl in his father's employ when he had been born. She had picked him up when he had fallen, smacked him when necessary, wiped his tears, cuddled and cajoled him, and later, as he grew older, treated him with deferential respect. She thought him omnipotent and no doubt believed that had he wished to do so, he could have closed his doors single-handedly against not only Major Meyer but the entire might of the Wehrmacht.

He poured himself a glass of wine, glad that his cellars were still full. There was still a lot for them to be grateful for, he reminded himself. Normandy was not suffering from the severe food shortages that were afflicting the rest of France. Butter, cheese, and eggs continued to be plentiful. Even after feeding the Germans, there were enough chickens for the pot, enough milk and cream. His fingers tightened around the stem of his glass. He had not yet suffered in the war and guilt surged through him. He had no sons facing death fighting with the Free French. He himself had not fought, had not been injured. He had simply remained, as a de Valmy had always remained, on his land.

He pushed his plate away, his omelette scarcely touched. It could hardly be called his land any more, when it was under the heel of the Germans. His helplessness infuriated him, and

11

there was no way that he could give vent to his frustration. He rose savagely, and ignoring the startled looks of his wife and daughter, abruptly excused himself. Lisette anxiously jumped up, intending to follow him, but her mother laid a cool, restraining hand on her arm.

"No, *chérie*. He needs to be alone. Leave him for a little while."

The door closed sharply behind him, and his footsteps could be heard crossing the hall in the direction of the library. Mother and daughter looked at each other for a moment and then, unhappily, continued with their meal.

Later, as they sat together in the front salon, Lisette wondered again why Major Meyer had been posted to Valmy. Perhaps he had been given a special assignment. André had said that the major's Horch had been accompanied by outriders. Surely that indicated he was a man of importance. The fire spat and crackled, the scent of pine logs filling the high-ceilinged room. Her mother's head was bent low over her embroidery, a slight frown puckering her usually smooth forehead. Lisette tried to return her attention to the book she had been reading, and failed. The Allies were desperate for information regarding the coastal defenses. If the defenses were the reason for Major Meyer's presence . . . Her book slid to her knees. Major Meyer was occupying her father's rooms: his bedroom, his study.

Sharp footsteps rang out distantly on the black and white flagstones of the medieval hall—brisk, decisive footsteps that she had never heard before. Her mother's hand paused—the needle held high over her work—her eyes flying to the door. There was a long, ominous silence; then the heavy outer door opened and slammed shut. Seconds later the Horch's engine revved into life.

Her mother's relief that the major had not walked in on them was evident. Lisette was too busy thinking to share that relief. For the moment, Major Meyer was alone at Valmy. But for how long? Surely he would need a batman, an aide. His rooms might never again be empty. She might never again have such an easy chance.

"I think I'll go to bed early, Maman," she said, rising to her feet. Her gentian-hued sweater and deeper toned skirt emphasized the color of her eyes and the blue-black sheen of her hair. She kissed her mother lightly on the cheek, wishing she could comfort her, then walked quickly from the room. If she hesitated, she was lost. He had only arrived this morning. If she were discovered, she could always say it was a mistake . . . that she had expected to find her father in his study.

The library door was closed, her father obviously still brooding over the day's events. There was no sound from the dining room or the kitchen. Marie retired early. She would be in bed by now, her arthritic toes on a comforting hot bottle. The stone stairs wound upward. An oil lamp had been placed on the sill of one of the arched windows set deep into the wall, and it gave out a soft pool of light. She hurried past it and on up to the next floor that housed her father's suite of rooms. She hesitated outside the bedroom door, then walked on. She had to be quick, and there was more likelihood of papers being on the study desk than on a yet unused bedside table.

She paused outside the study door. It would be locked— surely it would be locked. Scarcely daring to breathe, she closed her hands around the doorknob and turned and pushed. The door opened easily. Unhesitatingly, she stepped inside and walked quickly across the moonlit room to her father's Biedermeier desk. It looked abnormally neat: her father's habit was to leave letters and bills scattered at random, and the precisely arranged blotter and ink stand were clear indications that the desk was no longer his. The wide, shallow drawers contained only stationery. Major Meyer had clearly not yet settled in. There was a connecting door between the study and the bedroom. Her search so far had taken only a minute, probably less. She still had plenty of time.

The blue bedroom was silvered by the moonlight. It fell palely on the Rembrandt etching above her father's bed. Her stomach muscles tightened. The etching needed removing before the German cast covetous eyes on it. As she neared the bed, she saw that very few possessions had been scattered around to proclaim ownership. There was a gold cigarette case and an expensive looking lighter on the bedside table, and she saw with curiosity that they were both monogrammed, the interlinking initials worn smooth with age and constant handling. Hurriedly she opened the bedside drawer. There was a slim volume of poetry, a novel by Zola, and a diary. She riffled through the diary, wondering whether she should take it and knowing that she dare not. What she was looking for were official papers—something with recognizable place names; something that she could memorize. A suitcase stood at the foot of the bed, not yet unpacked. She bent down beside it, trying to open the catch, and then she froze. The study door to the corridor had opened. Her heart began to slam against her breastbone in thick, heavy strokes. Perhaps it was Marie coming in to turn down the major's bed. Perhaps it was her mother, checking that he had all that he required, or her father . . .

Her nails dug deep into her palms. There had been no knock at the door. Only one person could have entered her father's study, and that was its present occupant, Major Meyer. She stood up, her pulse pounding, backing away to the door that led into the corridor. It was seven or eight yards away. The connecting door was open, and she saw his shadow as he crossed to the desk—heard the rasp of the drawer opening. She took another step backward, and another. She had to keep her nerve. If she turned and ran, she would be heard. She had to open the door slowly, carefully. She took another step and stumbled against a bedroom chair. Her hand flew out to steady herself, her mouth rounding in a gasp of alarm.

It took Dieter Meyer just two strides to reach the connecting doorway and punch on the light. His eyes flashed to her empty hands, to the still closed door behind her, and then he leaned nonchalantly against the wall, arms folded, eyes narrowed. "Just what the hell," he asked in perfect French, "do you think you are doing?"

Her hand tightened on the back of the chair. "I—Supper," she said, her breath coming in harsh gasps. "I wanted to know if you wished to have supper."

He was not at all what she had expected. There was no monocle, no steel-gray hair. His masculinity came at her in waves. The jacket of his field uniform was open at the neck, cut perfectly across broad shoulders, and the Knights Cross of the Iron Cross decorated his breast. She didn't move for fear he would seize her. She knew that the ease of his stance was deceptive. He had entered the room with all the speed of a natural-born predator.

"You're a liar," he said smoothly.

14

His hair was blond, cropped short, as thick and coarse as the coat of a dog. His face was clean cut, hard boned; the jaw line strong, the mouth finely chiselled—sensitive as well as sensual: the face of a man who read Zola. She thrust the thought away. He was a German. She didn't care what he read. Her initial shock was over. She was in command of herself again.

"Yes," she said, with a slight Gallic shrug. "I am. I came into my father's suite because I was curious."

At her insolence, a flicker of admiration flashed in his eyes and was immediately suppressed. "These rooms are no longer your father's," he said, his voice snaking across her nerve ends like a whip. "If I find you in, or near them again, I will have you arrested. Is that understood?"

The menace in his voice was naked and a frisson of fear ran down her spine. He was not a man to make idle threats. She backed instinctively away from him toward the door.

"I understand you perfectly," she said tightly, her hands closing around the doorknob, the vast, silk-draped bed yawning between them. "Good night, Major Meyer."

His brow quirked, and she was immediately furious with herself. What deep-seated code of good manners had prompted her to say good night to him? Cheeks burning, she spun on her heel, slamming the door behind her, wishing him in hell.

She had behaved foolishly and without thought. Paul would have urged her to be more careful. It would be twice as hard now to slip into his room in the future. He hadn't believed her when she had said she had entered them out of curiosity. He had known what she had been trying to do, and he had also known that she had failed. She shivered as she hurried toward her own room. What would he have done if he had walked in on her holding his diary? Would he have sent her to Gestapo headquarters in Caen? Would she have thrown her life away on an impulsive and ill-thought-out plan of action? For the first time, she realized how much she had risked and how thoughtlessly. She entered her own room and sat down on her bed, hugging her arms around her. The next time she would be far more careful . . . and successful.

She saw him again in the morning. He was in the hall as she descended the stairs, a field gray greatcoat over his uniform, his cap under his arm as he drew on gauntleted gloves. Her eyes coldly met his. She wasn't going to fall into the trap of good manners again.

"Good morning, Mademoiselle de Valmy," he said, his eyebrow arching, as if he knew of her intention and it was amusing him to defeat it.

Her lips tightened, and she gave him the merest inclination of her head, sweeping past him into the breakfast room on a tide of anger.

He was mocking her! She had heard it in the lazy tone of his voice, seen it in the gleam of his eyes before she had swiftly turned her head away. When she seated herself at the breakfast table, she found to her fury that her hands were trembling. She clasped them together tightly. She had no intention of becoming a target for his sadistic amusement. No doubt he thought she had spent the whole night in fear of what her parents would say when they discovered she had entered his rooms. Well, she hadn't. She had slept soundly, regretting only her clumsiness.

From the high-arched windows, she could see the chauffeur-driven Horch sweep round the circle of lawn fronting the château and cruise down the drive at high speed. Her eyes narrowed. Hitler's glamour soldier had neither impressed nor intimidated her; he had only strengthened her determination to be of far greater service to the Resistance.

Her father's face was lined and drawn as he joined her at the table. For a moment she thought that Major Meyer had already spoken to him. Then he smiled, saying with false cheerfulness, "Our guest is at least civil."

"Only on the surface," Lisette retorted tartly, remembering the coldness of his eyes when he had threatened her with arrest.

Her father helped himself to a croissant. "He's highly decorated. The Knights Cross of the Iron Cross isn't awarded easily."

"For goodness sake, Papa! You sound as if you admire him!"

"I don't," her father said in a pacifying tone. "I detest everything he stands for. I'm simply trying to find a way to tolerate him."

Lisette toyed with the knife on her plate. She had to tell

him. If she didn't, Major Meyer would have a sizable advantage over her. She put down her knife and said carefully, "I did something stupid last night, Papa. I went into Major Meyer's rooms when he left the house."

Every vestige of color left her father's face. "You did *what?*" He pushed his chair away from the table, looking at her as if she had taken leave of her senses. "Don't you realize that man could have us all turned out of Valmy? Don't you realize that he could have you *shot* if he ever found out?"

"He did find out, Papa," Lisette said, miserable at the distress that she was causing him. "He came into the room while I was still there."

"Dear God," her father murmured, rising to his feet, his face gray.

She moved quickly, rounding the table and hugging him tightly. "I'm sorry, Papa. Sorry that I got caught."

"But not sorry that you did it?" her father said, a curious tone in his voice. His hands tightened on her shoulders. "What did Meyer say to you?"

"That I must not go near his rooms again."

"And you won't." His voice was tight. "What were you hoping to find, Lisette?"

She sat down again slowly. "I don't know. Maps. Papers. Something to indicate why he has been stationed here."

Her father sat opposite her, his expression grim. "And what would you have done with the information?"

The room was very quiet. She could hear a clock ticking and the distant sound of Marie moving about in the kitchen. "I would have told . . . a friend who would have been interested."

"Paul Gilles?" he asked quietly.

The pupils of her eyes dilated with shock. He grasped her hand tightly. "I'm not a fool, Lisette. I know what goes on in my own village. I know who the collaborators are; I know who the members of the Resistance are."

"Then why don't you *help?*" she asked fiercely. "The Allies may not invade in the Pas de Calais. They may invade here. And if they do, they will need every last bit of information about the coastal defenses, about troop movements."

"If such information is at Valmy, then *I* will find it," her father said softly. "Not you, Lisette. Is that understood?"

17

Her eyes were suspiciously bright. "Yes, Papa," she said, feeling the burden of secrecy that she had lived with for so long lift from her shoulders. "But you cannot meet Paul as inconspicuously as I can. You must let me continue doing the things that I *can* do."

"And you must promise me never to cross Major Meyer's path again."

Their eyes met and her throat tightened. There were no more unseen barriers between them.

"I promise, Papa," she said, not realizing how vain a promise it would prove to be.

2

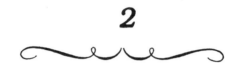

A week later, Field Marshal Erwin Rommel descended on Valmy, his large black Horch convertible flanked by a motorcycle escort, his aides' cars in his wake. There were no preliminary civilities as he entered the château. He marched across the flagstoned hall, a short, stocky figure in a heavy greatcoat, his silver-topped marshal's baton under his arm.

"Let's get to work, Meyer," he said impatiently, pulling off his gauntlets and slapping them against his palm. "We have only one real enemy, and that is time."

"Yes, Herr Feldmarschall," Dieter said respectfully, clicking his heels and leading the way into Valmy's grand dining room.

The maps were spread out on the twenty-foot table. Drinks had been set out on a handsome Louis XV chest, but Rommel ignored them. He had no time for fripperies. He strode straight to the table and stared grimly down at the maps.

"Well, Meyer, what do you think?" He personally had asked for Dieter Meyer's transfer to Normandy. He knew the family, knew the man. Dieter was the kind of officer he liked—hardheaded with intellect and imagination as well as courage.

"The war will be won or lost on the beaches, Sir," Dieter said bluntly. "We'll have only one chance to stop the enemy and that's while he's in the water . . . weighed down by equipment and struggling to get ashore. Our main line of resistance must be on the coast. There's only one way to smash such an attack if it comes and that is by meeting it head on."

Rommel growled in agreement "And do you think this is where an attack will come, Meyer?"

"Reports from captured Resistance leaders indicate it is."

"And the nightly air attacks on the Pas de Calais?"

"A bluff," Dieter said with cool certainty. "The Allies are trying to draw our attention from the real target."

Rommel nodded. It was a strategy he would have used himself. Get the enemy to deploy their strength on a false target, leaving the real target lightly protected.

Dieter saw the lines of strain on his commander-in-chief's face and knew the reasons for them. No matter what was said publicly, the Third Reich was in deep trouble. Thousands of Allied bombers were pounding Germany. Russia's massive forces had driven into Poland. Allied troops were at the gates of Rome. Everywhere the great armies of the Wehrmacht were being driven back and destroyed. Germany was not yet beaten, but an Allied invasion would be decisive.

It was here on the coast that the future of Germany would be decided. The high command thought that the attack would come at the Pas de Calais, but Dieter had that gut feeling they were wrong. To outwit the Allies, it was necessary to out-think them. And in attempting to do so, he had become more and more sure that the attack would not be in the obvious place—not at the narrow crossing being bombed with such zest, but on the vast, open beaches of Normandy.

Rommel swept his baton from the Scheldt in the Netherlands down across Normandy to the north front of Brittany. The possible invasion front was vast, and all of it had to be protected. He slammed his baton into the palm of his hand and began to stride the length of the room. "You've been here four days, Meyer. You've inspected the coast. What more can be done to defend it?"

"The low level of the land and the Vire estuary can be

19

more fully exploited," Dieter replied unhesitatingly. "More areas can be flooded. That will make it impossible for parachutists or glider-borne infantry to land. The open fields inland can be riddled with booby-trapped stakes and trip wires. That should give them a bloody enough welcome."

Rommel nodded. He hadn't underestimated his young officer. He continued to pace the beautiful inlaid floor. "See to it, Meyer," he said. "And see that every bluff and gully leading from the beaches is mined—every pathway, however obscure. We must leave nothing to chance." He clapped Dieter's shoulder. "The future of Germany is in our hands," he said gravely. "We must not let her down."

He swept from the château with the same speed and lack of fuss with which he had entered. His handsome face somber, Dieter watched the Horch skim down the linden-flanked drive. Their intelligence services had not been able to discover the Allies' plans. Yet Resistance leaders would have to be alerted in order to coordinate the attack. If it was to be in Normandy, the local underground leaders would be the first to know. His mouth tightened. That meant he would have to liaise with the Gestapo at Caen and Bayeux.

He wheeled on his heel, gravel scattering as he marched back into the château. His was an old German family that could trace its name back for hundreds of years in the *Almanach de Gotha*. His father had been a soldier, and his grandfather a soldier before him. They were members of the officer caste who hated the Nazis, and when it came to the Gestapo, Dieter shared their contempt. He wanted to have as little truck as possible with his country's bully boys.

She was walking toward the foot of the main staircase when he entered the hall. Her hair was windblown, soft dark tendrils brushing against her cheeks; she was wearing brown slacks and a cashmere sweater that had seen better days, and there was mud on the low heels of her shoes. She kept her bicycle in one of the deserted stables at the rear of the château, and he judged that she had just returned from one of her frequent trips to Sainte-Marie-des-Ponts. Her eyes, large and dark in the pale perfection of her face, met his coolly, and an impulse of sensuality went up like a flare inside him.

He wondered what the devil it was about her that he found so arousing. He was thirty-two, and his taste had never run to virgins. Before the war, his social circle had been high and fast-moving; the women he took to bed were glamorous sophisticates. Innocence had never held any charms for him. Yet ever since entering Valmy, he had been electrifyingly aware of the comte's young daughter.

The blaze of defiance with which she had faced him in her father's rooms had sexually disturbed him. He had never seen eyes so dark and brilliant, lashes so long and curling. There was a brightness to her, a vividness, that he found intensely arousing. It was as if she were lit by an inner flame, and he found his gaze being drawn to her time and time again. She was very French—carelessly elegant. Even in the crumpled slacks and old sweater, there was an air of chic about her—a style that had nothing to do with what she wore and everything to do with the way she wore it.

She had paused, one foot on the bottom stair, the thrust of her hip and the long line of her leg unknowingly provocative, her shining black hair held away from her face with two heavy tortoiseshell combs, her violet-blue eyes hostile.

He barely glanced at her, striding across the hall and entering the grand dining room with its array of maps. There were enough willing Frenchwomen without deflowering the daughter of his reluctant host. He gazed down at the maps, penciling in large areas, a deep frown furrowing his brow. More land east of the Vire could be flooded, and more guns placed on the cliffs, their barrels aimed, not toward the sea but directly down at the beaches so that they could fire at point blank range along the lines of assaulting troops. His pencil faltered, her face dancing insidiously in his mind. Her mouth was full and soft, like the petals of a rose. He wondered what it would be like to kiss her, then cursed with annoyance. Damn the girl. He had other, far more important things to think about. He renewed his concentration—studying the maps of the coastline, identifying areas of weakness—determined that if the Allies invaded, they would be thrust back into the sea.

Lisette ran up the stairs to her room, a small pulse pounding in her throat, the breath tight in her chest. His presence filled the château. It was no longer their home, but his. He moved through the rooms with utter assurance, ordering locks to be fitted on the double doors leading to the grand dining room, requisitioning yet another room that overlooked the Channel, curtly civil, always menacing.

She closed her bedroom door behind her, walking across to the window and staring out over the windswept headland to the sea. Paul was still working on the repairs to the defenses at Vierville, no doubt doing so on Major Meyer's orders. The aides had come to Valmy as she had known they would. The cobblestoned courtyard at the rear of the château was rarely empty of staff cars and motorcycles, and the old servants' quarters around the courtyard now housed a score of soldiers.

She leaned her face against the cool windowpane. Rommel's sweeping visit to Valmy had confirmed her suspicions that Major Meyer's task was to oversee the coastal defenses . . . which meant the German high command was increasingly suspicious that an attack by the Allies would be directed against Normandy. She drummed her fingernails against the glass in frustration. It was surely the kind of news that London would be interested in, yet without Paul, she had no way of passing along the information. For her own safety and the safety of others, she did not know who Paul's contact was. It was the way the Resistance survived and flourished: secrecy was its lifeblood. Even the leaders rarely knew one another except by code names, and never did one group know what another was doing. If betrayal came, it could not spread. Restlessly, she turned away from the window. An invasion was only rumor, but it was one the Germans believed. If it were true, it would be vital that they have no knowledge of where and when the attack would take place. Prior knowledge would doom it to disaster. And in Valmy, on the grand dining room table, might be the very maps and papers that would tell the Allies exactly how much information the Germans had about their plans.

Her eyes sparkled with impatience. Her father had promised he would garner what information he could, but the rooms occupied by Major Meyer were locked and a sentry stood on duty outside the double doors of the dining room. No easy opportunities for spying were going to present themselves. Opportunities would have to be made. She opened the bedroom door, walking quickly and quietly along the corridor and down the stairs to the library.

"We must talk, Papa," she said, not sitting down. "In the gardens, not in the house."

Henri de Valmy nodded. Field Marshal Rommel's visit to

Valmy had shaken him. Whatever Meyer's task, it was obviously an important one, and he could feel the precarious safety of their lives rapidly slipping away.

The sentry on duty outside the dining room eyed them with hostility as they crossed the hall. It was as if *they* were the usurpers. A flare of white rage surged through Lisette, and she had to clench her jaw in order to remain silent. The Germans were everywhere: tramping up and down the winding stairs that led to Major Meyer's study, grinding their cigarette stubs beneath their heels as they paced the terraces, littering the drive with their presence. Her father took her arm gently as they walked through the kitchen and out into the courtyard beyond.

"They must be endured," he said quietly, yet again. "It is the only way we will survive them, Lisette."

"I hate them," she said fiercely as they crossed the cobblestones, the February sun chill. "They've permeated Valmy with their presence. I don't think we'll ever be free of them."

"We will," her father assured her, his austere features grim. "And until we are, we must be grateful for the major's civility."

Beyond the courtyard, a long lawn sloped away toward a terrace and the sunken rose gardens. As they began to walk toward them something tight caught in Lisette's throat. She hated Major Meyer most of all. It was easy to be contemptuous of the others. They didn't rob her of breath when she unexpectedly encountered them. He had a way of looking at her that totally disconcerted her. His very presence scorched her nerve ends. It was because of him that the others were here, because of him that their home was no longer their own. And her reaction to him was intense.

"We have no reason to be grateful to Major Meyer for anything," she said, a throb of passion in her voice.

Her father led the way down the moss-covered steps that led to the formally laid out rose beds. In summer they were vibrant with color. He liked old-fashioned roses—full-blown Gloire de Dijon, pale-flushed Ophelias. Now the rose bushes were gaunt and bleak, only the fat green buds promising the glory to come.

"Valmy has many treasures and none of them have been

despoiled," he said patiently, wishing that he had put on a jacket for the sunshine gave no warmth. "We haven't been asked to move into the servants' quarters to make room for his men. Neither you nor your mother has been treated . . . disrespectfully." He passed a hand across his eyes. My God. When he thought of some of the stories he had heard about the occupying forces, the wanton destruction and brutality, the rapes . . . At least Meyer's men were disciplined.

He had walked into the kitchen some days ago in the Major's wake. Marie had been transferring a heavy casserole from the oven to the table, and two soldiers had been lounging in her way. The casserole was hot, and there was no other surface upon which she could set it down. She had said "*Excusez moi,*" and the soldiers had deliberately obstructed her, laughing at her distress as her gnarled hands began to lose their grip on the heavy dish. Meyer had stepped into the kitchen, ordering them to apologize instantly and, mortified, they had done so.

Henri had found the incident interesting. The soldiers' misdemeanor had been trivial, but it had earned them Meyer's contempt. That contempt had filled their eyes with misery as they had backed from the room. Meyer had not apologized to him for his men's conduct. He had not needed to. He had shown quite clearly that no liberties of any sort would be taken while he and his men occupied Valmy, and Henri had been grateful.

"The major has asked me to join him for a cognac after dinner this evening," he said as they walked down one narrow pathway and up another.

Lisette stopped short, horrified. "You promised me that you wouldn't be taken in by glib good manners, Papa! Have you forgotten who he is? He's a *German!* He has no *right* to be at Valmy! To ask you to share a cognac with him in your own house is an insult! Surely even you must see that?"

"And if being insulted means I enter his rooms?" her father said, quirking a silvered eyebrow.

Lisette regarded him doubtfully. "Will he? Is that why you accepted his invitation?"

"He very well might, and whether he does or not, the more time I spend with him, the more likelihood there is of my obtaining information for Paul."

24

Lisette slipped her arm through his and began once more to walk at his side. "He'll never tell you anything," she said with certainty. "He isn't the type, no matter how much cognac he drinks. The information we need is behind the locked doors of the grand dining room."

"Yes," her father said thoughtfully. "One set of keys and one guard. . . . Not impossible odds, surely."

Lisette smiled at him affectionately. "Not if we are determined, Papa," she said. As they continued to walk the deserted rose gardens her head was high, her eyes bright with the light of battle.

The next morning Lisette cycled down through the beech woods to Sainte-Marie-des-Ponts, looking at the flowers with kindlier eyes than she had a week ago. Major Dieter Meyer was directly responsible to Rommel for the strengthening of the coastal defenses. That much she now knew for certain. With a zing of elation, she skimmed over the bridge, past sharply yellow daffodils and deep purple crocuses. From now on she would be more than just a courier: she would be an informer. And with luck, her information would be important.

Pollarded trees lined Sainte-Marie's streets, linking pleached branches, their buds already bursting with green. She cycled over the cobblestones and into the square, leaning her bicycle against the side of the café. It was spring, probably the last spring they would spend under German occupation. It was a heady thought, and she hurried into the café, her spirits rising even higher as she heard the familiar tone of Paul's voice.

He was leaning against the zinc-topped bar, talking to André, his shabby corduroy trousers still discolored by the dust of Vierville. He was bespectacled, tall and thin, his shirt and jacket sleeves never quite reaching to his angular wrists. He had been born and bred in Sainte-Marie and was a popular though unconventional schoolmaster. The children were at lunch now, and Paul was in the village café, as usual. It was the one place all gossip reached, sooner or later.

Lisette's gaze met Paul's briefly, and he smiled an acknowledgment while continuing his conversation. Lisette looked around the café. Madame Chamot and Madame Bridet were sitting at a corner table, their shopping bags at their feet, half drunk cups of chicory in front of them. Old Bleriot was sitting alone, wheezing over a baguette, and a soldier stood near the doorway, munching a croissant, his eyes on the square outside.

"An anisette, André, please," she called out as she sat down at the table with the two women.

"Good morning, Lisette," said Madame Chamot, her black serge coat buttoned up to the throat, her steel-gray hair pulled tightly into a bun. "How is the comtesse, your mother?"

"Very well," Lisette replied, wishing that the soldier would go so that she could talk to Paul.

"I am glad," Madame Chamot said, but her voice expressed disbelief. How could the fastidious and refined Comtesse de Valmy be well when her home was overrun with pigs? She glared venomously in the soldier's direction as he wiped the crumbs from his mouth with the back of his hand, and sauntered back out into the street.

"*Salauds*," she said expressively. "Did you see that, Madame Bridet? He never even offered to pay for his drink or his croissant. I wish I were a man! I'd show them!"

"If you could terrorize the Boche the way you terrorize your husband, the war would be over by Easter," André said, his grin wide as he placed a small glass of anisette in front of Lisette.

"Bah," Madame Chamot said disgustedly, rising to her feet and picking up her bags. "I've more fighting spirit in me than you have, André Caldron! You should be ashamed of yourself, feeding the Boche free of charge! Good-bye, Mademoiselle Lisette. Come along, Madame Bridet, there is work for us to do. We cannot be idle all day like some I could mention." Weighed down by their shopping, the two elderly housewives struggled out into the street as André returned to the bar, and Paul crossed quickly to Lisette's table, sitting opposite her.

"I've heard about your guests. What is it like? Is it very bad?"

Lisette pushed a dark tendril of hair away from her face. "It's bearable," she said, her eyes dark with distaste. "Major Meyer has commandeered the château, and his men are quartered in the servants' rooms around the courtyard."

"You'll be under much greater surveillance. It could make things difficult," Paul said, thinking of her vital runs to Bayeux and Trévières.

"I don't think so. No one takes any notice of me. Why should they? The major does not take orders from the GHQ at Vierville, Paul. He is responsible directly to Field Marshal Rommel."

Paul sat very still, his eyes sharp. André had turned his back and was whistling to himself as he restocked the bar. The old man was dozing. "His task is to strengthen the coastal defenses," Lisette went on. "Rommel himself came to Valmy three days ago. He and the major spent nearly an hour together in the grand dining room. There are maps in there, Paul, I'm sure of it. Maps and plans."

Paul felt in his pocket for a cigarette and matches.

Her voice held conviction. "The major has had locks put on the doors, and a sentry is on duty outside them twenty-four hours a day. The information *must* be vital, Paul. Rommel was not paying a social call."

Paul regarded her thoughtfully. He knew very well what she was suggesting, but she was inexperienced and, if she were caught . . . He thrust away the memory of the entire Argent cell being lined up and shot at Gestapo headquarters in Caen because of a weak link in their chain.

"It's too dangerous," he said, holding his cigarette inward between his thumb and forefinger, taking short, sharp puffs while his mind worked furiously. If what she said was true, the information Major Meyer had access to was of incalculable importance. Obtaining it and transmitting it to the Allies could mean the difference between success and failure for the long-awaited invasion forces. And defeat would ensure that the Nazi dream of a thousand-year Reich would become grim reality. His skin turned cold. Lisette was too young, too inexperienced to be entrusted with a mission of such enormity.

"A well-trained agent must be infiltrated into Valmy as a maid or a cook," he said tensely.

"It won't work, Paul. It would arouse too much suspicion."

"It *must* work," he said fiercely. "We have to know what those devils are planning. How much they know of the Allies' intentions."

A slight frown puckered her brow. "But if Rommel is focusing his attention on Normandy, surely that is to our advantage? Everyone knows that when the attack comes, it will be at the Pas de Calais."

Paul Gilles's eyes met hers, the pupils mere pinpricks. "No one," he said steadily, "knows when the invasion will take place, or where. But if, just if, the Desert Fox has guessed correctly, then the results could be catastrophic."

Despite the warmth of her coat, she shivered. It was as if the whole future of France had suddenly been placed on her and Gilles's shoulders.

"The major is too sharp, too intuitive to accept a new maid or cook at face value," she said, her knuckles clenching as she remembered the agonizing moment in her father's bedroom when his hard gray eyes had stripped her naked, knowing instantly the reason for her being there, disbelieving with contempt her futile lie. "His suspicions would be immediately aroused, and security would be tightened to such an extent that not even a mouse would be able to get into the grand dining room." She leaned toward Paul, her eyes urgent. "Papa is already beginning to gain his confidence. The major has invited him to share a cognac with him after dinner this evening. If Papa can help us, Paul, he will. He has given me his promise."

Paul stirred uneasily on his metal chair. As far as he was concerned, the comte could have done much more far sooner. Sharing an after-dinner cognac with the Boche smacked of collaboration, not espionage.

"If your major is one of Rommel's golden boys, the information he has access to will be vitally important. We must obtain it. Your father is not a member of the Resistance. He has no experience at Resistance work. The task must be entrusted to one of our own, Lisette."

Her eyes sparked angrily. "Major Meyer is *not* my major, Paul Gilles! And my father is utterly trustworthy. I would stake my life on him!"

A wry smile touched Paul's thin lips. "By taking him into our confidence, we will *all* be staking our lives on him," he said dryly.

Her flare of fury subsided. What he said was true. She was reacting again with her heart and not her head. She pushed her hands deep into the pockets of her coat and stared out of the open door of the cafe. On the far side of the tree-lined square, a German soldier lounged arrogantly astride his motorcycle. The two elderly women had parted company and

28

were carrying their shopping home. Madame Pichon was hurrying off in the direction of the Telliers where young Madame Tellier was once more about to give birth.

She had waited for over a week to see Paul, confident that when she did so, he would tell her what must be done. And now that he had, she was rejecting his advice, confident that she knew better—that she and her father did not need his help, that all they needed was for any information they obtained to be ferried to the Allies through safe channels. She sighed and pushed a strand of hair away from her face. Paul was right. Neither she nor her father was an expert at espionage. Her one attempt had been shamefully bungled, and she had no way of knowing if any attempt her father made would meet with any greater success. An expert *was* needed, and it was up to her to give Paul all the support he needed.

She drew her gaze away from the distant German and the sunlit square and back once more to Paul. "What is it that you want me to do, Paul?" she asked gracefully, conceding defeat.

Paul grinned. His sexuality was so low key that it scarcely ever troubled him, yet he had long ago fallen under Lisette's spell. Her directness and honesty beguiled him, as did the long sweep of her lashes against the pale perfection of her skin. If he believed for one moment that she thought of him as anything but an older brother, he would have had no hesitation in putting his bachelor days behind him.

His grin faded. It was fortunate that Lisette regarded him with only sisterly affection. Comte Henri de Valmy would not regard a village schoolmaster as a suitable choice of a husband for his only daughter. He shrugged the dream aside and said in a practical vein, "Is Marie the only help you have at Valmy?"

She nodded.

"Who does the cooking?"

"Maman."

Paul tried not to show his surprise. It had not occurred to him that the ice-cool, elegant comtesse was familiar with her own kitchen.

"Then tonight, when your father joins the major for a cognac, he must say that your mother's health is not robust and that the occupation of her home has taken its toll . . . that with the major's permission, he would like to employ a niece of Marie's as a temporary cook."

"Has Marie any nieces?" she asked, raising a sleek eyebrow quizzically.

Paul laughed. "She has now. Don't worry about questions being asked of Marie or of anyone else. That is my concern. Just make sure that your father lays the groundwork well."

"And when Marie's 'niece' arrives?" Lisette asked, rising.

"Say nothing to her. She has come from Caen to cook. Treat her as a cook."

Lisette hesitated, still frowning, her hair falling forward in two glossy wings at either side of her face as she looked down at him. "And if an opportunity should present itself that only I or my father can take advantage of?"

Paul's thin, bony face looked suddenly old for his years. "Take it," he said briefly. "Good-bye, Lisette, and good luck."

She walked outside into the chill sunlight, wheeling her bicycle onto the cobblestoned road, her earlier optimism dissipated. The moment Marie's so-called niece entered Valmy, all their lives would be at risk, not only hers and her father's, but her mother's as well. If only—she thought, pushing down on the pedals, bicycling away from the square and through the narrow streets toward the bridge—if only there was an easier way. But try as she might, she could not think of one.

The soldier lounging astride his motorcycle watched her leave the café and then settled back to wait a little longer. Not until Paul left did he kick the machine into life, and before Lisette had reached the beech woods, he had roared out of the village in the opposite direction, circling round to the road barred to civilians that snaked along the cliff tops to Valmy.

"You're quite sure that seeing him was the purpose of her visit?" Dieter asked sharply as the private stood at attention in the study that had previously been Henri de Valmy's retreat from the world.

"Yes, Sir. She spoke to two old women but only briefly, and her eyes were on Gilles. As soon as the women left the café, Gilles came over and sat at her table."

"For how long?"

"Thirty-seven minutes, Sir."

Dieter frowned. It could have been a lovers' tryst, but he doubted it. He couldn't quite see the aristocratic Lisette de Valmy pursuing an alliance with a gangling schoolmaster.

Still deep in thought, he dismissed the private. He had made the unpleasant trip to Gestapo headquarters at Caen and had discovered that the Sainte-Marie-des-Ponts schoolmaster was high on the list of suspected members of the local Resistance. And Lisette de Valmy had cycled purposefully from Valmy to meet him for an intense conversation the moment he had been released from forced labor at Vierville. Dieter sat down at the large Biedermeier desk, tapping a silver pen thoughtfully on its surface.

Lisette de Valmy's name had not appeared on any of the lists of known or suspected members of the Resistance, yet she had a bicycle and spent long hours visiting villagers both in Sainte-Marie-des-Ponts and the surrounding countryside. The local patrols probably took very little interest in her comings and goings. It was all highly suspicious and his jawline hardened. He hoped passionately that his instincts, always acute, were playing him false.

"You mean that he is having *dinner* with us?" Lisette asked her father, aghast. "You can't mean it! You can't expect us to sit down and *eat* with him!"

"He's here, and we must make the best of it," her father said patiently. "So far, he has treated us with respect, and we can do no less than follow suit."

Lisette tried to speak and couldn't. Her throat was choked with distaste and panic . . . and something else, something too dark and fearful even to acknowledge.

"I can't," she whispered at last. "I would feel like dirt . . . like a collaborator."

Her father put his arm around her shoulders. "You have no need to, my love. It will give us an even better chance to convince the major that your mother's health is fragile and that extra help in the château is a necessity."

"He won't believe you," she said, her voice so low it was almost inaudible. "I told Paul that he would not believe us, but he hasn't met him. He doesn't understand."

"Of course he will believe us," he said serenely. "It is virtually the truth, so why should he disbelieve us?"

She remembered the way Major Meyer's eyes had held hers across the silk-draped bed. "Because he is a man who will never be taken in by falsity," she said, turning away as a flash of fear rippled down her spine.

Out of the habit of a lifetime, she changed for dinner but did not go down to join them. The pretense that he was a guest and not a ruthless, despotic invader would have been more than she could endure. She paced her bedroom restlessly, staring repeatedly out the window toward the inky blackness of the Channel. If only the English and the Americans would cross it! If only ships and planes and battalion after battalion of soldiers would bridge the narrow sea separating France from England! She pressed her fingertips against the icy coldness of the window pane. Such a narrow stretch of water, and yet Hitler had not been able to breach it. England still remained free. Her heart caught at the word. One day France, too, would be free.

She turned away from the window, clasping her hands tightly, wondering if her father had already broached the subject of an additional member of the household staff to Major Meyer. Would he give permission? And if he did so, would he permit her father to engage someone personally? Anxiety gnawed at her. Whatever else Major Meyer was, he was not a fool. She could imagine him agreeing smoothly to her father's suggestion to hire a cook. Then, as her father thought the battle won, she could almost hear him continuing to speak in the hard, dark voice that sent shivers down her spine: he himself would employ a suitable woman. Oh, yes. And he would know he was demolishing a scheme, defeating her father, and undoubtedly find the episode cynically amusing.

"Damn him," she whispered fiercely.

The hands on her small ormolu and porcelain clock stood at nine-fifteen. Surely the major would have left the breakfast room where they ate all their meals now? Enduring his presence at dinner must have been agonizing for her fastidious, well-bred mother. Unable to stand the suspense any longer, Lisette opened her bedroom door and walked quickly along the landing and down the winding stone stairs that led to the hall.

The door of the breakfast room was ajar, the room empty. With a sigh of relief, she crossed the hall and entered the main salon. For a moment, shock held her motionless. The high-ceilinged room glowed in the light of the log fire and the oil lamps that her mother liked. Her father was standing at ease in front of the fire, a pipe cupped in the palm of one hand, the other thrust into his trouser pocket as he said genially, "Lisette is the skier in the family. We have spent many vacations at Gstaad." He paused, looking up at her, his eyes meeting her shocked ones with sudden, crippling embarrassment.

Major Meyer was sitting in the high-winged leather chair to the left of the fireplace, a glass of cognac in his hand, the top buttons of his tunic undone, a relaxed expression on his normally granite-hard features.

For a moment there was a strained, taut silence with only the major continuing to look at ease, and then her father said awkwardly, "Come in, *ma chère*. I was just telling the major what an excellent skier you are."

She sucked in a deep, steadying breath and moved forward. They needed the major's permission to bring a stranger into Valmy. A stranger who would defeat whatever end he was working toward. She sat down, straight-backed, at her mother's side, her cool outward composure revealing none of her inner turmoil.

Dieter's eyes flicked across to her and then back once again to her father. He had been both relieved and disappointed that she had not joined them for dinner. He had known, of course, why she had not done so. Her father's urbane explanation that she had a headache would not have deceived a twelve year old. She had been unable to face sitting down to eat with the invader of her home and country. He hadn't blamed her in the slightest. If he had been in her position, he would have reacted in much the same way, possibly worse.

Conversation at dinner had been stilted at first. The comte had done his best to pretend that he was a voluntary host with an invited guest, but the comtesse had been unable to join him in the charade. Good breeding had determined that she be polite, but it was an icy politeness that would have frozen anyone less assured than himself. The assurance did not come from the power he wielded. It came from the inborn knowledge that socially their worlds and background were quite similar.

He was from a long line of Prussian aristocrats, a great landowning Junker family in the traditional mold. The first world war had altered their way of life but had not destroyed it. His family home had been a moated castle on the outskirts of Weimar, feudal, magnificent, and unbearably cold and unsanitary. His childhood summers had been spent there, but his mother seldom moved from her lavish and comfortable apartment on the fashionable Unter den Linden. By the time Dieter was nine, he was an assured and sophisticated Berliner.

Family tradition destined the eldest son for a military education, but Dieter's father—shamed by the terms of the Versailles treaty, appalled by the great inflation of 1923 that had made so many fortunes worthless—broke with tradition and, instead of sending Dieter to a military academy, sent him to the most expensive and exclusive boarding school in Europe—Le Rosey in Switzerland—where his schoolmates' blood was as royal as the Wittelsbach blood in the distaff side of his family. Le Rosey had insured that no one, least of all a mere comte and comtesse, could make him feel a social inferior.

Though for political reasons Dieter no longer sported the aristocratic 'von' before his surname, it had taken the comte only seconds to realize that his unwelcome guest was his social equal. The knowledge eased him. The major paraded none of the usual Nazi pretentions. In another place, in another time, Dieter Meyer was a man he would have liked greatly. In discovering that the Major shared his passion for polo and had played on the most prestigious circuit in Germany, he had forgotten the man was his enemy. Only the shock and accusation in his daughter's eyes brought him back to reality.

"Major Meyer skied at Gstaad regularly before the war," he finished lamely as Lisette sat still and silent, her face a polite, frozen mask. "He used to stay at the Steigenberger."

Lisette winced. The Steigenberger, Gstaad's most luxurious hotel, standing in chocolate-box grandeur on the south-facing slopes, had been the setting for many childhood holidays. The knowledge that Major Meyer had also frequented it tarnished her many happy memories. Her father's eyes were pleading. He needed her cooperation. Perhaps he had not yet gained Major Meyer's permission to engage Marie's 'niece' as cook.

She turned her head slowly toward the major, her heart beating fast and furious. "How nice," she said politely, but the words did not come out cool and indifferent as she had intended. Her voice seemed to be filled with smoke, and there was an underlying throb to it that would not be stifled.

He had resolved not to take the slightest notice of her. She was too disturbing, too innocently provocative. A pine log fell and cracked, sending a flurry of sparks up the great chimney, filling the room with pungent scent. Her remark scarcely warranted a comment. With an imperceptible shrug, he turned to her, about to make some meaningless rejoinder. His eyes met hers, and desire sliced through him—desire so naked and primeval that it stole his breath.

Her hair fell in one long, smooth wave to her shoulders, held away from her face on one side tonight with an ivory comb. Her eyes were thick-lashed pools that drew him down and down, robbing him of logic and common sense. The high-necked sweater and country tweed skirt that she habitually wore had been discarded. Her dress was of rose-red wool, the neckline deeply cowled, the skirt clinging gently to her hips and flaring out around her knees. Her hands were clasped in her lap, narrow and well shaped, the beautiful almond-shaped nails unpolished. Her legs crossed lightly at the ankles, long and slender, bereft of stockings despite the chill draughts that lurked in every corner of the château. He remembered the heavy stockings she wore in the daytime and knew with what contempt she would refuse silk ones if he were to offer them, just as she would reject with contempt anything that he offered her.

"The proprietors are family friends," he said. The tight control he was exercising over himself made his voice sound harsh.

The room seemed to have closed in on Lisette. She knew the proprietors well. They weren't the kind of people to entertain Nazi sympathies, yet it wasn't the shock of her family and Major Meyer's having aquaintances in common that was making her feel so faint. It was something else—the same, nameless emotion that overcame her whenever she was in his presence.

She had hated before but never with a passion that made her feel physically weak. She had hated the Germans when they had first invaded. She had hated them when over two-thirds of the villagers of Sainte-Marie-des-Ponts had been marched off for forced labor. And she had hated them when she had known that they were to defile Valmy. But it had been a cold, murderous hatred, a hatred that she was in command of. She was in command of nothing when Major Meyer looked at her with his hard gray eyes, his body as lean and lithe as that of a panther about to spring on its prey.

She tried to speak again, but the words would not come. Her father and mother had receded into a hazy distance, and she was conscious only of Major Meyer—of blond hair gleaming like dull gold in the firelight; of the abrasive, masculine lines of his face; of broad shoulders and the lightning flashes on his collar; of strong, well-shaped hands as they cradled his cognac glass; of the sense of power under restraint. His masculinity overwhelmed her, and suddenly she understood. In a moment of clarity so agonizing that she cried out loud, she knew what the emotion was that confounded her whenever she was in his presence. It was not hatred. It was physical desire.

"Lisette, are you ill?" Her father was stepping toward her anxiously.

She rose to her feet, fighting for air, her face deathly pale. "No . . . Please . . . Excuse me—" Shaking violently, she fended away her father's arm, knowing only that she must escape from the room—escape from Major Meyer's presence, escape from a truth too monstrous to live with.

3

Dieter fought the almost overwhelming instinct to leap to his feet and stride after her. His powerful arm muscles clenched as he remained where he was, one hand holding the glass of cognac, the other still clasping the ankle of a booted foot as it rested with apparent ease across the knee of his other leg.

The comtesse had been busy with her embroidery. At her daughter's strangled cry, the work had fallen from her hands, and now her gaze met her husband's in alarm.

The comte gave her the merest frown, intimating that she behave as if nothing untoward had happened, and said, with an underlying note of strain in his voice, "My daughter's headache is obviously still troubling her, Major Meyer. Please forgive her abrupt departure."

Dieter nodded, barely trusting himself to speak. Waves of shock still reverberated through him. It was as though he had touched a live wire. He had to tighten his hold on his ankle in order to prevent his hand from trembling.

"I have some aspirin in my room," he said, controlling his voice with care, appalled at the intensity of the sexual desire that had swamped and almost submerged him.

"Thank you, Major Meyer," the comtesse said as she rose, the skin taut across her finely sculpted cheekbones, "but I have a supply myself. Perhaps you would excuse me while I find the aspirins and take them to Lisette?"

"Of course." This time his voice was sharp edged. Anger had come hard on the heels of desire. He was a man who prided himself on always having his emotions under tight control. That he had momentarily lost that control was, to him, unforgivable.

"Le Rosey explains your flawless command of French," the comte said, striving to recover the easy atmosphere that had existed before Lisette had entered the room and then left it in so extraordinary a manner.

The slight, almost imperceptible shrug of Dieter's shoulder was Gallic. "It is my second language," he said, suddenly bored with the evening, annoyed by the comte's blatant desire to please.

Henri shifted his weight uncomfortably from one foot to the other. The rapport that had so unexpectedly sprung up between them had been irretrievably lost. If he failed in his task, it would be Lisette's fault, not his. He cleared his throat. "My wife is not very strong, Major Meyer. Before the war we had a large staff, but since then, things have become very difficult. Lisette helps admirably, but the château is large, and my wife is beginning to feel the strain. Marie has a niece who would be willing to come and take over most of the chores in the kitchen . . . with your permission, of course."

Dieter swirled the cognac around in his glass, suddenly wary. "Is Marie's niece a village girl?" he asked with apparent lack of interest.

"No." The comte's reply was uncomfortably swift. "She's from Caen . . . a good girl . . . reliable."

Dieter held the comte's gaze steadily for a moment. "Are her papers in order?"

"Oh, yes, yes," the comte said eagerly. Too eagerly.

Dieter felt disappointment settle cold and hard deep in his gut. Henri de Valmy, a man who had probably never lied in his life, was lying now. He drained his cognac, setting the empty glass carefully on the side table. "Then you had better tell her to come immediately," he said, his voice so indifferent that Henri de Valmy suppressed a heartfelt sigh of relief.

It was done. The girl would be here, within Valmy. The first task of his self-appointed mission was complete.

"The polo at Deauville before the war was the best in Europe," Henri said, resuming the earlier topic that had seemingly bridged the barriers between them. "I played myself until I broke my wrist. It's an infuriating thing to happen to any player. I never had the same strength again."

His voice was filled with regret, and Dieter's eyes darkened. Damn the man. He should never have allowed even the merest cordiality to have sprung up between them. They were enemies. Oppressor and oppressed. A second ago de Valmy had lied to him, and there could only have been one reason for such a lie. Now, amiably, he was trying to gain his sympathy for an accident that, if it had happened to him, would have filled him with equal regret and frustration.

He glanced at his watch and rose to his feet. "It is eleven o'clock and I still have work to do," he said abruptly. "Good night, Comte de Valmy."

Swiftly he strode from the room, wishing he had never entered it. First of all, Lisette de Valmy had disconcerted him so profoundly that even now his chest felt tight, as if an iron band constrained it. Then Henri de Valmy had lied to him, and all his doubts and suspicions as to Lisette's activities had been reawakened. He wanted the Resistance groups all along the coastline routed out, watched, and questioned. He wanted any information, however slight, that would give him a clue to the enemies' plans. But he did not want to see Lisette and her father escorted to Gestapo headquarters at Caen. Never, even when he had served at the Russian front, had he longed so intensely for the war to be over.

He stared somberly down at the long table and the large-scale maps of Calvados spread open upon it. Away to the east was Deauville, where Henri de Valmy had played polo. He wished to God that polo was still being played there—that there were no mines deforming the beach, no pillboxes frowning out over the elegant Promenade des Planches. He knew grimly that he would never play there—that Lisette de Valmy would never cheer him on from the stands, a ridiculously large summer hat on her cloud of dark hair, a pretty silk dress enhancing her slender figure. He swore savagely under his breath. His task was to make sure that Deauville remained firmly under German occupation. Polo belonged in another world—a world he sometimes doubted he would ever see again.

Lisette had fled blindly to her room, self-disgust and loathing weighing her down like a tangible force, crushing the breath from her body, choking her sobs as she slammed the door of her room shut behind her, leaning her weight against the centuries-smooth wood, sliding down against it, her arms hugging her shaking body.

She wanted him. Dear God in heaven, she wanted him—wanted to feel his hard, lean body against hers; to feel the spring of wheat-gold hair against the palms of her hands; to hear the dark, rich voice murmuring her name. She pressed her hands to her face, fighting for calm. She wasn't sane. She couldn't be. She was in the grip of hysteria. If she waited for a little while, the moment of madness would surely pass. She would realize that she would no more long to copulate with a German than with a pig.

One moment passed, and then another. The violent trembling that had overtaken her like a seizure steadied. She found she could breathe without having to gasp for air. She leaned her head against the wood and waited for the relief of laughter at her foolishness. It did not come. Only the truth faced her. Unbelievable. Unacceptable. Unendurable.

She never knew how long she sat there, huddled on the floor, her back against the door. Her mother came and knocked and asked if she was all right—if she needed an aspirin. She had replied yes to the first question and no to the second, and had made no effort to open the door. After a little while her mother had gone away, and she had remained, unmoving, in the darkness.

She had never been in love, but she knew it wasn't love that was devastating her now. How could it be? She hadn't spoken more than a dozen words to him, and those had been angry and scathing.

She hugged her knees tighter against her chest. It was surely what the Bible referred to as sinful lust. She shuddered. Nothing she had ever heard or read had prepared her for this. It was as if her body were completely divorced from her mind. Logic and sanity screamed that never, ever, could she bear to be touched by a man who had occupied her country, her home. Yet if she closed her eyes and thought of him, heat surged through her, and she found herself wondering what it would be like to touch his skin, inhale the male fragrance of him, to see the hard gray eyes grow dark with passion.

At last, unsteadily, she rose to her feet. She alone knew her despicable secret. No one else knew, nor would they ever know. She would continue to live and behave as if the truth had never been brought home to her. He was her enemy and he would remain her enemy. She would treat her physical weakness as if it were a disease. She would fight it, conquer it and one day she would be free of it. Slowly she undressed and climbed into bed, staring into the darkness for hour after hour, painfully coming to terms with the knowledge that there existed within her a person she had never even remotely imagined. Only when the night sky pearled into gray, presaging dawn, did she finally fall into a restless, troubled sleep.

"Marie's niece makes a commendably fine omelette," her father said two days later at breakfast. He glanced at his daughter as he spoke. She had been looking extremely pale lately, almost ill. "Are you sure you won't have one, Lisette?"

She nodded, continuing to sip at her chicory, ignoring the warm croissants on her plate.

A shaft of worry troubled him. "Are you feeling well, Lisette? Do you still have your headache?"

"No, Papa. Please don't look so anxious."

"But you're not eating properly, Lisette. You're bound to feel unwell unless you eat. Isn't there anything at all that you would like for breakfast?"

He sounded so concerned that she managed a wry smile. "A cup of genuine coffee instead of this ghastly chicory."

He grinned ruefully. "I'm afraid even Elise can't manage that."

"Elise. Is that her name? I haven't seen her yet. What is she like?"

Young, he wanted to say. Too young for what she has to do. The reality of her arrival had filled him with fresh doubts and fears.

"Pretty," he said, and pushed his plate away, his appetite lost.

They sat together silently, both wanting to discuss the girl's arrival and its implications, but too conscious of the danger of being overheard to do so.

"I think I'll cycle into the village this morning," Lisette said at last. "The daffodils are out in the woods. They look glorious."

His eyes met hers. What she was really saying was that she hoped to see Paul Gilles and let him know Elise had arrived safely and without arousing suspicion.

"Yes," he said unhappily, aware again of frustration and impotence. "The forsythia too has bloomed early. I think I'll go and cut some for indoors. A blaze of color will cheer us up."

The linden trees flanking the drive were already beginning to take on a verdant haze. The tight green buds were unfurling, and the fresh, clean scent of spring was strong in the air. Once out in the open, Lisette could breathe more easily. There was no chance here of suddenly rounding a corner and being confronted by him.

She cycled down the long, graveled drive, surprising a gray squirrel that scampered quickly out of her path. The late February wind had softened to a breeze. It blew refreshingly against her face, tugging at her hair, tinging her pale cheeks with a hint of color. At the end of the drive she swung left toward the village, free-wheeling down through the beech woods to the high-hedged lanes of Sainte-Marie.

The village was in sight when the chauffeur-driven Horch came down behind her, hard and fast. She pulled over as far as she could toward the steeply banked hedgerow, but the powerful car gave her no room. Her front wheel swerved, ramming into the grassy bank and sending her flying from the saddle. The bike fell heavily against her; as it slithered to the ground, the handlebar gouged her thigh, leaving a hideous trail of blood in its wake.

Through a sea of pain she was aware that the car had screeched to a halt, that someone was running to her aid.

"*Sind Sie schon gut?*"

The harsh voice was familiar but the words made no sense. There was a ringing in her ears, and colors and shapes zigzagged crazily.

"*Gott im Himmel! Are you all right?*" His voice was urgent, his arm tight around her shoulders, his eyes brilliant with anger and worry.

"Yes . . . I . . ." She tried to pull away from him, but it was impossible. She seemed to have lost all her strength, and there was something hot and sticky running down her leg.

"Good God, you could have been killed!" He swung his head round, shouting at his petrified chauffeur to open the rear door of the Horch, and then, as she gasped aloud in protest, he swung her up in his arms, striding with her to the car, the blood on her legs smearing his immaculate uniform.

"No . . . Please . . . I can walk." Her head was spinning with concussion, with shock, with the desperate need to free herself from his touch.

"Don't be ridiculous," he said curtly, laying her on the leather rear seat of the Horch. "You couldn't walk a step."

She caught a glimpse of the white, frightened face of the chauffeur and felt a surge of pity for him. He looked like a man whose career had come to a very sudden end.

"Please . . . ," she said again weakly. There was blood on the luxurious interior of the car, on his uniform, and on his hands. He edged into the seat beside her.

"Can you sit up if I help you?" he asked. "I want to take your coat off and see how badly you've been hurt."

She tried to protest but couldn't. His arm slid once more around her shoulders, pulling her against him so that her head was resting on his chest. She could hear his heart beating, smell the faint aroma of the spice and lemon cologne that he used, and knew with terror that her nightmare of physical capitulation was on the verge of becoming reality.

"Please . . . ," she gasped again. "You must let me go. I'm all right. It's only a graze."

"Stop being childish," he said peremptorily, ignoring her protests, easing first one of her arms out of her coat and then the other, with stunning gentleness.

"Can I help, Sir?" the chauffeur asked nervously.

"For Christ's sake, give me the first aid box!"

The chauffeur had been too dumfounded by the major's reaction to the accident to have thought of the first aid box. He stumbled from the car, hurrying round to the trunk, wondering what the devil all the fuss was about. He had recognized the de Valmy girl, of course, but even so, he saw no reason for the major to behave like a man possessed simply because she had been thrown from her bicycle.

"Please, you must let me go," she said, trying to pull away from him, her voice stronger as the wave of dizziness that had engulfed her receded.

"Not until I've seen how badly hurt you are," he said grimly, "and I can't do that until I've taken your stockings off."

"*No!*" This time her protest was so vehement that he paused, disconcerted. There was no trace of the ice-cool disdain with which she usually treated him. Her eyes were wide as she shrank back against the leather seat, and with a shock he realized how deep her detestation of him must be. Physical revulsion was not a reaction he was accustomed to. That he was experiencing it now, when he had allowed his own feelings for her to surface, infuriated him. "You'll damn well do as you're told!" he said in a raspy tone. He took the first aid box from the chauffeur, flicked the lid open, and was relieved to see a plentiful supply of bandages.

Lisette's temper flared at his high-handed manner. She wanted to tell him to go to hell, but her throat was so tight that no words would come. She closed her eyes, fighting for control as he whipped off his gloves and thrust them toward the chauffeur. He must not touch her intimately, she thought. It would be beyond endurance, beyond forgetting.

"You can't . . . I won't let you," she uttered hoarsely as he knelt at her side and with a gentleness that nearly robbed her of her senses, lifted her skirt high to her hips. Her lingerie displayed none of the serviceable qualities of her bloodied woolen stockings or tweed skirt. Her brief panties were unmistakably Parisian. He sucked in his breath sharply. A wisp of creamy-beige satin trimmed with fragile lace barely encased

43

the soft mound of her pubic hair. Crisp dark curls escaped enticingly only inches from his fingers. Desire, merciless and urgent, rocked through him.

"Shouldn't we take her back to the château, Sir?" the chauffeur asked, trying to redeem his reckless driving by being helpful.

Dieter swore beneath his breath, aware that it was just as well the chauffeur had reminded him of his presence. The rape of an injured French girl would hardly have been something to look back on with pride.

"Yes," he said through gritted teeth. "Just as soon as I stop the bleeding."

He began to ease down one of her stockings, and as his fingers touched the naked flesh of her inner thigh she moaned, a tremor running through her.

"I won't hurt you," he said, his voice smoke-dark with suppressed passion. "I promise."

She turned her head away from him, tears of shame stinging her eyes. It wasn't pain that had caused her to tremble. It was something far, far worse. Something she would die rather than allow him to see.

Slowly, with exquisite care, he eased the tattered remnants of her stocking down to the knee. The old-fashioned, unprotected metal handlebar had gouged deep into her thigh, slicing the flesh open in a long, ugly gash. A muscle twitched in his jaw at the sight of it. Quickly he reached for a sterile cotton pad, pressing it against the wound, which he bandaged with swift dexterity.

She lay unmoving, her head averted, her hands tightly clenched. Soon it would be over. She would forget his concern, his care. She would not leave it to Elise to betray his plans to the Allies. She would betray them herself. It would be her revenge on him for the assault he had made on her body and her senses.

The bandage at her thigh was secured. His hands moved lower, easing the bloodied wool over her knee and down her leg. Summoning the last vestige of control that was left to her, she opened her eyes, pushing herself upward on the elbow of one arm. There was another deep gash at her knee and long, raw grazes the length of her leg.

"I can bandage my knee myself," she said stiltedly.

He glanced up at her, one eyebrow slightly raised. "I'm sure you can, but I can do it much more efficiently. My hands," he said pointedly, "are not trembling. Yours are."

Her cheeks flooded with humiliated color. "It was the fall . . . the shock . . ."

Curious, he hesitated for a fraction of a second before pressing a cotton pad against the gash on her knee. That her fall had caused her state of shock was so obvious, it hardly warranted explanation. Yet her voice had been fiercely defensive. He slid his hand beneath her calf to support the weight of her leg as he reached for another bandage. As he did so, he heard again the small, desperate gasp of breath that he had previously thought was caused by pain.

Slowly, very slowly, he raised his eyes once more to hers. The pupils were still widely dilated, pansy-dark in the pale ivory of her face. Excitement, sure and hard, seized him. The tremor that had run through her body when he had first touched her had not been of pain. It had been the same age-old, primitive response that had flared through him when he had first confronted her across the vast, silk-draped bed.

She saw the expression in his eyes change, saw the realization and the answering heat, and she knew there was nowhere to run to, nowhere to hide.

"Don't touch me." She panted desperately. "Please don't touch me!"

A smile formed in the corners of his mouth. Her protest was one he had no intention of heeding. From the very first, he had suspected that beneath the ice was fire, and now it was palpable. He could both see and feel it. Quickly, carefully, he bound her knee, every sexual nerve end in his body raw with desire. There would be complications. However badly she wanted him, she would not submit easily or without guilt. But it would be submission. It would not be violation, the careless rape so many of his compatriots freely indulged in.

"Don't be afraid," he said and took her hand in his.

The nightmare was here and now, all around her. She could see the blond hairs on the back of his wrists, the strong, well-shaped fingers.

"No . . . ," she whispered as he slowly turned her hand over, palm upward, raising it to his mouth. "Please, no . . ."

His hard, hot mouth seared her flesh. She shuddered,

closing her eyes, wanting his hands once more on her naked thigh, on her breasts—wanting to submit totally and irrevocably. His thumb and forefinger cupped her chin, tilting her face upward.

"Look at me," he commanded, his voice thick with unassuaged passion, and as her eyelids flickered open, he drew her toward him.

She could feel the slam of his heart against hers, smell the clean, sharp fragrance of his cologne. She wanted to score his back with her nails, to sink her teeth into his neck and taste the sweat of his body, to have him take her then and there on the rear seat of the Horch.

"Give me your mouth."

The moment of capitulation had arrived. Time, as she knew it, stood still. Her pulse thundered in her ears, and then she lifted her head high and spat full in his face.

"*Never!*" she hissed, her eyes burning. "I shall never give you anything, Major Meyer!"

She heard him suck in his breath, saw his jawbone clench, his eyes blaze; and then he said, his voice dangerously confident, "You will, Lisette, and both you and I know it."

Her mouth was dry. One more word, one touch of his hand, and her hard won victory would be lost. She moved away from him, and as she did so, pain sliced through her and thick, dark blood began to seep through the bandage on her thigh.

"*Get back to Valmy as quick as you can!*" Dieter yelled to the chauffeur and, ignoring her vain protests, seized hold of more cotton wool, pressing down hard on the vein in her groin.

The chauffeur, who had been watching them with wide-eyed incredulity, hastily revved the car into life and careened round at the first opportunity. So that was the lay of the land: Major Meyer and the comte's eighteen-year-old daughter. He wouldn't have believed it if he hadn't seen it with his own eyes. He wondered if anyone else knew. He had heard no rumors, no gossip. He pressed his foot down hard on the accelerator. No wonder the major's fury had been white-hot when the Horch had knocked her to the ground.

Lisette could not see clearly. The major's face danced

before her eyes, and no matter how hard she tried, she no longer had the strength to pull away from him. Her head slumped against his shoulder and his arms closed tightly around her.

"Faster, man!" Dieter shouted as the blood continued to pour dark and thick, saturating the bandages and swabs.

The Horch screamed out of the high-hedged lane and into the beech woods, and Dieter grabbed a rarely worn scarf, using it as a tourniquet. His eyes were dark with fear, and Lisette knew that the fear was for herself. In that moment, weak and semiconscious, she forgot about the uniform that he wore—forgot about the war. He had become her refuge and her strength, and she leaned against him, secure in the knowledge that he would take care of her—that he would always take care of her.

"You're going to be all right, *Liebling*," he said as they roared down Valmy's long, formal driveway, skidding to a halt outside the brass-studded oak doors. "Trust me."

There was such a depth of feeling in his voice that his chauffeur stared at him, stunned. The major was known to be mercilessly tough and had come through Kiev and Sebastopol earning one of the highest decorations for valor that the German state could bestow. Never, as long as he had been his chauffeur, had he known him to yield an inch in any situation. And now, because this slip of a girl was injured, the major's hard-boned face was ashen.

Keeping his thoughts to himself, he sprang out of the driver's seat, sprinted round to the rear door and sprang to attention as the major stepped out onto the gravel, the girl in his arms.

Marie was hurrying toward them, her eyes wide at the sight of Lisette's disarrayed skirt, at the blood, and at her indecent proximity to Major Meyer's chest.

"Get a doctor!" Dieter shouted to his chauffeur as he strode through the flagstoned entrance hall to the stairs. "Take outriders with you and bring him back instantly."

"My God, what's happened?" Henri cried, running in from the gardens, his face white, the pruning shears still in his hand, forsythia blossoms clinging to his jacket.

"She fell off her bike," Dieter replied shortly, not hesitating in his swift stride toward the stairs. "She's bleeding badly. I need pads. Linen. Anything."

Henri took one look at his face and did not demur. With Marie at his heels, he ran in the direction of the linen cupboards.

Dieter didn't take Lisette to her own room. He was unsure which of the bedrooms in the east wing was hers and had no intention of wasting precious time by asking. Besides, it seemed only natural that the bed he took her to should be his own.

As he laid her on the blue silk counterpane, she said so faintly that he could hardly hear her, "I don't know your name."

He looked down at her pale face and the dark spread of her hair over the pillows.

"Dieter," he said, his voice tight.

A ghost of a smile touched her lips. Dieter. It was a nice name. She tried to repeat it, but she was being sucked down into a vortex of brilliant colors and black rushing winds, and then her mother ran into the room, Marie hard on her heels, and the colors vanished and only darkness remained.

Doctor Auge, the local doctor, was bewildered: a chauffeur-driven Horch to take him to Valmy, outriders, the demand for his presence issued not by the comte but by the Wehrmacht officer in residence? It was most unusual, and he was filled with apprehension as he hurried through Valmy's medieval entrance hall and up the winding stone stairs.

"My daughter fell off her bicycle," the comte was saying to him as he ushered him along the uneven oak floor of the upper landing. "We've been unable to stop the bleeding."

"Where is the wound?" Doctor Auge asked, puffing for breath.

"High on her inner thigh."

Doctor Auge increased his speed. It sounded like the artery. If it was, there was no telling how much blood had been lost. He paused at the open bedroom door, bushy eyebrows flying upward. The comtesse was kneeling at one side of the bed, holding her daughter's hand, and a German officer stood on the other side, blood smearing his uniform, every line of his body tense.

The doctor looked swiftly across to the comte in alarm. What in God's name had happened that the comte had flinched from telling him? Or maybe dare not tell him? He found no

48

enlightenment. Henri de Valmy did not look at him but strode quickly into the room, saying peremptorily, "The doctor is here."

A tourniquet had been applied to Lisette de Valmy's thigh. Bowls of warm, disinfected water stood ready for his use. He dragged his attention away from the sinister figure of the major and tried not to think how the injury had been inflicted. Of one thing he was sure—it had been no innocent accident. Innocent accidents did not attract the attention of the Wehrmacht, and the major's eyes were dark with an anxiety equal to that of the comte's.

The counterpane was heavily stained with blood, and the girl was unconscious. He hurried to the bed, setting his ancient black bag down at his side, aware that the German was watching him with hawklike intensity. Nervously, he began to remove the sodden bandages. If Lisette de Valmy died, he did not want the responsibility placed at his door. He eased off the large pad of cotton staunching the blood and breathed an imperceptible sigh of relief. It was bad, but the artery had not been severed. It was an injury well within his competence to tend.

"The water, Madame," he said to the comtesse, and, rolling up his sleeves, he set to work.

Even when the last stitch had been inserted, the German did not leave the room. The doctor put away his needle and wondered again what the truth of the matter was. The injuries had not been caused in the process of rape. There was no sign of sexual abuse. Nor had the deep, jagged gash been caused by a knife. Taken together with the cut on her knee and the raw grazes to her shin, it was consistent with what the comte had claimed: a bicycle accident, the unprotected metal handlebar slicing deep into the girl's flesh.

He closed his bag and rose to his feet, unrolling his sleeves. "She should not be allowed to put any weight on it for several days. The wound needs to be kept clean, Madame, until I come again to remove the stitches."

"And when will that be?" It was the German, and his voice was a whiplash in the still room.

Dr. Auge was acutely aware of the impressive decorations that hung on the narrow band of black ribbon about the officer's neck, of his rank, and of his powerful personality. "A week

. . . ten days, Major," he said nervously, glad that his task was finished and eager to escape from the major's presence.

"Mademoiselle de Valmy lost a great deal of blood," the major said. "I would appreciate it if you would call each and every day until she is quite recovered."

It wasn't a request, it was a command, and he knew better than to attempt to refuse it. "Of course, Major," the doctor said hurriedly. "I shall be here in the morning. Good-bye, Monsieur le Comte, Comtesse. Good-bye, Major."

He had fully expected the major to warn him against talking of his visit to the château, but with the assurance that he would be at Valmy the following morning, the major dismissed him from his attention.

Dr. Auge scuttled from the room with gratitude. He didn't trust what he didn't understand, and he didn't understand the relationship of the four people he had left in the bedroom.

Lisette lay back against the pillows, deep circles beneath her eyes. The moment she had regained consciousness, she had been aware of Dieter's continuing nearness and had been filled with terror at the comfort it gave her. She dared not look at him. To look at him would be to surrender.

"You need to rest now, *chérie*," her mother was saying solicitously, straightening the bedcovers.

Her father cleared his throat. "I'd better carry Lisette into her own room first, my dear," he said gently.

The comtesse looked up at him startled, then a faint flush heightened her cheekbones. In her anxiety she had forgotten the room was no longer theirs.

"Of course, how foolish of me . . ."

"Lisette stays here," Dieter said smoothly. "It would be dangerous to move her and risk opening the wound again. I will see to it that my clothes and personal possessions are removed until she has recovered."

"Thank you, Major Meyer," Henri said with gratitude. "We appreciate all that you have done. Your prompt action probably saved Lisette's life. If she had been left where she fell, bleeding so profusely—" He shuddered at the image his words conjured up, and his wife said, "Marie will move your things for you, Major. Elise has prepared a light lunch. Perhaps you would like to share it with us before resuming your duties?"

"Thank you," Dieter said, aware how hard it must have been for her to issue such an invitation.

The comtesse turned once more to Lisette. "I'll send Elise up with a tray. You must have something, *chérie*. A sandwich and a hot drink at the very least."

They were leaving the room. In another minute he would be gone.

"The room that used to be my mother's would be, I think, the most suitable for you," her father was saying to him. "It isn't as large of course, but it overlooks the Channel."

She had only to keep her eyes averted from him for another second and her personal battle would be won.

"Thank you," Dieter was saying to her father. "That sounds most suitable."

His shadow fell across the bed. She could smell the faint aroma of his cologne. He was looking down at her. Waiting.

"Lisette?" The tenderness in the deep, dark voice ripped wide her best intentions and sent them scattering. Slowly, inevitably, she raised her eyes to his and the whole pattern of her life shifted and changed.

He took her hand and raised it to his lips, numb with shock. Nothing in his previous experience had prepared him for such a moment. He had made love to countless women. He had enjoyed them and forgotten them. Now, too late, he knew that Lisette de Valmy would never join their ranks. Her combination of willfulness and vulnerability had awakened in him an emotion he had not suspected he possessed. He felt protective toward her. Responsible. He wanted her not only for now but for as far into the future as he could see. It was as if a fist had been smashed hard into his breastbone.

Unwillingly, he released her hand, following Henri de Valmy from the room. There was only one way that such an ambition could be achieved. His mouth quirked at the corner. He wondered just how Henri de Valmy would react to the news that the enemy of his country, the invader of his home, wished to marry his daughter.

The door closed behind them and Lisette lay weakly back against the pillows. She loved him. It was as simple and fundamental as that. No matter how hard she tried to apply logic to what had happened between them, she would fail. Logic and reason had played no part at all in their personal drama.

A shaft of pain seared through her thigh, and she braced herself against it, wondering how long it would be before the wound healed and the future had to be faced—a future of loving a German but not collaborating with him against her country, a future of such divided loyalties that her brain reeled at the mere thought of them. Her hands tightened into fists. There would be a way. There had to be. And together they would find it.

4

Within ten minutes Elise had entered the room with a tray. She was younger than Lisette had anticipated, with pale, fair hair tied in a band at the nape of her neck, and a pretty, intelligent face.

"I've brought you soup and sandwiches and a hot drink," she said with a friendly smile, setting down the tray on the bedside table. "Though you look to me as if a glass of brandy would be more beneficial."

Lisette managed a grin. "I certainly don't want the soup and sandwiches. Do you think you could discreetly get rid of them?"

"I don't see why not, if it means the comtesse having one less worry. She looks like a ghost, having to endure Meyer's presence at the lunch table."

The light in Lisette's eyes died. This was how Dieter would be talked about, and she would have to accustom herself to it. "Have you been to Sainte-Marie before?" she asked, changing the subject.

Elise shook her head, removing the cup from the tray. "No, I'm a city girl."

And now she was a member of the Resistance. The things that could not be spoken of hung between them for a long moment and then Elise said with sudden fierceness, "I heard what happened to you. They do it for fun. The little Savary boy was run down by a staff car a week ago. He died yesterday."

Lisette remembered the little Savary boy. He had been undersized for his age but had more than made up for his stature in energy. An ebullient, irrepressible child, he had been Paul's despair in the classroom. She turned her head away, feeling sick.

Elise crossed the room, looking out of the high, deeply draped windows to the courtyard below. "They'll pay for what they've done to us," she said with steely determination. "It won't be long now. A few more weeks, a few more months, and then there won't be a German alive on French soil."

Only hours ago, Lisette would have fervently endorsed that statement. Now she wanted to say, "*Not all Germans. Not Dieter.*" Instead, she said, "What happened to me was an accident."

Elise turned from the window, looking at her with incredulity. "You don't really believe that, do you? It was merely Meyer's little piece of sport for the day."

Lisette held Elise's eyes steadily. "It was Major Meyer who gave me immediate first aid and made sure the doctor came quickly."

Elise shrugged. "Perhaps that also amused him," she said equably. "Don't be fooled into thinking he is any different from the others. He isn't. He would have left you to die with the same ease with which he brought you home."

She knew Elise was wrong, but it was futile to tell her so. Her head ached and she felt unbearably tired.

"Meyer is going to Vierville to inspect the new defenses," Elise said, recrossing the room and picking up the unwanted tray. "With a bit of luck he'll stumble over one of his own trip wires and blow himself to eternity." She flashed Lisette a conspiratorial smile. "And if he doesn't kill himself today, perhaps we can arrange that he does so tomorrow."

She left the room, and Lisette closed her eyes against the pain building up behind them. She felt as if she were being torn apart. Nothing that had happened had changed her fervent patriotism. She desperately wanted the Allies to invade, and she knew she would do anything, take any risk, to ensure that the invasion, when it came, was a success. She wanted Germany defeated and France free. And she wanted Dieter Meyer alive. Defeated, maybe bloody, but above all alive. She stared out of the window—her eyes bleak, her heart heavy—hating the war with passionate ferocity.

Dr. Auge came the next morning and confirmed that the little Savary boy had died. He was still in her room when the motorcycle escort tore down Valmy's drive. From the courtyard below came the sound of running feet. Voices were raised and doors slammed.

"What on earth . . . ," the doctor began, his rheumy eyes apprehensive.

"Go to the window," Lisette said urgently. "See what is happening."

Quickly doing so, he squinted down into the courtyard where motorcycles and staff cars were parked ready for use. "The Germans are running around like crazed ants," he said bewilderedly. "Anyone would think that Hitler himself had just arrived."

"Not Hitler," Lisette said, her eyes bright. "Rommel!" She tried to swing her legs from the bed and join him at the window, but Dr. Auge hastily left his vantage point in order to stop her. "Oh, no, you don't," he said firmly. "No walking or even standing on that leg for at least another day."

High heels could be heard approaching, and a second later the comtesse entered the room, calm and elegant despite the disruption caused by the unexpected visitor.

"Is it Rommel, Maman?" Lisette asked swiftly, her thoughts flying to the locked grand dining room and the maps and plans that would be laid on the table.

"Yes." Her mother was dismissive. The Germans could throw themselves into a frenzy because of their general's arrival, but she was certainly not going to do so. "Are you happy with the way the wound is healing?" she asked Dr. Auge, crossing to the bed.

Dr. Auge was gazing at her wide-eyed. Rommel! Perhaps only rooms away! He loosened the collar of his shirt with his fingers.

"Yes, Madame," he said, trying not to show his consternation. "There is no sign of infection. There will be a scar, of

54

course, that is to be expected, but I foresee no complications. Young flesh heals easily."

"A fact for which we may be very thankful," the comtesse said, and at the tremor of relief in her voice, Dr. Auge wondered if she was as cool and unemotional as he had believed.

"I will call again tomorrow, Madame," he said, picking up his bag and jacket. He bid them good-bye, determined to leave by the side door as inconspicuously as possible. The comtesse might be dismissive of Rommel's presence in her home, but he did not share her composure. The thought of running the gauntlet of the general's aides made him feel sick with fear.

"Is he in the grand dining room with Major Meyer?" Lisette asked as her mother sat at the side of the bed.

The comtesse nodded. She had no desire to talk of Rommel. She wanted to forget the presence of Germans in her home. "Marie's niece is very pleasant," she said, steering the conversation determinedly to the minutiae of domesticity. "I wonder why Marie never mentioned her before or suggested that she might come to Valmy. Heaven knows, we could have done with an extra pair of hands these last three years."

Lisette's heart began to slam in short, thick strokes. Her mother was so innocent, so unsuspecting. Yet if Elise were caught trying to gain entry to the grand dining room, she too would suffer the consequences. Horror at the prospect of what those consequences would be nearly paralyzed Lisette. She thrust the images away, striving for normality as she said, "Has papa retrieved my bicycle yet?"

"Major Meyer sent one of his men for it yesterday," her mother said, her voice carefully controlled, revealing none of the confusion that the major's recent actions had aroused. It had been impossible not to be grateful to him for the immediate aid that he had given Lisette. Yet she did not want to be grateful to him. Asking him to join her and her husband for lunch had been a mistake. She had seen him not as a German, but as a person. It had been profoundly unsettling.

"Is it still usable?"

"I doubt it," her mother said, suppressing a shudder at the memory of the mangled front wheel and the dried blood caked on the lethal handlebars.

Lisette frowned in concern. Without a bicycle she could do nothing. "Perhaps papa can fix it . . . or Paul?"

"Perhaps," her mother said. She had no desire to see the bicycle fixed. She wanted Lisette at Valmy, not cycling around the countryside for hours on end, becoming overfriendly with schoolmasters and café proprietors. She pressed the tips of her fingers to her aching temples. Dear Lord, what a mess it all was. If it hadn't been for the war, Lisette's eighteenth year would have been spent in Paris. There would have been parties, balls, suitable young men.

"Elise told me that François Savary was knocked down and killed," Lisette said, her mouth suddenly dry. "Do they know who was responsible?"

Her mother set aside all futile thoughts of Paris, the Champs-Elysées, and couture clothes. "It was a German staff car from Vierville," she said, picking up her embroidery, her voice hard with bitterness. "The driver didn't even stop."

Vierville. Lisette felt a relief that she would not admit to. "*Salauds,*" she said, her eyes dark, thinking of the unknown driver and the body of the small child in the country lane.

Her mother didn't chide her for her language. It was an epithet she would have liked to have had the release of using herself.

She stayed with her daughter until lunchtime, until the sound of fevered activity once more filtered up from the courtyard and the slamming of doors reverberated throughout the château. Seconds later, there came the sound of motorcycles being revved into life, and though they could not see, they both knew that Rommel's short, stocky figure was marching out of Valmy, toward his car. The comtesse held her embroidery motionless in her lap. Lisette could almost hear Dieter's voice bidding his farewells. What had they talked of? What plans had they made for repelling an Allied invasion force? Did they know when the invasion would come? Where? Car and motorcycles surged away, spitting gravel, then silence hung heavy in the high-ceilinged room.

The comtesse stood up and walked across to the windows, looking down into the now quiet courtyard. "I had almost forgotten that Major Meyer was a German and an enemy," she said, her voice oddly flat. "Rommel has reminded me. I shall make quite sure that in the future I do not forget."

Lisette envied her mother the ease of her decision. A faint fragrance of lemon and spice cologne clung to the pillows, and she had only to close her eyes to see him looking down at her—to see the wheat-gold shock of blond hair; the gray eyes that could be so glacial when angry, so dark when filled with desire; the broad, powerful shoulders and lean hips—to be overcome once again by the overt masculinity and strength that she had fought so hard and powerlessly against.

Her mother looked across at her pale face and said contritely, "I shouldn't have stayed with you so long, darling. I've overtired you. I'll leave you now so that you can get some rest."

Lisette did not contradict her, but she knew it wasn't tiredness that was making her feel and look so ravaged. It was the grim knowledge that, by attempting to discover and disclose to the Allies the plans being discussed by Rommel and Dieter in the privacy of the grand dining room, she would be betraying the only man she could ever envision being in love with.

When Elise came in with her tea tray, she pushed herself up against the pillows, sensing at once that Elise had news for her. "What is it?" she asked urgently. "Did you see Rommel? Have you thought of a way of entering the grand dining room?"

"I saw him," Elise said, her face almost as pale as Lisette's, "and I've thought of a way. It won't be easy and it leaves a lot to chance, but it's a risk we must take." She set the tray down on the bedside table and whispered quickly, "I'm going to cause a diversion that will leave the grand dining room unguarded, and I'm going to do it soon. There's no time to wait for an opportunity to present itself. Meyer could be called away from here at any time, and when he goes, the plans and documents that are important enough to warrant Rommel's interest, will go with him."

"How are you going to cause a diversion?" Lisette asked, full of sudden foreboding.

Elise's eyes didn't flicker. "I'm going to start a fire in Meyer's apartment," she said coolly.

Lisette's eyes widened in disbelief. "You're crazy! A fire won't ensure that the dining room is left unguarded, and even if it is, it will only be for a very short space of time."

"Time enough," Elise said with frightening certainty.

57

Lisette stared at her incredulously, her anger growing. "You're mad!" she hissed, wondering how Paul Gilles could possibly have judged Elise to be more competent than herself. "Not only will you destroy Valmy, you'll gain nothing by doing so! What are the Germans going to think when the panic is over and the maps and papers are missing? They're not going to think a passing hitchhiker dropped in and snitched them! They're going to know damned well why the fire was started, and they're not going to have to look very far to find out who was responsible. We'll all be shot! My mother and Marie included!"

"They won't shoot anybody," Elise said equably, "because no maps, no papers, nothing will be missing. I shall photograph what I find. No one will know that anyone has even been in the room."

Lisette's breath was coming short and sharp. "It isn't possible! It's crazy, ill thought out . . ."

"It's a chance," Elise whispered fiercely. "Dear God, Germany's Inspector General of Defense in the West has been discussing military strategy only rooms away, and you're quibbling about the danger!"

"I'm not quibbling about the danger!" Lisette retorted furiously. "I'm quibbling at risking failure!"

"We won't fail," Elise said. "It's going to be as easy as falling off a log."

"Does Paul know your intentions?"

"He gave me the camera. How I get in and out of the room is my own affair."

"It isn't," Lisette said savagely, thinking of her mother. "It's mine as well, and I'm not going to sign my parents' death warrant because you're too hot-headed to listen to reason!"

"You have no choice," Elise said infuriatingly. "It's going to be days before you can even move from your bed."

Lisette's eyes flashed and she gritted her teeth. It wasn't going to be days, it was going to be hours, but she saw no reason why Elise should be informed of her plans.

"Have you told my father what you intend to do?"

"Not yet. The fewer people who know, the better. I've told you because you're the person who's going to have to sit tight on the camera in the immediate aftermath. If any suspicions are aroused, and there is a search, I doubt Meyer will think this room suspect or have his men toss you onto the floor in order to search under your mattress. I don't envy you your conquest, but he's sweet on you. I've overheard him asking after your welfare twice now."

"You're imagining things," Lisette said coldly, a shiver running down her spine.

Elise gave her a sudden, disconcerting smile. "I'm not. I'm very perceptive. I wouldn't have thought a copy-book soldier like Meyer would have been capable of ordinary human emotions, but it seems that where you are concerned, he is. Don't let it panic you. We can use it to our advantage."

"Yes," said Lisette bleakly, determined to see Paul Gilles at the first opportunity. "I'm sure we can."

When Elise left the room, she swung her legs from the bed and determinedly tried to stand. Elise's scheme was just the kind of careless operation Paul had been so insistent they avoid. The stakes were too high to allow for failure.

Sweat broke out on her forehead as she took first one step and then another. And if the Germans *didn't* know the Allies' plans, that information, too, would be vital to London. Her thigh throbbed, the blood pounding, and she reached the window with relief. Somehow she had to walk or ride into the village and speak to Paul. A young corporal was wheeling a motorcycle away into one of the disused stables. Dieter's staff car was parked on the cobblestones, gleaming and polished and frustratingly inaccessible. Elise had said she planned to act soon. But how soon? Surely the best time would be immediately after one of Rommel's visits, and there was no telling when his next flying visit would be. The feeling of foreboding she had felt when Elise entered her room with the tea tray deepened into fear. Had Elise told her of her plans because she intended to act almost immediately? Was there going to be no time to speak to Paul? No opportunity to come up with a safer, surer way?

There was a firm rap on her door, and she flew around to face it, her eyes wide, half expecting to meet the news that Valmy was on fire.

"What are you doing out of bed?" Dieter asked peremptorily, his dark, rich voice smoking across her senses. "Auge told you not to walk on it yet."

"I needed to walk on it," she said unsteadily. "I was getting so stiff I could hardly move."

59

His presence seemed to fill the room. He was in uniform, his cap and gloves held correctly in the crook of his arm, the decoration for valor that Hitler had placed around his neck gleaming in the late afternoon sunlight. He closed the door behind him, placed his cap and gloves on a chair, and walked toward her.

"I tried to visit you earlier, but your mother was insistent that you needed rest."

She tried to speak and could not. He was going to touch her and her mental capitulation would become physical reality. The blood drummed in her ears and she pressed herself back against the window.

He stood mere inches away from her, then slowly reached out, tilting her face to his, tracing the pure outline of her cheekbone and jaw with his forefinger. "Don't be afraid," he said, drawing her toward him, his voice thickening. "I'm not going to hurt you, Lisette. Not now. Not ever."

A shudder ran through her, and she gave a low, soft moan as his arms closed around her and his mouth came down on hers in swift, unfumbled contact. For one brief, vain moment, she tried to resist and pull away, but he held her easily. As his lips burned hers, hard and sweet, her body molded itself to his of its own volition. Her hands moved up and around his neck, her lips parting as she lost her breath in the passion of his mouth.

Nothing mattered any more—not the uniform that he wore, not the language that he spoke, not even Valmy. All that mattered was that she knew, with an instinct ages old, that she had found the other half of her being—the one person without whom she would never again feel whole.

"I love you," she whispered helplessly as his hot, urgent mouth moved to her throat and her shoulders. He slipped the strap of her nightdress free, his fingers caressing the soft warm flesh of her breast.

The silk fall of her hair brushed his hand and tenderness, terrible in its intensity, trembled within him. He wanted to plunder her body, to assuage his deep, driving need of her with ferocious lovemaking; yet when he lifted her in his arms and turned with her toward the bed, it was with passion tightly reined.

She was still pale from the blood she had lost. It would be

days before her stitches were removed, days before he could make love to her without inflicting pain. With a gentleness he had never before experienced, he laid her down on the bed, stunned by the knowledge that he would wait—and wait willingly.

He took hold of her hands, drawing her fingertips up and pressing them against his lips. All of his adult life, he had had as many women as he had chosen to reach out for: sophisticated, clever, beautiful women that he had taken and discarded with ease. Not one of them had possessed Lisette's vibrancy, her allure. Just looking at her sent his pulse pounding and his heart racing.

A smile crooked the corner of his mouth. His family would be outraged. His friends would think he had taken leave of his senses. A Frenchwoman. He could almost hear their remarks, see their disbelief. His shoulders lifted in an imperceptible shrug. He was not a man who cared what others thought of him. He was a hardened man of the world who knew what he wanted. And what he wanted was Lisette de Valmy.

"It won't be easy for you," he said, sliding the strap of her nightdress chastely up and onto her shoulder, fighting the urge to cup the perfect weight of her breast in his palm, knowing that if he did so all restraint would be lost.

There was ownership in his fingers and a shiver ran down her spine. "What won't be easy?" she asked, noticing for the first time the small scar that ran through his left eyebrow, the tiny lines at the corners of his eyes and mouth.

"Marrying a German."

She gazed up at him, her mouth rounding on a gasp of incredulity. "*Marrying?*"

His eyes gleamed. "Of course. What other alternative is there?"

The alternatives were legion and they both knew it. German officers did not marry French girls. They took them as spoils of war. Sometimes they seduced them. Sometimes they even loved them. But they did not marry them.

"But how . . . where?"

He hooked a finger under her chin, lowered his head, and kissed her long and deeply. "Don't you worry about that," he said at last. "Leave it all to me."

61

She grasped his hand. "No!" she cried in sudden fear. "My parents . . . The villagers . . ."

His smile faded. "There's no need for you to concern yourself about retribution from the villagers," he said tightly. "As for your parents . . . they won't like it any more than mine will. But they'll accept it. They'll have no choice."

She shook her head and the late afternoon sunlight danced in her hair. "I don't care what the villagers think of me, or what they might say or do. But I do care about my parents. They will be regarded as collaborators. You may be able to protect them now, but you won't be able to protect them when the war is over."

Her words hung between them. When the war was over. It meant different things to each of them. For Dieter, it meant the subjugation of the British. The surrender of the Americans. A France permanently under German control. A France where no retribution could be taken by the populace against those who had bowed to the inevitable and had joined forces with their conquerors.

To Lisette, it meant a France that was free. A France no longer under the heel of Nazi domination. A France where those who had collaborated would be seen as traitors and treated as such.

They stared at each other, French and German, and the war rose up between them like a high, bloody wall, separating and dividing. At the expression on her face, Dieter's jaw clenched. "Oh, no," he said savagely, reaching out for her and pulling her against him. "We're not going to fall into that trap, Lisette. Let the war take care of itself. It has nothing to do with you and me, and we must never allow it to. I shall tell your parents that we are going to marry, but there is no need for anyone else to know. Not yet. Perhaps not ever." He pressed his mouth against her hair. He would take her to Berlin. There would be difficulties, but none that he could not overcome.

His voice was the voice of a man accustomed to making decisions and not having those decisions questioned. She leaned against him, sliding her arms around the lean tautness of his waist, resting her head against his chest; the sense of refuge that she had felt when his arms had closed around her in the rear of the Horch returned in full force. His lips brushed her temples, her cheeks, and then closed hungrily on her willing mouth, and she knew that no power on earth would ever separate them. Not family. Not country. Nothing.

"Love me," she begged in hungry, hoarse tones she scarcely recognized. "Please love me!"

His muscles tensed as he exerted every last vestige of his iron-strong self-control. "No," he said, pressing her back against the pillows, his strong hands cupping her breasts, his mouth a mere fraction from hers. "Not while you're so weak that you can hardly stand."

"Then when?" Her shamelessness devastated her.

A grin tugged at his mouth. "When Auge says you no longer need his services. We'll go out for the day, far from Valmy. We'll have lunch and champagne and . . ." His voice deepened and she trembled against him. "We'll make love. There'll be no going back. Not ever."

She bent her head and kissed his hands. He stroked the satin-soft fall of her hair and left her quickly, not trusting himself to remain.

He frowned as he ran lightly down the stairs and crossed the flagged hall toward the grand dining room. His interview with Henri de Valmy would not be pleasant, and his interview with Field Marshal Rommel would take nearly as much courage as a straight run into cannon fire. German army regulations forbade marriage between servicemen and subject races. He shrugged dismissively. The German ambassador to France had married a Frenchwoman, and what was good enough for a potbellied ambassador was good enough for him.

The sentry on duty clicked his heels and saluted smartly as he strode past him and into the tapestried dining room. With a wry grin, he seated himself at the twenty-foot table, wondering who would be more appalled at his news—the comte or the field marshal.

A report to Rommel lay on the table waiting for completion. It was his personal estimate of the Allies' intentions. When it had been evaluated by Rommel, it would be sent with Army Group B's weekly report to Oberbefehlshaber West, Field Marshal von Rundstedt's headquarters, and from there, suitably embroidered, it would become part of the overall theater report and would be forwarded to the Oberkommando der Wehrmacht, Hitler's headquarters. God alone knew what would happen to it then. There were times when he believed that everything sent to OKW was destroyed unseen. Certainly no notice was taken of Rommel's repeated requests.

His face was grim as he picked up his pen. Rommel needed panzer divisions. No matter how many mines and booby traps were planted, the coastline could not be rendered safe without the backup of panzers. But the panzer divisions were being held in reserve far from the coast, and the führer insisted on retaining them there under his personal authority. Von Rundstedt could not move them, and Rommel, who had fought with such success with panzers in North Africa, could not move them.

Dieter's frown deepened. They needed at least five panzer divisions to counterattack an invasion. In the beginning of an assault, their presence would be vital. He worked steadily for three hours, forgetting all about Lisette and his personal difficulties, concentrating on the problem of when and where the Allies would attack, and how they would best be repelled.

Rommel had been tense and edgy when he had descended on Valmy because of the grueling hours that he worked and the nightmare suspense of constantly watching and waiting for moves from across the Channel.

"There's still no sign of an attack," he had said, pacing the dining room fretfully. "I'm beginning to think the Anglo-Americans have lost confidence in their cause, Meyer."

Dieter had not agreed with him. The Allies had not lost confidence. They were simply waiting. And when the moment was right, they would strike. But *where?* He clenched his hands into fists of frustration. Hitler had made it known that he thought it would be Normandy, and for once, Dieter was in agreement with his führer. Rommel and the other chiefs of staff favored the Pas de Calais.

He leaned back in his chair, ringing for coffee, studying for the thousandth time the aerial reconnaissance photographs spread out before him. Wherever the Allies invaded, they would need air cover, and the effective range of their Spitfires was 150 miles. That ruled out anywhere west of Cherbourg. It would be impossible to unload an army beneath steep cliffs, and that ruled out further vast sections of the coast. And the sea crossing would, of necessity, have to be short. All of which indicated the Pas de Calais. And yet . . .

His eyes narrowed. The Pas de Calais was too easy, too obvious. It was the Normandy beaches that would make an ideal landing site. They were not as heavily defended as the Pas de Calais, and the Allies would be well aware of the fact. Certainty, cold and hard, settled deep in his gut and he knew beyond any doubt, that Normandy would be where the invasion would take place.

But when and where?

In January, German intelligence had informed the chiefs of staff that they knew of a two-part signal that would be used to alert the Resistance immediately prior to an invasion. Rommel had treated the information with contempt, but General Canaris had been adamant that the information was correct and that all radio messages by the Allies be monitored with scrupulous care. Dieter had thought it a strange message to indicate the invasion of a continent. The first signal was to be the opening line of "Song of Autumn" by the 19th-century French poet, Paul Verlaine—"The long sobs of the violins of autumn." The second signal was to be the second line—"Wound my heart with a monotonous languor."

He had found a book containing Verlaine's poems in the château's library and had flicked through them with mild enjoyment. But he did not believe that Verlaine's words would herald the decisive battle for the German Reich. Grimly, ignoring the lateness of the hour, he picked up his pen once more and continued with his report.

At hourly intervals, Lisette walked gingerly from the bed to the window and back again, spurred on by the urgent necessity of being able to walk or ride into the village and speak to Paul. Elise had to be prevented from acting carelessly. If she did so, she would be caught. No information from Valmy would reach the Allies, and there would be no future for any of them. She leaned her forehead against the window, knowing that by serving her country she was betraying Dieter. "But not to death," she whispered fiercely. "Please God, never that." The information would be passed in the hope that it would help an Allied victory. Only with such a victory could they ever hope to live freely and openly together.

At Valmy? Could she ever live freely and openly with a

German at Valmy? Knowing the answer, she turned, sick at heart, and walked slowly back to her bed. The Rembrandt gleamed palely in the moonlight. Elise, when she had brought up her supper tray, had remarked savagely that all Germans were thieves and barbarians. Lisette had remained silent, knowing too well the treasures that had been stripped and looted from France, and knowing that, while Dieter Meyer was in residence, Valmy's treasures were safe.

The word "collaborator" seemed to whisper in the air around her and her eyes blazed. She was *not* a collaborator. She was not working with the enemy for her country's defeat. She knew that she would die rather than do so. And she would die, too, still loving Dieter. The knowledge came calmly and certainly, filling her with inner strength.

She turned to the books that he had left on the bedside table: Zola's *Nana*, a collection of poems by Paul Verlaine, Turgenev's *Father and Sons*. It was a strange collection for a soldier. She picked up the leather-bound copy of Verlaine's poems, noting the faint pencil mark at the side of "Song of Autumn," wondering why a poem of unrequited love had so appealed to him. She read until she fell asleep.

Elise woke early. As she moved quietly and efficiently about the kitchen, preparing breakfast, she could hear the faint chime of the church bell in Sainte-Marie-des-Ponts ringing the Angelus. Another night of curfew was over, and it was the 1363d day of Occupation. She knew that Lisette thought her scheme rash, and yet she could think of no alternative. She had to gain entrance to the grand dining room. She removed a *baguette* from the oven, filling the kitchen with the fragant aroma of newly baked bread. It had to be done in Meyer's absence. He was far too sharp to fall for any diversion, however skillfully planned. And if Meyer was absent, it meant that the ornately carved doors would be not only guarded, but locked.

She reached into a cupboard for a jar of honey. Only Meyer had a key, and she had not even toyed with the idea of removing it from his possession to make a copy. The lock, when the door was left unguarded, would have to be picked, and picked quickly.

She made herself a cup of chicory and leaned against the

stone sink, sipping it thoughtfully. Her ability with her fingers was the reason she had been detailed to Valmy. Her father had been a locksmith, and he had taught her his trade. It was a skill she had put to good use in her Resistance work. She wondered how many computations and permutations the lock had. If it was a five-lever lock, it would take perhaps ten minutes to profile, maybe fifteen—fifteen minutes that she did not have. From the far side of the château came the sound of running feet and motorcycles being blasted into life. She emptied the remains of her chicory down the sink and lifted a heavy, cast-iron omelette pan from the shelf above the stove.

No diversion she could stage would keep the grand dining room unattended for fifteen minutes. Lisette's horror had been justified. Yet the alternative would mean the de Valmys' death warrant, as well as her own. The sentry would have to be killed. There would be no disguising that the dining room had been entered, and spiriting the undeveloped film out of Valmy and out of the district would be a near impossibility.

The door flew open and Marie half fell into the room. "There's a house-to-house search taking place in the village," she gasped, her bosom heaving, her face white. "They're looking for a British pilot who made a forced landing outside Vierville two weeks ago!"

"Will they find him?" Elise asked tersely.

"Who knows?" Marie's arthritic fingers plucked agitatedly at the hem of her apron. "If they do, there will be arrests, deaths. Someone will talk, and then someone else will talk, and then where will we be?"

Elise cracked an egg savagely into the omelette pan. God willing, no one would talk; but if there were arrests, the price of silence would be high.

Dieter slammed the telephone receiver down hard on its rest. An hour ago general headquarters had woken him demanding that he instigate a full-scale search of Sainte-Marie-des-Ponts. An arrested Resistance member, under interrogation at Gestapo headquarters in Caen, had given information. An airman was being hidden at a safe house in Sainte-Marie. Dieter had curtly demanded that he be given more details but had been told that the informant had died under questioning.

"Imbeciles!" Dieter had snarled to himself, dressing and

issuing orders in cold fury. Their brutality sickened him. Subtle and intelligent questioning might have taken longer but would eventually have yielded far more.

"Beer-hall Nazis," he muttered savagely as he slammed out of his room, knowing full well that he would have to go into Sainte-Marie himself to supervise the search.

"Good morning, Major," the comtesse said politely as their paths crossed at the foot of the stairs. "Everyone seems to be awake exceptionally early today. Lisette is already fretting for Dr. Auge's arrival."

He paused. His car was waiting in the drive. His presence was needed in the village. "Perhaps I could see her before I leave the château?"

The question was purely rhetorical. The comtesse froze and said stiffly, "If you wish, Major Meyer."

He had already turned on his heel, and as he took the stairs two at a time, the comtesse fought down a surge of panic, hurrying toward her husband's room, more than ever disturbed by the major's interest in Lisette.

Dieter knocked sharply on the bedroom door and entered, relishing Lisette's expression of disbelief and pleasure. "Did you sleep well?" he asked, striding toward the bed.

Beneath her nightdress, the soft curves of her body were clearly visible.

"Yes . . . I . . ." Anything else she was about to say was left unsaid as his lips silenced hers. It was a long, deep kiss. Fierce and hungry. Infinitely satisfying. When at last he raised his head, there was heat in his eyes.

"So this is how you look first thing in the morning," he said huskily, smoothing her tousled hair away from her face.

Her smile was happy, sensuous. "What an unfair way to find out. Are you disappointed?"

A dimple lurked at the corner of her mouth and he kissed it. "No," he said, pushing the bedclothes aside and easing her legs to the floor. "I doubt I will ever be that."

He drew her to her feet, pressing her lithe young body hard against the length of his. Desire rushed through her so strong and urgent that she gasped aloud, standing on her toes to fit herself more perfectly against him. His fingers tightened in her hair, his happiness so deep-founded that it filled him with amazement. Love had struck him when he had least expected it—in the middle of war, and in an enemy land.

"I shall speak to your father tonight," he said, brooking no argument. She trembled, and he half lifted her against him, breathing in the sweet, clean fragrance of her hair and skin, kissing her with a passion that blinded all reason. The early morning sun streamed in, bathing them in golden light. When he raised his head from hers, looking down into the perfection of her face, he knew it was a moment that would remain in his memory forever.

"I love you," he said fiercely, stunned by the truth of his words. "Never forget it," and then he turned on his heel, striding swiftly from the room, wrenching himself back to his duty and the distasteful task awaiting him in Sainte-Marie-des-Ponts.

Lisette was still standing in the center of the room when Dr. Auge entered. He had passed the major on the stairs and, mindful of the situation in the village, had fairly scampered along the corridor and into the comparative sanctuary of Lisette's bedroom.

"Whatever is the matter, Dr. Auge?" she asked as he loosened his waxed shirt collar, his forefinger trembling convulsively.

"The village has been sealed off," he said, looking over his shoulder nervously to make sure that no one was listening behind him. "The Boche are conducting a house-to-house search for an Allied pilot. God knows what will happen if they find him."

She stared at him, stunned, the happiness draining out of her. "How long have they been searching?" she asked, feeling cold, and empty, and sick.

"Since dawn."

Ice seeped down her spine. While she had been in Dieter's arms, the Germans had been rampaging through Sainte-Marie. She wondered if he knew of the search and realized that he must. That was where he had gone now: to the village.

"Excuse me," she said to Dr. Auge, pushing past him, running for the door. She had to see Dieter before he left the château. She had to know.

"Mademoiselle!" Dr. Auge called out in protest. She ignored him. She ignored the throbbing pain in her leg, the fact that she was wearing only her nightdress and had not even a robe around her shoulders. She could hear cars screaming to a halt. Voices were raised, loud and harsh. She felt as if she were drowning—as if the very life was being squeezed out of her.

"What on earth . . . ," she heard her father exclaim from the hallway, then she was at the curve of the stairs. Valmy's massive oak door burst open, and all her hopes and dreams shriveled and died.

The Germans had captured three of them: a weary, gaunt-faced young man she had never seen before; Paul Gilles, his face bloodied, his glasses smashed; and André Caldron.

She gave a strangled, inarticulate cry.

"We've got them, Major," one of the soldiers said and thrust them forward so that they fell, hands tied behind their backs, at Dieter's feet.

5

Silence thundered in the ancient, sun-dappled hall. Henri de Valmy had wrenched the library door open, intent on running to the scene of the disturbance. At the sight in front of him, he froze on the threshold, his eyes widening in horror.

The soldiers stood at attention—young and broad shouldered, prime specimens of Aryan manhood—as they waited for acknowledgment from their commanding officer for a mission speedily and satisfactorily accomplished.

Paul and André had been thrust forward with such force that they sprawled before Dieter full length. Only the airman had retained his dignity. Forced to his knees, he regarded Dieter with insolence and then turned his head, looking up the graceful sweep of stairs to where Lisette stood in her ivory silk nightdress, her face ashen, her heart pounding as she fought for breath and strength. There was no fear in his eyes, only curiosity; then Dieter moved, and the tableau was broken.

He walked to the foot of the stairs, his face a sculpted mask. Lisette's fingers slipped and slid on the polished wood of the banister. She tried to speak, to move toward him, but could do nothing. It was as if her very life were being counted away in seconds—hopes and dreams running out with the sands of time, leaving a dark, immeasurable void in their wake that nothing would ever fill.

He lifted his head to hers, and in his eyes, she saw reflected her own all-encompassing despair. There could be no more compromise, no further pretense.

He halted, one foot on the bottom stair, his body so taut that the tendons in his neck were clenched into knots. The sun shone on his blond, cropped hair. She could see the white line of the scar that ran through his eyebrow and that her finger, only a little while before, had so lovingly traced.

"Let them go," she whispered, leaning her weight against the banister, sliding down weakly against it until she, like the men in the hall, was on her knees. "Please, for me . . . for us."

A nerve throbbed at his jaw line. A spasm of pain, so devastating that he wanted to cry out loud, flared through his eyes; then he turned away from her, and she knew that her plea had been in vain.

"Take the Englishman to Caen," he said curtly.

"No! Please, no!" she gasped, horror deepening and multiplying.

"Immediately!" he snapped to the officer, ignoring her. It was a sentence of death.

The Englishman was wrenched to his feet, and for a brief moment, he looked once more in her direction, and there was a glimmer of a smile about his mouth. "Thank you, Mademoiselle," he said, inclining his head before he was savagely hustled away.

She heard her father's hopeless protest, Marie's strangled sob, and then Paul and André were dragged to their feet.

"Paul!" She hauled herself to her feet, stumbling down the stairs, oblivious of her naked arms and shoulders, and the revealing thinness of her nightdress.

"Stop her!" Dieter ordered her father, his face chalk white.

Henri de Valmy moved swiftly, taking the stairs two at a time, wrapping his arms restrainingly around her.

"Paul!" she cried again, struggling futilely.

He turned his head to hers, his face pale, his eyes expressionless.

"You can't help them this way," her father whispered, tightening his hold on her. "We must speak to him on his own. Not in front of his men!"

"Take them away," Dieter rasped out, his jaw clenched, the skin tight across his cheekbones.

They were led away, and she heard a harsh, rasping cry of pain and knew that it was her own.

"Come along," her father was saying urgently. "He's not sending Paul and André to Caen until he has interrogated them himself. There's still time."

The sound of Paul and André's feet drumming on the cobblestones as they walked away under heavy guard reverberated on the still morning air. Dieter was alone in the hallway. Slowly he turned his head and looked up at her, his eyes revealing the enormity of his rage and frustration and defeat.

She was sobbing, the tears rolling mercilessly down her face and onto her nightdress. He wanted to seize hold of her, to kiss away her tears, to blind her to reason and reality.

"Free them," she pleaded again, her desperation so naked that his heart twisted in his breast. Her plea was not just for the lives of Paul and André; it was for their own lives, their own future.

His eyes were black pits of despair. They had no future. He was a German and an officer, and he could not do as she asked.

"Take her to her room," he said bleakly to Henri; then he turned and walked into the grand dining room. The hall was once again empty, save for the sunbeams and the dancing motes of dust.

She stared after him for a long, disbelieving moment, and then, half blinded by tears, she began to stumble back up the stairs. She had to dress. She had to make him change his mind.

Dr. Auge started fearfully as she rushed into the room. He

had heard the disturbance and seen first the Englishman being led away, then Paul Gilles and André Caldron. "What is happening?" he asked in panic. "Is the village safe? Are there to be reprisals?"

"They have arrested Gilles and Caldron," Henri said heavily. "There's no telling what will happen next."

Dr. Auge mopped his perspiring forehead with a large handkerchief. Executions were what could happen next, and the Boche had a habit of selecting their victims with terrifying impartiality.

"I'm going down to speak to him," she said feverishly. "He must let them go, Papa! If he sends them to Caen, they will be shot!"

Deep lines scored Henri de Valmy's face from nose to mouth. "No," he said. He felt old before his time. "That is my responsibility, Lisette."

She stepped behind a large screen and pulled her nightdress over her head, dropping it to the floor. Hurriedly, she dressed in a lavender wool sweater and a violet tweed skirt. "No, Papa," she said, her voice queerly abrupt. "It's mine."

She slipped on a pair of sandals, then eased around the screen, motioning to her father to precede her into the corridor. She turned slowly to face him, her eyes dark with pain.

Her father shook his head. "My dear child, how can the responsibility to speak to the major possibly be yours?"

"Because, until a few minutes ago, I was going to be his wife."

She saw the shock in his eyes, the disbelief. And then the disbelief faded, and she moved swiftly away from him.

She hurried toward the head of the stairs, forcing herself not to think of her father's shock and pain. It was Paul and André she had to think of, Paul and André she had to save from execution.

The Englishman was beyond her help. Dieter had sent him to his death as surely as if he had shot him in Valmy's courtyard. How many other deaths was he responsible for? How, until now, had she managed to close her eyes to the reality of his uniform? How could she possibly have envisaged sharing his bed, bearing his children?

73

The answer seemed to scream at her from the walls, and she pressed her hands over her ears in an attempt to blot it out physically. It was because she loved him, because she would always love him. But love was no longer enough. Not now. Perhaps not ever.

As she crossed the hall toward the sentry-guarded door of the grand dining room, Elise stepped out of the library carrying a tray. Her small, pointed face was white, but her hands were steady. Their gazes held, speaking untold volumes; then Elise hurried away toward the kitchen, and Lisette approached the sentry, saying with fierce determination, "I would like to speak to Major Meyer, please."

"*Nein*," the sentry said, not deigning to look at her. The grand dining room was sacrosanct. Not even officers went in there.

Panic bubbled up in her. She had to speak to him before he ordered that Paul and André be taken to Caen. "I insist," she said, her eyes flashing, her chin tilting defiantly.

"*Nein*," the sentry growled again, barring her way with the butt of his rifle.

Two of the soldiers who had been in the party that had captured Paul and André tramped into the hall.

"*Schafft sie fort*," the sentry said to them bad-temperedly. "Take her away."

The men laughed, seizing hold of her with ribald comments.

"Let me go!" she shouted furiously, and then louder and in desperation, "Dieter! *Dieter!*"

The door was pulled open with such ferocity that the soldiers staggered backward. He stared down at her, his lips bloodless. He had known that she would come, but even now, he was not prepared for the things they would have to say to each other.

"Inside," he said to her curtly, and then, to the disconcerted men, "*Genug!*"

Very little had changed in the high, hammer-beamed ceilinged room. The beechwood floor still gleamed as sunlight streamed in through the stained-glass windows. The huge stone fireplace was still decorated with polished brasses and heavy iron firedogs, and the twenty-foot dining table around which countless generations of de Valmys had feasted still stretched away down the center of the room. Only now there were no silver candelabras on its polished surface. Instead there were maps and sheaves of paper, and a workmanlike desk lamp.

The door closed and they were alone. Lisette turned and faced Dieter. He was the same person who, only an hour earlier, had taken her in his arms and told her he loved her and talked of their marriage. He knew he still loved her, and there would never be any marriage. They had thought they were stronger than the war and the circumstances of their lives, and they had been proved cruelly wrong.

"You should have stayed in your room," he said, his voice raw with the bitterness of their defeat. "You shouldn't have seen what happened. You shouldn't have known about it."

He didn't move toward her or try to take her in his arms, and she was grateful.

"I have known Paul Gilles and André Caldron all my life," she said, her voice throbbing with the emotions warring within her. "There is no way that I wouldn't have found out what happened."

"It needn't alter anything," he said savagely, his eyes blazing, *"Mein Gott!* Why should an Englishman and two damned Frenchmen destroy our future? It's insane!"

She shook her head, feeling suddenly older than he, and wiser. "It's not insane," she said, her eyes brilliant with unshed tears. "It's reality."

"Gott im Himmel!" he cried, his fist slamming down hard on the table. "We're at war! I had no alternative but to send the Englishman to Caen!"

"And Paul and André?" she asked, her eyes burning into his. "What will you do with them?"

She looked so delicate, so fragile, and yet he was aware more than ever of her core of inner strength. She had dressed hastily. There was no comb in the glossy black sheen of her hair to push it away from her face, and it dipped forward at her cheekbones, falling to her shoulders in a long, smooth wave. The soft wool of her sweater clung provocatively to the high fullness of her bare breasts, and he felt his manhood harden and swell. He wanted her, and he'd be damned to hell before he would allow the events of the morning to rob him of her.

"Paul Gilles and André Caldron knew the risks they were

75

taking when they sheltered the Englishman," he said, and she could see the heat in his eyes and his naked need for her. "Forget them, Lisette. Forget that it ever happened."

He moved toward her and she stepped backward, her bare legs and sandaled feet making her look as vulnerable as a child. "Let them go," she pleaded. "Isn't it enough that you have the Englishman?"

She could retreat no farther. Her hands were pressed against the paneled wall.

Lights danced in her hair and his senses were filled with her natural fragrance. "They are members of the Resistance," he said, his voice thickening as he leaned his body against her, pinning her against the wall. "They have to be questioned."

His hands slid up and under her sweater, cupping the delicious weight of her breasts. She drew in a deep, ragged breath, her pupils dilating.

"Will you free them?" she panted as his thumbs brushed the pink tips of her nipples, and her body screamed in an agony of pain and ecstasy. His eyes were dark with passion.

"No," he said, and lowered his head to hers, certain of his sexual domination over her.

It was over. Finished. She tilted her head back and, her heart breaking, spat full in his face. "Murderer!" she hissed, twisting away from him, running for the door. *"May you rot in hell!"*

"Jesus God!" His face was sheet-white. He sprang after her with terrifying speed, and she slammed the door on him, racing past the startled sentry, sobbing for breath, knowing that if he caught her he was quite capable of raping or killing her.

He seized hold of the door handle, then smashed his other fist into the wood above it. He had lost her. From the moment his troops had burst open Valmy's doors and thrust the Frenchmen at his feet, he had known that he had lost her. To pursue her was futile. He spun on his heel, marching back to the table, slamming his fist into his palm time and time again as he damned Gilles and Caldron and fought for control over his rage and frustration.

He halted abruptly, his blood running cold. Paul Gilles and André Caldron. He had wanted to question them for the same reason the Gestapo wanted to question them. To gain every last scrap of information about the Resistance network in and around Sainte-Marie-des-Ponts. Even if they did not talk when he interrogated them, they would talk once they reached Caen. Only the exceptionally brave, or exceptionally stupid, remained silent. They would give information, and they would give names. In that moment, all his suspicions of Lisette's bicycle rides and Elise's presence in the château crystalized into certainty. He knew, without a shadow of doubt, that the names Gilles and Caldron would give would include Elise Duras and Lisette de Valmy.

He cursed viciously. Headquarters already knew of the men's arrest. There was no pretext on which he could release them. Yet to send them to Gestapo headquarters at Caen would be to deliver Lisette herself into the hands of the SS.

The thought made him go cold with terror. He had to act and act quickly. Gilles and Caldron could not be allowed to reach Caen alive. The danger to Lisette was too great.

He strode toward the telephone, intending to order the immediate formation of a firing squad, and then paused. To execute them out of hand when Gestapo headquarters had specifically requested they be sent there for questioning would be crass stupidity. Far fewer suspicions would be aroused if they were shot while trying to escape.

His knuckles whitened. What he was going to do would sever himself from Lisette irrevocably. Her fury now was not for him but for the action he had taken. Once blood had been spilt, it would not be fury that filled her heart but cold, unyielding hatred. Yet it had to be done. For her sake, it had to be done.

He moved quickly, taking a small bunch of keys from his pocket and crossing to the nearest window. A steel-mesh security grille prevented entry or exit. It was hinged to the window frame on one side, locked on the other so that it could be opened in case of fire. Swiftly he unlocked it top and bottom. The stained-glass window behind it opened outward, the windowsill a mere three feet from the ground.

There were no carefully tended rose gardens on this side of the château, no stables or courtyards with loitering soldiers. The land shelved, bleak and bare, toward the cliffs, and he saw that low clouds were scudding in, suffocating the sunlight and shrouding the land in mist. His eyes narrowed. Only a fool would imagine escape lay that way, but the slim chance would surely be preferable to Gilles and Caldron than the certainty of what awaited them in Caen.

Grim-faced, he pushed the unlocked grille gently against the window pane and crossed to the telephone. "Have the schoolmaster sent in to me," he ordered curtly.

He wondered how Gilles would stand up to questioning. He was a thin, ineffectual-looking creature, but his type often showed the most resilience. He hoped to God that Gilles broke down and told him about Lisette's involvement. If he did so, it would make what he had to do so much easier. The last thing he wanted was to respect Paul Gilles.

There was a sharp knock at the door. He paused for a brief second before calling, "*Eintreten.*" If he were in Gilles's position, he would suffer the worst that the sadists in Caen could devise and not breathe a word that would bring harm to her. But then he loved her. Her life meant more to him than his own. And because of Gilles and Caldron, she wished him in hell.

He swore beneath his breath as the door opened, and Paul Gilles and his escort entered the room. Gilles's broken glasses and bloodied face made him a pathetic sight, but his eyes burned defiantly.

"Bastard!" he shouted as, his hands still tied behind his back, he was yanked unceremoniously toward a chair.

Dieter asked the escort to leave the room and regarded the schoolmaster curiously. There had been a time when he had wondered jealously if Lisette had been emotionally involved with this Gilles, but now he saw that was impossible, for the unprepossessing Frenchman had nothing whatsoever to offer a woman. He flicked open a packet of cigarettes. He knew, before he started, that he was going to learn very little from this man. There wasn't the time to wear him down, either mentally or physically. But gathering information was no longer his purpose. His purpose was to make sure that Paul Gilles never reached headquarters in Caen. His purpose was to make sure that the name Lisette de Valmy was not screamed out under torture to the SS.

"Who, in Sainte-Marie-des-Ponts, takes messages for you?" he asked. It was a voice that Lisette would not have recognized. A voice hard with menace.

Paul looked at him with loathing. The questioning was civilized enough now, but he knew very well to what depths it would descend.

"You're wasting your time. You'll get nothing out of me. Not now. Not ever."

Dieter, knowing the interrogation methods of Caen, regarded him pityingly. "Don't be a fool. Tell me what I want to know."

Paul spat derisively. Dieter glanced at his watch. The airman would be nearly at Caen by now. Very soon the telephone would ring, and there would be a demand to know where the two captured Frenchmen were.

"Don't be so confident that you will not talk, Gilles. Braver, better men than you have done so," he said, and slowly and explicitly he began to tell Paul Gilles exactly what he could expect in the prison cells in Caen.

He could see fear spark in the Frenchman's eyes, but to each and every question he only repeated, "You're wasting your time. I won't talk. Not ever."

"Lisette de Valmy takes messages for you, doesn't she?" Dieter said suddenly.

The pause before Gilles answered was infinitesimal, but Dieter was thunderingly aware of it and knew that the SS at Caen would have been aware of it too. For all his brave words, Paul Gilles would break under questioning. If the SS got hold of him, they would, with terrifying rapidity, get hold of Lisette too.

The telephone rang shrilly. He knew, even before he answered, who it would be. "Good morning, Major Meyer," the commandant at Caen said smoothly. "We appear to be two prisoners short."

"Gilles and Caldron are here in Valmy."

"The questioning of suspected Resistance members is a task that is to be carried out here, Major. Is that understood?"

"Yes, Commandant," Dieter said, his voice cold with dislike.

"Then I will expect them here within the hour, Major."

The line clicked and was dead. Dieter waited a second, then dialed his lieutenant's number. "Send Caldron in," he ordered. He turned once more to Gilles. "Caldron may be more willing than yourself to talk of Mademoiselle de Valmy's

79

involvement with the Resistance, especially if in doing so, he thinks he will save his own skin."

The fear in Paul Gilles's eyes deepened, and Dieter knew with sudden certainly that it would be Caldron, not Gilles, who would break first under questioning. Caldron, on no account, must reach Caen.

When the middle-aged café proprietor was thrust into the room, and Paul Gilles once again seized by the guards, Dieter said easily, "Please leave him, Lieutenant Halder."

Halder looked at him oddly but complied, and Paul Gilles was abruptly released.

"*Danke schön,*" Dieter said, and as the door closed behind the escort, he turned to the apprehensive André Caldron and said tersely in his immaculate French, "Tell me the extent of Lisette de Valmy's involvement with the Resistance."

André stared at him stupidly. He had expected to be questioned about the airman, about addresses of other safe houses along the escape chain. "I don't know what you mean," he said blusteringly.

"I think you do," Dieter said softly, his eyes narrowing. "And you're going to tell me. That is, you will tell me if you don't want to go to Caen."

There was sweat on André's thick upper lip, and Dieter knew that he was going to talk. He felt suddenly sick. He didn't want to hear the words confirming his suspicions. He didn't want to know. His hands shook slightly as he lit another cigarette. He had to know. For her own sake, if she was involved, he had to know how deeply.

He walked toward Caldron until the perspiring Frenchman was only inches away from him. "If you want to go free," he said, the menace in his voice naked, "Tell me about Lisette de Valmy."

Within five minutes the words came spilling from the big, bull-necked Frenchman as easily as from a child. Paul Gilles, white-faced, shouted obscenities at his compatriot until he was hoarse. Lieutenant Halder, hearing the disturbance, knocked and inquired whether his assistance was needed and was sent brusquely away. The last thing Dieter wanted was for anyone else to hear Lisette's name on Caldron's lips.

"I've told you everything I know about her," the Frenchman panted at last, his face shiny with sweat. "Can I go now?"

Dieter wanted to vomit. Without having a hair of his head harmed, the creature in front of him had told him enough for him to have had Lisette immediately arrested. The man's cowardice was beyond belief.

"*Bastard!*" Paul Gilles was screaming at Caldron, his face contorted with hatred. "*You miserable, yellow-bellied bastard!*"

"Tell me about Elise."

Caldron looked blank. Dieter's eyes flicked toward Paul Gilles. His shouted obscenities had ceased. He looked as though he had stopped breathing. Dieter didn't need to see or hear any more. Caldron knew nothing of Elise, but Gilles did. And he no longer had any time in which to question Paul Gilles.

Slowly and deliberately, he walked toward the window. He didn't like what he was going to do. There was a meanness to it, a deceit, which was not in his character. A shot in the back was no way for a man to die. Thin white lines etched his nose and mouth as he swung the window open and tossed his cigarette stub far out over the grass. He was doing it because he had no choice. Not if he wanted to safeguard Lisette. And to safeguard Lisette, he would have razed Sainte-Marie-des-Ponts to ashes.

He spun on his heel, walking back to them, the window open behind him, the breeze gently lifting the edges of the heavy damask curtains.

"Can I go now? I've told you all I know," Caldron whimpered.

"No," Dieter said icily. "You leave for Caen in ten minutes."

Caldron blanched. "You promised!" he gibbered. "You gave your word!"

Dieter ignored him. He wasn't worth wasting breath on. He looked across at Paul Gilles and felt pity for him. He didn't deserve to die with such a coward. "Caldron's shame is his alone," he said brusquely, "not yours." Then he turned on his heel and left the room, Caldron's frenzied protests still ringing in his ears.

The sentry looked at him disconcertedly but knew better

than to say anything. If Major Meyer had left two Frenchmen in a room with highly sensitive documents, it was because he had a good reason for doing so.

Dieter flicked open a packet of cigarettes. One minute passed, and then two, and still no sound had come from behind the closed doors. His lighter spurted into flame and then there came the barely audible sound of a booted foot scraping the windowsill and the soft thud as a body dropped to earth.

"When you shoot, shoot to kill," he ordered the sentry, whipping the door open, springing across the room to the window.

Paul Gilles was already thirty yards away, head down, running dementedly. André Caldron lumbered behind him, weaving unsteadily, his balance hampered by his bound wrists.

Dieter lifted his firing arm and took careful aim. He felt no compunction at all in shooting down the man who had so cravenly implicated Lisette in the hope of saving his own skin. With cool deliberation he fired, and André Caldron fell to the earth, his skull shattered. He did not know whether it was his shot or the sentry's that brought the still running figure of Paul Gilles to the ground in a bloodied heap, nor did he want to know. It was enough that it was done. Over. Lisette's name would not now be added to the list of French men and women suspected of being members of the Resistance. Slowly he lowered his arm, the pistol heavy in his hand, and turned. Halder and a squad of men were running across the hall and into the room. Tersely he ordered them to retrieve the bodies, and then he saw the gleam of her hair as she pushed between the soldiers, fighting her way into the room.

She broke free of the last of them and stood before him, her eyes wide with horror, her slender body trembling. "You've killed them!" she gasped, and a dreadful shudder ran through her, convulsing her. "Oh, my God! You've killed them!"

He looked into the ashen perfection of her face and knew that he could say nothing. He could never tell her why he had shot them. The burden was not hers to carry. "Take her away," he said quietly, his voice raw with weariness.

She arched her spine as she was seized, her hair tumbling

around her shoulders, her eyes betraying the depth of her anguish.

"*Murderer!*" she shouted, the cry sounding as if it had been torn from her heart, and then louder, in potent, raging hate: "Murderer! *Murderer! MURDERER!*"

6

Elise came to her room an hour later. "He suspects," she said tightly. "He's ordered me to leave. Now. Immediately."

"He can't suspect you! If he suspected you, he would have had you arrested and shot you as he did Paul and André!"

"He suspects," Elise repeated, shocked by Lisette's grief-ravaged face. She remembered the rumors she had heard concerning Lisette's relationship with Paul Gilles and for the first time wondered if they were true. "He won't allow anyone else into Valmy, not unless it is purposely to trap them. Goodbye, Lisette. I've no more time. I have to go."

Lisette stepped toward her. "Where is the camera?" she asked urgently.

Elise looked gaunt. "In my bag."

Lisette's finely etched nostrils flared. "You'll be searched," she said tightly. "Give it to me. Let me hide it."

"It's too dangerous," Elise protested, but there was indecision in her expression.

"Give it to me," Lisette insisted with such passion that Elise blinked. This was a new Lisette, a creature of steel and determination and implacable will.

She bent down to the bag at her feet and unzipped it. "It's inside there," she said, pulling out a tin of dried milk.

"Is it loaded with film?"

Elise's eyes widened. "Yes, but . . ."

"Whom do I pass it on to?"

"You can't do it, Lisette," Elise said, aghast. "You won't be able to get into the room. It's an impossible task."

"I can try," Lisette said fiercely. "And if I succeed, I need to know whom to give the film to."

They heard the sound of booted feet tramping into the hall and querying voices. Elise backed away toward the door. "I must go. They're looking for me."

"*Whom do I give the film to?*"

Else paused for a fraction of a second, and then said in a rush, "Jean-Jacques, the Bar Candide, Bayeux. Good-bye, Lisette, and good luck."

She ran from the room, hurrying along the corridor and down the stairs. A few seconds later there was a slam of a door and then silence.

Lisette sat down on the bed and opened the tin, pressing her fingers down amongst the soft granules until they came up against something hard and solid. Her eyes burned. She would do what Elise could no longer do. She would ensure that the Allies knew exactly what Dieter Meyer's plans for them were, and she would render them worthless. Paul and André's death would not go unavenged, not even if it cost her her own life.

Five days later, the body of André Caldron was buried in the churchyard of Sainte-Marie-des-Ponts. Dieter had abruptly informed the comte that no one from Valmy would be allowed to attend the service. It wasn't Lisette or her father who flagrantly disobeyed him, but the comtesse.

"But you hardly knew Caldron," Henri protested, anxiety lining his face.

"It's a matter of principle," Héloïse de Valmy said quietly, setting a small black pillbox hat on the smooth upsweep of her chignon. "He died at Valmy. I have a duty to attend his funeral, and no one, certainly not Major Meyer, is going to prevent me."

"My dear, I know how you feel, believe me, I do. But Meyer is not a man it is wise to cross."

Héloïse de Valmy adjusted the wisp of veiling across her eyes. She looked as though she were about to dine at the Ritz, not attend the funeral of Sainte-Marie's café proprietor. Her long, slim legs were encased in black silk stockings. She had hidden the stockings away three years ago, intending to wear them on the day of liberation. André Caldron and Paul Gilles's death, on the grounds of her home, demanded that they be worn now. Her black suit was by Balmain, bought on her last shopping trip to Paris before the outbreak of war.

"He'll stop you," her husband warned. "He won't allow you to flout his orders."

Héloïse said nothing. She picked up her prayerbook, the fine, aristocratic bone structure of her face ageless. Henri regarded her with aching tenderness. She never ceased to amaze him. She hated turmoil and discord and retreated from it whenever possible, yet now, because her own code of conduct demanded it, she deliberately was going to arouse and face Meyer's wrath.

"I haven't told you that I love you for a long time," he said, walking across to her and kissing her gently on her temple. "But I do, my dear. With all my heart."

A slight flush touched her cheekbones. "Thank you, Henri," she said and then, as he stepped with her toward the door, "No, Henri, don't come with me. This is something I wish to do alone."

She paused at the head of the stairs, suppressing a slight tremble, then descended, her outward composure flawless.

Dieter had known very well what she would try to do. In her own way she was spirited and as willful as her daughter. As she crossed the hall, he opened the door of the grand dining room, his shadow falling across her. "Where are you going?" he asked quietly.

"To André Caldron's funeral." Her flute-clear voice was icily chill. There had been a time when she had warmed toward him, invited him to dine with them, imagined that here at last was a German who was different—a German who was not a Nazi. She had been wrong.

Dieter regarded her with a mixture of admiration and irritation. She had an amazing figure for a woman of fifty. Looking at her, he knew very well the kind of woman Lisette would become. At the thought of Lisette, pain flared behind his eyes. He said brusquely, "I gave orders that no one from Valmy was to attend."

She had been standing looking straight ahead, not deigning to glance in his direction. Now she turned, and her blue-gray eyes held his steadily. "I am aware of your orders, Major Meyer."

"And you refuse to obey them?"

"If you wish to prevent me from attending the funeral of the man you shot dead, then you will have to do so physically."

Dieter sighed. He wondered what she would say if he told her that the man whose funeral she wished to attend had cravenly named her daughter as a member of the Resistance. "Very well," he said tightly, "I'll see to it that a car is brought round for you."

"You can't imagine that I would arrive at the funeral of one of your victims in a German staff car, Major Meyer. I would rather crawl there on my hands and knees!" She walked quickly away from him, her exquisitely coutured back rigid, her high heels tapping on the flagstones.

He returned to the report he was trying to finish, but his concentration had deserted him. He could think only of Lisette. With nerves stretched to breaking point, he slammed out of the château, striding round to the stables where his Horch was garaged, and ordered his chauffeur to drive him to Vierville.

The defenses were still not satisfactory. They needed more concrete, more steel, more swiveling cupolas for the bunkers and blockhouses in order that the arc of fire from their guns would not be restricted.

Lisette's face rose up before him and he groaned, wondering how long it would be before his terrible need of her abated. He needed another woman. He needed lots of women. He had a weekend leave due to him. As the Horch sped through the deep-hedged lanes, he decided to go to Paris. The prospect did not elate him. He didn't want the sophisticated, experienced women who had made previous leaves so relaxing. He wanted Lisette.

Her face burned at the back of his mind. He remembered the way her heart throbbed beneath his caressing hand, the low laugh that caught in her throat, the soft sensuality of her mouth. Then he remembered the passion of her hate and deep, simmering rage for its cause consumed him. The Englishman had been nothing to either of them. She, herself, had been responsible for Paul Gilles's death. If she had not so foolishly involved herself with the Resistance, there would have been no need for Gilles to have been silenced.

He had yet to tell her that he knew of her Resistance activities. It was a confrontation that he dreaded. He had seen her only once since the shooting. It was she who had asked to see him, and he had hoped for a moment that she had come for a reconciliation. She hadn't. She had come to tell him that Paul Gilles was to be buried at Valmy.

"Shouldn't that be a request?" he had snapped when his first flare of shock had subsided. She had remained frigidly silent, her eyes darkly ringed, her face deathly pale. He wondered if she had lost as much sleep as he, and hoped savagely that she had.

"Why the devil should Gilles be buried at Valmy?"

"He had no family of his own. He died at Valmy. It is fitting that he should be buried at Valmy." Every line of her body had been taut with tension, her voice as tight as a coiled spring.

She had been wearing a dress he had never seen before: a narrow sheaf of black wool crepe with long sleeves and a high neck, its stark simplicity unadorned by jewelry or accessories. Her hair had been drawn back away from her face, tied at the nape of her neck with a velvet ribbon. She had looked incredibly beautiful. The breath had caught in his throat, and for a second, he had not trusted himself to speak, then he had asked tersely, "Is there consecrated ground at Valmy?"

"Yes, there used to be a small chapel near the gatehouse. De Valmys have always been buried on de Valmy land."

"And now Paul Gilles is to join them?"

She had flinched at the hatred in his voice, then had said steadily, "Yes."

He had been unable to bear her nearness any longer. "Then bury him at Valmy!" he had said explosively, and marched from the room, rage and frustration and jealousy warring deep within him.

The priest had come from Sainte-Marie-des-Ponts, and Paul Gilles had been buried in the de Valmy family churchyard.

The day after the funeral, Dieter had had his chauffeur stop at the gatehouse and, driven by a devil he couldn't name, had walked over to the grave. Flowers had been freshly planted. Blue grape hyacinths and mauve honesty and sharply yellow forsythia. The tumbledown walls of the chapel were covered in wisteria and clematis and wild rose bushes, and he knew that in summer the air in the little churchyard would be heavy with fragrance. It was so quiet that he had heard the distant roar of the sea and the birds calling to one another in the nearby beech woods. This was where, one day, Lisette would lie: Lisette and her children, and her children's children. He had turned abruptly on his heel, striding back to his car. He had to stop thinking about her. It was over. Finished. He had suffered from temporary insanity, and now he was well again.

The Horch slid to a halt on the clifftops of Vierville. He stepped from the car onto damp grass and stared out over the sea. The English Channel. The moat that had protected England. The wind blew in from the west, bitingly cold, hurling the waves over the shingle. He tried to think of the task at hand—the coastal defenses, the Atlantic Wall; but he could only fume at his inability to banish her from his thoughts as he had so many other women before her. At thirty-two, hardened and sophisticated, he had experienced the *coup de foudre*—the thunderclap of unreasoning, instant infatuation—and he could not free himself from it. His eyes narrowed. He didn't tolerate weakness in others, and he would be damned if he would tolerate it in himself. From now on she would cease to exist.

Lisette shoved the tin of powdered milk far back into the cupboard in the pantry, behind tins of other dried foods. It looked less conspicuous there than hidden in the drawer of her dressing table. She knew that with Elise's departure, her father had assumed that all attempts to infiltrate the grand dining room had been abandoned, and she did not disillusion him. Whatever needed doing, she would do alone.

Her leg had begun to heal, and Dr. Auge no longer came to the château. She mended her bicycle herself, hammering out the mangled frame, soldering new spokes to the wheels. It was March now, and tulips bloomed in sheltered corners of the garden. She had pruned the roses, cutting out diseased and frost-damaged wood, working until dusk. It was easier not to think when she was tired, and to think was to open herself to such terrible emotions that it was as if she were being rent apart.

She rarely saw him, and when she did, she saw also Paul and André, their hands bound behind their backs, lying in crumpled, blood-stained heaps. He went to Paris on leave, to Rommel's headquarters at La Roche-Guyon, and on inspection trips. But whenever he was away, the security remained as tight as ever. Sentries were now at Valmy's gates. No one could enter or leave without running their gauntlet. Lisette lived in a prison.

She cycled twice to Bayeux, and both times she knew that she had been followed. She did not go to the Bar Candide. She lingered over an anisette at a street café before cycling the long, weary way home. Elise had been right. Dieter had been suspicious and still was. He was waiting for her to expose other members of the maquis. Paul and André's death had not been enough. She felt ill with the need for revenge. It was as if her very soul demanded a purging.

By the time she had reached Sainte-Marie, her leg hurt so much that she had to fight back tears of pain. It had been a wasted journey. She toiled up the hill through the beech woods wondering when she could again attempt it. She had to let Elise's contact at the Bar Candide know what it was she intended to do. She was too exhausted to brave the snide looks and glances of loitering soldiers by wheeling her bicycle round to its customary place in the stables. She leaned it against the outside wall of the kitchen and hauled herself through Valmy's deserted lower rooms and to her bedroom.

It was five o'clock in the afternoon. Her mother would be resting, her father taking his usual walk. Marie had said that she was going to visit Madame Chamot who had been ill with bronchitis. Weary with defeat, she crawled into bed fully dressed, and closed her eyes. She would not try to make the trip again, not until she had completed her self-appointed mission and the camera was full of vital film waiting for development. Sleep tugged at her conscious mind. She was hazy and floating, forgetting the hate that she clung to for survival every waking moment of every day. His face swam into her mind, strong and caring. She felt again the curious rapport, the feeling of being completely at one with another human being. "I love you," he had said. "Love you . . . love you . . ." She could see him, taste him, smell him.

Footsteps rasped on the cobblestones of the courtyard below her window. "Are you leaving for Caen immediately, Major?" Lieutenant Halder asked, his voice slicing through the still air of late afternoon.

Her eyes flew open, and there was sweat on her brow. She had been dreaming. She had believed that the horror had never happened, that he had walked out of her room after kissing and holding her, and that there had been no search in the village—no airman to be found and captured.

"Yes. There have been more arrests. The local maquis seem to be primed for an invasion on this part of the coast. I want to hear for myself what they have to say."

Her breath came fast and shallow. Her German was not good, but the question had been unmistakable. "And the airman we captured in the village, Sir?"

"As you might expect, he knew nothing at all about local activities. He was shot two days ago." His voice was crisp, matter of fact: the voice of a stranger and an enemy.

The lieutenant spoke again, but she could no longer hear what he was saying. Their footsteps faded, and she gazed up at the ceiling, rigid with pain.

Shot. As Paul and André had been shot. She wondered if the Englishman, too, had been shot in the back. A great shudder ran through her body. She had given herself to Dieter Meyer mentally and physcially, and even now—when sleep robbed her of the safeguards that sustained her, at some deep, primeval level that she was powerless to control—she was still his. Bile rose up in her throat, and she swung her legs off the bed, fighting down wave after wave of nausea and self-loathing.

He was going to Caen. Now. Immediately. He would be away for at least two hours, possibly longer. If she was ever going to take the risk of storming the grand dining room, surely this was the time to do it.

But how? The question had racked her every hour of every day since Elise had left. The only person who could give her help was the unknown Jean-Jacques, and she had been unable to make contact with him. She had to have a key, and only Dieter had a key. There were no duplicates, not even for the sentries. Her head ached, and she pressed her fingers to her throbbing temples. If she had become his lover, there would have been opportunities for her to have removed the key from his possession. He would have taken off his jacket, his breeches. The blood pounded behind her eyes, and she sprang to her feet with an inarticulate cry, thrusting the image away from her. She had not become his lover. She would never become his lover. Never, never, never!

A car engine revved into life, and she stood, waiting, until it faded into the distance. He had gone. She waited for a feeling of exultation, but it did not come. There was only cold and pain and a desolation so terrible that she knew it was destroying her.

She turned away from the bed, knowing that sleep was an impossibility. If she closed her eyes, she would see the crumpled bodies of Paul and André, the face of the airman as he had looked up at her seconds before he was dragged away to his death in Caen, and Dieter's eyes, hot and urgent, as he pleaded with her to forget them—to forget that it had ever happened.

She walked decisively out of the room. She would prepare tea. She would walk around the outside of the château and check again that all the grilles barring the grand dining room windows were locked. They had been left unlocked once. It was not beyond the realm of possibility that accidentally they would be left unlocked again. She remembered the expression in the lieutenant's eyes when he had realized how Paul and André had made their escape. He had been stunned at the carelessness that had made so vital a room insecure. Such carelessness would not be allowed to happen again. Her sortie would be a waste of time. The grilles would be locked, and her movements watched; but she had to do something. She had to keep busy, keep moving.

As she approached the head of the stairs, she saw that the hall was still and silent, the face of the young sentry on duty impassive. She looked down at him with hatred. He had no right to be in her home, to be fouling it with his presence. As she watched him from the shadows at the top of the stairs, he shifted his stance, glancing down at his watch. Her pulse quickened. He was bored, and his commanding officer was well on his way to Caen. Perhaps . . . perhaps . . .

"Please God, let him desert his post," she prayed silently. "Please, *please.*"

The sentry looked once more at his watch and then, with a barely perceptible shrug of his shoulders, strolled away from the grand dining room toward the front door. She saw him remove a packet of cigarettes from his trouser pocket, then he swung Valmy's great oak door open wide and stepped out into the late afternoon sunlight.

Her breath was so tight in her throat that she could hardly breathe. If he remained in the open doorway, she would be unable to do anything. She saw him pause, look right and left, then step briskly away in search of a less conspicuous spot in which to enjoy his illicit smoke.

The door was unguarded, but it was still locked. Her heart began to hammer fast and light. If Elise had been here, Elise could have taken advantage of the situation. Elise could have picked the lock, could have gained entry to the room. She began to hurry down the stairs, her legs trembling, her hands filmed with perspiration. There had been one act of carelessness. The window grille had been left unlocked. If the door should be unlocked too . . .

"Please," she prayed feverishly. "Oh, please, God, let it be unlocked! Let this be my chance!"

There wasn't a sound in the empty entrance hall. It was as if Valmy had been deserted, abandoned. If only the ornate doorknobs on the carved double doors opened to her touch . . .

She ran fleet-footedly across the hall and grasped hold of them, praying as she had never prayed before in her life. With eyes closed, she turned and pulled, and with old, familiar ease they opened wide. She gasped and half fell, the blood drumming in her ears and behind her eyes. The miracle had happened! She had been given her chance! The camera. She had to have the camera!

She spun on her heels, hurtling down the corridor toward the kitchen. The sentry would not be long. He would smoke one cigarette, perhaps two, and then he would return. She half fell against the kitchen door. Five minutes. She had perhaps five minutes in which to retrieve the camera, return to the room, and photograph whatever documents she could find. She scrabbled for the door handle, yanking it open, racing across the room to the cupboards.

Her fingers slid and slipped over tins of chicory, tins of carrots. Dear God! Why couldn't she move faster? She grabbed the tin, pushing the lid off, granules of dried milk spilling to the floor as she extricated the camera. She clutched it tightly to her chest. How long had she taken? Sixty seconds?

Two minutes? As if the hounds of hell were at her heels, she leaped once more for the door, running full speed down the corridor. Time! All she needed was time!

The grand dining room doors still stood open. The hall was still deserted. She gave a strangled sob. Just a few more minutes! Only a few more minutes! She darted into the room, her hands trembling violently as she closed the doors behind her. She had to be calm! She had to work swiftly and efficiently. There was a map of the coastline on one wall, and on the table, a blotter and an ink stand with a tidy pile of paperwork beside it. At least she wasn't faced with such an array of documents that she had to spend time judging which were of vital importance and which were not.

She hurried round the corner of the long, polished table. The papers were in meticulous order and would have to be found in meticulous order after she had left the room. She could not allow carelessness now to defeat her chance of success. She was going to win. She was going to serve her country, help the Allies, render worthless all Dieter Meyer's carefully laid plans.

On top of the pile of papers was a memo to Field Marshal Erwin Rommel, commander-in-chief, Army Group B. Taking a deep steadying breath, she focused the camera, pressed the shutter . . .

"You idiot," he said quietly from behind her. "You empty-headed, stupid little idiot."

She spun round so suddenly that the papers scattered to the floor. She couldn't breathe. Couldn't speak. He was walking toward her, and through her terror, she was aware that there was no rage on his face or in his voice. Only deep weariness.

"You cannot really have believed, Lisette, that the door to this room would have been left unlocked and that the sentry would have abandoned his post, just at the precise moment you were about to descend the stairs."

She fought for composure, for air. "The window grille was left unlocked. . . . I took a chance. As Paul and André took a chance."

He halted a mere two yards from her and said, his voice oddly flat, "You fell into a trap. As Paul and André fell into a trap."

There was no more room for terror. Another emotion had taken its place. An emotion far more terrible. She seemed to shrink visibly before his gaze.

"I don't understand you," she whispered, her eyes dilating, her face chalk-white.

He wanted to take her in his arms and comfort her. Instead he said cruelly, "You cannot for one moment believe that Gilles and Caldron's escape was chance. The grille was left unlocked, the window opened purposely so that they would attempt to escape—and be shot while doing so."

She had thought that she had come to terms with horror. Now she knew that it was not so, that it was a bottomless pit whose depths could never he plumbed. She shrank back against the table, sending another flurry of papers showering around her.

"Why?" she choked. "What kind of man are you?"

He looked at her long and silently, then he sat on the corner of the table, one gleaming booted leg swinging free, the other touching the floor. "I did it for you," he said abruptly, the lines around his mouth hardening. "You were responsible for their death, Lisette. You and your stupid, childish attempts to be a heroine for France."

She didn't speak, didn't move. Silence stretched between them, and he knew when it ended her innocence too would have come to an end.

"Paul Gilles was a local Resistance leader. You were a courier. If Gilles had ever reached Gestapo headquarters in Caen, how long do you think it would have been before I was ordered to arrest you?"

"Paul Gilles would never have betrayed me," she said, and his heart ached at the brave certainty in her voice.

"Paul Gilles didn't," he said tersely. "It was Caldron who betrayed you."

He saw her flinch, saw her valiant attempt to mask her feelings, and knew that the private battle he had been waging was lost. He would never be able to pretend that she didn't exist. It was not humanly possible.

He rose and stepped toward her, his eyes dark. "Listen, Lisette," he said in a quick urgent voice, "you must, please, make some effort to understand. What I did, I did for you. Gilles and Caldron would have died anyway. They would have died after days, perhaps weeks, of torture. Instead they died quickly and cleanly here at Valmy."

"Cleanly!" She recoiled from him, her eyes blazing in her stricken face. "My God, *cleanly!* How can you say the word? You murdered them! You murdered Paul and André and the Englishman! You're an animal! No different from the SS sadists in Caen! You're a murdering, filthy *Nazi!*"

Rage at the circumstance in which they found themselves, fear for her safety, frustration at her inability to understand, all overcame him. His hand sliced through the air, slapping her across the face with such ferocity that she fell to her knees. "Jesus God!" he shouted, furious with himself for what he had done, furious with her for goading him to it. "Why can't you see sense? Caldron betrayed you and Caldron died! Paul Gilles would far rather have died at Valmy than in a stinking prison cell knowing that he was taking you and perhaps untold others to their death!"

She was sobbing, blinded by her tears, the marks of his fingers rising in scarlet, ugly weals across her cheekbone. "And the airman?" she gasped. "Can you justify his death as well?"

He dropped to his knees in front of her, seizing her shoulders so savagely that she moaned in pain. *"To hell with the bloody airman!"* he thundered, and as she cried out in protest, his mouth came down on hers, hard and powerful and unyielding.

From the moment he had laid hands on her, he had known that there was no going back. His physical desire for her was too great. The electric excitement that had spiraled between them from the very first convulsed him. He pressed her beneath him, plundering her mouth, uncaring of her tears and her fists beating on his shoulders. All his life he had had whatever he wanted, and he wanted Lisette. He had been prepared to dismay his family, outrage his friends, defy army regulations in order to make her his wife. She alone, torn apart by divided loyalties, had thwarted him, and she was going to do so no longer.

He caught hold of her wrists, pinioning them high above her head with one hand. With the other, he opened his pants, then tore away her skirt, the creamy beige satin of her slip until he reached the exquisite lace that lay beneath and the soft, sweet velvet of her flesh.

95

Desire roared through his veins. He heard her cries, saw the desperation in her eyes, and then, his own eyes so dark they were almost black, he crushed her beneath him, parting her thighs viciously, thrusting deep inside her in an agony of relief.

7

She was moaning beneath him, her face wet with tears. His breath came in harsh rasps. God in heaven, what had he done? To what depths had he sunk? He eased his weight from her, looking down at her, knowing that she had fought him to the bitter end.

"Lisette?" He raised his hand to wipe away her tears, and she jerked her head to one side, her hair spilling across her face, fanning out over the carpet.

"Lisette," he said again, his voice raw with urgency. "Lisette, look at me. Listen to me."

She was rigid, the long lovely line of her throat taut, her knuckles clenched, her face beaded with sweat, her skin so pale it was almost translucent. He knew he had hurt her. He had taken her as if she were a whore, taken her with a brutality that sickened him. Blood trickled down her inner thigh. Blood and semen inextricably mixed.

"Let me help you," he said, leaning back on one knee, taking hold of her shoulders.

She gasped aloud, pushing herself away from him, scrambling to her feet. She gathered up her skirt, stepped into it, and faced him. *"Don't touch me!"* The pupils of her eyes were widely dilated, utterly opaque, the irises a petrified, pristine gray. *"Dear God! Don't touch me! Not now! Not ever!"* She was free of him, running and stumbling to the door.

He rose unsteadily to his feet. Rape. It was a resort he had never before descended to. The act of men he despised. His face, where she had clawed at him with her nails, was scratched and bleeding. The top two buttons were ripped from his jacket. They lay on the floor, scattered among the reports and memoranda that had fallen from the table. Slowly he bent down and began to pick up the disordered sheets of paper that he had left for her to find. None of them would have been of any interest to the Allies. The memo she had been in the act of photographing was merely to confirm that he would be in Paris from the 22nd to the 26th of the month.

He picked up the camera, wondering who had given it to her. Paul Gilles? Elise? He would take no steps to find out. To pursue the matter would be to bring Lisette's name to the attention of the Gestapo. For all official purposes the incident had never happened.

He stared broodingly at the camera in his hand. And for unofficial purposes? It would be easy enough for him to behave as if nothing had happened. The rape of a Frenchwoman was hardly a crime he need lose sleep over. Yet it hadn't been the rape of just any Frenchwoman. It had been the rape of the woman who had aroused emotions in him he had never suspected existed, the woman he had fallen irrevocably in love with. His vow that she would cease to exist for him had been impossible to keep. He might as well have vowed to stop breathing.

His face grim, his eyes bleak, he set the camera on the table and left the room. He had to see her, had to speak to her. The nightmare they had plummeted into had to come to an end.

She ran up the stairs and along the corridor like a blind thing. She mustn't think! Mustn't think! Mustn't think! She half fell into her room, slamming the door behind her, the back of her hand pressed hard against her mouth to silence her rising screams. She mustn't think! If she thought, she would go mad! She would lose her reason.

The strength that had sustained her flight failed her. She sank to her knees, sobbing, gasping for breath, crawling toward the bed like a wounded animal. She had fought him! She must think of that and of nothing else. She collapsed against the bed, unable to rise to her feet, her arms stretched out across the coverlet, the tears streaming down her face and neck. She had fought him . . . fought him . . . fought him . . .

The door opened behind her, and she knew that she was lost. Drowning. Beyond all help.

"Go away," she choked out, lifting her head from her hands, turning her swollen, tear-streaked face to his. "Oh, dear heaven, go away!"

His eyes were so dark they were almost black. He had never apologized to anyone, ever, in his life. "I'm sorry," he said, and his voice was naked with suffering. "Forgive me, Lisette . . . please."

His thick blond hair was tousled. His hard-boned face was white and drawn, scored by livid scratchmarks. The top of his jacket gaped open, and she could see the pulse beating in his throat, smell the sweat that had dried on his body as he moved toward her.

"Don't touch me," she said hoarsely, shrinking back against the bed. "Please, please don't touch me!"

"I love you," he said, and his hands were on her shoulders, drawing her to her feet. "I know how much you hate me, Lisette. I know I've given you every reason to hate me . . ."

A great shudder ran through her body. The waves had closed over her head. There was no further hope. "I don't hate you," she whispered. "I hate myself." And as she raised her eyes to his, understanding rocked through him.

"Oh God," he said and crushed her to him. "Lisette . . . my love. *Lisette!*"

There was no escape. There never had been. Her arms slid up and around his neck, her mouth parted helplessly beneath his, and as he lowered her once more to the floor beneath him it was with the gentleness of absolute love.

"I won't hurt you . . . I promise I won't hurt you . . ."

Her sweater and skirt lay tangled with his uniform—lavender and gray, violet and black. She trembled in his arms, overcome by the beauty of his masculinity, by the smoothness of his skin, the hardness of bone, the lean tautness of rigorously exercised muscle. The touch of his hand as he caressed the curve of her body from her neck to her hip bone rendered her half senseless with pleasure. It was like flying, like nothing she had ever known.

He entered her, and her heart moved. With all the skill and patience of an accomplished lover, he took her slowly, step by step, to a country she had never dreamed of. Her body was like molten gold. It flowed, white-hot, into his. She no longer had any sense of identity, any sense of separate being. She was dissolving, disintegrating—her voice calling his name over and over again.

The following days and weeks were the strangest, most bittersweet of Lisette's life. Dieter did not tell the comte and comtesse of their affair as he had originally planned to do. Paul Gilles and André Caldron's death made it impossible. Neither his men nor the comte and comtesse guessed at their true relationship. He knew that after what had happened, it was better for Lisette that they didn't.

They met at night, in the room that had been her grandmother's, the room overlooking the sea. Always, afterwards, when she thought of their lovemaking, she remembered the distant sound of the sea as it surged up onto the shingles, and the light from an oil lamp glowing softly in the darkness.

They talked about their childhoods. He told her of walks with his father in the flower-filled Tiergarten, the heavy scent of the pear and apple trees only yards away from the Kurfürstendamm, chocolate cakes brought from the Hotel Sacher in Vienna, iced lemonade at the Hotel Adlon in Berlin.

She told him of a sheltered childhood spent at Valmy, of family holidays in St. Moritz, of her convent schooling at Neuilly, of the finishing school in Switzerland she would have gone to had the war not intervened.

They talked of books and music. He liked Zola and Kafka and jazz; she, Flaubert and Chopin. They talked of anything and everything, but they did not talk of the war. In the lamplit confines of their turret room, the war did not exist.

They drank the vintage champagne that Dieter would not have dreamed of being without, even on a battlefield, and calvados, the heady cider and apple cognac that her father brewed. Dieter was a man who smiled rarely, but she knew by the expression in his black-lashed eyes when he looked at her, by the touch of his fingers on her flesh, that his happiness was as deep as her own.

She never tired of looking at him—at the line of his eyebrows, the angle of his jaw, the crisp corn-gold thickness of his hair. She wanted to be with him forever—to share his life, to sleep with him every night, and to wake with him every morning. She wanted the war to end. She wanted to know what the future held for them.

He knew what it held. It held the invasion, and he both yearned for it and feared it. Yearned for it because, if the Allies were repulsed, it would be months, perhaps years, before they could launch another such attack. Germany would be able to concentrate her entire strength on throwing back the Russians. Britain would crumble under the horror of the new V-1 rockets, and Churchill would be forced to sue for peace. There would be a future for him and Lisette.

He feared it because if the Allies were not repulsed, if they surged inland, then Germany's defeat was inevitable. And in that defeat there would be no future at all. Not for him.

He knew she didn't understand that yet, that she believed when the invasion came, win or lose, they would remain together. He had not the heart to disillusion her. He wanted nothing to darken their fragile, perhaps fleeting, happiness.

He had a radio in his study at the château, and every night, before meeting Lisette in the lamplit glow of the turret room, he listened in over earphones to the hundreds of messages the BBC broadcast after their regular news broadcasts. All were coded. All were in French, Dutch, Danish, or Norwegian. Messages to the Underground. Messages that made no sense, except to the people to whom they were directed.

Night after night he waited for the coded message to the French Resistance that General Canaris believed would signal the invasion of France. Night after night it failed to come. He knew, when it did, there would be no more meetings for them in the turret room above the sea.

All through April the weather was mild and calm—ideal weather for the invasion forces. But the Channel remained empty of ships, the horizon clear.

On April 26th, he received a memorandum stating that morale in England was at an all-time low. It was reported there had been cries of "Down with Churchill" and demands for peace. He hoped to God it was true.

By the beginning of May, there was still no sign of the British and American invasion, and he said to Lisette, "They're not going to come, *Liebling*. They're going to sue for peace without invading."

She shivered in his arms, pressing herself close to the long, hard length of his body, and he knew that she could not share his relief. Without an invasion, France would not be free. His arms tightened around her. She wanted the impossible: a German defeat that would not take him from her.

"I'm sorry, *Liebling*," he said, knowing how much she hated all references to the things that divided them. "But we must talk of it. If I am wrong, and if the Allies do invade, then it will be impossible for you and your parents to remain at Valmy."

Her head had been resting on his chest. She sat up suddenly, her hair spilling over her shoulders and naked breasts. "Leave Valmy?" Her tone was incredulous.

He raised himself up on one elbow in the large bed. "If there is an invasion and it takes place here, then you cannot possibly remain. The whole of Normandy will be a battlefield."

"You will remain."

"I'm a soldier," he said gently, reaching out and cupping her cheek.

Her eyes were dark in the paleness of her face. "And the villagers? Will they be given a chance to leave?"

"They will be ordered to leave," he said, drawing her down once more against him. "Civilians are nothing but a hazard in battle conditions."

They lay silent, each with their own thoughts, each knowing that those thoughts could not be expressed. To express them would be to face each other across the great abyss of their divided loyalties.

"We should make arrangements," he said at last, stroking her hair. "Do you have any relatives, any friends that you could go to?"

"My father's brother lives in Paris."

"Then that is where you should go."

She twisted once more to look at him. "Now? So soon?"

A muscle flexed at the corner of his jaw. He didn't want her to go. Once she went away, there was no telling when, or if, they would be reunited. But she couldn't stay at Valmy, not

101

if the Allies invaded. It would be too dangerous. His arms tightened around her.

"It would be for the best," he said quietly. "In case I am wrong and they do still come."

In the distance the waves could be heard ebbing and surging along the deserted coastline.

"Will we have any warning?" she asked curiously. "Will we know beforehand?"

He thought of the message to be transmitted to the Resistance. "No," he said, vowing that when the war was over he would never lie to her again. "There will be no warning."

They lay in the lamplit darkness, arms entwined, and he thought once again of Rommel's words, spoken so long ago it seemed: "The Anglo-Americans have lost confidence in their cause." If they had, how long would it be before they knew for sure? How long before they sued for peace? Before a semblance of normality returned to the world? He wanted all the things he had previously derided as bourgeois: marriage, children. And he wanted them in a world that was at peace.

She saw the familiar white lines of tension etch the corners of his mouth. "What is it?" she asked, loving him so much that it was a physical pain. "What are you thinking about, Dieter?"

"About you. About us."

"Then be happy, not unhappy," she said, and rolling over in one swift movement she pressed her naked body against his, lifting her arms around his neck, kissing away the lines of strain.

Their bodies were their refuge. In their lovemaking there were no divisions, no yawning gulf stretching between them that could not be crossed. There was only happiness and delight and unity. "I love you," he said hoarsely, folding his arms around her, twisting her beneath him. "Never forget it, Lisette. No matter what happens. Never forget . . ."

More intelligence reports came stating that the British were demanding Churchill's resignation and their government's surrender. He wondered how accurate they were. All the British he had ever met had been mulish and pigheaded. He couldn't imagine any of them surrendering, no matter how lost their cause. And thanks to Germany's folly in attacking

Russia, their cause was no longer lost. Germany had over-reached herself. She had not enough men, enough planes, to fight a war on two fronts. He knew damn well what he would do if he were Churchill. He would attack now, in the underbelly that was Normandy, and he knew, with terrible foreboding, that if he did so, he would, within weeks, be in the heart of the Fatherland.

Dieter met Henri de Valmy the next morning as he was striding across the cobblestones toward his Horch, and Henri was returning from his prebreakfast walk. "Excuse me, Comte de Valmy, could I have a word with you, please?" he asked civilly.

Henri stiffened. Ever since the shooting of Gilles and Caldron he had had as little to do with the major as possible. "If you wish," he said coldly.

"Not here," Dieter said as he signaled to his chauffeur that he was no longer needed. "Somewhere a little more private."

"The library?" Henri suggested, trying not to show unease.

"No, let's walk." He began to stride out of the courtyard and toward the terrace that led down to the rose gardens, wondering what would happen if he were to ask the comte for his daughter's hand in marriage. His mouth tightened. He knew what would happen. The sky would fall in. Henri would shoot not only him, but Lisette as well. Yet there had been a time when telling him had been a possibility: before the airman had been captured. He cursed silently and then, as they began to walk down the moss-covered steps, he said, "As you know, most of the villagers along the coastline have been evacuated for security reasons. The remainder are also going to be asked to leave."

"And . . ."

"And I am going to have to ask you and your wife and daughter to leave the area also."

"For security reasons?" Henri asked tightly, trying not to betray his distress.

"No." Dieter stopped and turned toward him. "If the Allies are going to invade, the invasion date cannot be far off. It will be safer for you and your family if you are not in Valmy if and when they land."

103

Henri's fists clenched. "Any danger we face does not come from the British," he said pointedly.

"Nor from me!" Dieter snapped. "I'm giving you orders to leave Valmy, and I'm explaining to you my reasons for doing so. Good God, man, you can't want your wife and daughter to be caught in the middle of a battlefield!"

"No, and I don't want them homeless and dispossessed as hundreds of thousands of other people are, all over Europe!"

"Some of those dispossessed and homeless are German! British bombs have gutted Berlin!"

"And German boots have marched all over my land. Don't ask me for sympathy, Major Meyer. You will not receive it."

Dieter's rage was at himself, for having allowed himself to be goaded into an emotional betrayal of his feelings. His nostrils flared as he took a deep, steadying breath, then he said with tight control, "I understand you have relatives in Paris."

"Yes."

"Then I suggest you go to them."

"Life is not easy in Paris, Major Meyer. There are shortages there. Life is better for my family here at Valmy."

"Not if the battle for Europe takes place in and around Valmy," Dieter said harshly.

"If that happens, then it will be you and your men who will be in danger, Major Meyer. Not my wife and child."

"Stop being so bloody obtuse," Dieter said in a low, rasping tone. "There will be bombs and tanks and rocket fire. Civilian casualties will be as heavy as military casualties."

"I wasn't aware that civilian casualties worried you, Major Meyer," Henri de Valmy said quietly.

The reference to Gilles and Caldron was unmistakable. Dieter went pale. "You will do as I say," he said tautly, not trusting himself to continue the conversation. "You will make arrangements to have your family out of Valmy and out of the area." He spun on his heel and strode back over the gravel to the château and his car.

Henri sat down shakily on a wooden garden seat. Dear Lord. Had he really spoken to a German officer in such an insulting way? He felt ill. Why on earth had Meyer stood for it? He wasn't the kind of man to allow liberties to be taken. The more he thought of it, the more bizarre their angry exchange of words seemed. He could understand them being ordered away from their home for security reasons. Very few people living so near to the coastal defenses had been allowed to remain. But to be moved for their own safety in case of an attack by the invasion forces? It was all most odd.

He mopped his face with his handkerchief and rose unsteadily to his feet. Meyer, usually so disciplined and self-controlled, had seemed almost to be under stress. Could it be because he knew the invasion was imminent? Henri dismissed the idea almost as soon as he had thought of it. Meyer was not a man to panic at the thought of battle. He held the Knights Cross of the Iron Cross. His courage was proven.

Then why? Was he really genuinely concerned about their safety? There had been a time when such a thought would have been feasible. Despite the circumstances under which Meyer had come to Valmy, Henri had instinctively liked him. The man was a Berliner, of course—hard and smart, just like his city—but there had been integrity there as well, or so he had thought. Then had come the shootings. Revulsion coursed through his veins. That action of Meyer's had damned him. Whatever his reason for demanding that they leave Valmy, it couldn't possibly be out of concern for their safety. His initial impressions of the man had been wrong. There was no integrity, no humanity.

He began to walk wearily back toward the château. He needed to speak to Héloïse. If the invasion forces were going to land on their beaches and not in the Pas de Calais, then they needed to make plans. He had already determined that no force on earth would persuade him to move his family to Paris, but it would make sense to move them a few miles inland until the Allies were established and the Germans were on the run. He refused to think of the alternative—the Allies pushed back into the sea and France chained to her occupiers without hope of release.

From the window of her room, Lisette saw her father walking back across the dew-wet terrace. He looked perturbed, his eyebrows pulled together, deep lines creasing his forehead. She resisted the urge to hurry out to him and slip her arm through his. She had problems of her own that morning, problems that she had to resolve before she spoke to anyone.

She turned away from the window and closed her hands across her stomach. Common sense told her that she should be distraught, that of all the feelings she should be experiencing, joy was not one of them. But she couldn't help it. She was having a baby, Dieter's baby. She was carrying a tangible part of him in her body. No matter what happened, they would be bound together, through their child, for always. Her problem was not in the existence of the baby, but of whether she should tell Dieter of it. He was deeply worried already about what would happen to her if Normandy was turned into a blood-bath. If he knew she was pregnant, his worries would increase. Yet she wanted to tell him of it. The baby would be born out of their love for each other. It would grow up in a world where, God willing, there would be no fighting. They would not live in France or Germany. She knew now that no matter what happened, neither country could be their home. They would live in Switzerland. The Allied invasion would be successful: Germany would be defeated. Dieter would put away his uniform and never wear it again. They would be an ordinary, happy family, building a new life for themselves in the aftermath of the war. That was the future. But what of the present?

Her parents would have to be told, and she knew how the news would devastate them. They would not be able to understand, and they would not be able to forgive. The villagers would eventually know. She would be branded as a collaborator. Her child would be reviled and spat upon. Valmy would no longer be a home and a haven to her. She had sacrificed Valmy on the day she had entered Dieter's arms, and she did not regret it. She could not. She had committed herself to him for the rest of her life.

The interview with Henri de Valmy had shaken Dieter considerably. He had been appalled to discover that the comte's opinion of him mattered. He wanted the man for a friend, not an enemy. He had stormed back to his car, barking commands at his men, sweeping off to inspect the flooded areas around the Vire, and cursing again the capture of the Allied airman that had made good relations with Henri de Valmy an impossibility.

His bad temper persisted all day. He returned to the

château to find a memo on his desk stating that OB West now firmly believed that the invasion would take place at the Pas de Calais on or around the fifteenth of May, a week away. He wondered what information the intelligence services had received to make them so sure of the place and the date. If it was accurate, Lisette would be far safer at Valmy than in Paris. He wrote his report of the day's inspection trip in a firm, hard hand. The waiting was beginning to wear on his nerves. He only hoped it was wearing on the nerves of the Allies as well.

He finished his report and poured himself a drink, wishing the war were over, that he were in Berlin with Lisette, that he could take her out for a meal on the Kurfürsten-damm—take her to the theater, to a nightclub. There were times when just thinking about her almost took his breath away. He had never believed it possible to love anyone so much. The dark, vibrant quality of her beauty devastated him. Everything about her was soft and feminine and elusive, and he knew he would never tire of her. She had seeped into his blood and into his bones and had become a part of him. He looked at his watch. It was ten to seven. There were nearly two hours to go before she could slip away to meet him in the lamplit solitude of the turret room. With difficulty, he turned his mind back to his work and the report that was awaiting completion.

"Meyer has demanded that we leave Valmy," Henri said to his wife and daughter that evening at dinner.

Héloïse's knife and fork clattered down onto her plate. "Leave?" she repeated, aghast. "Why should we leave? Where would we go?"

"Please don't distress yourself, my dear. I have no intention of complying with his demand. At least, not in the way that he envisions. However, I do think we should discuss where you and Lisette could retreat to if the invasion takes place here."

"You said it would take place in the Pas de Calais," his wife said, her cheeks bloodless, her eyes wide.

"So it very well might. But we should be prepared for all contingencies. I've been giving it some thought, and I believe the best plan would be for us to join Marie's family in Balleroy."

"Have you spoken to Marie about it?"

"Yes. She says that we would be more than welcome."

"And when would we go?"

"We would go if Meyer persists in ordering us to go. And we would go if the situation here becomes impossible for civilians."

"Otherwise we stay at Valmy?"

Her husband's eyes held her steadily. "Yes, my dear. Otherwise we stay at Valmy."

Lisette felt limp with relief. Balleroy was only a little over sixty miles away. Even if she could not persuade Dieter to let her remain at Valmy, she would only be a day's journey away, and her parents would be safer there than on the coast if there was an attack.

"Are you happy about going to Balleroy if it is necessary, Lisette?" her father asked, his eyes concerned.

"Yes, Papa," She hesitated, then said, "Though there might not be an attack. They may not come. They may sue for peace without invading."

Her parents stared at her, stunned by the dreadfulness of such a prospect. "Oh, no, Lisette," her mother said at last, recovering her power of speech. "They have to come. They *must* come."

"Who put such an idea into your head?" her father asked. "Marie?"

"No." She looked at them, loving them so much that her heart ached. "Major Meyer."

It had to be done. His name had to be mentioned. She couldn't just tell them that she was carrying Dieter's child without giving them some warning, some inkling of a relationship between them.

There was a long silence, then her father said unsteadily, "Does Major Meyer make a habit of confiding in you, Lisette?"

"Yes," she said, rising to her feet, her legs trembling. "I like him very much, Papa." She could say no more. Her mother's lips were as bloodless as her face. Her father looked as if he had been struck.

"But you can't!" Her mother's voice was agonized. "Not after what he did. You can't! It isn't possible."

"I'm sorry, Maman," she said quietly, "but I do," and she walked from the room, tears at the distress she was causing them burning the backs of her eyes.

He was waiting for her when she entered the turret room. The sheets were turned down on the big brass bed, the lamps on the stone sills in the deeply embrasured windows glowing softly. He walked quickly to her, folding his arms around her. "I thought you were never coming," he said, drinking in the sight and the sound and the scent of her.

She laughed softly. "It's only five past nine, my love."

"Those five minutes seemed like an age."

"They're over now." His lips were hard and sweet against hers. She could feel his heart beating hard, feel the tension and strain leave his body as he pressed her close against him. It was like coming home. It was all she would ever want or need.

As he raised his head from hers, he said suddenly, "You've been crying."

Her fingers interlocked tightly with his. "No, I haven't," she lied gently, not wanting to burden him with the grief she felt at her parents' distress. "I have a cold coming, I think."

"Then you need a hot drink with honey and lemon."

"Maybe," she said, smiling, "but I don't want you deserting me to rummage around in Marie's kitchen making me one."

"Then have a brandy." He crossed to the antique cabinet that had been discreetly converted to hold drinks.

She curled up on the bed while he poured a French brandy and a calvados. The room had become their world. It was high in the turret, far away from the main body of the château. Her grandmother had made the room her retreat, using it as both a bedroom and a sitting room, and since her death it had not been used. Everything was pearl gray: the silk on the walls, the thick carpets, the heavy velvet drapes at the windows. Dieter's books scattered the bedside table, and there was a small, silver-framed photograph of his mother on the dresser. Lisette looked at it reflectively. It showed a laughing woman, with soft blonde hair framing her face, kneeling on the grass with a flat of flowers by her side. No doubt she would be appalled when she knew that her son was to marry a French girl—a French girl who was already carrying his child.

"You're looking very serious, *Liebling*," he said, handing her the brandy.

"I was thinking about your mother," she said as he settled himself down next to her, pulling her close. "About how unhappy she will be when she finds out that she is to have a French daughter-in-law."

His mouth crooked in one of his rare smiles. "My mother has a great capacity for adjusting to surprises. And she trusts my judgment. She won't be unhappy, *Liebling*. Not once she has met you. How could she be?"

A chessboard and chessmen lay at the side of the bed, and she leaned across, drawing it toward them, not wanting him to see the doubt in her eyes. "Your queen is still in danger," she said teasingly. "Have you any plans for rescuing her?"

Her hair had fallen forward over her shoulders, and he lifted it back, away from her face, loving the heavy, silky feel of it in his hands.

"Yes," he growled softly, moving a knight to protect his queen. "But let the chess wait," and he slid her down beside him, his body already hard, his fingers at the buttons of her blouse.

She stretched herself out beneath him as he kissed her throat, her bared breasts. She would tell him tonight. In a little while. After they had made love.

8

She lay with her head in the crook of his shoulder, her fingers tracing a line down his chest, through the mat of crisply curling blond hair to the taut, hard muscles of his belly and the darker, stronger curls beyond.

"I have something to tell you," she said gently as the warm night air filled the room, carrying with it the fragrance of roses.

In the palm of her hand his sex stirred, and she moved her hand lower, to the lean muscles of his thighs, not wanting to arouse him again so soon—not until after she had told him.

The room was very still. A firefly danced around the flickering light of the lamp and in the distance the waves could be heard surging rhythmically up and down the deserted beach.

His arm tightened around her shoulder. "What is it, *Liebling?*" he asked tenderly.

She raised herself up on one elbow and looked down at him, her hair shimmering like silk in the lamplight.

"We're going to have a baby."

His eyes flashed wide. "A *what?*" he thundered, pushing himself up against the pillows.

"A baby," she said composedly.

"*Mein Gott!*" His gray, black-lashed eyes were incredulous. "Are you sure? How long have you known?"

She twisted herself back onto her knees, her hands clasped lightly on her lap. "I've only known for a couple of weeks, but I'm quite sure," she said, her pose and gravity that of a dark-haired, pagan Madonna.

She saw all the emotions that she herself had first experienced chase across his face: stunned disbelief, dawning comprehension, exhilaration, and lastly, overriding anxiety.

"What will you do? How will you manage? We're bound to be separated. The deadline for the completion of the defenses is June 18th. After that I could be sent anywhere . . ."

A smile tugged at the corners of her mouth. "I'll manage like any other woman having a baby in the middle of a war. I'll manage even better if I know that you are pleased about it."

He pulled her to him, an expression of such fierce love in his eyes that her heart rocked in her chest.

"You know how pleased I am, *Liebling*. And you know how concerned I am for your safety, for the baby's safety."

She said tentatively, "Even if the Allies land, we will be safer here than in Paris, Dieter. The shortages there are truly terrible, and I couldn't bear to see Paris abject and defeated."

He had known all along that she did not want to go. He took hold of her shoulders, squaring her to face him, his expression grave. "If Valmy becomes the center of a battlefield, you cannot remain, Lisette. The coastline will be bombed with the same kind of ferocity with which they are bombing Cherbourg and Caen."

111

"My father has spoken to Marie. Her family lives at Balleroy. We will go there. It is far enough inland to be safe and yet near enough for me to return within a day."

He nodded. The comte was right. Balleroy would be a far better place for the comtesse and Lisette than Paris. Their eyes held, violet and gray, both thinking of the coming baby, of the future. She clenched her hands tightly. "Oh, God, how I wish we both wanted the same thing!" she cried passionately. "I can't bear it when we talk of defeat and victory, and we both know that victory for one is defeat for the other!"

He took her hands, sliding his fingers between hers. "We do want the same thing," he said gently. "We want peace."

Her eyes were bright with tears of frustration. "There can never be peace under Hitler! Never! The Allies *have* to be victorious, Dieter. Surely you can see that?"

His face was somber. Slowly he released his hold of her and rose from the bed, crossing to the marble-topped cabinet to pour himself a drink. She hugged her knees tight against her chest, knowing that now she had started, there was no way of stopping. She had to carry on inexorably to the end, no matter what the price.

"We have to want the same thing for the future," she said fiercely. "We have to want the same thing for our child. And I would rather he was never born than he should live his life under a monster like Hitler!"

The abyss was out in the open, yawning between them. His face closed, shuttered, the powerful lines of his naked body tense.

Fear caught and clutched at her heart. Only a short while ago anything had seemed possible. Now she felt as if at any moment she might be plunged into a ravine that was bottomless. He swirled the brandy around in his glass, and then, extinguishing the lamp, he pulled back the heavy drapes and stared silently out over the headland and the sea.

He trusted her completely. Her loyalty was now to him utterly, as his was to her. He loved her. She was carrying his child. She was going to be his wife. "Our child will not live under Hitler, Lisette," he said quietly, not looking at her, staring out into the darkness. "Within a few months Hitler will be dead."

He heard her swift intake of breath and turned toward her, his handsome, hard-boned face tense. "Germany cannot afford Hitler any longer, Lisette. He is destroying her."

"I don't understand . . ." she whispered, her eyes wide. "How can you know that he is going to die?"

He moved to her swiftly, taking her hands in his, his voice quick and urgent. "Responsible army officers and leading civilian leaders are going to overthrow him. He will be seized, tried, and executed. Then Germany will make peace with the United States and Great Britain."

She let out a long, shuddering breath. "Are you one of those officers?" she asked, already knowing the answer.

He nodded, feeling overwhelming relief at admitting it. "Yes. When the government of a nation is leading it to its doom, rebellion is not only a right but a duty. Hitler and his SS thugs aren't fit to lead Germany. Bad decision after bad decision has been made. Attacking the Soviet Union was madness. We need a man of honor to bring us out of the nightmare we have been plunged into."

"Who?" Lisette asked dazedly. "There is no one . . ."

"Rommel," Dieter said, his eyes bright, his wheat-gold hair silver in the moonlight. "Rommel will replace Hitler. He's strong enough to prevent civil war from breaking out between the army and the SS. There *will* be peace, Lisette! The minute Hitler is seized, Rommel will contact General Eisenhower, and all further bloodshed will be forestalled. A peace treaty will be signed, and then they will join with us in throwing back the Russians. There will be peace all over Europe before the year is out."

Her heart was slamming against her chest. She could hardly believe what she was hearing. "What if anything goes wrong?" she asked, her lips dry.

He tensed. If anything went wrong, then he and von Stauffenberg and every other member of Black Orchestra, the group pledged to free the Fatherland of Hitler and Nazism, would die slowly and agonizingly in a Gestapo torture chamber dangling from a noose of piano wire.

"Nothing will go wrong," he said tightly, drawing her to her feet and holding her close against him. "Germany will be free of the brownshirts she has had to live with for all these years. There will be no more Goebbels, no more Himmlers.

113

No more men who have never set foot on a battlefield sending hundreds of thousands to die futilely on the Russian front. The Gestapo will be crushed, and the army will be able to operate freely under men like von Rundstedt and Rommel. Germany will emerge bruised and bleeding but with honor." He cupped her face with his thumb and forefinger and tilted it upward so that her eyes met his. "We will be able to live with ourselves and with each other, Lisette. In order to do that, no risk is too great."

Her arms tightened around him. The ground was solid beneath her feet. There was no abyss. There never would be again.

"I love you," she said fiercely as he lowered his head to hers, bending her in toward him.

"That's good," he murmured, kissing her, "because I'm going to take you to bed again." He scooped her up in his arms, carrying her with ease across to the rumpled, inviting, brass-headed bed.

He had known, the minute she had told him about the baby, that he would have to speak to her father. He could be withdrawn from Normandy at any moment. He had to make sure that she would be taken care of, that the comte knew his intentions were honorable.

The next morning, before he left the château for his day's duties, he sent a request to Rommel for a personal interview. The field marshal would not be pleased, but he would be sympathetic. Since they had mutually committed to Black Orchestra, they were bound in a loyalty of the highest kind.

As he stepped from the château into the brilliant May sunshine, he saw two figures, arms linked, walking across the terrace and toward the rose gardens. He frowned in concern. It was Lisette and her father, and he knew, instinctively, what she was telling him. For the first time in his life, he was uncertain of what to do. He had envisioned telling the comte himself, making sure that Lisette met with no parental abuse. They began to walk down the wide, shallow steps that led to the gardens, and he was torn with indecision. Logic told him that his place was at her side. Emotion made him hesitate.

There was something about the closeness of the two figures, father and daughter, that excluded him. He wondered how he would feel in another twenty years if he were having such a conversation with *his* daughter. His fists clenched. He was damn sure he wouldn't want the bastard who had made her pregnant intruding on their private conversation. The very thought made his muscles tighten. *Mein Gott!* Any man who laid a finger on his daughter would find himself with a broken neck! He allowed himself a grim smile, knowing how his reaction to the hypothetical situation would have amused Lisette, then turned sharply on his heel, walking toward his car. He would talk to the comte later that evening. Alone.

"I don't think I want to hear what it is you have to tell me," Henri said as they walked down the moss-covered steps.

"I'm sorry, Papa, but it has to be said."

He halted at the foot of the steps, turning to face her. "Has it?" he asked gently.

She nodded. There were blue shadows under her eyes. She had slept very little, lying awake and wondering how best she could break the news to him, how least she could hurt him. "There isn't an easy way of telling you," she said as they began to walk down a graveled pathway that led between lush-budded Ophelias and Gloire de Dijon.

"No, I don't suppose there is," he said, pausing to take a pair of pruning shears from his pocket and clipping an early flowering, milk-white bloom for his buttonhole. "It's Major Meyer, isn't it?"

"Yes," she said quietly. "I'm in love with him, Papa."

His hand shook, an expression of pain flaring across his face, and she said urgently, "It isn't as bad as you think. Please listen to me. Let me explain."

He walked away from her, toward a wooden seat that in another week would be half-hidden by roses. "How can you explain?" he asked, sitting down heavily. "He's a German. He shot Paul and André. What possible explanation can you have for consorting with a man like that?"

She sat down beside him, taking one of his hands. "He shot Paul and André because of me, Papa," she said unsteadily. "The burden of their death is mine. I will carry it all my life. I would do anything, give anything, for it not to have happened. But at least I understand *why* it happened, Papa! The responsibility was mine as well as Dieter's."

115

"How could it possibly have been yours?" he asked in stunned disbelief.

"Dieter . . . Major Meyer . . . knew that I was a courier for the Resistance. And he knew that was why Elise had come to Valmy, what her mission was. When Paul and André were arrested, there was no way he could release them. Gestapo headquarters at Caen already knew of their existence. And Major Meyer knew what sort of interrogation they would face when they were taken there." She paused, her face white. "He was terrified that Paul or André would give my name under questioning. And in fact, André did give it to him. I, too, would have been arrested. It was because of *me* that he allowed them to escape in order to shoot them without the Gestapo becoming suspicious of his motives! It was *my* fault! If he hadn't fallen in love with me, it would never have happened." Her face was ravaged by grief and guilt.

"Are you sure that he knew Elise was a member of the Resistance?" Henri whispered, horrified.

She nodded, wiping her tears away with her hands. "Yes. He knew what she was trying to do. He knew all along that she had come to Valmy in order to gain entrance to the grand dining room and copy or photograph the maps and papers in there."

Henri passed a shaking hand across his eyes. His face was ashen. He had been responsible for Elise's presence at Valmy. If the girl had been arrested, killed . . . "And he let her go?" he asked incredulously.

Lisette's eyes were fierce in her tear-stained face. "Yes, he let her go. He would have let Paul and André go as well if he could have done so. Please try and understand, Papa. I would never have wanted him to do what he did. I'm not very brave, but I would far, far rather have been arrested and taken to Caen than live with Paul and André's death on my conscience. But I didn't know about it. Dieter had only minutes in which to make a decision. If Paul and André went to Caen, then the chances were that within hours there would be an order for my arrest too. My arrest, and Elise's arrest. Your arrest. Perhaps even maman's . . . What he did wasn't right, Papa, but it was the only thing he could think of in the circumstance. Please try and understand."

Her father suddenly looked old, his face lined, his

shoulders bowed. "I understand," he said at last. "But I can't forgive it. I can't forgive any of it. Not their presence in my home, in my country. Not the abomination of their creed. Not their arrogance. Not the blood that is on their hands and that nothing will ever wash away. There are so many other people you could have fallen in love with, Lisette. Why Major Meyer? Why a German?"

"I don't know," she said quietly. "I just know that I have, Papa. Nothing that anyone says or does can change it. I love him, and I want to marry him."

"Marry him?" He stared at her as though she had taken leave of her senses. "But you can't marry him, Lisette. Germans don't marry French girls."

"I'm having a baby," she said quietly, "and I'm going to marry him, Papa."

"But my dear child, he won't marry you!" he said, anguished. "Such a promise is meaningless!"

She squeezed his hand tightly. "It isn't, Papa. He asked me to marry him long before he knew about the baby. Long before there *was* a baby."

Henri closed his eyes. She was his only child. He couldn't disown her, couldn't cast her off. He tried to remember his first, instinctive feelings about Major Meyer. He had liked the man. He had sensed strength there, and courage. Then had come the shootings. He wondered if Lisette would have been arrested if Paul and André had been taken to Caen. It was very likely. No one could say for sure who would talk and who would not when subjected to the treatment the Gestapo meted out. In which case, at the cost of Paul and André's lives, Lisette had been spared arrest and interrogation and death. He sighed deeply, wondering what he would have done if he had been placed in the same position, what Paul Gilles would have done. There was no answer. There was no way he could know. He could only guess.

"It won't be easy," he said, opening his eyes. "Whether the war is won or lost, you will not be able to raise the baby at Valmy, not if his parentage becomes common knowledge."

"The war will be over soon, Papa," she said, wishing she could tell him of the plot to overthrow Hitler, of Dieter's part in the conspiracy. "When it is, we shall live somewhere clean and untainted. Somewhere like Switzerland."

Henri smiled and patted her hand. "Yes," he said, rising. "Of course you shall, *ma chère*. When the war is over."

When Dieter arrived back at Valmy at dusk, Henri was waiting for him. "My daughter has told me of her relationship with you," he said without preamble as Dieter strode into the flagstoned entrance hall. "I naturally cannot condone it, but for her sake I shall tolerate it."

"Thank you." Dieter inclined his head not knowing quite what to say next. He understood that the comte was deeply hurt and that he was behaving with dignity in what was, for him, an intolerable situation. "Will you join me for a drink?" he asked.

Henri shook his head. "No. I have no desire to alter our relationship in any way, Major Meyer."

Dieter regarded him reflectively, wondering how best to continue. "You know that I want to marry Lisette?"

"Yes." Henri's voice was stiff. "She told me about the coming child."

"I would like to tell you about it also," Dieter said gravely, "but not in an entrance hall. Please join me for a drink, Comte de Valmy, so that we may talk."

Henri hesitated and Dieter took his arm, propelling him gently in the direction of the study. "I have already written to Field Marshal Rommel requesting an interview with him at which I will ask his permission for the marriage. That permission will be given, I'm sure."

"The marriage cannot be conducted here," Henri said as Dieter opened the study door. "If it becomes public knowledge, Lisette would be branded as a collaborator. Both she and the child would be ostracized."

"I am aware of all the difficulties that Lisette and I will face," Dieter said quietly, walking across to the drinks cabinet.

Henri stared at him. "You?" he asked. "What difficulties can you possibly face?"

A slight smile touched Dieter's mouth. "I have a mother, Comte de Valmy, and I doubt very much she had envisaged having a French girl for a daughter-in-law."

"Ah, yes, probably not," Henri said, disconcerted. It hadn't occurred to him that German officers had mothers. And

118

if they had, it had certainly not occurred to him that they might care what they thought.

"Please don't worry," Dieter said. "Her shock and disapproval will be short-lived. What will you have to drink? A brandy or a whisky?"

"A brandy please," Henri said, feeling in sore need of one. He had intended having as few words as possible with Meyer. He had certainly not anticipated discussing the man's mother. By the grace of God, he only had managed to prevent himself from asking if Meyer and his mother were close. He shook his head, knowing he was tired and had aged years over just the last few months.

"I have to ask what you intend for the future," he said, making an effort to bring the conversation back to a proper footing.

"Of course." Dieter found the comte's dignity and formality in the bizarre circumstances in which he found himself, endearing. It would, he thought, swirling his brandy around in the glass, be easy to become very fond of his future father-in-law. "Let me say, first of all, Comte de Valmy, that I am very much in love with Lisette."

Henri looked at him, startled. He had long ago judged Meyer to be a man of deep reserve and few words. He had not expected such a public declaration of his feelings.

"Falling in love with her is not a thing that I would have done by choice," Dieter continued frankly. "But there was no choice. I met her, and though I tried hard not to, I fell in love with her."

His eyes met Henri's, and Henri sat down suddenly in a leather winged chair. There was no denying the depth of feeling in Meyer's voice—or the sincerity in his eyes. He was as much in love with Lisette as she was with him.

"If only . . ," he said helplessly. "If only you weren't a German!"

Dieter's lips tightened fractionally, and he put down his glass on the desk. "I *am* a German, Comte de Valmy, and I am very proud of being a German. But if it is any comfort to you, I am not and never have been a Nazi."

The room was quiet for a long time, then Henri rose heavily to his feet. "Then I do not envy you your moral dilemma," he said quietly. "Good night, Major Meyer."

Dieter watched him leave the room, then turned and poured himself another glass of brandy. His moral dilemma had been solved by his commitment to Black Orchestra and its avowed intention to remove Hitler from power. But Henri was right not to envy him. The strain of waiting for news from Berlin was crushing.

"What is it that Colonel von Stauffenberg intends to do now?" Lisette asked as they sat before a log fire in his room, waiting for the messages that followed the BBC news broadcast from Britain and that they now listened to together each evening.

"As a staff officer to General Olbricht, von Stauffenberg has access to Hitler's conference room. He will smuggle in a bomb concealed in a briefcase."

"But when? Why doesn't he do it right away?" she asked impatiently, resting her head against his chest.

"It isn't easy," Dieter said gently. "Hitler is pathologically suspicious of everyone around him. He changes his timetable constantly. He leaves meetings early or he does not turn up at all. But the opportunity eventually will present itself, and von Stauffenberg will take advantage of it."

"Pray God it's soon," she whispered as his fingers slid caressingly through her hair. "Before the Allies invade and hundreds of thousands more men are killed and injured."

Above her head, his expression was grim. It had to be soon. Every day, every hour, he expected to hear that von Stauffenberg had placed the bomb and that their mission had been successful. His task then was to join Rommel immediately and escort him to Berlin. During the following three hours, communications from Hitler's headquarters to the outside world would be severed.

The news broadcast came to an end, and the messages to Resistance units all over Europe began.

"The Trojan War will not be held," "Molasses tomorrow will spurt forth cognac," "John has a long moustache"—the list went on and on, but there was no quote from "The Song of Autumn" by Paul Verlaine. As the messages came to an end, Lisette hugged her knees with relief. For the invasion to be launched now, when Hitler was so near to being removed, would be the most needless and terrible waste of life. The news from Berlin had to come first.

"How much more time can we possibly have?" she asked, turning toward Dieter.

He shook his head, his wheat-gold hair bronzed by the fire. "I don't know. The weather was perfect for a landing all through May. The long-term forecast now isn't good. It could be next month before they come."

"And by then von Stauffenberg will have seized his chance?"

"Yes." He felt isolated and cut off from his fellow conspirators. Stülpnagel was in Paris; Strölin was in Stuttgart. He needed to talk to someone to make sure that the plot was going ahead. "I think I will go to Paris this weekend," he said, his eyes narrowing as he stared into the fire. "I need to speak to Stülpnagel." His arm tightened around her. "And I will make arrangements for the wedding. You'll not be able to delay telling your mother any longer."

"It is papa who doesn't want me to tell her," she said as his hand cupped her breast. "And I promised not to. Not for a little longer."

"It doesn't matter," he said, his voice thickening as his hand slid down and across the still flat smoothness of her stomach. "There will only be you and I at the wedding. And the baby . . ."

His lips touched hers, gently and then with increasing urgency. She shivered in delight, sliding her arms up and around his neck, refusing to think of what would happen to him if the plot on Hitler's life failed, if the conspiracy was revealed. Refusing to think of anything but the immeasurable joy of his body, hard and strong against hers, of the heat of his lips on her hair and on her skin; of the utter delight of giving, and in that giving, receiving treasures that she knew would be stored up in her heart forever.

It was a damp, misty morning when Dieter left Valmy for Paris. Wrapped in a blue velvet robe that had been her mother's last Paris-bought gift for her, Lisette had risen early to say good-bye to him. He had kissed her in the privacy of his study, tracing the outline of her face with his forefinger, committing every tiny nuance of gesture and expression to memory.

"Be safe, *Liebling*," he had said huskily. "I'll be back in three days—four at the most."

He had walked outside to his car, and she had been overcome by such a feeling of loss and of impending disaster that she had run after him, flinging her arms around his neck, uncaring of his watching chauffeur.

"Be careful!" she had urged, hugging him so tight that her arms hurt. "Please, please be careful!"

Gently he had lifted her arms from around his neck. "I'll be careful," he said. "And I'll be back. I give you my word."

He had stepped away from her and into the car, and she had stood in the center of the graveled drive, watching as the Horch went down its long length and turned right, disappearing from view. The damp had made her shiver. It was the first day of June, but it seemed to Lisette, watching Dieter speed away from her, that summer had never been further away.

That evening, alone, she listened on his radio to the BBC news broadcast and the messages that followed. "Sabine has just had mumps and jaundice," said the clear, unemotional voice from London. And then: "The long sobs of the violins of autumn."

She froze, her heart slamming against her chest. It came again. "The long sobs of the violins of autumn," and then, "The children are bored on Sundays. The children are bored on Sundays."

She could hardly breathe. Her throat was so tight that she thought she would choke. Dieter was in Paris and the invasion of Europe was imminent.

9

She stood for a few seconds, overcome by the enormity of
the message she had just heard, and then turned, running
from the room and along the long corridors to her father's
study.

He was sitting at his desk, staring bleakly down at a large-
scale map of France, a glass of calvados in his hand.

"It's come, Papa!" she said breathlessly as she burst in on
him. "The message to the Resistance that the invasion is
imminent!"

He looked up at her, bewildered. "What message? I don't
understand."

She quickly crossed the room to him. "Dieter told me of a
message that the British would send immediately prior to the
invasion. It is to come in two parts. The first part was broadcast
from London a few minutes ago."

Her father rose unsteadily to his feet. "Do you mean that
you have been listening to the BBC?" he asked incredulously.
"Here? At Valmy?"

She nodded, the dark fall of her hair lustrous in the
lamplight. "Yes, Papa, I listen every night. With Dieter."

Henri passed a hand across his eyes. The punishment for
possession of a radio was fierce: deportation to a labor camp or
execution as a spy. And Lisette was not only listening to
banned broadcasts but was doing so with a German officer!
There were times when he doubted if he would ever be able to
adjust to the situation between Lisette and Major Meyer. He
found it far too disorientating.

"When are they coming?" he asked, trying to collect his
scattered wits. "More important still, *where* are they coming?"

"I don't know, Papa. But the message was to alert the

Resistance to begin sabotaging rail and road links to the coast. Dieter believes that the invasion will take place here in Normandy. You must leave now, Papa," she said urgently. "You must take maman to Balleroy."

"We must *all* go to Balleroy," Henri said, his voice shaking with emotion. "This invasion will be the most massive battle in French history!" His hands gripped hers. "I can hardly believe it, Lisette! After all these years of waiting and hoping. At last they're coming! France will be free!"

She hugged him tight, knowing he was near tears. "You must leave first thing in the morning, after curfew ends. Dieter has left papers enabling you to pass freely on the roads. You will have no trouble at the checkpoints."

"*We* will have no trouble," he corrected her.

She drew away from him gently and shook her head. "No, Papa. I'm not going with you. I'm going to stay at Valmy until Dieter returns."

The exhilarated color that had flushed his cheeks drained away, leaving him ashen. "You can't stay here on your own," he protested. "It's unthinkable! We must either leave together or not at all!"

Her gaze unfalteringly held his. "No, Papa," she said again, with a determination that brooked no argument. "I'm not leaving Valmy without saying good-bye to him. Please don't ask it of me. I will stay here until he returns, and then I'll make my own way to Balleroy."

"Your mother will never agree to it," he persisted vainly. "The invasion could come before you are able to leave. You could be cut off here in the middle of a battlefield. Trapped."

"There is no need to tell maman of the message or what it means, only that you are going on a visit to Balleroy and would like her to go with you. Tell her now, Papa. And Marie. You will need to leave early in the morning, before the roads become congested with troops being ferried to the coast."

His shoulders sagged. He knew that to argue further was hopeless. "Is there anyone we should try and get in touch with?" he asked defeatedly. "Anyone we should tell about the message?"

She shook her head. "No, Papa. The people for whom the message was meant will have received it and will be acting on it. Dieter ordered the evacuation of Sainte-Marie-des-Ponts a week ago. There is nothing that we can do but wait."

He heard the tension in her voice and his heart went out to her. He knew that she was thinking about Dieter. The battle they had longed for and was now imminent was one in which the man she loved could very well lose his life. He sighed again. Nothing, not even the prospect of an Allied victory, was simple any more.

"I'll go and tell your mother and Marie now," he said awkwardly, not knowing what comfort he could give her. "With God's good help, this battle will be the last."

She looked down at the map of France spread out on his desk. "I hope so," she said fiercely, her hands clenching in the pockets of her skirt until the knuckles showed white. "With all my heart, I hope so, Papa."

She slept very little that night. At two she heard the familiar and distant sound of bombs falling over Cherbourg. She waited, rigid, for the attack to spread, for more planes to fly across the Channel. They did not come. The bombers dropped their nightly load and returned to England, ack-ack guns firing in their wake.

Her parents and Marie left at seven the next morning. Lisette had expected Lieutenant Halder and his men to be tense with expectation, but the activity in the château's courtyard was no more hurried than normal. If they had been informed during the night that an attack was imminent, they were showing no signs of it.

"Henri, I'm sure it isn't necessary for me to go with you," her mother protested as her father settled Marie and a large basket of eggs in the rear seat of the family's battered Citroën.

"Nevertheless, my dear, you are coming," Henri said firmly, glad there was at least one female member of his family over whom he still had authority. "The Duboscqs have offered us shelter if we have to leave Valmy. It is only good manners that we should thank them for doing so."

"But Lisette will be on her own all day . . ."

"Good-bye, Maman," Lisette said, opening the front door of the Citroën for her and kissing her cheek. "Don't worry about me. I shall be perfectly all right."

Her father slammed the rear door on Marie and looked at Lisette, his eyes anguished.

"Please, Lisette . . . Change your mind. Come with us."

"No, Papa," she said with the same firmness with which he had spoken to her mother. "I shall be perfectly safe at Valmy. And I shall be with you very soon. I promise."

Her mother was winding down the window, looking up at her curiously, and Lisette knew that in another moment her suspicions would be roused. She stood back, flashing them a brilliant smile, waving cheerfully. "Good-bye Papa, . . . Maman. Good-bye Marie."

Her father stepped heavily into the driving seat and revved the engine. There was nothing more he could do. Her mind was made up and nothing on God's earth would change it. His responsibility was now to his wife. It was better that Héloïse was at Balleroy and that Lisette had promised to join them there, than that Héloïse, too, should remain at Valmy and run the risk of being caught in the middle of a bloody and murderous battle.

The Citroën, unused for nearly two years, creaked into life and rolled and jolted over the cobblestones of the courtyard toward the stone archway that led out onto the linden-flanked drive beyond.

Lisette waved until it had disappeared, as she had waved when Dieter had left. This time her isolation was complete. There was no one for her to talk to now, not even Marie. She turned on her heel and walked quickly back into Valmy. Lieutenant Halder would know that her parents and Marie had left Valmy, and that she was alone. It was not a pleasant thought. She wondered how long it would be before Dieter returned. He would have heard the message last night as she had. With luck, he would be back by lunchtime, perhaps even earlier.

She made herself a cup of chicory and stood sipping it in the kitchen. Nothing that she had expected to happen was happening. There was no sign of alarm, no black staff cars screaming down the drive, no telephones were ringing. Lunchtime came and went, and Dieter did not return.

The turret room gave the best view over the windswept headland and the sea. She stood at the window for hour after hour, but the Channel remained empty of ships, the waves heaving and surging with a heavy swell. Dusk fell, and she returned to the kitchen and made herself an omelette, and then, tense with expectation, she tuned the radio to the BBC London.

Through the whining and roar of static she listened to the news and then the familiar voice from across the Channel said in perfect French, "Kindly listen now to a few personal messages."

Lisette sat on the floor, hugging her knees as message after message was broadcast, and then at last it came: "The long sobs of the violins of autumn." She waited, the breath so tight in her chest that she could hardly breathe. No second part came. The first line of Paul Verlaine's poem was repeated, and then another, entirely different message was broadcast.

She turned off the radio and let out her breath unsteadily. It hadn't come. Perhaps German Intelligence had been misled. Perhaps there wasn't a second part to the message at all. Perhaps the message did not even mean what they believed it to mean. With her head aching, she walked back down the winding stone stairs to her own room. She had told her father that waiting was all they could do. And the waiting, for a little longer at least, would have to continue.

It continued for far longer than she had anticipated. All through the next long, lonely day, German activity continued as normal in and around Valmy. That night the message was broadcast again, as was a message for all French residents living along the coast: "You are urged to abandon your homes temporarily and move far inland to a safe place," a solemn British voice intoned. "Repeat: You are urged . . ."

But Dieter did not return, and the Germans at Valmy betrayed no signs of apprehension.

On Sunday night, there was a fierce storm. Tiles on Valmy's roofs were hurled to the ground. Gale-force winds rattled the deep-set windows and hurled sheet after sheet of rain against the leaded panes. Despairing, Lisette lay in bed. A fleet could not set sail in such ferocious weather. It could be days before the Channel was calm again, and then the tide would perhaps be wrong for a landing. Dieter had told her that there were only a few days a month when the tide and moon would be right for the Allies. Was that why he had not returned to Valmy? Did he know that in spite of the message, a landing was impossible?

She pummeled her pillow and once again tried to sleep. It was impossible. He had left Valmy intent on speeding up Black Orchestra's plans to annihilate Hitler. In the three days that he had been away, he could have been arrested, even killed. She had no way of knowing what was happening to him. She could only wait—and wait—and wait.

The next morning the sky was bright and clear with only the broken blossoms in the rose garden testifying to the ferociousness of the storm. She braved the hard, curious eyes of the Germans by walking around to the stables for her bicycle. There was no excuse now for bicycle rides. Sainte-Marie-des-Ponts was deserted. Only one or two farmers, obstinate to the last, had been allowed to remain, and that mainly so they could still supply milk and fresh eggs to the militia. She wheeled her bicycle over the cobblestones of the courtyard and through the archway onto the graveled drive, expecting at any moment to be stopped.

Lieutenant Halder turned sharply in her direction, his eyes narrowing. She lifted her head high, her chin firm. If he wanted to stop her, he would have to do so physically. A private called "Halt" and began running toward her, but Halder barked out a restraining order. The private slowed to a standstill, watching hostilely as she pressed down on the pedals and rode away from them.

She had no intention of going far. She did not want to be away from Valmy when Dieter returned, nor did she want to miss any message that might come from him. At the far end of the drive, she turned left, away from the village and toward the sea. She wanted to see for herself if extra troops had been posted, if the cliff tops were bristling with men.

She cycled as near as possible to the giant rolls of barbed wire that closed off the cliffs. Two soldiers were squatting outside a pillbox, playing cards. Another was patrolling, keeping a lookout for any approaching officers. It was all very curious. There was no sign that tanks were being ferried to the coast, or extra men. No sign of any extraordinary activity at all. Yet for three consecutive nights, the message from London to the Resistance had been broadcast loud and clear. Why, then, were the Germans not in a state of high alarm? Was their confidence such that nothing could shake it?

Depressed and anxious, she cycled back toward Valmy.

The day had grown hot and sultry. The storm of the previous evening had cleared nothing from the air. If anything, it seemed even more oppressive. To her right the sea glittered, surging with a heavy swell, the waves creaming on the beaches, the steel spikes and bars that Rommel had ordered embedded in the sand, rearing skyward grotesquely.

If Hitler did not die . . . if the Allies came . . . then Dieter would fight against them. He would fight, not for Hitler, but for Germany. He would be responsible for the deaths of men who were coming to free France. And he, too, would very likely die. The monstrousness of it all sickened her. She halted, then wheeled her bicycle to the verge of the road and into the field beyond, where she threw herself down on the grass.

Time. It was the one thing they desperately needed, and the one thing they did not have: time for von Stauffenberg to carry the bomb into Hitler's headquarters, time for Rommel to assume the mantle of leadership, time in which a peace treaty could be signed, time in which the coming battle could be averted.

She blinked up at the sky and the scudding clouds, overcome by the terrifying certainty that time was not going to be kind to them. It was going to betray and defeat them. Minute by minute, it was leading them not toward happiness, but toward disaster.

That evening, for the fourth time, she listened alone to the radio. "It is hot in Suez. . . . It is hot in Suez," the voice of the announcer said clearly. "The dice are on the table. . . . The dice are on the table." She waited, her heart racing, and at last it came, the second part of the message that Dieter had told her would presage the invasion of Europe: "Wound my heart with a monotonous languor. . . . Wound my heart with a monotonous languor." She drew in a deep, shuddering breath, and as she did so, there came the sound of a powerful car approaching Valmy at speed.

She leaped to her feet, running out of the room and down the spiral stone staircase. It had to be Dieter. It couldn't possibly be anyone else.

She flew along the corridor to the head of the stairs. Distantly, she heard the car doors slam, heard him wishing his chauffeur good night. There was no urgency in his voice, no strain. As she reached the head of the stairs, he stepped into the huge, medieval hall beneath her, and she knew, instantly, that he had heard nothing.

He looked up in her direction, sensing her presence immediately.

"Good evening, Major," the sentry on guard outside the grand dining room said courteously.

"Good evening, Corporal," Dieter said. He removed his cap and gloves and tossed them to one side, then ran up the stairs two at a time. "I missed you," he said fiercely, crushing her against him.

She looked up at him, her eyes large and dark. "You don't know, do you? The message—It's been broadcast four times since you left. Tonight, just minutes ago, the second part was broadcast."

The grin of delight at having her in his arms again vanished. "I don't believe you!" he said. "It isn't possible."

"There was also a message to all civilians living near the coast. We were told to move inland for safety. Papa has taken maman and Marie to Balleroy. I said I would join them later . . . after I'd seen you."

He gripped her hand tightly, striding quickly toward his room. "What the hell is going on?" he asked savagely. "There's been no news of it! Not a whisper!"

He slammed into the room, punched on the light, and strode to his desk and the telephone.

"The signal Canaris warned would presage the landings has been broadcast for four nights!" he barked at Halder. "What orders have been given from headquarters?"

Lisette could hear stunned amazement in Halder's voice. His reply was that none had been given.

Dieter severed the connection, his face grim. "You're sure, quite sure, about what you heard?"

She couldn't speak. It hadn't occurred to her that the Germans were unaware of the message. Information about it had come from German Intelligence. It was inconceivable that they hadn't listened to it and acted upon it. But if they hadn't heard . . . If it was she who brought it to their attention . . .

"Oh, God," she whispered, her face white, knowing the treachery she would be guilty of. "Don't tell them, Dieter. Please . . ."

"I have to!" His eyes were agonized. "Von Stauffenberg can't act until the beginning of next month. We have to be in a position of strength when Hitler is removed so that Rommel can negotiate a peace that will be honorable to Germany. If the Allies succeed in invading France, there will be no peace with honor, only defeat."

He began to dial again. She didn't know whom he was calling. It didn't matter. She moved with lightning speed, seizing the telephone wire as he said tersely, "Major Meyer speaking. The Canaris message—"

She wrenched at the wire with all her strength, ripping it from the wall, yanking the telephone from his desk, and sending it crashing to the floor.

"I'm not sorry," she gasped defiantly as he whirled round on her. "I had to do it! I couldn't let you tell them if they didn't already know!"

His face was sheet-white. *"Mein Gott!"* He kicked the telephone out of the way, seizing her shoulders. For a terrible moment she thought he was going to hit her, then he groaned, pulling her against him. "I understand," he said, his voice choked. "And you must be understanding for me, Lisette." He looked down at her, and in his eyes she saw all his love for her, all his concern, all his fear for her safety. "I'm going down to the coast. I don't know when I will be back. As soon as it is light, you must make your way to Balleroy."

She nodded, overcome by the feeling that time had run out, that these few moments were all they were ever going to have.

"I love you!" she said fiercely. "Oh, God, my darling. *I love you!*"

His mouth came down on hers, hard and sweet, and then he was gone, sprinting along the corridor and down the stairs, snatching his cap and gloves, slamming open the door, and running for his car.

Two hours later the first planes began to roar overhead. She turned off the lights, pulling the heavy blackout curtains to one side, her eyes straining skyward. There were more of them than she had ever seen at one time before, certainly more than was usual for the nightly bombing of Cherbourg. She stood alone in the darkened room, hugging her arms tight

131

against her chest as wave after wave of low-flying aircraft flew over Valmy. It was beginning. The invasion of France by the Allies was under way.

Dieter's Horch careened at breakneck speed down the narrow lanes that led to his observation bunker. The sky to both the east and west was red with flares, the sound of bombing unmistakable. The Horch swept through the outer perimeter of the coastal defense zone and rocked to a halt. Seconds later, with Halder and two gunnery officers hard on his heels, he was scrambling quickly up a steep, sand-covered track behind the cliffs.

"They're bombing Le Havre as well as Cherbourg," Halder said panting hard. Dieter grunted but did not slacken his pace. The track to the bunker was treacherous in the darkness. Coils of barbed wire hemmed it in on either side, and beyond the barbed wire were mile after mile of mine-fields. The slit trench they were making for was almost at the top of the cliffs. He dropped down into it with agility, taking the concrete stairs beyond two at a time, sprinting down underground passages to the large, single-roomed bunker below.

The three men manning it swung around to him in surprise. He wasted no time on explanations, striding past them to the high-powered artillery glasses that stood on a pedestal opposite one of the apertures. Slowly, moving the glasses from left to right, he scanned the bay. There was nothing: no lights, no sound, not even an errant fishing boat on the silk-dark surface of the sea.

"There's nothing there," he said tersely to Halder. "But there will be. I'd stake my life on it."

He strode to the field telephone and dialed headquarters. "Meyer here," he said in answer to a sharp query on the other end of the line. "The Canaris message was broadcast only minutes ago. Have you been apprised of it?"

His lieutenant colonel sounded amused. "No, my dear Meyer, we have not. Please don't sound so anxious. I really don't think the enemy is stupid enough to announce its arrival over the radio."

Dieter blanched. "That message is vital to our security!"

he hissed. "It means that we can expect the invasion within forty-eight hours!"

"Then get down to the coast and keep me informed," his lieutenant colonel said laconically. "Good night, Meyer."

If the man had been in the same room, Dieter knew he would have shot him. Savagely, he asked for a connection to Rommel's headquarters at La Roche-Guyon.

He was informed that the message had been received, that no immediate action was being taken. The field marshal had taken leave: he was visiting his wife in Herrlingen, near Ulm.

Convulsed with fury, Dieter slammed down the telephone. The work of Counterintelligence had been for nothing. Germany had been given the opportunity to be ready and waiting when the Allies invaded, and the opportunity had been squandered. Within hours the Allies would be storming ashore, and the German army was sitting on its backside, doing nothing. It didn't bear thinking of.

He seized the artillery glasses once again. In daylight, from this position a hundred feet above the beach, the whole of the Bay of the Seine could be seen, from the tip of the Cherbourg peninsula to Le Havre. Even now, in the moonlight, he had a formidable view. But the sea was still empty. There was nothing to be seen.

It was the longest night of his life. For months he had done all that he could to fortify the beaches of France. Now there was nothing more he could do. He tried hard not to think of Lisette. To think of Lisette was to be consumed with fear for her safety, and fear was the last thing he wanted to feel or communicate to his men. He used the field telephone constantly, checking on his units, determined that any soldier landing on a Normandy beach would never leave it. They would be repulsed as Rommel had always said they would be: in the water. The fighting would not spread beyond. It would not touch Valmy.

The telephone rang stridently. "Paratroopers have been reported on the peninsula," his lieutenant colonel barked, no longer sounding amused. "Alert your men, Meyer."

"Yes, Sir," Dieter said tightly, refraining from telling him that his men had been on full alert for hours.

"The sky is beginning to lighten, Sir," Halder said as he slammed the telephone receiver back onto its rest.

Dieter walked across to him and swung the artillery glasses once more over the vast sweep of the sea. There was a heavy, low-lying mist. White-capped waves roared ceaselessly shoreward. His glasses swung slowly across the dark mass of the Cherbourg peninsula and then back once more across the bay. The sky was dulling to gray, long fingers of light presaging dawn. He was just about to lower the glasses when he halted, every muscle and sinew freezing.

They were coming. Ship after ship was taking shape and substance as the mist and clouds and the night ceased to hide them. There were hundreds of them, thousands of them. More ships than he had ever dreamed possible. A mighty armada filled the horizon from east to west. An avenging force so terrible in its beauty that the breath caught in his throat.

"Jesus God," he said softly. "Take a look, Halder. You'll never see such a sight again."

He handed the glasses to Halder, but still he could see them. Pennants flying, battle ensigns streaming in the wind. His lieutenant lowered the glasses and turned to face him, his face white.

"It's the end," he whispered. "No force on earth could repel an invasion of that size!"

"You're wrong, Halder," Dieter said grimly. "We can. And by God, we're going to!" He strode once more over to the telephone and rang headquarters. "It's the invasion," he said brusquely. "It's here. All ten thousand ships of it!"

The bombing continued all night, sometimes far off over Cherbourg, sometimes frighteningly near. Lisette left Dieter's study and ran up the stone spiral staircase to the turret room. In daylight, the entire headland and the sea beyond were clearly visible from the high-arched windows. Now all she could see were clouds scudding across the face of the moon and the planes, wave after wave of planes. She opened the window and leaned out and saw the sky to the east and the west was streaked with flame: Cherbourg and Le Havre, both burning.

The night seemed interminable, and then slowly, almost grudgingly, the darkness began to pearl, presaging dawn. Through the early morning mist, the headland and the lip of the cliff took on shape and substance, and she leaned farther out the window, straining her eyes seaward. At first she could see nothing, then a sliver of light cleaved the sky and there they were. Ship after ship. Massing the horizon. Uncountable. Unimaginable.

The sliver of light cracked and broke. Dawn seeped over the horizon, and a dull gold glow rippled over the hundreds and thousands of ships and men that had come to free France. There was one long second of silence, one moment in which everything was perfectly still, then the roar of guns crashed out across the water, and planes swooped in low, bombing as they came.

She ran to the radio, tuning it to London, pressing her ear against the set in order to hear above the deafening noise.

"This is London calling," a voice said faintly through a roar of static. "I bring you an urgent instruction from the supreme commander. The lives of many of you depend upon the speed and thoroughness with which you obey it. It is particularly addressed to all who live within twenty miles of the coast. Leave your towns at once. Stay off frequented roads. Go on foot and take nothing with you that you cannot carry easily. Get as quickly as possible into open country . . ."

A shell exploded, so near that she could hear nothing more. Common sense told her to run for the cellars, but from where she was she could see the beach, see the ships as they neared the shore. Recklessly, she crossed once more to the window, the concussion of the shoreline guns reverberating through the soles of her shoes.

The noise and clamor and smoke were so dense that she could barely distinguish anything. The glass in the windows exploded inward, a shard catching her on the forehead. Planes continued to scream overhead. Guns from the German shore batteries blazed out over the water, met by devastating fire from the battleships. She pressed her hands over her ears, gasping for breath as smoke-blackened air billowed around her.

Then she saw the streak of flame as a plane keeled away from formation, its tail on fire. It screamed down, over the cliffs, heading in a sickening spin for the beech woods beyond Valmy. She saw one parachute open and then another. Heard the rattle of machine-gun fire and knew that it was being directed at the helpless figures in their harnesses.

She didn't stop to think. To think would have caused her to be paralyzed by fear. She ran from the room, down the twisting stairs, running along the passageways, running, running down the main stairs, out into the kitchens, struggling with the heavy rear door, hurling herself outside into the inferno that was now Normandy.

Machine-gun and artillery and mortar fire from the beach assailed her senses. Dust and smoke and burning cordite filled the air. Blood from the cut on her forehead trickled down into her eye, and she dashed it away, running through the gardens to the fields.

Planes continued to roar overhead, bombing the shore batteries, overshooting and raining their cargo down onto meadows and fields. She saw the first parachute balloon into the woods and then the second. Gasping for breath, she vaulted the low hedge that separated the kitchen garden from the wilderness beyond and kept on running, running, toward them.

Enraged, Luke Brandon cursed as machine-gun fire ripped into his leg. Jesus Christ, but this wasn't the way he had intended to set foot on French soil. He was going to be killed without having fired a shot in retaliation. He tried to see if his copilot had been shot, but Colley's chute was already billowing down between the trees.

His lips tightened as he rated their chances of survival. As a spotter pilot, his last message to the battleship *Texas* had been that truck convoys were moving rapidly toward Saint-Marie-des-Ponts, the village only half a mile from where he was going to land. The Germans would be so thick on the ground that there would be no escaping them, not with a smashed and shattered leg. The trees were only seconds away. He clenched his teeth against the pain and crashed into them.

His parachute was trapped high above him. For a few vain seconds he swung backward and forward, then managed to unclasp his harness and tumble in bloody agony to the ground. Someone was running toward him. He could feel the earth vibrate, see the movement of the trees. He drew his pistol and waited. However many of them there were, he'd see to it that he took one of the bastards with him.

Lisette raced to the first body and faltered. She had never seen anyone dead before. He was young, not more than eighteen or nineteen, and there was a surprised look on his face. She stood for a second, gazing down at him, trying to catch her breath, then began to run into the woods.

He was lying on his stomach at the foot of a tree, his weight on his elbows, a pistol held unwaveringly in both hands. She burst out of the surrounding undergrowth and stood panting, gazing down into the Webley's barrel.

For a terrified moment she thought he was going to shoot. His fingers tightened on the trigger, a spasm of incredulity crossing his face, then he dropped the pistol weakly to one side.

"Excuse me," he said, and his French had the clipped, precise accent of an Englishman. "I thought you were a German."

She ran to him and knelt at his side. "Can you stand? Can you walk?"

A lock of dark hair fell forward over his brow as he shook his head, grimacing with pain. She hooked her arm under his. "Lean on me. Quickly."

"No, I'd be too heavy. My copilot came down not far away. Find him. Tell him I need him."

"He's dead," she said steadily. "Now, lean on me and do as I say."

She saw bitterness and rage flare in his eyes, then he did as she told him, and she braced herself against his weight.

"Are you on your own?" he gasped, beads of sweat scoring his face.

She nodded. "Don't talk. There isn't time."

He was older than she, twenty-six or twenty-seven, with a cool, well-bred look that she thought of as being particularly English. Twice he lost consciousness, and she had to lower him to the ground, waiting for him to recover.

"Where the hell are you taking me?" He was gasping, and his face was ashen.

"To my home. To Valmy."

"But this way leads to the coast!"

"I know," she replied calmly, "but there is nowhere else that I can take you. Please don't talk any more. Save your strength."

He said something beneath his breath that she couldn't understand, and then their tortuous progress continued.

Out of the woods and into the fields. Out of the fields and into the gardens. Out of the gardens and into Valmy. By the time the kitchen door slammed behind them, she could barely stand. Her vision was distorted and blurred. Her breath came in harsh, savage rasps. She laid him down on the stone floor of the kitchen, then staggered over to the sink and ran water into a bowl. He needed medical treatment, a doctor, and there was only herself. She hadn't saved his life yet.

10

The noise was indescribable. It was like being in the center of a volcano. Dust rained down on her. Smoke billowed in through every crack and crevice. Her ears hurt from the concussion of guns and cannon. She threw a handful of rock salt into the bowl of water before carrying it over to the semiconscious Englishman, knowing that when the Germans fell back from the beach, they would overrun Valmy. She had to stop the bleeding, had to hide him.

With a pair of kitchen scissors, she slit open the leg of his trousers, peeling the blood-stained cloth away from the mangled flesh. At the sight that met her eyes she flinched, her jaw tightening. Dear God in heaven, how had he managed to limp and crawl so far, even with her assistance?

"I can't take the bullets out," she said, kneeling at his side, her hair tumbling around her shoulders. "I'm going to clean the wound and stop the bleeding . . ."

"What time is it?" His voice cut across her, surprisingly strong.

"Nearly seven."

He winced with pain as she began to sponge leaves and grass and debris from his bloodied leg.

"How far is it to the beach?"

"A little under a mile."

His eyes registered shock. "We were told there were no civilians so near to the coast."

His head and shoulders were braced against the kitchen wall as she continued to clean the worst of the dirt away, the water in the bowl deepening from rose to scarlet to ghastly crimson.

"There aren't many," she said. "A few farmers. That's all."

"And yourself?"

"Yes." She offered no explanation. She was too busy tightening her stomach muscles against her reaction to the awfulness of his leg and thigh wounds. She staunched the blood with towels and then ran for sheets, rending them into strips, binding the gaping flesh with swift, trembling fingers. By the time she had finished, his face was gray.

"You can't stay in the kitchen," she said as she leaned back on her heels. "Germans could burst in at any moment."

His lean face tensed against the pain. "So could the Americans," he said, attempting a smile. "Is there a vantage point? A place where we can see who is approaching?"

"Upstairs." Her voice was doubtful as she regarded his leg.

"Then I'll have to ask you to be my crutch again," he said, and this time his smile was steadier. "My name is Luke Brandon. I owe you my life. Thank you."

She hooked her arm under his, taking his weight.

"What's your name?"

"Lisette," she replied, bracing herself as he leaned against her.

He sucked in his breath as pain knifed through him, then said jerkily, "I like it. It suits you. It's very pretty."

A smile touched her lips. For the first time since she had found him in the woods and seen his bloodied leg, she was convinced that he was not going to die. Dying men did not, surely, pay their nurses compliments.

"We have to go into the entrance hall, to the main staircase. It's a long way."

He nodded, gritting his teeth, fighting against the longing

to collapse where he stood. He'd been lucky. He didn't want his luck to come to a sudden end and be taken unawares by a party of Germans. It was seven o'clock. The Americans would have control of the beach. They would be coming ashore. He would be able to get expert medical aid and move inland with them. He certainly wasn't going to allow himself to be shipped back to England. The stairs stretched out unendingly before him. He drew a deep breath. They had to be climbed. He had to be able to see what was happening.

They were drowned in noise. Submerged by it. "Are those our guns?" she shouted as Valmy's stout and ancient walls shuddered.

He nodded grimly. "That bombardment is coming from the battleships. They're annihilating the German gun batteries. There won't be a German left alive by the time they've finished."

She gave a small cry and stumbled, and he had to fling himself across the banister to maintain his balance. "Don't be frightened," he said, seeing how white her face was, how large and dark her eyes. "Another few minutes and the war, for you, will be over."

"When the Germans surrender, they'll be taken prisoner, won't they?" she asked urgently. "They won't be shot?"

She looked as though she were about to faint, and he didn't blame her. They could hardly make themselves heard over the roar of exploding shells. He heaved himself painfully up another step. "Germans aren't in the habit of surrendering," he said comfortingly. "Don't worry. They won't trouble you again after the Americans gain Omaha."

"Omaha?"

He leaned on the banister, panting for breath. "That's the code name for the beach down there. American units are taking it. The British and Canadians and Free French are farther east, beyond Arromanches."

"But you're not American," she said as she half carried him down a wood paneled passageway and into a large, blue, silk-lined room.

"No," he said with a painful attempt at a smile. "I'm English."

He looked out through the shattered panes of the large windows, and his smile vanished. He could see the headland

and the distant sea, but there were no American troops swarming ashore, no U. S. tanks trundling up from the beach, rolling inland. Instead, German shore batteries were blazing devastatingly down on to the beach: antitank guns raked the water with murderous fire; machine gunners decimated the incoming Americans before they could even clear the landing ramps.

"Holy God," he whispered. "They're pinned down! They're not going to make it."

He sank to the floor, staring out over the headland, at the hell that was Omaha. Beyond the landing craft, the battleships *Texas* and *Arkansas* directed a blistering barrage of fire against the German gun positions, but the guns still blazed. More men were disgorged from the ships—the 29th Infantry Division, the 1st Infantry Division—battle-hardened men who had crossed the beaches of North Africa and Sicily and Salerno. But they were not crossing Omaha. The shoreline was thick with bodies. The water heaved with them. And still they came, hurtling down the landing ramps and into the water, struggling for the shore.

She knelt at his side and wondered if she would ever again be able to think the Channel beautiful. It was red with blood, the tide high, four-foot waves tossing and bucketing the landing craft as German bullets rained down on them. She closed her eyes, saying a silent and fervent prayer for the men on the beach . . . for Dieter.

A blast rocked her back on her heels.

"*Go back downstairs,*" Luke shouted to her as plaster and debris rained down on them.

She shook her head. "*No,*" she shouted back stubbornly over the deafening roar of guns and mortar. "*I'm staying here!*"

All through the long, blood-soaked morning, they crouched on the floor of the bedroom, lifting their heads whenever they dared, their eyes straining through clouds of dust and smoke to see what was happening down on Omaha.

Luke had expected the Americans to pull out. He had expected at any moment that the ships standing off the coast and full of men waiting to land would move to the other beaches, the beaches being assaulted by the British and Canadians. They didn't do so. The battleships came even closer to shore, firing flat trajectory salvos toward the batteries.

Allied fighter bombers swooped down on the German positions, bombing and strafing. Slowly, incredibly, over the
bodies of the dead, men came ashore and stayed ashore.

"They're going to do it!" Luke said tautly, dragging
himself once more to the window. "The Big Red One is coming
through!"

Lisette stared at him, thinking that his carefully accented
French was at last beginning to let him down. "The Big Red
One?" she asked.

He flashed her a grin of elation and relief. "That's the
nickname for the regiment down there. They're the toughest
outfit that the Americans have, and they're winning through!"

Her eyes were still full of fear. "Are they taking prisoners?" she asked, crawling over to him as another salvo of
bombing shook the château to its foundations.

"If you had some binoculars, I could probably see. As it is,
all I can tell you is that they're on that beach, and any minute
now the Germans will be falling back."

Her pretty face was flecked with soot marks, wracked with
strain. He wondered what the hell she was doing in a large,
rambling château, alone in an area of high German security.

"Where are your parents?" he asked, easing his flying
jacket off, revealing the shoulder flashes of an officer.

"Balleroy. It's about sixty miles south of here." There was a
trace of huskiness in her voice that he found irresistible. When
he had first seen her, he had wondered if he was hallucinating.
He had expected a party of Germans and instead, the most
beautiful girl he had ever seen had run through the woods to
him and hauled him to safety. Even now, he had to keep
looking at her to make sure that she was real.

"Why aren't you with them?" he asked curiously.

She shrugged delicate shoulders, her violet-dark eyes
bleak. He had never before seen eyes the color of amethysts.
"I am to join them," she said at last. "When it is safe to do so."

She had promised Dieter that she would go at first light.
It had been impossible. Now it was too late to go. She would
not leave until she knew he was safe. Her hands tightened in
her lap. He *had* to be safe. The Americans would sweep
ashore, and Dieter and his fellow officers would surrender.
They would be taken prisoner. He would be safe until the end
of the war, until the peace came and their life together could
begin.

Luke noted her clenched knuckles and said comfortingly, "It won't be long now. Another hour, maybe two. Those Germans are going to wish they'd never set foot on French soil."

Tendrils of hair curled damply against her forehead and cheeks. She pushed a strand away and changed the subject, saying unsteadily, "What were you doing when you were shot down?"

"Spotting for the battleships. Relaying to them the targets they should be aiming for."

He had a pleasant voice, calm and controlled, the voice of a man who would consider it ill-bred to panic. He was unexpectedly dark haired for an Englishmen, but that was his only Mediterranean feature. His eyes were blue, their rain-washed vibrancy almost Nordic; his mouth, finely chiseled. His whole demeanor was one of cool confidence.

"The medics will want to use this place by nightfall," he said, the dark line of his brows pulling together. "They'll want water. Sheets. Anything that you have."

She tore her gaze away from the terrible drama of Omaha. "I'll go downstairs and check the water. If it's cut off, I'll have to pump it from the stable yard."

"Don't go outside!" he yelled, but she was already running to the door, and his voice was lost as more planes roared overhead.

Pictures had come off walls; lamps had smashed. Glass crunched beneath the soles of her shoes as she ran along the corridor and down the main staircase. The doors of the grand dining room, guarded so diligently for so long, looked bereft without a soldier fronting them. It would be easy now to break them down: easy and pointless. The Germans' plans to repel the invasion were now obsolete. She ran past them and into the kitchen. As in the upper rooms, all the windows had been shattered. Smoke had blackened Marie's carefully scrubbed floor, and debris had been blown in, smashing against walls and cupboards. She picked her way carefully through pieces of still hot metal and turned on the taps at the sink. Only a trickle of water ran down over her hands and fury knifed through her. She should have filled every pan and bowl with water while it was still running. Now she would have to pump it up, bucket by bucket, from the stable yard. She ran to the door, pulled it open, and stood, frozen in horror, as four Germans raced toward her across the cobblestones.

"Hold your fire!" Dieter yelled into the field telephone to his gun batteries. "Don't give away our positions! Wait till they hit the beach!"

The observation bunker shuddered around him as shells blasted into the cliff face. Through swirling white dust he saw the Allied planes fly in, wingtip to wingtip in perfect formation: Spitfires and Thunderbolts; Mustangs and Lancasters; Fortresses and Liberators. There were hundreds of them. Thousands of them. So many that it seemed as if the sky could not possibly hold them all. They flew straight in over the massive fleet, strafing the beaches and headlands, zooming up, sweeping around, and strafing again.

A shell smashed into the cliff face immediately below the bunker, and he was blasted from his feet, hurled backward against the concrete wall, deluged with dust and dirt and concrete splinters.

"Are you all right, Sir?" Halder yelled as he scrambled to his feet, his face bloodied, and his uniform ripped. Another salvo of shells landed on the cliff above them, and into the swirling clouds of white dust, an avalanche of earth and stone shattered through the bunker's apertures.

"Keep at your post, Halder!" Dieter yelled. "See if any of the batteries have been hit!"

All around him, men were picking themselves up from the floor. No one seemed hurt. "Back to your positions!" he shouted, and seized the glasses.

"No one has been hit, Sir," Halder shouted through the choking swirls of fine white dust. "They're waiting for orders."

"Tell them to hold. I want those landing ships directly beneath us before we fire."

He looked through the glasses at the landing craft, tossing and bucketing as they neared the shore. They were almost in range. Another three minutes . . . another two. He began to telephone fire orders to his guns: "Target One, all guns, range four eight five zero, basic direction twenty plus, impact fuse."

Another salvo from the battleships hit the cliff face. Masonry fell from the ceilings, choking dust swirled through the apertures, men were thrown back against the concrete walls.

Dieter remained at his position. The bunkers had been designed to withstand direct fire from the sea. His guns were still in action, and they were going to stay in action. Men scrambled back to their feet. In their batteries, his gunnery officers waited for his order. One minute . . . thirty seconds . . . The gray shoal of landing craft rocked down onto the shore. Landing ramps hit water. "Target One," Dieter rasped into his handset. *"Fire!"*

By eleven-thirty he knew it was hopeless. Despite the artillery and mortar fire raining down on them, the Americans were gaining the beach. Pockets of them were scaling the bluffs, weaving upward through the minefields, running over the dead and dying. A battery on his left flank was knocked out by bazookas. A battery on his right had been captured.

"Troops formerly pinned down on beaches now advancing up the heights," he said to his batteries. "The ammunition convoy has been wiped out. There will be no more supplies. Prepare for close combat."

They were defeated and he knew it. They had needed the backup of the panzer divisions Hitler had so insistently kept from them. The Americans were now storming the cliffs. There was no longer any hope of throwing them into the sea. They had landed on French soil, and they were going to remain on French soil.

Lisette's face burned in his mind. He could see her eyes, brilliant with love for him; her wide, full-lipped mouth; the glossy, silk-dark fall of her hair. She would be safe. The Americans would take Valmy. "I'm sorry, *Liebling,*" he whispered beneath his breath, then he turned to his men. "Prepare to leave the bunker and engage in close combat with the enemy," he said tersely, and then to Halder, "Let's go! Let's give it to those bastards!"

Lisette slammed the door on the German soldiers and ran for the stairs. They burst in behind her, knocking her to her knees, rampaging through the kitchen, their skin and clothes rank with sweat and burning cordite. They raced for the stairs and the upper rooms that would give them ideal firing positions. She struggled to her feet, running after them into the flagstoned hall, shouting a frantic warning to Luke Brandon as they began to surge up the stairs.

An officer wheeled on her in fury. He seized her arm and hurled her across the stone floor, then raised his rifle to shoot.

She didn't see Valmy's massive oak door burst open. One second she was sprawled upon the floor, facing the barrel of the German's rifle; the next, the door was rocking on its hinges and Dieter stood there, firing from the hip.

The three Germans on the stairs whipped around, staring at the scene below them with stunned incredulity: at the Wehrmacht major, his face bloody, his uniform ripped; at the officer he had killed, a German officer.

At the top of the stairs Luke hauled himself up against the banister and began to fire. Taken by surprise, dead and dying, the Germans reeled and slithered down the steps. Lisette heard Dieter call her name, saw him take a step toward her, and then, as she screamed at him not to shoot, Luke raised his pistol and fired. Dieter plummeted to the floor, blood spurting from his chest. She stumbled and fell across to him, still screaming. He moved his head, saw her. A smile tugged at the corners of his mouth.

"*Dieter! Don't die! Oh, please God, don't let him die!*" She was sobbing, kneeling beside him, cradling him in her arms.

"I'm sorry, *Liebling*," he whispered. "I didn't know you had another protector here."

Her eyes were wide with terror. Blood was pouring from his jacket, soaking her blouse, oozing onto the floor around them.

"Don't talk. Save your strength! I'll get bandages."

"It's too late, *Liebling*," he whispered weakly. "I just wanted to come . . . and say . . . good-bye." The breath was harsh in his throat. She held him tighter, her hands sticky with his blood.

"No, *chéri!*" she cried fiercely. "You're not going to die! I won't let you!" She turned to where Luke Brandon was swinging his injured body down the stairs with the aid of the banister. "Help me! For God's sake, help me!"

"I don't understand . . ." He looked down at the dying German in Lisette's arms, at the others he had taken from the top of the stairs, and at the German officer who had been facing Lisette with his rifle raised: a German officer who had been shot through the heart, shot by someone other than himself. "I don't understand . . . ," he repeated bewilderedly.

"Get bandages," she sobbed. "Please!"

"No," Dieter said gently, his fingers curling around hers, holding her fast. He sensed but could not see the Englishman standing above him. "Take care of her until it's over," he said raspily, the blood thick in his throat. "Take care of her . . . and the child." He could feel the breath leaving his body. Feel his lifeblood deserting him. He looked up at her for one last time. Her eyes were full of tears. Beautiful eyes. Eyes that a man could drown in. Die in. "I love you, *Liebling*," he said. His head fell against the soft swell of her breast, and his fingers opened, losing their grip, sliding away from her.

She had lost him. She had known all along that she would lose him. She felt her heart break and her courage fail. She had loved him with all of her heart, with all of her might, mind, body, and strength. And now he was gone and she was alone. She sobbed his name, holding him close, tears raining down her face. There would be no more dreams, no more visions of a future together.

Luke Brandon swung himself down the last step and said awkwardly, "Who was he?"

"Dieter Meyer," she said, raising her grief-ravaged face to his. "My lover."

"A *German?*" His straight black brows rose incredulously.

She looked down at the still figure in her arms. "Yes," she said, and there was no trace of shame or apology in her voice. "A German."

Even ravaged by grief, she was beautiful. There was a vibrancy about her, an honesty that he could not associate with a collaborator.

"Are you a Nazi sympathizer?" he asked, struggling for understanding.

"No," she said, rising to her feet, her slender body heavy with the weight of her loss. "And neither was he."

Luke Brandon stared at her. "I don't understand. He was a German, wasn't he? A major?"

"Yes." She had to get something to cover him with. She couldn't move his body from the hall by herself. She would have to wait until help came. She walked into the salon, stepping over the dead Germans that Luke had shot down, and returned with a vast, hand-embroidered tablecloth that

147

had been specially made for the grand dining room. Gently, she spread it over him, then said quietly, "He was one of a group of German officers and high-ranking civilians intent on removing Hitler from power."

Luke sucked in his breath, "My God," he said. "And just how were they going to achieve that?"

Her voice was oddly flat. It didn't seem to matter any more. Nothing mattered. "A bomb was to be placed in Hitler's headquarters. Afterward, Rommel was to assume power and seek a peace treaty with the Allies. They wanted to do it before the invasion was launched, but the opportunity did not come." There were blue shadows beneath her eyes. "Time ran out," she said, turning her head away from him, her voice laced with pain.

Luke's mind was racing. British Intelligence might or might not know about such a plot. Either way, he had to pass on Lisette's information at the first opportunity. He looked at her. Her face was pale, like carved ivory. She was near to collapse, and he cursed his bullet-ridden leg, wishing he could help her move Dieter Meyer's body from the bloodstained flagstones.

"The child he spoke of," he said tentatively. "Is it your brother? Your sister?"

She shook her head and her hair spilled forward, full of soft light. "No," she said with devastating dignity. "He meant our child. The child that I'm carrying."

Luke felt as if he'd been punched hard in the chest. A year ago she would have been little more than a child herself. "Won't that be hard for you?" he asked, disconcerted. "An illegitimate baby fathered by a German?"

Something flashed in the amethyst eyes, and he recognized it as courage that had prompted her to run out of the château under shell fire and bring him to safety. "It will be hard for my parents. I'll go away, far away. If Dieter had lived, we would have gone to Switzerland. Perhaps I will still go there. When the war is over."

The pain in her voice seared him. She had risked her life to save his, and he had killed the man she loved, the father of her child. He was seized by the fierce desire to make amends, to take care of her.

"Even after the war is over, life is going to be very

difficult, Lisette. Let me help you. Don't go to Switzerland. Come to England."

He didn't know who was the most stunned by what he had said, Lisette or himself. She stared at him as if he had taken leave of his senses.

"What do you mean?"

He caught hold of her hands. It was crazy. Insane. But he was filled with the dizzying certainty that what he was doing was right. He wanted to make reparation to her, and he wanted something more. He wanted her for himself.

"Marry me," he said urgently. "The baby can be born in England. Dieter Meyer asked me to take care of you, and this is how I can best do it."

She drew her hands away from his and rose unsteadily, her eyes wide with disbelief. "No . . . It isn't possible. You don't know what you are saying . . ."

With every passing moment he was more and more sure. "I do. I want to marry you. I want to do what Dieter Meyer asked of me. I want to take care of you."

Her beautiful face was pale, her eyes bruised with grief. "No," she repeated, backing away from him. "I know why you are asking me and I'm grateful, but it isn't possible."

"You will be branded as a collaborator," he said brutally. "Reprisals against all those who consorted with the Germans will be fierce. You owe it to the child to make a new life for yourself. I'm offering you the opportunity, Lisette. Don't turn it down!"

Dieter's body lay only yards away from them. She looked at it, the tears coursing down her face. "No," she said. "It isn't possible, Luke. I'm sorry."

He accepted defeat only temporarily. He would ask her again, when Dieter Meyer's body had been decently buried, when she was able to think more clearly.

Once again he became aware of the noise around them, of the deafening staccato of machine-gun fire and the roar of exploding shells. A score of running feet charged toward them from the rear of the château.

"Clear all the rooms!" an American voice yelled, and Luke lowered his hastily raised rifle.

"Jesus Christ!" The young lieutenant colonel at the head of the running squad of men halted in his tracks as he burst out

149

of the passageway and into the hall. He stared from the dead Germans to the injured Luke.

"Looks like you've been busy," he said with a grin. "Don't move. Medics are on their way." Then his eyes widened as he looked beyond Luke and saw Lisette.

She stepped forward, dead Germans all around her, the floors and walls of her home spattered with blood. "Welcome to Valmy, Colonel," she said with exquisite politeness, holding out her hand to him. "Welcome to France."

Greg Dering wondered if he were asleep and dreaming. They'd been told there were no civilians so near to the coast. He'd certainly not expected to be greeted by a dark-haired, dark-eyed French girl who looked as if she had stepped from a painting by Raphael.

"Pleased to be here, Ma'am," he said, his grin widening, and as he was on French soil, he raised her hand to his mouth with a flourish.

With his steel helmet crammed on curly brown hair and knives hanging from his hips and tucked into his jump boots, he reminded her of a medieval pikeman. She felt a rush of warmth toward him. "Do you want to use my home as a medical station, Colonel?"

"We certainly do. A truck is on its way right now with equipment and medics."

He had a friendly face, easygoing and uncomplicated. He turned to his men. "Get these bodies out of the way, boys."

The Americans, automatic rifles slung across their chests, Colt revolvers strapped to their hips, began unceremoniously to drag the dead Germans by their heels to the door.

"No!" She ran across to Dieter's body, standing in front of it, her face white. "Please, no!"

"What's the matter?" the young lieutenant colonel asked curiously.

Luke saw the anguish in her eyes. He knew that, in another few seconds, Dieter Meyer's body would be ignominiously thrown onto a pile in the courtyard outside. The heavy, hand-embroidered cloth covered him completely. "He isn't one of them," he said swiftly to the American. "A family friend, I think. She needs help to bury him."

Greg Dering nodded. He was commandeering her home. It was the least he could do. "Help the lady with her friend," he said tersely to two of his men, then, rewarded by a look of deep gratitude from Lisette, he ran up the stairs, two at a time, to check out the upper floors.

She buried him in the de Valmy family churchyard beneath the shade of a wild cherry tree. All around her was the noise and mayhem of battle, but by the time the cherry tree flowered again, she knew there would be peace. The clean sea winds would blow over his grave, and wild roses would cover it with blossoms. She knelt back on her heels, her hands caked with the soil she had dug.

"Good-bye, my love," she whispered, her face wet with tears. "*Auf Wiedersehen.*"

11

The bombing and shelling continued unabated. The two Americans who had helped dig Dieter's grave had long since sprinted back to the cover of the château. They were in France to kill Germans, not bury them.

Lisette rose from her knees, seared by a grief that could not be given vent to, not while thousands of injured men lay in helpless agony on the nearby beach. Wearily, she wiped away her tears and turned toward Valmy. There was work to do. The château had to be turned into a makeshift medical center. There would be time for grief later, all the time in the world. A pall of thick, acrid smoke swirled round her, and she began to run. There was water to draw and boil, linen to tear into bandages, wounds to clean—and until the American equipment arrived, only rock salt and chlorine bleach with which to clean them.

* * *

"What the hell happened on Omaha?" Luke yelled to Greg Dering as he dragged himself across the floor to a window, a rifle in his hand.

"The seas were too high," Greg yelled back grimly, watching from an adjoining window as a party of Germans, retreating from the beach, swarmed toward them. "We landed thousands of yards from where we should have, right below the German guns. A third of my men were killed before they even reached the beach."

Luke wiped his forehead with the back of his hand. The Americans designated to Omaha were battle-hardened troops, experienced men who had landed previously in North Africa and Sicily. If they had taken such a pounding, he dreaded to think what the situation was like on the British and Canadian invasion beaches farther east.

"Do you think we're going to make it?" he asked tersely.

"We'd better," Greg responded, steadying his rifle, preparing to fire. "If we lose this one, we lose the war." The first of the Germans came into range and simultaneously both men fired.

For over an hour it was impossible for Lisette to run out into the courtyard and draw the desperately needed water. The Germans were determined to take Valmy and use it as a defensive position, and the fighting was hard and bloody.

"*Keep down!*" the young lieutenant colonel had yelled at her, and she had done as she was told.

Bullets rained through the shattered windows, beating on the inner walls of the château like hail. Mortar shells exploded, sending flying metal through the air. She could hardly see or breathe, or hear. Cordite stung the back of her throat, smoke and dust burned her eyes, erupting hand grenades deafened her. A soldier at the far window was hit in the stomach, and as he screamed, she ran to him. She tore off her petticoat and used it to staunch the thickly spurting blood.

"*Get down!*" the lieutenant colonel yelled at her frenziedly, but she had ignored him, dragging the soldier away from the window as rifle fire whistled past her.

It lasted for seventy-five minutes and seemed to last for an eternity.

"Got the last of the bastards!" Greg Dering said triumphantly as the final German gun was silenced. He spun away from the window and sprinted across the room to Lisette.

"Is he dead?" she asked fearfully as he dropped down on one knee by her side.

"Not yet." He reached savagely for his sulfa pack. Christ Almighty, where were the medics? They'd wanted him to secure the château for them and he'd done so. Now he needed equipment.

"Trucks and tanks are making it off the beach, Sir!" one of his men yelled. "They're heading this way!"

Greg breathed a sigh of relief. Once the tanks made it from the beach, there would be no pushing them back. The battle would be half won. He emptied his sulfa pack into the gaping wound, knowing that unless experienced medics reached the château fast, the young private was doomed. He turned his attention to the slender young girl at his side.

"Are you all right, Mademoiselle?" he asked urgently, his eyes filled with concern.

She nodded. Her hands and petticoat were saturated with the blood of the injured American. "Yes," she said tightly. "But this man will die unless he gets help soon!"

"The medics are on their way," he said, wondering how many thousands had died already. Christ, what a shambles it was. Nearly half the amphibious force scheduled to support the assault troops had foundered. Under the pounding of the heavy sea, one after another of the landing craft had flooded and been sucked down beneath the waves, taking hundreds of men with them. It had been a debacle, the water thick with dead and dying. He had torn himself free of the surging surf and hurled himself and his men onto the bloodied beach and up the cliffs beyond. Now, thank the Lord, others were following. He could hear the roar of approaching trucks and tanks. The noise of jeeps almost drowned the incessant whine of German 88s. And in the midst of all this carnage, there was the girl at his side.

Her eyes were haunted, her face ashen, and he remembered the dead Germans he had found on entering the château. His stomach muscles tightened. Her country had been occupied for three years. There was no telling what she had endured in that time. War for the French had been much more intimate than war for the British and Americans. The

French had had to live with the Germans. Jackboots had marched their streets, invaded their homes.

A truck screeched to a halt outside. "Medics, Sir!" someone shouted.

"Tell them there's a severely injured man in here," he yelled back, then touched her shoulder gently. "It's nearly over," he said, wondering if she realized it yet. "You're free now. You've been liberated."

She looked up at him, at the uniform that was American and not German, at the strong, kind, uncomplicated face. He meant well. He was trying to comfort her in the only way he knew how.

"Thank you," she said, but her eyes remained bruised with grief. Free. It was a relative term. She had lost her freedom when she had given her heart to Dieter, and she knew she would never again be truly free.

The medics rushed into the room, and she rose to her feet as they gave the unconscious American immediate aid. Within minutes other trucks were following the first—trucks full of appallingly wounded men, trucks full of medical equipment. Swiftly, Valmy was turned into a field hospital.

She showed the medical orderlies where fresh water could be drawn. She helped them set up their crude operating theater in the grand dining room. She bound up Luke Brandon's leg after the bullets had been removed and had the relief of knowing that his life was no longer in danger. For hour after hour, through the long day and even longer night, she toiled with the medics, cutting away mud-stained battledresses and bloody boots, swabbing wounds, even giving injections. There were wounds caused by gunshot, by mortar blast, by mines, and by incendiaries—wounds so horrifying that she never knew from where she drew the strength not to flinch and turn away.

"That's a good girl," the doctor said as she held a drain steady while he stitched up the stump of a leg he had amputated. "You make a fine nurse, Mademoiselle."

When Greg Dering returned from a bloody sortie inland, she had been on her feet for over twenty hours. "That's enough," he said firmly, taking her arm. "You must have some rest. When did you last eat? . . . last have a cup of coffee?"

A flicker of amusement touched the dark depths of her

eyes. "My last cup of coffee was three years ago, Colonel," she said wryly, pushing a damp tendril of hair away from her face.

He stared down at her, his sun-bronzed face grim. She looked like a ghost, her eyes darkly ringed, her face deathly pale. "Well, you're going to have one now," he said firmly, and led her out of the fetid, makeshift operating theater and into the small cubbyhole of a room that was serving as his temporary headquarters. There were incendiary burns on the backs of his hands and arms, but they could be treated later. They were fleabites compared to the injuries of the men massing the château's rooms and corridors. Entire platoons had been wiped out on the beach, and the day's fighting to establish a bridgehead had been fierce and bloody and, so far, unsuccessful.

He pushed her gently down onto the only chair in the room and lit a primus stove. His task was to link up with the troops who had stormed ashore on the beach code-named Utah, some fifteen miles to the west. The town designated for the merging of forces was Carentan. It was small but of vital strategic importance. Not only was it a rail center, but Route Nationale 13, the major highway between the port of Cherbourg and Paris, ran straight through it.

He spooned coffee from his ration pack into an incongruously delicate coffee cup bearing the de Valmy coat of arms. It was now invasion day plus one, and Carentan should have been taken. Without it, the push to Cherbourg was impossible. He wiped a trickle of sweat and grime from his forehead. The Germans had flooded vast areas of marshland leading to the town, and the only access was by a narrow causeway. Their casualties, when they renewed their attack, would be high.

"Here, take this," he said, turning to Lisette, the cup of hot coffee in his hand.

She was asleep, her legs curled childlike beneath her in the deep armchair. There were smudges of smoke on her cheeks and forehead, and her sweater and crumpled skirt were coated with dust and flecks of dried blood. She looked very young and very defenseless and, even in sleep, exquisitely graceful. Quietly, he picked up his army greatcoat and lowered it gently around her shoulders.

There was something about her that was totally European. He loved the slight tilt of her head when she spoke, the

155

husky quality of her voice, the long, shining fall of her hair. She was as different from the girls back home as chalk was from cheese. Luke Brandon had told him she had saved his life, dragging him from the woods to the château under heavy fire from strafing planes. He couldn't imagine how she had done it. She looked too delicate and slender to lift any weight heavier than herself. For a long moment he looked down at her, then he tenderly tucked his coat in around her knees and left the room, his expression thoughtful.

When she awoke, Lisette stared in puzzlement at the army coat covering her. Then she remembered that the lieutenant colonel had brought her into this room to make her a cup of coffee. It stood, cold, by the primus stove. There was still gunfire, but now it was more subdued and not aimed directly at the château. Instead it was reverberating over the fields and woods that separated Valmy from Sainte-Marie-des-Ponts. She threw the coat to one side, appalled at her weakness at falling asleep, and ran back to the operating theater.

"Is there fighting in the village?" she asked as she helped strip off an infantryman's blood-soaked uniform.

The medic nodded grimly, his face gaunt and gray with fatigue. "There's no more resistance on the beach; troops and equipment are coming ashore freely, but we've not pushed the Germans back far. It's still touch and go."

As many of the wounded as possible were ferried out to the destroyers standing offshore, and winched aboard. Many more died before they could make such a journey. Thirty men died in her presence that morning. She was numbed by the horror. Field hospitals had been set up behind the beaches. Medics tended the wounded wherever they fell, but there were not enough of them. Mines exploded underfoot. Sniper and machine-gun fire came from every hedge and ditch. For every yard they pressed inland, an American soldier died.

She cleaned wounds, staunched blood, held the hands of the dying, and sometimes, when she thought she could bear no more, she thought of the kindness of the toughly built American with the friendly eyes.

Luke Brandon fumed impotently. He wanted to join up with the British forces in the east, but his smashed leg made the task a near impossibility. If only there was some transport.

A truck, a car—*anything*. But all American transport was intent on forging a way through to the west and Cherbourg. He could only remain at the château and pray to God that they succeeded.

Route Nationale 13 ran arrow straight over the swamps and flooded fields, its crown some six feet above the murky, swirling water. Greg knew that he and his men were cruelly exposed, but there was no alternative approach to Carentan. The causeway, as they called the narrow ribbon of asphalt, had to be crossed. It offered them nowhere to dig in, nowhere for them to take cover or to pause to regroup. German paratroopers raked them with withering fire. A Luftwaffe dive-bomber zoomed down on them. Mortar shells decimated their long strung-out column. Inch by bloody inch they crawled forward, and as they did so, Greg Dering clung fast to the image of a slender figure curled up in a chair—a slender figure he was determined to know better before he shook the bloodied soil of Normandy from his heels.

At Valmy, day and night merged into one. When it was physically impossible to stand on her feet any longer, Lisette snatched a few precious hours of sleep curled up in the armchair in Greg Dering's cubbyhole of a room, wondering where he was and if he was still alive.

Water from Valmy's well was brought up ceaselessly, but there was never enough. As soon as the nearest inland town was safely in Allied hands and the medics were told there was water there, they transferred equipment and wounded in a fleet of trucks.

She watched them go with a mixture of elation and panic: elation that the Germans were receding so rapidly from Normandy, and panic at the prospect of no longer being able to submerge her grief in backbreaking physical work.

She hugged her arms around herself as she stood in the damp chill of early morning, and the last of the trucks rumbled away down the graveled drive. Dieter was dead. She would never see him again. It was a reality that she had to face and come to terms with. Behind her Valmy waited, thick with memories—memories of their confrontation in the grand dining room; of their heady, magical lovemaking in the turret room; of his body in her arms, his lifeblood staining the ancient flagstones a ghastly crimson. She could not step back in there. Not yet. Luke Brandon had remained behind, still determined to join up with the British forces at the first opportunity, but his presence would not be enough to provide the solace she craved. The Red Cross truck disappeared at the end of Valmy's drive in a cloud of dust, and she turned decisively, taking the small path that led away from the château and out over the headland to the beach and to the sea.

The giant rolls of barbed wire that had prohibited it for so long were ripped and flattened by the weight of Allied tanks. The dead had still not been buried. They lay, German and American, beside the charred and twisted remains of knocked-out vehicles.

She raised her face away from the carnage and toward the vast, clean sweep of the sky. It was going to be a hot day. Already the early morning chill was melting away, and the sun, striking through the thin cotton of her blouse, was warm. Ships still darkened the sea, bringing more men ashore, taking aboard the injured, unloading more tanks and trucks, more equipment. It was seven days since they had come ashore. The British were in Bayeux and pushing on to Caen. The Americans held all the coastal towns from Colleville to Ste. Mère Eglise and, according to Luke, were now pushing on to the important port of Cherbourg. They had come ashore and they were staying ashore. She remembered Dieter saying that the only way they could be repulsed was if they were repulsed on the beaches. He had fumed at Hitler's reluctance to allow Rommel control of more panzer divisions. If those divisions had been available, she knew that the devastation around her would have been the devastation of an American defeat, not that left in the wake of their victory.

If she closed her eyes, she could almost hear his voice. His face burned in her memory, strong and abrasive, the black-lashed gray eyes ablaze with love for her. The sobs she had suppressed for so long rose in her throat and could be contained no longer. She threw herself down on the grass and sobbed and sobbed, her heart breaking, her clenched hands beating the earth in a paroxysm of grief.

She knew now that there had never been a future for them. They had been living in a make-believe world that time and circumstance would have brought to an end, even if he had not died. Fate had not meant them to be together, to be happy. Her breath came in harsh, shuddering gasps. She raised her head from her arms, knuckling away her tears, staring sightlessly out over the heaving gray waves. For a little time at least, they had cheated fate. They had loved each other fiercely and passionately, compressing a lifetime's loving into a few, precious months. And now it was over.

Wearily, she rose to her feet. Above her, wisps of cirrus clouds flecked the sky. From the direction of Vierville came the faint sound of a church bell ringing. Her hands closed across her stomach. There had been an end and now there was a beginning. She was luckier than most. She had her child to look forward to, Dieter's child: a child with corn-gold hair and warm gray eyes, a child he would have been proud of.

When she returned to Valmy, the lines of strain and grief that had etched her mouth and shadowed her eyes were smoothed away. Luke opened the door for her, leaning heavily on his crutches.

"I was worried. I didn't know where you were," he said as she walked with swift and easy grace toward him.

"I went for a walk. Not far. There are church bells ringing in Vierville."

"It isn't safe," he said tersely. "When the Americans moved out, they warned us to be careful. They think there are still pockets of Germans hiding in Sainte-Marie-des-Ponts."

"I didn't go into the village. I walked up onto the headland," she said, a small, reassuring smile touching her mouth.

He caught his breath. It was the first time he had seen her smile. The glow that it gave to her dark beauty devastated him. He had made his impulsive offer to marry her out of guilt and the desire to protect her, but he knew now that it was an offer he would have made, even if he hadn't been responsible for the death of Dieter Meyer.

"We need to talk, Lisette," he said, following her into the château's large kitchen. He watched her as she began to make two cups of coffee from the rations the Americans had left behind.

She nodded, thinking he wanted to talk to her about the progress of the invasion. "Have the British taken Caen?" she asked curiously.

He shook his head, his expression grave. "There's been no further news. It won't be an easy city to take. The Germans will hang on to it to the last bullet. It isn't Caen I want to talk about. It's us."

Her eyes clouded. "It's no use, Luke," she said gently, knowing very well to what he was referring. "I'm grateful for your suggestion, but . . ."

"Damn being grateful," he said, his straight, black brows flying together. "It isn't gratitude I'm after!"

A tide of color stung her cheeks, and he leaned his weight on his crutches, running his fingers through his hair, saying apologetically, "And it isn't just sex I'm after, either, Lisette. I can't stay here much longer. I have to join up with my own forces, even if it means crawling to them on my hands and knees. Once I'm back with them, it could be months before I can come back to you. I want to know that you will be here, waiting for me, when I return."

"You know I will," she said, and he felt his throat tighten.

"As my lover?" he asked, his blue eyes hot, his voice tense.

She shook her head and her hair shimmered like black silk. "No," she said, and his knuckles whitened on the struts of his crutches. "As your friend."

Frustration knifed through him. "That's not what I want," he said fiercely. "I want the kind of love that you gave to Dieter Meyer!"

Pain flared across her face, and he cursed himself for a fool, knowing that he had put their fragile, burgeoning relationship into jeopardy.

"I shall never give that kind of love again," she said, turning away from him, her eyes bright with anguish. "Not to you or anyone."

She picked up the pail used for carrying water from the courtyard and walked quickly toward the door, not wanting him to see her pain.

Impotently he watched her go, wishing to God he could throw his crutches to one side and run after her and seize hold of her. They had been together for seven days and seven nights. He had seen her under the most appalling stress. He had watched her as she returned from burying Dieter Meyer, her lover's blood staining her skirt. He had watched her as she had braved enemy fire, her courage never failing. And he had watched her as tirelessly and with exquisite tenderness she had nursed the wounded and comforted the dying.

Her dark beauty had a fragility that rendered him breathless, but he knew now that she herself was not fragile. She was made of fire and steel and heart and guts, and he wanted to marry her. His initial proposal had been prompted by guilt. He had shot and killed the father of her unborn child, only hours after she had fearlessly saved his own life. The dying Meyer had asked him to take care of her. It had seemed the least he could do, and marriage had seemed the most obvious way of doing it.

But now he wanted to marry her because he had fallen in love with her, because her grace and beauty and courage were almost more than he could bear. Once he joined up with the British forces to the east, there was no telling how long it would be before he could return to Valmy. He had to know that she would be here when he did so, that when retribution began against those who had consorted with the Germans, she wouldn't leave Valmy and be swallowed up with the hundreds of thousands of homeless wandering a war-ravaged Europe.

He had never thought of himself as a romantic, but the way they had met had surely been fate. He couldn't lose her now. It would be beyond bearing.

Lisette walked quickly across the cobblestones to the water pump and began pumping water fiercely. Luke's words had shattered all her hard won composure, and her grief was once again raw and terrible.

A truck began to rattle down Valmy's long, tree-lined drive, and she dropped the bucket, running apprehensively out of the courtyard and around to the front of the house. It was an American army truck, caked with grime, packed with remarkably jaunty looking soldiers. She raised her hand to her eyes, squinting against the glare of the sun as it swerved to a halt only yards away from her.

"The field hospital has been moved . . . ," she began. Then a husky figure jumped down from the tailboard and began to run toward her, and her eyes lit up with recognition and welcome.

It was Greg Dering, his olive-drab battledress thick with

161

dried mud and dirt, a helmet crammed on his head, a Colt .45 strapped to his hip.

"It doesn't matter," he said with a wide grin, his hands going around her waist. He lifted her from her feet and swung her around. "We're not in need of it!"

She laughed, infected by his high spirits, so much at ease with him that his familiarity seemed only natural.

"I'm glad," she said as he set her down on her feet again. "Luke will be so pleased to see you again. Has Carentan been taken? We've heard no news. Nothing."

He grinned down at her. There had been times over the bullet-ridden journey from Carentan to Valmy when he had wondered if he were in his right mind. He could easily have seen to it that someone else was detailed to mop up the lingering panzers in Sainte-Marie and the neighboring coastal villages. Instead, he was doing it himself because it would give him an excuse to see her again. And now that he was here and she was smiling up at him, he was fervently glad that he had done so.

"Is Brandon still here?" he asked as he began to walk with her toward the château.

"Yes. He's determined not to be shipped home as medically unfit. As soon as his leg begins to heal, he's going to join up with the British forces around Caen." She looked back over her shoulder to the men still in the rear of the truck. "Are they coming in? The medics left coffee behind. . . ."

He shook his head, his grin fading. "No. We're on our way to reconnoiter Sainte-Marie and the other coastal villages, to make sure there are no Germans hiding out behind us."

The light in her eyes died. "I hope there aren't," she said anxiously. "The villagers are beginning to move back into their homes. If there are still Germans about, they should be warned." She thought of old Madame Bridet and Madame Chamot and Madame Tellier, who had so recently given birth to her latest child. She had seen none of them since the fighting began. "Can I go with you?" she asked. "Some of the elderly villagers may need taking care of. They may be more comfortable at Valmy for the next few weeks than in their own homes."

"No," he said gently. "It's too dangerous."

Her eyes flashed stubbornly. "If I don't go with you, I shall have to bicycle down there alone and that will be far more dangerous!"

"All right," he said reluctantly, certain that in Sainte-Marie at least they would find nothing. "But only Sainte-Marie. Then I'm bringing you straight back. Is that understood?"

She nodded, smiling up at him as Luke opened Valmy's great oak door. A spasm of emotion crossed Luke Brandon's face. When she had left the kitchen, she had looked almost ill with the weight of her grief. Now, in Dering's company, a transformation had taken place, and she looked almost light-hearted. He suppressed the sudden flare of jealousy he felt. If Dering's arrival had cheered her, he was grateful. The huskily built American with his sun-bronzed face and easy grin was immensely likable. His own reaction had been one of immediate relief that Dering hadn't been killed in what must have been a bloody assault on Carentan.

"Colonel Dering is taking me into Sainte-Marie," Lisette said, picking up her cardigan and slipping it around her shoulders. "Some of the more elderly villagers may want to come to Valmy for a while, and there is room for them now."

Luke's eyes flashed across to Greg's. "Is it safe?"

"Safer than having her pedal down there on her bicycle," Greg said dryly. "We're conducting a mop-up operation on all the coastal villages. We don't want to leave pockets of Germans behind us."

"And Carentan?"

Greg Dering's square-jawed face hardened. "We took it yesterday," he said briefly. "At a high price."

Luke, aware of Lisette's continuing presence, did not ask him for details. The German 6th Parachute Regiment, one of the Reich's best, was based in Carentan. He could well imagine the loss of life that had ensued when they had confronted the U. S. 101st Airborne Division.

"If you see a spare jeep in Sainte-Marie, bring it back for me," he said as they prepared to leave.

"Will do," Greg said with a quick grin.

"And take care of Lisette," Luke added as she walked toward the waiting truck. "I intend to marry her as soon as this party's over."

"I'll take care of her," Greg said, his gaze holding Luke's

steadily, "but I have to tell you that I'm going to do my best to ruin your plans."

Luke's mouth tightened. He had guessed as much. There'd been no other reason for Dering to return to Valmy on so fleeting a visit.

Lisette sat in the front of the truck, wedged between the colonel and his smoke-begrimed driver, a helmet strapped uncomfortably to her head. Greg had insisted she wear it. They had encountered no sniper fire on the approach to Valmy, but it could come at any time and from any direction.

At the end of the drive they turned left, trundling down through the beech woods to the village. Scattered German and American bodies lay at the roadside, gaunt in death.

"Why haven't they been buried?" she asked unsteadily.

Greg's voice was tight. "Not enough time, not enough men, and many of the German bodies have been booby-trapped by their comrades."

Through the trees she glimpsed the Keiffer farm and the Bleriot farm, both smoke blackened. Her stomach muscles tightened. She knew that Jean Keiffer had not left the village. He had been one of the few people allowed to remain because of the milk and eggs from his farm, collected daily by the Germans. They bucketed down to the bridge, narrowly avoiding another army truck approaching fast from the opposite direction.

Greg waved it down. "Where are you going?" he yelled to the driver.

"Toward Vierville. There are reports of a squad of Germans lying low in the area."

Greg nodded. "We'll catch up with you later. Good luck."

The truck crashed into first gear and then through to second and third, speeding away in a cloud of dust and exhaust fumes.

"If they have just come through Sainte-Marie, it means the village must be clear," Greg said to Lisette, knowing how tense she was beneath her veneer of calm.

"I hope so," she replied fervently. "The two farms we passed had both been shelled."

"*Everywhere's* been shelled," the driver at her side said grimly, and then they were speeding over the bridge, and Lisette could see Jean Keiffer running toward them, a broad beam on his ruddy face.

"Welcome! Welcome!" he called out to them. "Long live the English. Long live the Americans! Long live France!"

She leaned across Colonel Dering to the window, calling down to him, "Have people started to come back into the village, Jean? Is there anyone who needs help?"

Jean flashed her a toothless grin. "Nearly everyone is back. The Laffonts never left. They spent two days locked in the cellar with their five children and their goats and hens! Old Madame Chamot has kissed so many American soldiers that she's lost count! It's marvelous! Magnificent!"

The truck lurched to a halt, and the soldiers jumped down from the tailboard, running quickly through the streets, checking that Sainte-Marie was as free of Germans as Jean believed.

"You are safe, Mademoiselle de Valmy?" Madame Bridet and her children came running toward her, throwing her arms around her, hugging her tight. "Thank the good God! And your mother and father? They are in Balleroy? Good, good, but I would not wish to be anywhere else but Sainte-Marie today! We are liberated at last! I can hardly believe it. I have hung the French flag from my topmost window. It is wonderful, is it not? No more Germans, damn and spit on them!"

Madame Bridet's hen coop had been blasted into extinction, and Lisette promised she would search out a replacement for her. Madame Lechevalier had broken her arm when half her kitchen had fallen in on her. Old Bleriot had been found drunk at the bottom of the garden, and it was widely believed that he had been there, in that condition, throughout the invasion.

"Feeling happier?" Greg asked her as she came out of Madame Chamot's gutted house, promising to return with linen and saucepans.

"Yes, everyone was safely inland when the village was being bombed and strafed. No one is seriously hurt, though they do say there was gunfire to the south of the village this morning."

Greg nodded. "Our errant handful of Germans, no doubt. It's time we hunted them down. I'll take you back to Valmy now. Are there any passengers wanting to come with us?"

"No. They're too grateful to be back in their own homes, even if they are falling down around them."

"Come on then, let's go." He took hold of her hand to help her once more into the truck and then paused. The rattle of machine-gun fire could be heard quite distinctly, coming from the direction of Valmy.

His mouth tightened. "What the devil . . . ?" He slammed the passenger door, ran around to the other side of the truck, and jumped into the driver's seat.

"What is it?" she asked fearfully, her hearing not as acute as his.

"I'm not sure," he said grimly. "But I'm going to find out."

As he revved the engine, his men scrambled into the truck's rear and then, not relinquishing the steering wheel to his driver, he pressed his foot down hard, careening out of the village, villagers and hens scattering before him.

As they took the bridge at the foot of the hill she heard it: a rattle of machine-gun fire, suddenly stilled. The sound had become so commonplace, she would hardly have given it attention if it had not been for the expression on Greg Dering's tight-lipped face. They took the hill at a rush, and she suddenly understood. It had come from Valmy.

"Quickly," she whispered, her hands clenching on her lap. "Oh, please, *quickly!*"

Even before they left the woods, they saw the smoke. It rose and curled in great black plumes, then the woods thinned out, the headland stretched before them, and Valmy stood in all its ancient splendor, burning furiously.

12

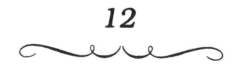

Sparks and ash floated toward them on the sea breeze. From the shattered windows, tongues of flames leaped skyward as the ancient hammer-beamed ceiling burned furiously.

They hurtled out of the last of the woods and toward the

entrance of the drive, the smoke catching the backs of their throats, stinging their eyes.

"*Hurry! Hurry!*" Lisette sobbed. They saw the U. S. army truck and the soldiers they had passed on the outskirts of the village, and Greg swerved to a halt. He threw open his door and ran to them. "What the hell happened?" he yelled as Lisette struggled in his wake, shielding her face with her arms as the heat surged toward them.

"Reckon the Germans moved in when you moved out, Colonel," a weary-faced captain said, his rifle still in his hand, "We met with heavy gunfire when we arrived. Two of our men are injured, one severely."

"Luke?" Lisette gasped. "*Where is Luke?*"

The Captain looked blank.

"There was an Allied airman in the château," Greg said to him tersely. "Have you seen him?"

The captain shook his head. "The Germans were in charge when we arrived, Colonel. Not many, about six, but they put up a fierce fight. Two of them were still alive when the grenades went in. Since then there's been no firing. Guess there won't be now."

Lisette spun away from him toward the holocaust that was Valmy, and Greg caught hold of her arm. "There's nothing you can do!" he yelled, holding her fast. "No one could possibly be alive in there!"

"But I have to see! I have to make sure!"

A stream of sparks rained down on them, and his fingers dug deep into her flesh. "It's no use! He's dead! The Germans would have killed him long before the grenades went in!"

There was a rumbling sound, as if Valmy's very heart was being devoured, then a great crash as the blazing beams toppled down into the red-hot furnace that had been the grand dining room. She stood, white-faced with rage and grief. She had saved his life, and now he was dead—as Dieter was dead, and hundreds and thousands of others were dead.

"What now, Colonel?" the captain was asking.

"Reconnoiter the surrounding villages," Greg said tersely. "I'll meet up with you at Isigny in an hour's time."

They were going, but she didn't turn around. Even the garden was burning. Rose petals shriveled and fell. Honeysuckle smoldered. Greg's hand tightened on her shoulder.

167

"Come along, Lisette. Nothing can be saved. It will burn itself out, given time."

Time. Seven hundred years of standing high above the beech woods and the sea. Seven hundred years of being proud and magnificent and inviolate. The hungry flames were shot through with blue and purple and green. She watched as they licked up to the tower room, as the heavy silk curtains caught and flared.

He pulled her gently away, and this time she did not resist him. "I'm taking you to Sainte-Marie-des-Ponts," he said firmly.

She nodded. She would stay with Madame Chamot. Later, when the roads were safer, she would join her parents in Balleroy. Beyond that, she could not even begin to think.

"I'm sorry about Luke Brandon," he said awkwardly as he held the door of the truck open for her.

"Thank you." Her voice was barely audible, her eyes anguished.

He wondered when they had first met, how long they had known each other. Downed Allied pilots were often obliged to live for months with the French families sheltering them.

They didn't speak again until they were nearing the bridge, and then she said, "Would you drop me off here, please? I'd like to have some time to myself before going on to Madame Chamot's."

He didn't want to drop her off anywhere. He wanted to keep her with him. He braked, and the truck rattled to a halt.

"Will you be okay?" he asked.

Her chin tilted upward fractionally, her dark hair swinging softly against her cheek. "Yes," she said, her voice filled with the determination not to be beaten. "Good-bye, Colonel Dering, and thank you. You've been very kind."

None of the things he wanted to say to her were even remotely appropriate. She had just buried some guy who was a family friend, perhaps even a relation. Brandon, who had wanted to marry her, was also dead. And even as he walked around and opened the door of the truck for her, her home was burning to ashes. His hands closed around her waist as he swung her to the ground. Letting go of her was one of the hardest things he had ever done.

* * *

"Are you sure there'll be no problems for you in Sainte-Marie?"

She looked up at him, touched by his concern for her. "I'm very sure," she said, the curve of her lips softening so that he could imagine very easily how she would look when she smiled. "Good-bye Colonel Dering."

He took hold of her hand and kissed it. "Good-bye," he said, and thought what a ridiculous word it was to be using when they were going to be together for the rest of their lives.

Madame Chamot was appalled by the destruction of Valmy and overcome by the pleasure of having Lisette as a temporary guest. Three days after the fire, the charred, burned-out shell of the château was cool enough to enable Lisette and old Bleriot to walk through the gutted rooms and for them to retrieve the odd and surprising objects that had escaped the flames: Marie's giant stone bread bin, a silver frame blackened by smoke that had once held a wedding photograph of her parents, a pewter vase.

There were no signs of the Germans who had perished in the blaze, and none of Luke, and there was no memento of Dieter in the bric-a-brac they collected. It was when she returned in the evening to Madame Chamot's that fate dealt her its last cruel blow. She was racked by weariness, exhausted both emotionally and physically, and at first she hardly noticed the dull ache low in her back. She understood only when she felt the warmth of blood between her legs.

She lay on the narrow bed beneath the eaves of Madame Chamot's small cottage and prayed for it to stop. It continued desultorily for three days, and when it ended she knew there could be no further hope of still carrying Dieter's child. It was the ultimate blow. She felt bereft and barren and raw with the hurt of all she had lost.

A week later, her father returned from Balleroy, and together they surveyed the ruins of their home.

"The outer shell is still intact," he said stoically. "The grand dining room can never be rebuilt, of course, but perhaps, in time, the other rooms can be made habitable once more."

"Where will you live until they are? Balleroy?"

169

"No," he said. "Here."

Her eyes shot open wide. "Here? But you can't! The roof has gone! The floors have gone!"

"The rooms above the stables are still intact. I shall live there. They are still Valmy."

His stubborn refusal to be defeated struck a chord deep within her. The rooms were smoke blackened, scarcely habitable. There was no electricity, no water save that from the pump in the courtyard. For the first time since she knew she was losing the baby, she felt a spark of purpose. "We'll *both* live here," she said fiercely. "We'll work on Valmy room by room, and we'll make it habitable again."

He patted her hand. "Your mother will not share our enthusiasm, but she is comfortable enough at the Duboscqs', and when the war is over it will be Paris she will want to return to, not Valmy."

Madame Chamot did everything she could to persuade Lisette to change her mind, but she was adamant. She was returning to Valmy. It was the only possible course open to her.

Old Bleriot visited them, bringing them the news he gleaned from soldiers still busy on the shoreline, ferrying fresh equipment and provisions ashore. At the end of June there were rumors that Cherbourg had been taken by the Americans. Lisette felt her stomach muscles tighten. The fighting had been savage. American casualties were reported to be high.

"I hope that he's safe, Papa," she said as they hauled charred floorboards from what had once been the small breakfast room.

"Who, *ma chère?*" her father asked, his back aching, his hands cut and scratched.

"Colonel Dering. The American who came to Valmy."

"So do I," her father said sincerely. Lisette had told him all about the American colonel who had been so kind to her; about Luke Brandon, the Allied pilot who had been shot down and who had died at the hands of the Germans. And she had told him, too, of the way Dieter Meyer had met his death.

For Lisette's sake, he felt regret at Meyer's death, but his regret was tinged with relief. There would be no difficult Franco-German marriage now, and, thank God, no need for one. His heart had gone out to her when she had told him that she had lost the baby, but only because he couldn't bear to see her so pale and wan. There would come a time when she would know that it was for the best. Meanwhile, all he could do was give her his love and his understanding and pray that, before very long, she would again know happiness—a happiness with no complications in its wake.

Misery stifled Lisette. There were days when she felt she could hardly breathe for it. There seemed to be no purpose in life, nothing to look forward to, nothing to hope or dream for. The handful of rooms above the stables were made habitable by diligent scouring and whitewashing, but it was obvious it would be many months, perhaps years, before they could move back into even a corner of the château. Her mother quietly announced she would not be returning at all. She understood and sympathized with her husband's reluctance to forsake Valmy, but she did not share it. When she left the Duboscqs', it would be to go to Paris. It was arranged that Henri would visit her there, perhaps even stay for months at a time, but never again would they live as a family at Valmy.

Her parents assumed Lisette, too, would leave Normandy for Paris when hostilities ended. She hauled another beam of charred timber from the ruins, dropping it on the cobblestones of the courtyard, trying to imagine a new life in Paris, and failing. It was as if misery had robbed her of imagination. She could not think ahead; she could only live each day as it came, finding pleasure in small things: the family of dormice that had made a home in the rubble, the wisteria that defiantly flowered against the smoke-blackened walls, the clean feel of the sea breeze against her face as she walked the headland.

There was no longer any fighting around Sainte-Marie-des-Ponts, but the battle for Normandy was far from over. In hedgerows and roadsides, crude wooden crosses marked the graves of the hastily buried dead. In the east, the British had still not taken Caen. In the west there were reports of fierce fighting as the Americans struggled to take St. Lô. It was still not beyond the realm of possibility that the Allies could be squeezed back into the sea, and she gathered every scrap of information she could about the invasion force's progress.

By the light of an oil lamp, she would sit at her father's side in the evening as he pored over a map of France, shading in the areas he believed to be in Allied hands.

"The Allies must break out of Normandy and take Paris by the end of the summer," he said worriedly, a deep frown furrowing his brow. "Once the winter weather sets in, high seas will make it difficult for them to continue ferrying in the provisions and equipment they need. And they can't break out of Normandy until Caen is taken."

Lisette hugged her knees, her thoughts not on Caen but on St. Lô. It was there that the Americans were fighting. There, in all probability, that Colonel Dering would be fighting. She hoped he was safe. If he wasn't, she would never know. There was no one who would write and tell her. She stared once more at the map, her eyes bleak. St. Lô was the headquarters of General Marcks, a German commander Dieter had admired unstintingly. The tough LXXXIV Infantry Corps was under his command. Though much smaller, it was possible that St. Lô would be as difficult to capture as Cherbourg had been.

She asked old Bleriot every day if he had gleaned any further news about troop movements inland, but he could tell her only that fresh troops were still arriving, St. Lô had not been taken, and his sciatica was so bad he needed to drink a jar of calvados a day in order to ease the pain.

Greg Dering had to admit that it was a hell of a time to have a woman on the brain. For three weeks he and his men had been continually under heavy fire. Exhausted, mud spattered, and unshaven, they had forded streams, crawled up wooded hillsides, and waded through marshy wasteland. They had been raked with machine-gun fire, lobbed with mortar shells, and confronted by tanks. They had endured the anguish of the screams of their wounded and had had to leave their dead behind them. The road to St. Lô was slippery with their blood. Greg knew when it was over, he wouldn't want to spend a day longer in France than was absolutely necessary, which meant he would have to marry Lisette now, as soon as there was a lull in the fighting—as soon as he could get a pass.

He wiped the sweat from his brow and continued to wriggle on his belly toward his objective, the farmhouse full of Germans. A French girl! His mother would love it. Daughter of an east coast millionaire, she thought the only culture in the world worth having was French.

Bullets whizzed past him. Heavy bursts of small arms fire continued to pin him and his men down. He had to make a crucial decision: either to order his men to start crawling toward the rear of the farm buildings and abandon much of the ground they had gained, or charge the farmhouse and risk getting the entire company wiped out in the process.

He shouted across to his second-in-command who was pinned down a short distance away from him, across a narrow dirt road. "We're going to get some artillery smoke on that goddamned farmhouse, Major! Then we're going to make a bayonet charge!"

It didn't occur to him that she might refuse him. Failure was a word that was not in his vocabulary. Beneath his easy-going manner was a confidence imbued by wealth and social prestige. His mother had been born into that world. His father had fought and clawed his way there. Greg had inherited characteristics from both of them: the recklessness and gut instinct that had prompted his mother to elope with a muscular lifeguard only days before her society wedding was to take place, and the fierce ambition and sheer tenaciousness that had lifted his father from the beaches of California to the presidency of one of its most powerful companies. He had learned early that instinct was a God-given gift to be followed. He was following it now. He was going to charge the farmhouse, and he was going to marry Lisette de Valmy.

As the hot, stifling days of July drew to a close, Lisette was overcome by an increasing restlessness. She tried to sublimate it in hard physical work, but it wouldn't be quenched. When it became unbearable, she would walk as near to the beach as troop activity permitted and stare out across the waves. The old Lisette, the pretty teenager in red beret and shabby coat, cycling the Normandy lanes on errands for Paul, had gone for good. There had been an innocence about her then that she knew she would never recapture. And there seemed no place in the life she was now living for the new Lisette—the Lisette who had loved so fiercely and passionately, the Lisette who had grown from childhood to womanhood in the lamplit glow of the small turret room.

She dug her hands deeper into the pockets of her skirt and turned away from the surging gray waves. For the first time in her life, they had failed her. They had not soothed and calmed her; they had merely intensified her feelings of frustration.

He was waiting for her when she returned, leaning with casual ease against the gateway that led from the drive to the courtyard, his curly brown hair thick and springy as heather, his smile vivid in his sun-bronzed face.

She stopped short, disbelieving her eyes, and then she began to run toward him, relief at his safety bubbling up inside her.

His heart began to bang against his ribs. She had drawn her hair away from her face, securing it at the nape of her neck with a ribbon. Beneath the dark sweep of her brows, her eyes looked even more startlingly violet than ever.

"Colonel Dering! What a lovely surprise," she exclaimed, running up to him, her face radiant.

His grin widened, his arms opened, and to her astonishment and his delight, she entered them unhesitatingly.

Shock reverberated through her. She had meant nothing sexual by her action. She had simply been pleased to see him, and it had seemed quite natural, when he had opened his arms to her, to enter them and hug him in welcome as she would have done her father. The instant she had done so, she knew there was a vast difference between her father and Colonel Dering. She put her hands against his chest, flushed and disconcerted, trying to distance herself from his hard, disturbing body.

He looked down at her, not smiling any more. His eyes were brown, dark and warm, with tiny flecks of gold near the pupils, and an expression that had nothing to do with mere friendship.

"I missed you," he said with stark simplicity. "I want to marry you."

She stood in the circle of his arms, and she didn't tell him he was crazy. Nothing seemed crazy any more. Life had ceased to exist by the old rules. War had stripped away conventional behavior, and primitive, urgent responses had become normal.

"I know nothing about you," she said, and even as she said it, she knew it wasn't true. She knew a lot about him. She knew that he was a man who commanded respect from other men. She knew that he was kind. She knew that she was physically drawn to him, that she liked him and felt safe with him.

He flashed her a dazzling, down-slanting smile. "That's easily altered," he said, not releasing his hold of her. "I'm a Californian. I'm twenty-seven. Financially sound. Mentally stable. And I've never been married. Will that do for starters?"

A gurgle of laughter welled up deep inside her. For the first time since Dieter's death, she felt warm and loving and alive, then her laughter faded. She turned away, breaking free of him, her eyes shadowed and full of pain.

"You don't know anything about me."

At the tone of her voice, a slight frown creased his brow. She had begun to walk toward the ravaged rose gardens, and he walked at her side, not touching her. "I know I'd have been a fool not to have come back for you," he said. "I know everything I need to know. I know that I don't make mistakes, that this isn't a decision I'm going to regret."

She stood still, looking up at him. The scent of the roses that had survived the fire was as thick as smoke in the July sunlight. With passionate fierceness, she wanted to touch him again, to purge her restlessness in the comfort of his arms, to feel alive again. She said quietly, "The man I loved and was going to marry died only a few weeks ago."

"I know," he said, reaching out for her hands and holding them fast. "Luke told me."

Her eyes widened with shock. It had not occurred to her that Luke Brandon had spoken to him about Dieter.

"I don't expect you to forget the past as if it never existed," he said gently, "but you can't live in it, Lisette. It's gone. It won't ever return."

"But I don't know how to stop loving him!" she cried, unable to contain her anguish any longer. "I don't know how to start to love someone else!"

A smile touched the corners of his mouth. "Let me show you," he said, drawing her to him with strong, firm hands.

She was overcome by a feeling of *déjà vu*. In just such a way had she entered Dieter's arms, barely knowing him, trusting her instincts, capitulating to a primeval sixth sense that overcame reason and rationality.

She looked up into Greg's sun-bronzed face. This time she was in command of herself. There was a choice. She could draw back if she wished. She could continue to live in restless isolation, tormented by the past and unable to envision a future; or she could alter her life as surely and as irrevocably as she had on first entering Dieter's arms. The choice was hers. All she had to do was make it.

Laugh lines creased the corners of his eyes and etched his mouth. His brows were thick, many shades darker than the honey-brown tumble of his hair. It was the face of a man with no self-doubt. A handsome face. Confident. Gregarious. Generous.

He held her securely, sliding one hand up the length of her spine, and into her hair, cradling the nape of her neck, raising her face to his. She shivered, an impulse of sensuality flaring through her as slowly, purposefully, he lowered his head to hers.

There was one flash of doubt, a surge of guilt that nearly overwhelmed her, and then her body yielded against the hard sureness of his, her arms went up and around his neck, and her mouth parted willingly beneath his, warm and sweet.

He was shocked at the fierceness of his response to her. He wanted to feel her flesh naked against him: the upthrust of her nipples in the palms of his hands, her hips grinding in passionate movement against his. The rose garden was deserted. All he had to do was ease her down beneath him, unbutton her blouse, push her skirt high. . . . He knew if he did, she would be lost to him forever. He had sensed her momentary doubt. She still loved Brandon. She had told him so when she had told him she needed time to learn to love someone else. If he went too far, too fast, too clumsily, he would frighten her away forever. She wasn't hungry for him yet as he was for her. He raised his head from hers, his eyes gleaming. She would be though, given time. She would learn to love him under the very best possible conditions: as his wife.

"In forty-eight hours I'll be leaving Normandy and moving toward Paris," he said, still holding her close. "I want you to marry me before I go."

The soft curve of her brows rose in disbelief, and then her lips curved into a smile. "That isn't possible. In France, weddings take time. There has to be a civil ceremony as well. Permission has to be granted. Banns have to be called . . ."

176

He hooked a finger under her chin, tilting the exquisite triangle of her face toward his. "I've already taken the liberty of obtaining permission, and Sainte-Marie's mayor is only too happy for the civil ceremony to take place without delay. The priest was very understanding about the banns. He's waiting to speak to you now. He's with your father, marking in the new lines of Allied control on a map of France."

"I don't believe you!" Beneath the thick sweep of her lashes her eyes were incredulous.

He grinned. "You'd better," he said, circling her waist with his arm, beginning to lead her back toward the courtyard and the stables. "Father Laffort is expecting to speak to a blushing bride-to-be."

"But how could you possibly have known that I would say yes?" she asked, full of laughter. "You hadn't even asked me!"

He took her shoulders, swinging her around to face him. "I'm asking you now. Will you marry me?"

As if to compensate for the flowers that had burned and died, those that had survived had bloomed with ferocious splendor. Their scent hung heavy in the afternoon sunlight. Bees droned slumberously. In the far distance she could hear the faint surge of the sea. Time spun out in a long, fragile moment.

She lifted her face to his, the dark fall of her hair shimmering glossily.

"Yes," she said. She was dizzy with recklessness as he exuberantly circled her waist with his hands, lifting her off her feet and swinging her around with a whoop of triumph.

When they walked into Henri de Valmy's makeshift sitting room above the stable, he stared at them in astonishment. Lisette's hand was held firmly in the American's, her eyes warm with an expression of happiness he had thought he would never see there again.

"I'm going to marry Colonel Dering, Papa."

Henri rose dazedly to his feet, leaving Father Laffort still sitting at the table with its large-scale map of France. "So he told me when he arrived, *ma chère*. But I must confess that I thought he had made a mistake. . . . "

The tall, toughly built American at his daughter's side

grinned. "It's not a mistake, sir. With your permission we'd like to be married now, before I move on toward Paris."

"But the paperwork . . . ," Henri protested faintly.

"I have my birth certificate, my medical card, and my permission to marry from my commanding officer," Greg said, taking a wallet out of the inner pocket of his combat jacket. "Father Laffort has no objections. He's happy to marry us right away if that is agreeable to you, sir."

Henri turned to Lisette. "Is that what you want, *ma chère?* Are you sure?"

She stepped toward him and took his hands. "Yes, Papa, I'm sure."

Henri lowered his voice discreetly. "And does the colonel know about . . ." He cleared his throat, leaving Dieter's name unspoken. Father Laffort's ears were sharp.

She nodded. "Yes, Luke told him."

Some of Henri's tension eased. If the American knew about Dieter Meyer, then there was nothing more to be said. If she wanted to marry him, he would not stand in her way. Better an American for a son-in-law than a German.

The wedding took place three hours later in Sainte-Marie-des-Ponts's tiny Norman church. Roses from Valmy, pale-flushed Ophelias, and creamy Gloire de Dijon massed the small stone windowsills and crowded the foot of the altar.

There were only eight people present: the mayor; Father Laffort, small and spry and enjoying the celebratory nature of his task after the grimness of the burials that had taken place; Madame Chamot, who had insisted that the bridal couple's few brief hours together after the wedding should be spent in the privacy of her cottage, while she absented herself on a visit to Madame Pichon: old Bleriot, washed and shaved and ramrod straight in a shiny pinstriped suit; Major Harris, who was acting as best man; Henri; and the bride and groom.

Lisette's dress was one that Madame Chamot had worn thirty years before at a garden party at Deauville. It was of cream lace, high at the throat, the sleeves extending in delicate points over the back of her hands, the long skirt cascading gently to the floor. She had swept her hair high, coiling it on the top of her head. Delicate tendrils curled at her temples and the nape of her neck. A wisp of veiling, purloined from one of Madame Chamot's summer hats, was held in place by a full-blown rose.

Greg's battle-stained uniform had been exchanged for one that was spanking clean and freshly pressed, a feat that had been harder to achieve than all Lisette's bridal finery. His confidence and easy manner had relaxed even Henri. When he thought of the anguish of the last few months, it was a marriage he could view with nothing but relief.

As dusk fell and candles flared they sang Lisette's favorite hymn, then Father Laffort stood before them. "Lisette and Gregory," he intoned, speaking slowly so that the American would understand. "You have come together in this church so that the Lord may seal and strengthen your love in the presence of the church's minister and this community."

The community, represented by old Bleriot and Madame Chamot, straightened their backs and stood stiffly in the ancient pews.

"Christ abundantly blesses this love. He has already consecrated you in baptism, and now He enriches and strengthens you by special sacrament so that you may assume the duties of marriage in mutual and lasting fidelity."

Lisette's throat tightened. She had believed that she would stand and hear these words with Dieter. For a second, a vision of what might have been swam before her eyes. Her fingers tightened on her posy of roses. She wasn't marrying Dieter. Dieter was dead. She was marrying Greg Dering: tough, laughing-eyed, generous-hearted. She was marrying him, and she was going to make him happy.

"And so, in the presence of the church, I ask you to state your intentions," Father Laffort said solemnly.

Greg looked down at her, and at the understanding and reassuring expression in his eyes she wondered if he had known what she was thinking. She smiled up at him, wanting to ease his concern, and then Father Laffort was saying, "Lisette and Gregory. I shall now ask you to undertake freely the obligations of marriage, and to state that there is no legal impediment to your marriage. Are you ready to do this, and without reservation, to give yourselves to each other in marriage?"

"I am," Greg said firmly.

Father Laffort smiled at her. "Lisette?" he prompted gently.

"I am." Her voice was low and clear, perfectly steady.

"Are you ready to love and honor each other as man and wife for the rest of your lives?"

"I am," Greg said without hesitation.

In the blue haze of twilight the candles flickered warmly.

"I am," Lisette said, lifting her face to the tall, broad-shouldered man at her side. His eyes were warm and sure, leaving her no room for doubt.

Father Laffort turned to Greg. "Please repeat after me. I do solemnly declare that I know not of any lawful impediment why I, Gregory James Dering, may not be joined in matrimony to Lisette Héloïse de Valmy."

Their eyes held, violet and brown, as they made their vows, and then he slipped his too-large signet ring onto the fourth finger of her left hand.

"You may kiss the bride," Father Laffort said.

Greg lifted the veil from her face and did so with commendable competence. Madame Chamot dabbed at her eyes, old Bleriot grinned, and Henri remembered Lisette's baptism and marveled at how quickly the intervening years had fled.

She gave her posy to Madame Chamot, kissed Major Harris and old Bleriot warmly on the cheek, and hugged her father tightly. There was to be no wedding celebration. In three hours' time Greg had to be back in St. Lô, preparing himself and his men for an early morning assault on their next objective—the market town of Torigni.

Major Harris, after wishing them all the happiness in the world, sped back to camp. Her father and old Bleriot walked off together up the hill toward Valmy, with the intention of sharing a bottle of calvados. Madame Chamot pressed the key to her cottage into Greg's hand and hurried off, flush cheeked, to spend the remainder of the night with Madame Pichon.

They stood in the deepening twilight, beneath the moss-covered lych-gate, man and wife. His arm circled her waist. "Would you like to begin your honeymoon, Mrs. Dering?" he asked gently.

She leaned her head against his shoulder, confounded by memories she had tried hard to suppress: Dieter carrying her into Valmy, her blood on his hands and his uniform. Dieter, his strong-boned face grim as he told her of the plot to assassinate Hitler. Dieter, his face transfigured by love for her as he twisted her beneath him in the lamplit glow of the turret room. She trembled, feeling as if she were about to commit an infidelity.

Greg slid his hands up to her shoulders, turning her toward him, sensing her distress.

"If it's too soon for you, too quick, I understand," he said, his tawny eyes dark with the passion he was curbing. "But we can't spend what little time we have together in the churchyard. Let's at least go to Madame Chamot's and talk."

She nodded, grateful for his understanding, tenderness surging through her.

He traced the line of her jaw with his finger, then lowered his head, his mouth brushing her hair line.

At the touch of his mouth, sensuality seeped along her veins, warming and reassuring. He was her husband. Only seconds ago she had promised to love him for better or for worse, in sickness and in health. They were going to build the rest of their lives together, have children, be happy.

His lips moved softly across her skin, dropping a kiss at the nape of her neck. She swayed against him, closing her mind to memories of the past.

"I'd like to begin our honeymoon," she said huskily, slipping her hand into his.

His arms tightened around her, his relief so great he could hardly speak. At last he said hoarsely, "Then let's go," and holding her close against him, he led her out of the darkening churchyard and into the narrow, cobblestone street that led to Madame Chamot's cottage.

13

Madame Chamot had been lavish in her preparations for their return. The sheets on Lisette's bed were fragrant with attar of roses, and there were tiny sachets of potpourri beneath the lace-edged pillows. Greg lit the oil lamp on the large mahogany dressing table. There was very little time, yet he was determined not to rush her. Better that they didn't make love at all than that they should do so without her willingness.

She stood in the center of the room, her heart beating fast and light as he took off his jacket. He walked over to the window and drew the curtains against the rising moon.

She was acutely aware of his body, of the whipcord muscles beneath his light cotton shirt, of the ease and grace with which he moved, despite his height and tough build. His sexuality stirred and excited her. There was something utterly sure about him, a confidence that disturbed and aroused. As he turned from the window she said unsteadily, "Would you undo my buttons for me, please?" Tiny and silk covered, they ran from the nape of her neck to the base of her spine.

Slowly he walked across the room to her, his breath tight in his throat. She was telling him that it was all right, that there was no need for him to keep a tight rein on the desire raging through his veins, that she was as ready for him as he was for her. His hands touched her shoulders, and a tremor ran through her.

"I love you," he said huskily, "you're the most beautiful creature I've ever seen or ever will see."

She raised her face to his, her eyes brilliant beneath the dark sweep of her lashes. She couldn't tell him that she loved him. Not yet. Not as she had loved Dieter. But she knew that she would love him, that love was already blossoming and burgeoning deep within her. And she knew that she could please him, that she could show her gratitude for his patience, for his understanding, for the love that he was already giving to her in such rich abundance.

Slowly she lifted her hands to her hair, pulling out the pins, letting the dark glory tumble to her shoulders, rippling and shimmering over the back of his hands.

He wound his fingers in the soft, heavy silkiness of it, pressing it against his lips, and then, his eyes smoldering with heat, he turned her around and one by one began to unfasten the tiny silk buttons, revealing the creamy perfection of her flesh.

The dress slid from her shoulders, to her breasts, to her hips, slithering into a pool of lace around her ankles. The curve of her hips, the soft roundness of her buttocks, covered only by a wisp of silk, sent his pulse pounding and the blood roaring in his ears. She was perfect. Exquisite. All he had ever dreamed of. He wanted to kiss every inch of her, to drive all thoughts of the past from her mind, to make her as hungry and greedy for his body as he was for hers.

He lifted the heavy weight of her hair away from her neck and kissed the milky smooth skin there, refusing to hurry. Slowly, caressingly, his fingers moved down her spine, lower and lower, until his strong, large hands cupped the dainty perfection of her buttocks and she gasped for breath, trembling beneath his touch as he turned her, in all the beauty of her near nakedness, to face him.

Her breasts were high and firm, fuller than he had imagined; the nipples, rose-pink, taut and erect, begging to be kissed. The blue-black triangle of her pubic hair curled enticingly over the restraining silk of her panties, and he groaned with need as he pulled her into his arms.

"It's going to be good," he whispered, his mouth brushing her temples, her eyelids, hot and sweet at the corners of her mouth. "Between us, it's always going to be good, Lisette."

She was on fire, stunned by her physical response to him. She felt like a small, wild animal, desperate for the comfort of copulation. She wanted to drown herself in his arms, to bury her hurt and pain, to submerge herself in a sea of sensuality.

His mouth was on her neck, her throat. She was tormented by longing. She wanted him to grind his lips against hers, to savage her mouth with his tongue, to plunder her body without thought of tenderness or care or consideration.

She twisted her mouth to his and in hungry, swift response, his tongue plunged past hers, his arms crushed her against him, and she found the oblivion she craved. There was no past. No future. Only his mouth on hers, his hands on her flesh, their bodies straining dementedly toward each other.

He scooped her up in his arms and strode with her to the bed. She sank onto the fragrant linen, half senseless with desire as he ripped off his shirt, his pants. The lean, tanned contours of his body gleamed in the soft light. A pelt of crisply curling hair darkened his chest. The white scar of a knife wound snaked down beneath his rib cage. She opened her arms to him, and the narrow bed rocked beneath his weight.

The heat of his body spread through her. She arched against him hungry for love, for relief from pain.

He gasped her name, his hands hot on her thighs, removing in one swift movement the offending barrier of fragile silk. He had intended being gentle, considerate, in control. Her pubic hair sprang against the palm of his hand. Her nipples burned his chest. With a groan he abandoned his intentions, parting her legs beneath him, plunging unhesitatingly into the dark, sweet softness of her, intent on a relief that was cataclysmic.

Her nails scored his back, his shoulders. He didn't wait for her, and she didn't need him to. Their cries merged and mingled, and when the point of momentary disintegration came, it was mutual: a physical and emotional explosion that convulsed both of them to the roots of their being. It wasn't what they had expected. It wasn't what either of them had anticipated or imagined.

He had thought he would need patience, restraint. She had thought she would have to pretend, be kind. Both of them had been wrong, and they lay, breathless and panting, weak with relief.

At last he raised himself up on one elbow, gazing down at her, smiling. "If it's going to be like that every time I make love to you, Mrs. Dering, I'm going to have to take out more health insurance. My heart won't stand it."

A bubble of laughter rose up inside her. She had made him happy, and in making him happy, she had eased her own hurt. With a sense of incredulity, she realized that love, like suffering, was not finite, that in her growing love for Greg, her love for Dieter was not diminished. Her fingers slid up the smooth, glistening contours of his back and buried themselves in the thickness of his hair. "There's only one way of finding out," she whispered, her eyes sparkling wickedly.

"Then let's not waste time," he said huskily, his hands caressing the full, delicious weight of her breasts, his body already hardening with the need to make love to her again.

They moved together slowly, rapturously. He was overwhelmed by the love he felt for her, consumed by it. She was the princess in the fairytales of his childhood: dark, seductive, hauntingly beautiful. When they reached again an unbearable summit of mutual pleasure and he heard her cry his name, his triumph was nearly more than he could stand. He felt in complete possession of her. No matter whom she had loved before, he was certain she was his now. She would be his for always. His wife. His love.

There was no time for sleep in each other's arms. No time for the endearments of satisfied love. Through the dark, silent streets there came the sound of a jeep fast approaching the cottage.

He hugged her close, knowing that in another few minutes he would be on his way back to camp, and that before dawn broke, he would be leading his men south to German-held Torigni.

"I have to go, my love," he said, his brandy-colored eyes dark with regret. "It may be weeks, months, before I'm back, but I will be back. I promise."

Her arms tightened around him in a spasm of fear. Dieter was dead. Luke Brandon was dead. She had lost her baby, her home. She couldn't bear the thought that Greg, too, might never return to her.

"Be careful," she said urgently as he gently removed her arms from his waist.

He grinned down at her. "Don't worry," he said with easy confidence, "I will be."

The jeep braked outside the cottage. Reluctantly, he rolled away from her, the bed creaking as he stood up. He walked over to the window and signaled down to the driver that he was on his way. "This time next year it could all be over," he said as he quickly began to pull on his clothes. "By July '45 you could be in California, wowing them with your French accent!"

She sat up in bed, her hair tumbling about her shoulders, her eyes widening. California. She scarcely had thought about it. Now that she was doing so, she felt such a mass of conflicting emotions she could hardly breathe.

His vivid smile flashed again. "You'll love it," he said reassuring. "Sun, sea. No memories."

Her fingers clutched at the sheets. No memories. No Valmy. No rain-washed skies over the beech woods. No corn fields or apple orchards.

The waiting driver revved the jeep's engine impatiently. Greg snatched up his jacket, his cap. She stumbled from the bed and he caught her against him. "Oh, God, how I love you!" he said, his mouth coming down hard and savage on hers.

In the street outside, the waiting driver slammed his hand hard on the jeep's horn. Greg tore himself away from her. "I'll be back," he said fiercely. "Be waiting for me."

"I will. I promise." Her voice was strangled in her throat.

He crushed her against him one last time, and then he was gone, running down the narrow stairs to the street, springing into the jeep, not trusting himself to look behind him as the engine roared into life and the jeep sped away toward the bridge and the darkened countryside beyond.

She stood for a long time at the window, staring out over the moonlit rooftops of Sainte-Marie-des-Ponts, accompanying him in her mind's eye for as long as she could. He would fight on toward Torigni. When the German defenses in western Normandy were destroyed, some American forces would drive south, into Brittany; others would swing eastward, forcing the Germans to withdraw across the Seine. She didn't know in which direction Greg would continue to fight. She didn't know when she could even begin to hope for his return.

She didn't sleep. When the first hint of dawn began to lighten the night sky, she dressed in sweater and skirt and low-heeled shoes, carefully made the tumbled bed, and quietly let herself out of the house.

The cobblestoned streets were silent. As she approached the bridge, she could hear cocks crowing lustily and the distant clang of milking pails. The grassy banks of the river beneath the bridge were wet with dew. A spider web gleamed silkily. Marsh marigolds and kingcups hung heavy, with golden, unopened heads.

She began to walk up the narrow, high-hedged lane toward the beech woods. There was something she had to do, a visit she had to make before she embarked on life as Mrs. Greg Dering.

The trees thinned and the husk of her home stood before her, gaunt and bleak, its beauty ravaged. She turned aside, and the long grass brushed her naked legs as she walked toward the churchyard and the cherry tree beyond.

A month later, in August, the Germans had still not been pushed back across the Seine. Information was scarce. Caen had been taken, but farther south, around Falaise, fighting was still fierce. Lisette had begun to feel unwell, sick and tired. When her period came, it was brief and scanty, barely noticeable. She knew that her father was worried about her, that if she didn't do something about her general feeling of malaise, he would insist that she join her mother in more comfortable living conditions at Balleroy. Reluctantly, she went to see Dr. Auge.

The doctor congratulated her on her wedding, examined her, and concealed his surprise at his diagnosis. He wondered who the father was. Certainly not the American who had stormed ashore on the sixth of June and she had married a month ago. She was at least twelve weeks pregnant. He curbed his curiosity. It was none of his affair. The American wouldn't be the only soldier cuckolded into rearing a child he hadn't fathered.

"The sickness will pass within the next week or two . . ."

"But how do you know?" she interrupted, puzzled. "What is causing it? What is the matter with me?"

Dr. Auge toyed with his pen. He didn't for one minute believe she was ignorant of her condition. She was simply trying to convince him, as she would have to convince everyone else, that the baby had only just been conceived, that when it was born, embarrassingly soon after her wedding, it could be described as premature. He sighed. He had thought she would have had more respect for his intelligence.

"You are approximately three months pregnant," he said unequivocally. "Sickness rarely continues into the fourth month and—"

"I can't be!" She was staring at him as if he had taken leave of his senses. "It isn't possible . . . My last period was only a few weeks ago . . ."

"Periods, much lighter than normal, sometimes continue irregularly all the way through a pregnancy," Dr. Auge continued, regarding her with interest. "Especially when there has been great emotional stress."

She rose unsteadily to her feet, her heart slamming hard and fast, the blood pounding in her ears. "Perhaps you are wrong about the dates, Dr. Auge," she said hoarsely. "Perhaps I am only a few weeks pregnant. A month pregnant!"

He shook his head, knowing that he had been wrong. She hadn't known. "There is no mistake, Madame Dering. The child must have been conceived some three months ago. In May."

So many emotions rushed through her that she could barely stand. She was having a baby. Dieter's baby. The child she wanted more than anything else in the world. And she was married to Greg. He would think that she had deceived him on purpose, that she had married him solely to give her unborn child a name.

"Oh God," she whispered, her face ashen. "Oh dear, dear God!"

"Madame Dering . . . ," Dr. Auge began anxiously.

She was no longer listening to him. She had to get out of the room. She had to get into fresh air. She had to think.

"I shall want to see you in four weeks' time . . . ," he was saying, but she had gone.

Dazedly she slammed the door of his office behind her. A baby. *Dieter's* baby! Her shock gave way to joy. She hadn't lost him completely. She would have his child. A part of him would be with her for always. And Greg?

She leaned against a plane tree in the village square. She would explain to him, tell him the truth. He already knew about Dieter. Luke Brandon had told him. He had been understanding, asking her no questions, promising only to teach her to love again. She felt the weight of her anxiety lift and ease. Luke Brandon had been prepared to marry her, knowing that she was carrying Dieter's child. Surely Greg, with his infinite generosity, would be equally understanding.

Her father stared at her, appalled. "A *baby? Meyer's* baby?"

"Yes, Papa," she said gently, wishing that she could ease his distress. "Dr. Auge says I'm at least three months pregnant."

"Dear Christ!" He groped blindly for a chair. "What will you do when Dering returns? What can you possibly say to him?"

Her face was pale and resolute. "I shall tell him the truth, Papa. There is nothing else I can tell him."

He raised his stricken face to hers. "The wedding was a month ago. I remember your mother telling me that Jean's wife regularly gave birth after seven-month pregnancies."

Her face tightened. She shook her head, her eyes clouding. "No, Papa," she said, knowing how deep was his anguish for him to suggest such a deception. "I would rather he left me than stay with me believing such a lie."

"He probably will, *ma chère,*" her father said unsteadily. "Another man's child. A *German's* child! It is more than you can expect any man to tolerate."

Anxiety sprang alive again, clutching at her heart. She didn't want to lose Greg. She was already more than halfway in love with him. The thought of a future without him appalled her. "It will be all right," she said fiercely, rising to her feet to make some coffee. "Greg will understand. I know he will."

Her father shook his head disbelievingly. She could have Dieter Meyer's child, or she could have a new life in America with Greg Dering. He couldn't see how she could possibly have both.

Two weeks later Paris was liberated. Her father wept for joy, forgetting his anguish about the coming baby. There was no champagne and so they celebrated with glass after glass of calvados. "Long live the Americans!" her father cried, holding his glass high. "Long live the Canadians! The English! *Long live France!*"

At the beginning of September she went with him to visit

189

her mother in Balleroy. Travel was still not easy. Apart from their old Citroën, there were very few vehicles, other than army vehicles, on the roads. White crosses at the roadsides proliferated. The fields were dotted with the carcasses of animals killed in the fighting, and the undergrowth and woods were thick with the remains of burned-out tanks.

Her mother was delighted to see her, delighted to be able to hear at first hand about her wedding. By tacit agreement neither Lisette nor her father spoke of the coming baby. There would be time enough for that when Greg returned and they were sure about what the future would hold.

By October, the rounding swell of her stomach could no longer be disguised. Madame Chamot and Madame Bridet congratulated her, apparently seeing nothing odd about the obviousness of her condition. Only Madame Pichon looked at her askance. She had delivered over five hundred babies. Like Dr. Auge, she knew very well that the coming baby had not been conceived on Lisette's wedding night. The Americans had only landed on the sixth of June. Madame Pichon pursed her lips. The Dering baby had obviously been conceived long before Colonel Dering had set foot on French soil. It was all very strange and intriguing, but she liked Lisette, and she discreetly kept her thoughts to herself.

In November, Lisette received a letter from Greg. His battalion was attacking German positions east of Aachen. In December, he was in the Ardennes, fighting a bloody battle against panzer divisions in heavily wooded country.

Life in Sainte-Marie-des-Ponts returned to normal. There were still soldiers about, but they were American soldiers. They patrolled the road junctions, guarded the railway bridges, and continued to ferry provisions and equipment from the beaches inland.

Lisette visited Dr. Auge once a month. The baby was due at the beginning of February. Auge still privately speculated about the father. He had never seen her in the company of village boys, apart from Paul Gilles. And young Gilles had been shot too early in the year for him to have been the father. It was all most intriguing, but his patient showed no inclination to confide in him. She was healthy, happy, and apparently looking forward to her husband's return. It was all very puzzling, but it was none of his concern. His concern was for the birth. She was very small boned and slim hipped, and he anticipated problems.

All through January, the fighting in the Ardennes continued. Units of the U. S. 1st Army and the British XXX Corps moved forward slowly, but the terrain was crucifying, the weather appalling.

"Units of Free French are reported to be crossing into Alsace," her father told her as they sat in their now cozy suite of rooms above the stables, a log fire burning pungently. "De Gaulle is determined that France will emerge from the war with pride."

There came the faint throb of a car engine. It grew louder, fast approaching Valmy.

She sprang to her feet, her eyes wide. "It's a car, Papa!"

"It's a jeep!" he said, rushing over to the window to peer out into the dusk-filled courtyard.

She ran from the room and down the whitewashed stairs, her heart racing. It was Greg. No one else would be visiting them in an army vehicle. Perhaps the news about the continued fighting in the Ardennes was wrong. Perhaps the Germans were in full retreat. She raced through the empty stable and out into the courtyard, the baby hampering her speed.

The jeep turned in through the stone archway, and she knew immediately that it wasn't Greg. She sagged with disappointment, tears stinging the backs of her eyes. She had been so sure it was him, so sure that her waiting was over.

"Don't I get a smile?" the tall, dark figure asked as he sprang from the jeep.

She gasped, staring in disbelief.

"I've dreamed of this reunion for months. You could at least look pleased to see me," Luke Brandon said, a lock of dark hair falling across his forehead, a smile on his lean face as he strode toward her.

"Luke! I don't believe it! We thought you were dead! Oh, Luke! *Luke!*"

She ran toward him in the gathering darkness. His arms closed round her, and before she could avert her head, he kissed her full on the mouth, a deep, passionate kiss full of need and longing.

"I thought I was going to be back too late to give this baby a legal entry into the world," he said thickly, raising his head from hers. "You have changed your mind, haven't you, Lisette? You're not still determined to go it alone?"

Slowly she lowered her arms and stepped away from him. It was too dark for him to see the expression in her eyes. He said confidently, "I knew that you needed time to get over Meyer's death . . . that when you had done so you would realize that a new life in England would be the very best thing for you. I still want to marry you, Lisette. Not just because of the promise I made to Meyer, but because—"

She couldn't let him continue. She lifted up her hand, and the too-large signet ring gleamed dully.

He stared at it and then at her. "I don't understand," he said blankly. "What are you trying to tell me?"

"I'm married, Luke," she said gently. "I've been married for four months."

He blanched. "I don't believe it! You couldn't be—" and then, incredulously, "*Four months ago?*"

She nodded. Always, when she had thought of his marriage proposal to her, she had thought he had proposed out of obligation to the promise he had given Dieter—out of guilt for being responsible for his death. Now, for the first time, she realized that it went deeper than that, that he truly wanted to marry her, irrespective of Dieter and the nightmare that had taken place at Valmy.

"I married Colonel Dering at the end of July," she said awkwardly.

"Jesus Christ!" He swayed slightly and then said, his voice harsh, "You didn't waste much time, did you? I thought you were convulsed with grief for Meyer. I thought you said you would never love again, the way you had loved him."

She didn't flinch beneath his bitterness. Her brilliant dark eyes met his steadily. "I did say that, and it's true. But I've discovered that there's more than one way to be in love."

"And are you in love with Dering?" His eyes were black pits in the gaunt whiteness of his face.

She stood silent for a moment, remembering how she had felt when she had believed he was driving the jeep, when she had thought that he had returned to her. "Yes," she said, and her voice held surprise. "Yes, I am."

He pushed a sleek, black lock of hair away from his

forehead. "And what about Meyer? Does Dering know all about him?"

For a long moment she couldn't speak. When she did the breath was tight in her throat, her lips dry. "Yes, you told him, Luke."

He stared at her incredulously, and even before he spoke, she knew there had been a terrible mistake. "I never breathed a word about Meyer to anyone. What on earth gave you the idea that I had spoken to Dering about him?"

There was no air in her chest. She felt as though she were suffocating. "He said he knew that I was going to be married. That you had told him."

The anger drained out of him. She looked so beautiful, so vulnerable. He said hoarsely, "I told him that I intended marrying you, Lisette. I never spoke to him of Dieter Meyer."

The courtyard was dark now, the January night air chill. She swayed slightly and his hands steadied her. "Does he know about the baby?" Luke asked.

She shook her head, unable to speak. She had thought he had known about Dieter, that he had been understanding of her love for a German. And all the time he had believed it was Luke Brandon she referred to when she had told him she had been in love, and that the man she loved had died. No wonder he had been understanding. No wonder he had asked no questions. The cold seemed to strike through to her very bones. She shivered, and Luke put his arms around her, holding her close.

"I was injured again when I escaped from the château, Lisette. I've been hospitalized for months. The war is over for me. I'd like to stay at Valmy for a little while, until you have the baby or until Dering returns."

"That would be nice," she said unsteadily, not daring to think what her mistake might cost her, what Greg's reaction would be when he knew the truth. She took a deep, steadying breath. Luke was no longer angry with her. He was offering his support and friendship. She managed a smile. "Come inside and meet Papa. He's heard so much about you. He won't be able to believe it when I tell him you escaped the Germans."

They walked toward the stable. "How did you get away?" she asked as they climbed the stairs. "When Greg and I arrived from Sainte-Marie-des-Ponts, the château was ablaze, and there were Americans here. They said they had been met with German gunfire."

"I saw the Germans coming and hauled myself out here, to the stables. When the gunfire started, I dragged myself out, under cover of it, to the gardens at the rear, intending to circle around and join up with the Americans. Someone must have seen me from the château. I was hit twice, in the chest and shoulder, and passed out. When I came to, it was dusk and Valmy was burning. I crawled off in the direction of the village, and a truck full of Americans gave me a lift. They were going to Bayeux. The medics there patched me up, and then I was moved north and hospitalized."

She squeezed his hand tightly. "I'm so glad you're alive, Luke. I can't tell you how hideous it was—Deiter dead, believing that you were dead, Valmy burning."

"Have you been living up here ever since?" he asked as they mounted the last step.

She nodded, and then her father was greeting them, his hands outstretched in welcome, his eyes bewildered.

"It's Luke Brandon, Papa," she said, introducing them. "He didn't die. He's here. Isn't it marvelous?"

"My dear young man! How magnificent. Do come in. There's no champagne, I'm afraid, but there're barrels full of calvados!"

In the first week of February Luke drove her to Bayeux in the Citroën, the jeep having been returned to the camp from where it had been borrowed. The baby was due in the next few days, and she wanted to do enough shopping to last them till the end of the month. They were approaching the market square when a girl her own age was dragged kicking and screaming from a nearby house into the street.

"*Collaborator! Traitor!*"

Within seconds, the street that had previously been nearly empty was a torrent of people. Luke tried to pull Lisette away, but it was too late. They were trapped in the middle of a shouting, chanting crowd.

"*Oh, dear God!*" Lisette cried frantically as the sobbing girl was hissed at and spat upon. "*Make them stop, Luke! Make them stop!*"

It was impossible and he knew it. All he could do was try to get her out of the crush before the real horror began.

"*Where's your fancy kraut boyfriend now?*" a pinstriped suited man yelled, throwing a rotten tomato full in the girl's terrified face. The tomato spattered, its rotten flesh oozing juice down her cheek, her chin. "*Whore!*" the man shouted exultantly. "*German's whore!*"

A wooden chair had been hastily dragged into the center of the cobblestoned street. Old women, their shawls crossed beneath their chins and round their breasts, fought their way forward to tug at a handful of the girl's hair, to scratch, to spit.

Lisette was engulfed by horror, drowning in it. "*No!*" she screamed as the still-struggling girl was tied to the chair, her hair seized and twisted cruelly. "*No!*" She tried to push her way through the crowd. "*Leave her alone! For God's sake, leave her alone!*"

The baby jumped and jarred in her womb. Luke caught her wrist, but she twisted away from him, intent on reaching the girl's side.

Collaborator! Whore! Traitor!

The words beat against her ears. Whatever the girl had done, it was no more than she herself had done. They had both had German boyfriends, and she, Lisette, was carrying a German's child.

"*Stop it!*" she shouted. "*You're animals! No better than the Boche!*"

She was hit viciously across the mouth, and blood spurted on to her hands, her coat. She half fell, only the force of the crush around her keeping her upright.

Putrifying fruit was thrown at the weeping girl—rotten eggs, offal. Lisette made one last vain effort to reach her, and then a placard with the word "Collaborator" daubed in red paint was hung about the girl's neck, and the women exultantly began to shear her hair.

"There's nothing we can do," Luke gasped when he finally reached her side. "Let's get out of here while we can."

The girl's hair fell to the cobblestones and a great cheer rang out. Lisette turned away, her face white. Luke was right. There was nothing they could do. The same scene was taking place in nearly every village and town in France. Sickness rose like bile in her. It was what she could expect if the villagers in Sainte-Marie-des-Ponts discovered she had been Dieter Meyer's mistress, if they knew the child she was carrying had been fathered by a German.

Pushing and panting, Luke elbowed a way clear of the mob. "Let's leave the market for another day," he said, hurrying her up the street toward the parked Citroën. "When they've finished abusing the pathetic victim they already have, they might start looking around for another and remember your protests."

She didn't argue with him. She was hugging her arms fiercely to stop herself from shaking.

"Are you all right?" he asked as he opened the doors of the Citroën and bundled her inside.

"No," she said, her hair disheveled, her voice unsteady. "The baby is coming!"

14

Luke took one look at her face and then put his foot down hard on the accelerator, racing out of Bayeux's cobblestoned streets and into the narrow, high-hedged lanes beyond.

"It will take me half an hour to get back to Valmy. Will you be all right until then?" he asked tightly.

"I should be all right for hours. First babies don't come quickly," she said reassuringly, bracing herself against a spasm of pain that was nothing like the gradual buildup which Dr. Auge had told her to expect.

Luke saw her hands clench in her lap, the knuckles whitening, and pressed his foot down even harder. He didn't know anything about the time sequence of first babies, but instinct told him that this one was not going to be long in arriving. He flashed through Le Calvaire and Mosles wondering how soon he could get hold of Dr. Auge or Madame Pichon.

"It doesn't feel . . . at all as I had expected," she gasped, pressing her hands to her bulging stomach.

Luke remember the crowd, the crush, her terrible distress at the scene they had witnessed. He didn't know what shock did to a woman in the early stages of labor, but in Lisette's case it certainly seemed to be speeding events up.

"Hold tight," he said grimly. "We're nearly there."

"You'd better be quick," she gasped. "This baby is well on its way!"

"*Christ!*" He slammed his foot to the floor, screaming up the hill toward the beech woods, a cloud of dust billowing in his wake.

He still had to get hold of Dr. Auge or Madame Pichon. It could take him thirty minutes, perhaps forty. And if the baby came while he was away? He couldn't leave her alone with her father. The unworldly Henri would be totally unable to cope, which meant that he, Luke, would have to stay with her while Henri drove the Citroën to Sainte-Marie-des-Ponts in search of the doctor or midwife. And if Lisette was right, and the baby was determined to arrive in a hurry, then in all probability he would be the one delivering it.

"*Christ!*" he said again, swerving out of the woods and plunging down the long, linden-flanked drive. He felt as if he were about to enter into combat, not knowing what to expect, what he would be called upon to do.

"Are you going to be able to talk me through this?" he asked tautly as they screeched to a halt outside the stables.

"I'm sure babies that arrive in a hurry do so with very little help," she said, trying to sound more confident than she felt. She clambered from the car, then halted suddenly as another spasm of pain knifed through her.

Luke ran to her side, slipping his arm around her waist. She leaned against him, panting for breath. The pain receded and she said urgently, "Help me up the stairs, Luke. I think time is running out."

He half carried her up the whitewashed stone stairs, shouting for Henri.

The comte rushed out of the room above them, staring down at them in alarm.

"What is it? What's the matter?"

"The baby," Luke said tersely. "It's on its way. Take the car and bring Dr. Auge or Madame Pichon back with you!"

Another wave of pain swamped Lisette and she groaned, swaying against Luke's supporting arm. "Quickly!" Luke shouted. "There's no time to lose!"

Henri didn't hesitate. He dashed past them, stumbling down the stairs and running toward the car.

There were beads of perspiration on her forehead. "It's coming!" she gasped, seizing his hand. "Oh, Luke, the baby's here!"

He got her into the bedroom and to the bed. She collapsed across it, panting, bearing down, unable to hold back. He tore open her coat, pushing her skirt high, pulling her panties down and ripping them from her legs. There was no time for hot water. No time for towels. No time for anything. The baby's head was at the mouth of her vagina.

"Gently, Lisette!" he urged as she groaned and the baby's head crowned. "*Gently!*"

The baby's head emerged. Luke saw tightly closed eyes, a wrinkled, scarlet face, a mouth already opening to draw breath. Lisette gave a great gasp, there was a rush of liquid, and to Luke Brandon's indescribable wonder, Dieter Meyer's son slid, squalling lustily, into his waiting hands.

By the time Henri returned with Dr. Auge, the baby was wrapped in a shawl and Lisette was suitably clad in a nightgown, cradling the child to her breast.

"Good God!" Dr. Auge said, pulling up short in the doorway. "Is there anything left for me to do?"

Luke grinned. "I didn't cut the umbilical cord. I thought you'd prefer to do that yourself."

Dr. Auge collected his scattered wits and bustled across to the bed. "And to think I thought this would be a difficult birth," he said briskly, taking the baby from Lisette's arms and laying it on the bed.

The baby, aggrieved, began to squall again. Dr. Auge removed the shawl and regarded him with satisfaction. "Congratulations, Madame Dering. You have a fine son. A little small, perhaps, but that is to be expected after the hardship of the last months." He turned toward them. "Have you some weighing scales?" he asked, certain that the baby's weight was to everyone's advantage.

"Five pounds three ounces," he said a few minutes later.

"He will need a little extra care, but he's healthy enough if the sound he is making is anything to go by. Put him to the breast. I'll call again tomorrow. *Au revoir, Monsieur le Comte. Au revoir, Madame. Au revoir, monsieur.*"

He hurried away, wondering who the Englishman was, and if he were the father. Somehow he doubted it. The Englishman's coloring was distinctive: black hair, blue eyes. The baby's hair was dark gold and, in Dr. ·Auge's opinion, destined to stay dark gold. No, the Englishman wasn't the father. And the husband wasn't the father.

He frowned as he threw his bag into the rear of his battered car. One solution had occurred to him, but he dismissed it as too bizarre, too ridiculous to be considered seriously.

"What are you going to call him?" Luke asked, sitting on the edge of the bed as she nursed the baby, her hair falling softly against her radiant face.

She smiled. "I'd like to call him Luke, after you."

He gave her a lopsided grin. "Don't do that, it would only confuse things more. Don't forget that Greg believes it was me you were in love with."

Her eyes darkened, her happiness draining away. "Will he mind very much?" she asked, desperate for reassurance. "He didn't mind when he thought that it was you I was in love with, but when he finds out it was Dieter . . ."

"I don't know," Luke said truthfully, turning his head away so that she could not see the expression that had flashed through his eyes. He hoped Greg Dering minded like hell. He hoped he walked out on her and never returned. When he had mastered his emotions he turned toward her once again. "Will it matter so much to you if he does mind?" he asked tightly. "If he finds the baby totally unacceptable?"

He wanted her to say no—that she wasn't in love with Dering, that she never had been, that she was happy now, with the baby, with him.

"Yes," she said, and beneath the dark halo of her hair her face was pale, her eyes anguished. "It would be almost more than I could bear."

His mouth hardened. He'd been a fool to have asked. But she was being loyal to a man she barely knew. He was certain, when Dering returned, she would be disillusioned. Until then, all he could do was to be supportive and loving. And wait.

She called the baby Dominic. It was a name that was French in origin and yet would not sound strange in California. A name that began with the same letter as Dieter's name. A name that had no other associations.

He was a placid baby, not reminding her temperamentally of Dieter at all. But there was no mistaking his paternity in the already firm lines of chin and jaw, the black-lashed eyes, and the burnished mop of dark gold hair.

A week after the birth she was cooking and cleaning and shopping in the market, the baby constantly at her side in the makeshift cot that her father had made.

In March, she received a brief and hastily written letter from Greg saying that his company was pressing on toward the Rhine. By the end of the month, the Rhine had been crossed, and Luke assured her that the war was in its final stages, that the Germans had no alternative but to surrender.

In April, Greg wrote her that American and Russian soldiers had met up on the banks of the Elbe. From the radio, borrowed from old Bleriot, they learned that Russian troops were advancing on Berlin, that the French First Army had reached Lake Constance.

"The surrender can't be much longer," she said, her eyes bright with expectation. "Once it is, it can only be a matter of weeks, perhaps days, before Greg returns."

She had misplaced her tortoiseshell comb and her hair dipped forward at either side of her face, brushing her cheeks. She was wearing a red silk shirt and a white linen skirt and looked as if she should have been on the Champs-Elysées instead of in a converted stable in Normandy.

"Where is Greg now?" Luke asked, forcing his voice to sound casual. He didn't want Greg Dering to return. He didn't want to witness a joyful reunion. He didn't want to risk facing the incredible: Dering's acceptance of Meyer's son.

Lisette looked at the last, hastily scrawled letter. "They're moving south, toward Munich. He expected to be at a place called Dachau the day after he wrote. I don't know where it is. I've never heard of it before. It isn't on any of the maps."

Luke hadn't heard of it either, but if the Americans were moving south so speedily, and if the Russians were in Berlin, then the end could only be days away.

It came a week later. They heard the news of the German surrender on the radio and almost simultaneously the bells in Sainte-Marie-des-Ponts's church steeple began to peal.

Luke lifted Lisette off her feet, swinging her round and round exultantly. Henri was nearly incoherent with joy. He kissed Lisette, he kissed Luke, he kissed the baby, he hung the *tricolore* from the window. It was over. The nightmare was at an end. The Germans had been beaten to their knees and Europe was once again free.

Greg returned to Valmy a month later. Luke and Henri were in the village, visiting old Bleriot who had fallen in a drunken stupor and broken his leg. Lisette was arranging roses in a bowl near an open window, the baby in his cot at her side. When she heard the note of the approaching engine she froze, her hand in midair. It was a jeep, an army jeep.

She left the roses. She left the room. She hurled herself down the whitewashed stone steps, through the archway, and onto the cobblestones. He was in uniform: strong, fit, and unbelievably handsome.

For a split second she faltered, then he saw her. He shouted her name, leaping from the jeep, his eyes shining, and as he sprinted toward her, her hesitancy vanished, and she entered his arms like an arrow entering the gold. Only when she was crushed hard against his chest did she admit to herself how frightened she had been that he would never return—that he would be killed, reported missing; that she would never see him again.

"Oh, I'm so glad you're back!" she cried joyfully, her arms tightening around his neck. As he looked down at her and she saw the flecks of gold near the pupils of his eyes, the tumble of his hair curling low over his forehead, she said chokingly, "I missed you, Greg! Oh, how I missed you!"

Relief rocked through him. It had been ten months since he had said good-bye to her, long enough for her to have changed her mind about the hasty wedding he had talked her into. He felt her press herself against him. She hadn't changed her mind, and she hadn't forgotten. The memories of their wedding night had sustained her through the long months of waiting as they had sustained him.

"No more partings," he promised huskily. "This time when I leave, you come with me," and then his mouth came down on hers, hard and hungry, and desire licked through her.

He swung her up in his arms, carrying her with devastating ease up the stone stairs, striding with her through the sun-filled sitting room where Dominic lay unnoticed in his cot, falling with her onto the bed in the room beyond. She tried to speak, to tell him about Dominic, but he gave her no chance.

"Later," he said hoarsely. "We'll talk later, Lisette. All I want to do now is make love to you. It's been so long. Too long."

His fingers were on the buttons of her blouse, his mouth on her lips, her throat. She abandoned the attempt to speak, astonished at the ferocity of her own need, her own passion and hunger.

He tore himself out of his uniform. Within seconds her blouse followed his shirt onto the floor, her skirt his trousers, her lace-edged French knickers his shorts. He was too impatient to wait until she removed her garters and cheap, rayon stockings. A tuft of night-black hair curled silkily against the fragile whiteness of her inner thighs. He groaned, burying his face in the sweet-smelling fragrance of her, his tongue hot and exploring. Her fingers tightened in his hair, her back arching with pleasure.

"I love you . . . love you . . . love you . . . ," she gasped, and knew with delight that it was true. When he mounted her and she opened for him, she shivered with ecstasy, wrapping her legs around him, wanting to hold him inside her forever.

Their climax was shattering, the reverberations going on and on until she thought she would die. As she looked up into his face, at his tightly closed eyes, at the expression of intense concentration, almost agony, furrowing his features, she was aware of a sensation she had never before experienced. Power and pleasure inextricably mixed. He was her husband. There was no shadow hanging over their love for each other, no darkness to blight the happiness they had discovered.

He collapsed on top of her, murmuring her name, his hand on her breast, and the baby, unaccustomed to being neglected for so long, gave a whimper and then a cry.

Greg jerked his head up. "What the devil is that?" he asked unbelievingly.

She was still trapped beneath him, her hair streaming over the starched white pillowcases. "It's a baby," she said, the blood drumming in her ears. "My baby."

He stared down at her in incredulity, then leaped from the bed, racing across the room and into the sitting room.

She scrambled after him, hastily pulling on her skirt and blouse. "I didn't tell you in my letters because I thought you'd be angry . . ."

"Angry?" He stood naked in the sun-filled room, the baby held high in his hands. "But he's magnificent! Incredible!"

She sagged against the doorjamb with relief and then he was saying, "When was he born? How old is he?"

"He's five months old. He was born in February. His name is Dominic."

Greg laughed with delight. "He's fantastic! Amazing! What did he weigh?"

Her surge of relief died rapidly. He hadn't understood. He had made a terrible mistake. "Five pounds three ounces," she said unsteadily. "Greg, he isn't—"

"That's pretty good for a short-term baby." Greg regarded Dominic admiringly. "My sister was short term. Born at seven months and weighing four-and-a-half pounds. My mother never thought she'd make it. This little fellow is going to make it all right. Just look how he's holding onto my finger!"

The baby, fascinated at being held so high in the air, was clinging tightly to Greg's finger, cooing cherubically.

She knew if she moved she would fall. "Greg, please, you don't understand. Listen to me . . ."

The Citroën roared beneath the stone archway and into the courtyard.

"I'll talk to you later," Greg said to Dominic. He laid him gently back in his cot and made a beeline for his clothes.

She couldn't tell him now, not with Luke and her father about to make their entrance at any moment. Luke. She still hadn't told him about Luke.

"Luke Brandon is with Papa," she said rapidly. "He didn't die. He escaped. He's been living here since January."

Greg halted in the act of buckling his belt. "*Brandon* has?"

203

She saw his mind immediately fly to the baby. Saw doubt. Uncertainty as to what their relationship had been. She ran to him and seized his arm. "Greg! I didn't love Luke! I never have! That was all a mistake! He's lived here as a friend . . ."

There came the sound of Henri and Luke climbing the stairs. Greg grabbed her wrists so hard she cried out in pain. "Is that true?" he asked urgently. "You never really loved him?"

"No. I love you!"

It was the first time she had told him so. His teeth flashed in a relieved grin. "That's okay then," he said, releasing her and pulling on his shirt. "In that case I can afford to be sorry for him."

"Lisette? Is Greg here?" her father called.

She pushed a strand of sweat-damp hair away from her face. "Yes, Papa," she said. She took a deep, steadying breath and walked from the bedroom into the sitting room. She would have to talk to Greg later. She would tell him then about Dominic's paternity, that he had misunderstood her when she said that she didn't love Luke, that she meant she had *never* loved Luke, that it had been Dieter Meyer she had been in love with—Dieter Meyer she had been talking about when she had told him, before their marriage, that she didn't know how to begin to learn to love anyone else.

"He arrived half an hour ago, Papa," she said, aware of Luke's face tightening at the sight of her disarrayed hair, her rumpled clothes.

"That's wonderful news. Is he on leave? Home for good?"

"I'm on leave, sir," Greg said, stepping into the room behind her.

"It's marvelous to see you again," Henri said sincerely, taking his hand and shaking it warmly. "How long is your leave? Twenty-four hours? Forty-eight?"

"Twenty-four," Greg said, turning to Luke and proffering his hand. "It's good to see you again, Brandon. I always thought you were too wily to be caught by the krauts."

Luke fought down his jealousy. "It wasn't easy getting away from them," he said wryly, knowing that however much he tried, he was never going to be able to hate the tall, handsome American. "What sort of war did you have after you left Valmy?"

204

Greg's brandy-colored eyes darkened. "The last few days were the worst. Have you ever heard of a place called Dachau?"

Luke shook his head. "Lisette said you mentioned it in one of your letters. What is it? A town? A village?"

The skin tightened across Greg's strong-boned face. "No," he said, and there was something in his voice that sent a shiver down Luke's spine. "It's a camp."

"A prisoner-of-war camp?"

Greg shook his head, his eyes narrow. "No, a concentration camp. One of the camps the Germans used for containing Jews and undesirables." He crossed to the window and stared down into the courtyard. "There were thousands of them there when we liberated it. Men, women and children, starved and tortured; thousands of human beings, little more than living dead." His voice shook. "You can't begin to imagine it. The stench; the bodies. The guards had fled, but the inmates hadn't fled. They couldn't flee. They couldn't walk."

He paused and then continued tightly. "There was one room piled to the ceiling with potties, little zinc potties. The mothers had brought them with them for their children. God knows where the Germans had told them they were going." He passed a hand across his eyes. "They didn't need those potties. When they arrived at the camp, they were gassed. Hundreds of thousands of them. Men, women, and children." His throat seized up and he couldn't continue.

They were looking at him in horror. Lisette's eyes were so widely dilated, her face so white, he thought she would faint. He said unsteadily, "Never, as long as I live, will I set foot on German soil again. Never will I stay in the same room with a German. Speak to a German."

The baby began to cry. Greg crossed to the cot, lifted him comfortingly in his arms, and Lisette crumpled, insensible, to the floor.

When she recovered consciousness, she was lying on the sofa and Greg was at her side, his face taut with anxiety. "I'm sorry, sweetheart. It was crass of me to tell you about that hellhole when you've just had a baby and aren't very strong." His hand was holding hers, warm and comforting. "Will you be able to make the journey all right?" he was asking. "I'm going to be stationed in Paris for the next six months. I want you with me, and I have to be back there by tonight."

Her father was standing against the fireplace, his pipe in his hand, his face strained. Luke was standing only a few feet away, his brilliant blue gaze burning hers. They were both waiting for her to tell him. She knew when she did there would be no future for her as Greg's wife. Luke would want her to marry him, but she didn't want to marry Luke. He was her friend, but she wasn't in love with him. She was in love with Greg.

Her hand tightened its hold on his. "Will I be able to bring Dominic to Paris with me?"

He grinned. "Hell, yes. I told you. There's going to be no more partings. Not ever."

She sensed Luke stiffen, every nerve in his body taut. Her father had begun to clean his pipe, his eyes carefully avoiding hers.

She looked up into Greg's strong, handsome face. If she hadn't fallen in love with him, she knew she would have told him the truth. But she had fallen in love with him. And she was terrified at the thought of losing him.

"I'm ready to travel whenever you want me to be," she said steadily.

She heard Luke gasp. Saw him take a quick step forward. Her eyes flew pleadingly to his.

"That's settled then," Greg said, rising to his feet. "I'll help you pack."

"I need to talk to you," Luke said to him, white-faced.

Lisette sprang to her feet. "No!" she said, her voice anguished. "Please, Luke!"

Greg looked slowly from Luke to Lisette and then back again. "Whatever it is, I don't want to hear it," he said quietly. Their eyes held for a long moment, then Luke shrugged. "It's nothing," he said tersely. "I was just going to ask if you could give me a lift as far as Caen. I've been here long enough. It's time I started to make my way back home."

They left Valmy at dusk. The ruins of the château stood stark and bare against the darkening sky. Her father held her tight, telling her not to be homesick. To be happy.

While Greg and Luke were piling cases into the jeep, she slipped away, running down the drive to the gatehouse and plunging through the long grass to the churchyard to say another, more difficult good-bye.

"Where's Lisette?" Greg asked, the last of the cases safely stowed away.

Luke shrugged. "Having a last look round I expect," he said, knowing full well that she was in the churchyard and feeling a flare of jealousy that was, for once, not directed at Greg.

When she returned, her father was holding the baby. She took him gently. "*Au revoir, Papa,*" she said, kissing his cheek. "I love you."

"*Au revoir, chérie,*" he said tenderly. "Have a good life with your American."

Greg was already in the driver's seat and revving the engine. "Good-bye," he yelled to Henri. "I'll bring her back to you on vacation, I promise!"

She sat in the front passenger seat, the baby on her lap. Behind her, in the rear of the jeep, Luke sat grim faced, his eyes bleak. "*Au revoir, Papa,*" she called again as the gravel crunched beneath the wheels. "*Au revoir!*"

15

The sun was still golden on the linden trees as they sped down the drive and past the gatehouse. Lisette hugged Dominic tightly. She was leaving. Tears stung the backs of her eyes. She had known for a long time that this moment would come, but she was still unprepared for it.

Greg was talking easily to Luke, asking him what he intended to do now that the war was over. She didn't listen to his reply. They were speeding through the beech woods, the sunlight filtering amber-colored through the leaves. She kissed the top of Dominic's head. Greg had promised her they would return. It was a lavish promise, but one she knew he would keep. He wanted her to be happy, and from now on she had to learn to be happy away from Valmy.

The streets of Sainte-Marie-des-Ponts were quiet as they flashed through them and she was grateful. She didn't want to say any more good-byes in case the tears she was holding back spilled down her cheeks. The poplar trees lining the streets, the high slate-roofed houses, were left behind them. They were out in the countryside, speeding toward Caen, and Luke and Greg were discussing de Gaulle. She could hear the underlying tightness in Luke's voice. He had not been able to say good-bye to her alone. She knew what he was feeling, and she wished that she could turn to him and tell him that she was sorry.

Though she was not in love with him, a deep bond had been forged between them. He was the only person in the world, apart from her father, who knew the truth about Dominic's paternity. She would never forget the help he had given her when Dominic had made his impetuous entrance into the world. She could be at ease with him because she had nothing to hide from him. He knew about Dieter. And he didn't care. He was the truest and dearest friend she would ever have.

As they approached the bomb-shattered suburbs of Caen, she wondered if she would ever see him again. If she came back to Europe, it would be to France, not England. Her throat hurt. She was going to miss him. In the few months he had been at Valmy, he had become part of her life. They roared into the center of the city and screeched to a halt amidst a cloud of dust and gasoline fumes.

"This is where we say good-bye," Greg said, shooting Lisette a swift glance. Her face was pale, her eyes suspiciously bright. He hoisted himself from the driver's seat to the ground. "I think I'll go in search of some *Gauloise*," he said nonchalantly. "I'll be back in a few minutes."

Lisette felt a rush of gratitude toward him. He was leaving them alone in order that they could say good-bye privately. It was the act of a man who not only loved her but also trusted her. As he strode away from them, Luke sprang from the rear of the jeep, swinging his kit over his shoulder.

"Write to me at this address," he said, handing her a piece of paper. "It's my mother's address. Wherever I am, she'll forward letters on to me."

"Thank you." As she took it from his hand their fingers touched. "If it doesn't work, if you're unhappy, write and tell me," he said urgently. "Promise me!"

She nodded. "I promise," she said, her voice unsteady. "But I'm going to be happy, Luke. I know I am."

Luke had discovered some very unpalatable things about himself in the last few weeks. He didn't want her to be happy with Greg Dering. That kind of unselfishness was Greg's department, not his. He wanted her to be as miserable as hell. He wanted her to recognize the mistake she was making and to rectify it by leaving Greg and joining him in London.

"I'll be waiting for you," he said fiercely, and he tilted her face to his, kissing her so hard that she tasted blood. She was shaking as he released her, as he heard Greg returning. His shadow fell across them.

"Guess this is good-bye, Luke," he said, and nothing in his voice indicated that he had seen their embrace or had been crucified by jealousy at the sight of it.

Luke took his proffered hand stiffly, then turned once more toward the jeep. "Good-bye, Lisette," he said thickly. "I'll miss you." Then he turned on his heel and strode away from them, not looking back.

"He's still in love with you, isn't he?" Greg said, a nerve ticking at his jawline as he swung himself back behind the steering wheel. She nodded, unable to speak. His hand closed over hers. "Just as long as it isn't mutual," he said, and put the jeep into gear, driving off through the rubble-strewn streets toward the main highway and Paris.

She said very little for the rest of the journey. She was tired, physically and emotionally. Too tired to appreciate at first the sumptuousness of the new house, a large and beautiful one in the 16th Arrondissement.

"Let me take Dominic," Greg said gently as he helped her from the jeep.

"Where are we?" she asked curiously.

His teeth flashed in a grin. "Home," he said. "At least it's going to be home for the next few months."

They approached a tall wrought iron gate set in a hedge,

and he unlocked and opened it, leading the way into a carefully tended garden.

"Who does it belong to?" she asked, intrigued.

"A banker. In the days immediately prior to the Occupation, he left Paris for the healthier climate of Geneva. The Germans appropriated it, and now we're renting it. There are two servants in residence, both elderly. They won't be much help with Dominic, I'm afraid. We'll have to look round for a nanny."

She smiled, the soft, effortlessly sensuous smile that turned his heart over. "That won't be necessary," she said, sliding her hand into his. "I looked after Dominic by myself at Valmy. I can look after him by myself here."

He didn't argue with her. He knew she hadn't realized yet how her lifestyle had changed. Paris was in holiday mood, drunk with the heady wine of freedom. Every night was party night. She would need new clothes, perfume, a reliable babysitter to care for Dominic while he wined and dined her in what was still the most beautiful capital city in the world.

Hand in hand, with Greg in full uniform, the baby held incongruously in the curve of his arm, they stepped up to the door of their new home.

It was a magnificent house. The floor of the grand entrance hall was of rose-tinted marble. The painting in the salon was by Monet. There were delicately inlaid Louis XV chests, velvet upholstered *chaises longues,* Persian carpets, and crystal chandeliers. It was all breathtakingly elegant and freezingly formal. Within twenty-four hours she had turned it into a home, filling it with masses of flowers.

They lived there for three months, and they were three of the happiest months of her life. Paris was *en fête* after the dark, stifling days of Occupation. The boulevards were thronged with pretty girls and American soldiers, the pavement cafés were festooned with flags and bunting, the tree-lined streets full of the sound of laughter. The war was truly over and the realization was exhilarating.

They employed a Savoyard girl as a nanny. She was young and pretty, and Lisette was able to leave Dominic in the evening, knowing he was being well cared for as she strolled with Greg through the dusk-spangled streets, dining at Maxim or Le Moulin, dancing until dawn at Le Quarante-Cinq. They saw her mother and often took her out.

Greg had insisted on buying her new clothes: a dozen new dresses, two suits, half a dozen hats, shoes, handbags, scarves, lingerie, a cornucopia of gifts that took her breath away.

"I've never seen so many new clothes all at once," she said, laughing, as she stood in the center of their vast bedroom, knee-deep in opened boxes and tissue paper.

He grinned. "Can you bear to open another box?" he asked, and sliding his arm lovingly around her shoulders he handed her a small, velvet-padded ring box.

The wool coat she had been trying on slid from her shoulders. Slowly, carefully, she lifted the lid. Inside lay a pink diamond, large and flawless, surrounded by smaller white diamonds and set delicately on a narrow gold band.

"Oh, it's beautiful, Greg," she whispered as he gently removed the ungainly signet ring she had worn for so long and slipped the glittering diamond in its place.

"Not as beautiful as you," he said huskily, his arms sliding around her, his mouth closing passionately on hers.

They left Paris for America in November. The chestnut trees were gaunt, the dome of Sacré-Cœur sharp against a rain-washed sky. She took one last look round her before stepping into the limousine that was to take them to the *Gare du Nord*. Paris had been an interlude. Now it was over and her new life, in a country half a world away, was about to begin.

They sailed on the *Liberté*. Simonette, the young Savoyard girl they had employed as a nanny, came with them. When Greg had asked her if she would consider accompanying them to America and working for them there, she had accepted unhesitatingly. They were her first employers, but she was convinced she would never find anyone nicer to work for than Madame Dering.

"This is a little different from the tub I came out on," Greg said with a grin as a steward escorted them into a wonder of gold and scarlet and Lalique glass.

"It's marvelous!" Lisette said with the husky note of laughter in her voice that so entranced him. "Like a palace!"

Her hair shone, wound into a sleek figure eight. Her incredible amethyst eyes sparkled. The mink he had insisted on buying her swung casually from her shoulders. Beneath it,

211

she wore a crimson cashmere sweater and a gray, narrow, exquisitely cut skirt. There were pearl studs in her ears and a rope of pearls around her neck. Her shoes were black crocodile, ridiculously high; her stockings sheer. She was so effortlessly chic, so lovely, so graceful, that he hurt with love for her.

He remembered how she had looked when he had first set eyes on her. The sweat-damp tumble of her hair. The deathly paleness of her face as she had stepped across the blood-spattered bodies of the Germans and welcomed him with heartbreaking dignity to Valmy and to France.

He had wanted then to make her happy, and he was confident that he had done so. Luke Brandon had written to her, and she had showed him the letter and also her reply. It had been loving and caring, but it had not been the letter of a woman to a man she still loved. She had been telling him the truth when she had said that she had never really been in love with Brandon. His surge of jealously when he had seen Brandon kiss her good-bye so passionately had been unnecessary. The emotion had all been on Brandon's part. Lisette wasn't in love with him. She never had been. He, Greg, had her love, and he was determined to keep it.

Lisette became aware of many things on their nine-day trip across the Atlantic. She had realized in Paris that Greg was wealthy, and the realization had filled her with pleasant astonishment. Now, for the first time, she understood that he was not only wealthy, but very wealthy, that the name Dering was one that was instantly recognized by their fellow passengers and accorded respect. She realized, too, that she was not alone in finding him devastatingly attractive, other women did do—beautiful, sophisticated women.

"My goodness, isn't that Greg Dering?" she overheard a willowy blond ask her female companion as she entered the *Liberté*'s cocktail bar a few paces behind them.

"Dering, as in banks and steel?" her companion asked, a carefully plucked and delicately penciled eyebrow rising speculatively.

"Yes, but curb your hunting instincts, darling. I read in *Paris Match* that he married a French girl shortly after D-Day."

Her titian-haired companion, exquisite in a dress encrusted with bugles of jet, gave a low-throated laugh. "My God, a war bride! How will the Derings react to that?"

"She isn't quite a little matchgirl, darling. Her father is a comte. Isabelle Dering is so unorthodox that she'll probably find it all terribly romantic and be absolutely delighted."

"Jacqueline Pleydall won't be," the other said dryly. "She was all set to become Mrs. Greg Dering the minute he returned home."

The blonde laughed, her gaze on Greg who was standing at the bar, his thick brown hair curling crisply at the nape of his neck, his shoulders broad beneath the expensive cut of his white tuxedo. "Yes, there'll be no warm welcome from *that* source for the returning hero." She ran the tip of her tongue speculatively around glossy lips. "He really is a dish, isn't he? I think I could be very accomodating. Given the chance."

Aware of several male heads turning appreciatively in their direction, the two women strolled into the rococo and gilt cocktail lounge. Lisette paused on the threshold, a slight frown puckering her brows. A war bride. Was that how Greg's family and friends would regard her? And who was Jacqueline Pleydall? Greg had never mentioned her, and yet it was obvious that they had been engaged, or unofficially engaged, before he had left America to fight in Europe.

She was oddly disconcerted. It had never occurred to her to wonder about the personal life Greg had led before they had met. Yet, he was an accomplished lover. She should have realized that there would be a woman waiting hungrily for his return, a woman for whom news of his French marriage would come as a bitter shock and disappointment.

Greg lifted his head a fraction and across the crowded room their eyes met. A blaze of happiness shot through her. He loved her and he had married her. She flashed him a dazzling smile and began to ease her way through the crush toward him, happy for herself, but feeling intensely sorry for the unknown Miss Pleydall.

That night, as she lay in bed flicking through the glossy magazines that Greg had purchased before they sailed, she came across a three-page article on Berlin. Greg was in the shower carrying on a conversation with her over the noise of gushing water, asking her if she intended visiting the gymnasium with him in the morning. She didn't answer him. Berlin, the city Dieter had loved so much, lay wasted and devastated.

Photographs showed a civilian population queueing in tattered clothing for bread and potatoes, waiting at standpipes for driblets of brackish water. The once proud city had been divided by the Allies into four occupation zones. American soldiers, chewing gum, swaggered through the Tiergarten where, as a child, Dieter had walked hand in hand with his father. British soldiers lounged outside the battered facade of the Hotel Adlon where, long ago, he had drunk iced lemonade.

She closed the magazine, sick at heart. How Dieter would have hated the occupation of his city, how he would have loathed the sight of Allied soldiers strolling at ease through the streets. Her stomach muscles tightened. Was Dieter's mother one of the weary women queueing for food? Was she, too, one of the dispossessed and homeless? She remembered the photograph that had stood on Dieter's dresser in the turret room: the laughing woman with the flat of flowers at her feet, the woman who had lost her son and who would never know she had a grandson.

"We'll go in the morning, before breakfast," Greg said, striding out of the shower, toweling his hair vigorously. He stopped suddenly as he saw her white face. "What's the matter?" he asked, crossing the room toward her, his eyes dark with concern. "Don't you feel well?"

She shook her head, not trusting herself to speak.

"I'll call the ship's doctor," he said, stretching out his hand to the telephone.

"No! Please don't, Greg. It's only a headache. I'll be fine by tomorrow."

He looked down at her doubtfully and she forced a small smile. "Please, Greg. There's no need to worry."

"If you're sure. What about an aspirin? A brandy?"

She shook her head again, her heart hurting with pain and grief. "No, all I need is some sleep. Good night, Greg."

"Good night, sweetheart," he said gently.

She squeezed his hand, and when he slid into bed beside her, she lay against him, but she didn't sleep. Not for a long time.

A week later they passed the Statue of Liberty at sunrise. "Oh, isn't she magnificent?" Lisette exclaimed, her eyes shining with delight. "I'd never realized she was so enormous!"

They leaned against the deck rails, and Greg slid his arm around her waist, hugging her close as the *Liberté* glided into the welcoming waters of New York harbor.

"Will we stay in New York?" she asked as they cleared customs. "Will we be able to see the Empire State Building and Central Park?"

He laughed, delighted with her enthusiasm, delighted to have left a war-ravaged Europe far behind him, and delighted to be once more on American soil.

"We can stay here as long as you like, sweetheart. We can have our honeymoon here."

Her eyes were bright, her voice teasing. "I thought our honeymoon was the voyage over."

"Our honeymoon is never going to be over," he said, his eyes gleaming in such a way that the breath caught in her throat. "Let's book into the Plaza and I'll show you New York."

Her first shock was how few people spoke French. The concierge at the Plaza spoke a few carefully pronounced phrases, but the rest of the staff were able to do nothing more than courteously wish her good day and good evening.

"I thought everyone would speak a little French," she said, a note of alarm in her voice. "How shall I manage when you are not with me? My English accent is terrible."

"Your English accent is delightful," Greg said truthfully, kissing the top of her head. "Everyone will adore your accent. And you."

She had been doubtful, but in the following days discovered that he was right. Everyone she spoke to beamed at her immediately and listened with immense patience as she sought the right words with which to express herself.

She liked New York. It was big and brash compared to Paris, and utterly alien compared to the villages and market towns of Normandy, but there was an excitement about it that she responded to. Everywhere she went she was met with friendliness, and she was stunned when she discovered that the friendliness was not always what it seemed to be.

They had run into an old college friend of Greg's in one of the art galleries. When Greg had introduced her as his wife, the American had greeted her effusively, telling Greg that he was damned lucky. After a little while, Greg and he had begun to talk of people and places that she did not know, and she had excused herself in order to go to the powder room. It was when she was on her way back to them that she heard the American say, "She's a stunner, Greg, but you were taking a risk, weren't you? From what I've heard of Vichy France not all French girls were violently opposed to the krauts!"

She thought Greg was going to punch him in the jaw. His fist bunched, his face went white, and then he spat, his eyes blazing, "Never speak like that about my wife or her country again! You know nothing about the French! Nothing about what they endured! My God, when I think what Lisette suffered at their hands . . . her home overrun with them . . . burying with her bare hands a member of her family killed by them . . ."

His friend looked uncomfortable. "You didn't tell me that. But *Newsweek* has been running pictures of French girls who didn't suffer, who collaborated. Girls who have had their heads shaved publicly in the streets. There was a lot of it going on out there while we were risking our necks to liberate them. That's all I'm saying."

The tendons in Greg's throat bulged. "Don't say it again!" he snarled savagely. "Now get the hell out of here!"

His friend backed away from him hurriedly. "Okay, okay, don't get so heated about it. A hell of lot of Americans died saving Europe from the shit it got itself into. When I meet anyone from over there, I just like to be sure whose side they were on, that's all."

Greg's patience snapped. He took a step forward and his friend turned and fled.

Lisette couldn't move. She was shaking. The hideousness had erupted so suddenly, so unexpectedly, just as the hideousness in Bayeux had erupted the day she had given birth to Dominic.

Greg turned, saw the stricken expression on her face, and walked swiftly toward her. He held her tight against him. "Don't take any notice of that cretin's stupidity. He doesn't know a damn thing about what went on in Europe and he never will."

"It's all right . . . I understand."

But she didn't understand. She didn't understand what he had meant by saying so vehemently that she had buried a member of her family with her bare hands, a member of her family who had been killed by the Germans. The only person she had ever buried had been Dieter. Greg himself had given her permission to do so. She felt sick and dizzy, wanting to question him and not daring to, fearful where any such questioning would lead her.

"Let's get out of here and have lunch," Greg said, aware that the altercation had made them a center of attention. She nodded, forcing a smile, but the day had been spoiled. She knew how very nearly it could have been a picture of herself in *Newsweek*, and she knew with what horror and revulsion Greg would have regarded it.

Two weeks later they left Grand Central Station for the three-day train ride to San Francisco. Greg had looked at her a little anxiously as the train inched out of the station and began to hurtle through New York. Whenever she thought she was unobserved, he had seen a strange look creep into her violet eyes, almost a haunted look. He wondered if it was because she was sad to be leaving New York.

"We can come back here any time we please," he said reassuringly. "There's no need to look so sad about leaving."

"I'm not sad," she had said quickly, slipping her hand into his. "I'm quite sure I shall love San Francisco and Dominic will adore the sun and the sea."

"He's already adoring the train," Greg said with a grin as Dominic gurgled delightedly in his carrying cradle.

She smiled, but as she turned her head away from him and looked out of the window at the suburbs flashing by, her smile faded. She had spoken the truth when she had said to him that she wasn't sad. Sad was no adequate description for the growing inner turmoil she had felt ever since the unfortunate encounter in the art gallery. She felt guilty. She was hiding the most important part of her past life from Greg, deceiving him in a way she had never intended. Luke had been right when he had urged her to tell Greg the truth, but she hadn't done so, and now it was too late. She had allowed him to think that another man's son was his child, and she had no alternative but to live with the consequences of that decision.

217

They changed trains at Chicago and then thundered on, across the vast plains of America toward Denver and the Rocky Mountains.

"This is my part of America," Greg said exuberantly. "Do you like it, sweetheart?"

"It's beautiful," she said truthfully. It *was* beautiful—great, soaring mountains capped with snow. But she couldn't help feeling homesick for the lush meadows and high-hedged lanes, the scudding clouds and windswept headlands of Normandy.

The next morning they woke to find the Rockies far behind them. The land was now flat, the hills in the distance gentle.

"We're nearly there," Greg said, and she sensed his excitement. He was coming home. His parents would be waiting for him. His sister. She felt a flash of panic and tried hard to stifle it. They were Greg's family. Her family now. The azure blue of the Pacific Ocean gleamed dazzlingly, and subconsciously reaching for comfort, she gently lifted Dominic from his carrying cradle and held him close.

"Are you ready, my love?" Greg asked as they prepared to leave the train.

"Yes." It was a beautiful December day. The sun was shining, the air crisp. She wore a dove-gray suit, a peplum emphasizing the minuteness of her waist, a white silk shirt tied with a loose cravat at the neck. Her shoes were gray suede, high and open toed; her only jewelry, the magnificent ring he had bought her and a double rope of black pearls that had been her grandmother's. She looked magnificent. Slender and petite. Totally chic. Totally French.

"Stop worrying," he said, seeing the anxiety in her eyes. "They're going to love you."

His family's welcome was ecstatic. Any fears she had that they would be disapproving and unhappy about Greg's unexpected marriage were quickly dispelled.

"We're so pleased to meet you at last!" his mother cried, hugging her tight. "Welcome to San Francisco, Lisette! Welcome home!"

She was a tall, amply proportioned woman, her chin firm, her eyes bright. This marriage was not the marriage she had wanted or expected, but if this was the girl her son had fallen

218

in love with, then she had every intention of being loving to her and supportive.

The instant she saw Lisette, any doubts she had about Greg's wisdom in marrying a girl of a different nationality and culture, a girl he must have barely known, vanished. She was exquisite. There was a natural grace about her that went straight to Isabelle Dering's heart. Lisette responded immediately to the older woman's warmth and sincerity, and she felt suspiciously like crying as Isabelle at last released her and turned to embrace her six-foot-two-inch-tall son.

"Thank God you're home safe," Lisette heard her say huskily, then Greg's father was kissing her welcomingly on the cheek.

"Welcome to San Francisco, Lisette. It's a little different here from Normandy, I expect, but I hope you'll be very happy here."

He was powerfully built like his son. There were deep lines running from nose to mouth on his deeply tanned face. His hair was gray, still thick and with a touch of the same unruliness as Greg's. His eyes were kind, his handshake firm.

"I'm sure I will be," Lisette said, overcome by the warmth of her welcome.

"Hi, I'm Chrissie," the pretty girl at his side said impatiently. "I've never seen *anyone* look so stunning! I feel as overdressed as a Christmas tree! Will you show me how to do my hair like yours? I feel all frills and curls, and *totally* without style!"

Simonette stood a foot or so behind them, a curious-eyed Dominic in her arms. Almost at the same moment, the Dering family became aware of him. Isabelle Dering drew away from her son, her eyes widening. Gregory Dering's brows were slightly raised as he waited for an explanation. Chrissie, aware that something momentous had caught her parents' attention, swung away from Lisette and on seeing Dominic her mouth rounded in a gasp of incredulity.

Greg grinned. "There's another introduction still to be made," he said, stepping toward Simonette and gently lifting Dominic from her arms. "Mom, Dad, meet your grandson, Dominic."

For a second no one moved, and then Isabelle Dering said weakly, "Oh, my goodness! I'd no idea. Isn't he *gorgeous!*"

She stepped forward. "Let me hold him! Why didn't you *tell* us, Greg?"

"I didn't want to load too many shocks onto you all at the same time," Greg said, his dark, rich-timbred voice amused. "Besides, I didn't know myself till a few months ago. He was born in February while I was fighting in Germany."

Isabelle Dering had taken hold of Dominic and was looking down at him, her face radiant. "He's beautiful, Greg! Absolutely beautiful! I can't believe it! Here I am, holding my first grandson in my arms!" She turned to Lisette, her eyes shining with tears of happiness. "Thank you, my dear. This is the nicest surprise anyone has ever given me."

Greg had slipped his arm around Lisette, and she knew that she dare not tremble, dare not give way to the emotions flooding through her. God in heaven, why hadn't she foreseen all this? Realized what his parents' reaction would be? She wasn't only deceiving Greg, she was deceiving his whole family! The enormity of what she had done nearly swamped her. She could not allow Isabelle Dering to continue believing Dominic was her flesh and blood. It was too monstrous a crime to perpetrate. Too obscene.

She knew that the blood had left her face, that she had to speak. To put an end to the fiasco she had plunged them all into. "There is something I have to tell you . . . ," she began unsteadily, her face white, her nails digging into her palms.

Greg's arm slipped around her shoulders. "The baby was six to seven weeks premature," he said easily. "I told her not to worry . . . that there would be no misunderstanding about that here." He flashed her a down-slanting smile, his arm tightening reassuringly around her. "We're accustomed to premature babies in this family, sweetheart. Look at Chrissie! Born at seven and a half months and given only a few hours to live. No one who was around when she was born would have thought she'd grow up into a lady basketball player!"

Chrissie threw him a playful punch on the chest. "Enough of the insults, big brother. Can I hold the baby? I can't believe it! I'm an auntie. What do aunties do? Can I take him for walks? Change his diapers?"

They were all laughing. Only Gregory Dering's eyes were speculative. The marriage had been in July, and the baby had been born in February. It wasn't a case of the baby being conceived before they were married, it was a case of the baby being conceived even before Greg had landed in France. No wonder the girl had looked so distressed. He gave her a swift look and relaxed, trusting the judgment that had made him a self-made millionaire. His new daughter-in-law wasn't a trollop. He'd stake his life on it. If they said the baby was premature, then they were speaking the truth.

"Let's get along home," he said, "A train station is no place for a family reunion."

"No . . . please. Just a minute . . ." She felt as though she were falling, as though the ground were dissolving beneath her feet.

"It's okay, honey," Greg said, his arm tightening around her shoulder. "They understand. There's nothing more to be said. Let's go home."

For one fevered moment she wondered if he knew, if he had known all along.

"No," she gasped as his father began to lead the way toward their waiting limousine. "They don't understand! You don't understand. Please listen to me, Greg!"

"Later," he said, the tone of his voice brooking no argument. "You're tired and overwrought. We can do all the talking in the world, later." He ushered her into the limousine, slammed the door behind her, and strode around to the other side.

She felt sick and dizzy. Chrissie was sitting beside her asking questions about Paris, about fashions—marveling at the magnificent pearls she wore. She tried to answer her, to collect her scattered wits, but her mind was whirling. *Did* Greg understand, or had he again misunderstood her, as he misunderstood when she had talked of Dieter and he had thought she was talking of Luke Brandon? She pressed a hand to her throbbing temples. If he knew, it was obvious that he wanted no one else to know, that he didn't want it spoken of.

Isabelle Dering was sitting in front of them, Dominic still in her arms. "His hair is beginning to curl just like yours," she said, turning her head around to speak to Greg.

"He's got my nose and mouth as well," Greg said, and at the pride in his voice Lisette knew with despair that she had been wrong. He had suspected nothing. His only concern was

221

that she did not distress herself over what he believed was his son's prematurity.

"The train station is in a pretty ugly part of town," he was saying to her. "It's not all like this. In a few minutes you'll see how beautiful 'Frisco really is."

"I've never been so happy in my life," Isabelle Dering said ecstatically. "My son home—safe and sound—a wonderful new daughter-in-law, and a grandson I'd only dreamed about. God is being very, *very* good to me."

Lisette felt as if she were shrivelling up and dying. The moment was over. Gone. To speak would be to destroy not only Greg's happiness but Isabelle Dering's as well. The burden of her guilt would just have to be borne.

"We're coming into the heart of the town now," Greg said enthusiastically. "There's the Golden Gate Bridge. Have you ever seen anything so lovely?"

"No," she said, forcing a smile, touched by his obvious love for the city that was his home.

The bay lay on their right, shining and still, dotted with boats and rimmed with hills. All around them were steep hillsides, the houses built on them looking like something out of a child's picture book. There was no uniformity of style, nothing remotely resembling the high, slate-roofed houses of Sainte-Marie-des-Ponts. Most of the houses were pastel colored: pale pink and blue, lavender and green, their gardens a riot of color.

"It's lovely, Greg," she said truthfully. "Like something out of a fairy tale."

"Wait till you see the house," Chrissie said, pleased that her beautiful French sister-in-law was impressed by their city. "Mom has supervised every detail of the decor for you. She says you can alter things around as much as you like, but she wanted it to look and feel like home for when you arrived."

Lisette looked from her sister-in-law to her husband not quite understanding. Greg squeezed her hand. "The bachelor apartment I lived in before I left for Europe wouldn't have been big enough for us. I asked Mom to arrange somewhere for us to come home to."

"You mean our own house?" she asked, her eyes widening. She had thought that they would be staying with his parents.

"That's exactly what I mean," he said.

"If you don't like the way I've had everything done, just call in the decorators and have them do whatever you want. There'll be no hurt feelings," Isabelle Dering said with a wide smile.

They sped up a steep hillside through swaths of trees, turned sharply to the right between high wrought iron gates, and drew up outside a large Spanish-style house. Lisette gasped. It was like being on top of a mountain: the bay and the town lay spread out before them, the Golden Gate Bridge glittering in the brilliant sunlight.

"Well, here we are," Isabelle said, stepping from the chauffeur-driven limousine, Dominic still held tightly in her arms. "I hope you like it, Lisette. Chrissie and I just loved getting it ready for you."

All the rooms looked out over the bay and the hills. The Mexican tiles in the kitchen were burnt orange and white, with exotic plants hanging from hooks in the rich wood ceiling. The living room was ivory-white, the sofas deep and comfortable, the low tables massed with flowers.

The dining room was formal, the drapes a vibrant blue against the wood-lined walls, the elegant dining table and chairs early 19th-century mahogany. There were six bedrooms, six bathrooms. The sheets were trimmed lavishly with handmade lace, the towels monogrammed. There were books in both French and English on the shelves, bowls of sweet-smelling potpourri, Redouté watercolors on the walls. It had been furnished with love and care, and Lisette felt her throat tighten as she turned toward her mother-in-law.

"It's beautiful," she said, her eyes shining. "Thank you so much."

Isabelle squeezed her hand. "It's my pleasure, my dear. I am not, though, going to allow you to enjoy it for too long today. A celebration lunch is waiting for us at Ocean View. From now on, Lisette, you have *two* homes: this one, and the family one at Pacific Heights."

Ocean View, the Dering family home, was palatial. They ate lunch in a dining room that would have done credit to Versailles. In the evening friends and other members of the family—aunts and uncles and cousins—came to dinner to meet her. It had been a long day, and by the time dinner was over, she was physically tired and emotionally drained.

So much had happened in so short a time. She was grateful for the interlude in Paris. A swift transition from war-torn Normandy to the glossy splendor of Pacific Heights would have disoriented her completely. Even now, she found it strange. It was as if the war had not touched the people sitting around the dinner table. There was no sign of suffering, none at all of hardship. She felt very alien from them all. She didn't come from their world, and she knew they would not be able to understand the world she came from: the world of cycle rides across country with messages for Resistance leaders; the ever-present fear of arrest or torture; the horror of finding herself in love with an enemy of her country; the listening in secret to the radio broadcasts from Great Britain; the desperate, daily longing for liberation. She was half a world away from home, and the happy, gregarious Americans seemed suddenly like creatures from another planet. With a stab of shock, she realized that she had had far more in common with Dieter, even though he had been a German, than she had with these people. She and Dieter had both been Europeans. He had understood her culture, her history. She was suddenly overcome by longing for him. His face burned at the backs of her eyes—strong and hard boned—his shock of wheat-gold hair cropped short, his black-lashed gray eyes fierce with love for her.

"Tired, darling?" Greg asked, smiling down at her.

She nodded. She hadn't felt so tired since the early days of her pregnancy. Her eyes widened. It was perfectly possible for her to be pregnant. Neither she nor Greg had taken any precautions to prevent a baby being conceived. If she gave Greg a baby that *was* his, surely her guilt would be eased? She felt suddenly light-headed and full of hope.

"Let's go home, Greg," she whispered softly, her hand sliding into his. "Let's make love."

16

The spasm of alienation she had felt at the celebration dinner faded. Greg's family and friends were enchanted with her, going to enormous lengths to make her feel at home. There were trips to Lake Tahoe, to the Yosemite National Park, to Monterey. Greg loved America, and he was eager that Lisette, too, should be in love with it.

Whenever he thought of Europe, he had to suppress a shudder. The scenes of poverty, of suffering that he had seen there still haunted him: the mile after mile of weary refugees, their worldly possessions in bundles on their backs; the bomb-blasted ruins of Caen and Cherbourg; the smoke-blackened walls of Valmy. He thanked God he had been able to take Lisette away from it all. He loved her deeply, and though he knew she hadn't been in love with him when they had married, he was certain that she was in love with him now.

She had retained the Frenchness that so delighted him— the grace and femininity, the effortless chic. He was intensely proud of her. His personal life was good. His professional life was good. He was damned lucky, and he knew it.

He had founded Dering Advertising before the war, helped by family wealth and his own considerable talent. It had been flourishing nicely and was grossing over a million dollars a year when the Japanese bombed Pearl Harbor. While he had been serving with the army, the agency had been placed in the capable hands of a subordinate, but no exciting new accounts had come its way. Greg had returned to find the business in the doldrums, but he was unperturbed. He knew the postwar world was ready and waiting for a dynamic new approach to advertising, and within months of his return, he was supplying it with zest.

He had been amused to discover that Luke Brandon had carved himself a niche with one of the largest London advertising agencies. When Greg had pitched for Chemico, an international account that would lift Dering Advertising from the small time into the big time, the account director of the London agency also chasing the account had been Luke.

"Did you know Luke had opted for advertising as a profession?" Greg asked Lisette one day as they sat with drinks by the pool.

A slight flush touched the delicate line of her cheeks. "Yes. I thought I'd told you."

Greg felt a twinge of unease and quelled it almost immediately. Brandon wrote to Lisette regularly, and she either showed him the letters when they arrived or left them lying casually on her desk. But there had been at least one letter that he knew she had not mentioned to him, one letter that had not been left lying around quite so carelessly.

"He spent a couple of months with a publishing company right after his discharge," she said, her voice betraying none of the inner emotion that had suddenly flared up inside her. "Then Thomson's offered him a job and he leaped at it." A smile touched her mouth. "He said publishing was a gentleman's profession and as such he didn't feel cut out for it."

Greg grinned. "It may have been once," he said dryly, "I doubt that it will stay so much longer. The postwar world is going to be far different from the prewar world."

Her smile deepened but did not touch her eyes. She turned her head away from him, staring out over the still, turquoise-blue water of the pool. Luke had told her about his switch of profession in the same letter that he'd asked her if she was happy with Greg. If she wasn't, he had told her to join him immediately in London. He still loved her, he wrote. He still felt that fate had brought them together and had meant them to stay together. He had asked about Dominic, and he had pointed out that in deceiving Greg, she would also have to deceive her son. He would never be able to know who his real father was. She would never, ever, be able to talk to him about Dieter Meyer.

She had destroyed the letter immediately, her hands trembling. The thought of not being able to tell Dominic about his father was a prospect that was already tormenting her. But there was nothing she could do about it. She was trapped by her own deceit, and every day the burden of that deceit grew, slowly crippling her.

She died a little every time Greg proudly introduced Dominic as his son, every time Isabelle said what deep happiness having a grandson gave her. But she didn't tell Luke of her growing distress. She wrote him a terse letter in which she told him never to ask her to leave Greg again . . . that she was happy . . . that she hoped soon to be expecting another baby . . . that her home was with Greg and always would be.

A month later she had received an equally terse note in reply. He was marrying. Her name was Annabel Lacey. He had known her before the war and had been dating her regularly since his return. He wasn't in love with her, but she was in love with him. She came from a wealthy background and had money of her own. It was, he had written savagely, a marriage very similar to her own. She destroyed that letter, too.

"His wife looks very pretty in the wedding photographs," Greg was saying, and Lisette dragged her gaze away from the pool, forcing a smile.

"Yes, she does. They were married at St. Margaret's, Westminster. I believe it's terribly grand there. It seems strange to see Luke in a morning suit and not in uniform."

Her fair fell softly to her shoulders as it had done when Greg had first met her. She looked very young, frighteningly fragile, and he reminded himself that she was still only nineteen years old. His unease deepened. She said she was happy. She said she loved him. But how could he be sure when sometimes, when she thought herself unobserved, her eyes clouded and her delicately winged brows drew together as if she were deeply troubled. Was it because of Luke Brandon? Was it the mention of Brandon's marriage that had so disturbed her a minute ago?

He remembered Brandon telling him that he was going to marry Lisette. He remembered also the naked suffering in Lisette's voice when she told him that the man she had loved had died and that she did not know how to begin to learn to love someone else. Later, after their marriage, she had told him that she had never been in love with Luke, but there were times when he was not so sure. She had certainly believed herself to be in love with him once. Perhaps her denials later had simply been for his benefit. After all, she was married to him by then. There could have been no going back to what might have been.

"You haven't forgotten we're going to a cocktail party at the Warners' at seven o'clock, have you?" he asked, wishing to God he could lay the ghost of his ever-recurring doubt.

"No." She glanced at the slim gold watch on her wrist. "I'd better go in and shower and change now."

He put down his drink and rose. His white silk shirt was open at the throat, his jeans hugged his hips tightly. "We'll both go in," he said, drawing her toward him. "There's time for a little more than a shower and a change of clothes."

Their lovemaking was a constant delight to him. He loved every inch of her body: the graceful curve of her neck, the creamy-smooth perfection of her breasts, the hand-span narrowness of her waist—even the long scar on her inner thigh did nothing to detract from her beauty. He had traced it gently with his finger the first time he had seen it, and she had stiffened, as if freezing inside. Sensing her distress, he told her that it wasn't unsightly, a mere sliver line on her flesh, but he knew she didn't believe him. The scar distressed her, and he had learned to say and do nothing that drew attention to it.

Thirty minutes later, in the cool dimness of their bedroom, she reluctantly slipped free of his embrace and rose from the bed, her body flushed from lovemaking.

"We're going to be late, darling. It's six-thirty already."

He raised himself up on one elbow, looking at her naked body appreciatively. "It was worth it," he said with a grin, tousled curls tumbling low over his forehead.

At the expression in his eyes, her heart somersaulted. She had thought she would never love anyone else as she had loved Dieter, and yet slowly, surely, she had begun to do so. And she realized with a shock that it was a much deeper love than the desperate passion she had shared with Dieter. She had never lived as Dieter's wife, never shared each day with him as she did with Greg. Dieter had taught her how to love. It had been his gift to her, and because of it, both she and Greg were his debtors.

She stepped into the shower, wishing for the thousandth

time that she felt free to tell Greg about Dieter—tell him how brave a man he had been; how fearlessly he had schemed to remove Hitler from power; how much, if he had met him, he would have liked him.

She dusted herself with talcum powder and sprayed herself with cologne. She mustn't think about it. She must think only of the things that were possible—loving Greg, making him proud of her. She zipped herself into an ice-blue dress that danced softly over her skin, slipped on ivory-kid pumps, and swept her hair high, piercing the neat twist she created with long, jeweled pins.

"You look sensational," Greg said admiringly, and a flare of happiness burst within her. She would think no more of Luke's letter to her. The past was the past, and she would not allow it to darken the joy of the present. Twenty minutes later her good intentions were shot down in flames.

"Nice to see you two," Frank Warner said welcomingly as he greeted them at the door of his colonial-styled mansion. "Come inside. You're just the people I want to help me with a discussion I'm having with Brad Dennington. He says that the war trials at Nuremberg are an unnecessary piece of exhibitionism. What do you think?"

"I think he's a fool," Greg said harshly, his face tight, a nerve jumping violently at the corner of his jaw. "It should be the entire German nation on trial, not just twenty-one hand-picked specimens."

"I'm not with you there," Frank Warner said, fixing them drinks. "You can't make a nation responsible for the crimes of a few. It isn't rational. I have a friend who is German by birth . . . lived in Los Angeles ever since he was a kid. You're saying he's as guilty as the animals in the SS simply because he's a German. He isn't. He's charming and cultivated and—"

"Bullshit!" Greg snapped with such savagery that his host instinctively took a quick step backward. "You don't know what you're talking about, Frank. I do. I was there. And what I saw you would never believe. The whole race is mentally sick. They have to be to have allowed the obscenities of Auschwitz and Dachau. Don't talk to me of charming, cultured Germans because there aren't any!"

Frank laughed awkwardly. He'd had no idea that Greg felt

so deeply, and he had certainly no desire to have his party founder on the rocks of German war crimes.

"Forget it," he said, clapping his hand on Greg's shoulder. "Let me introduce you to a friend of mine from New York. His company is thinking of changing its advertising agency. You may be able to help him out."

Greg took a deep, steadying breath, reaching down for Lisette's hand as Frank led the way across the crowded room to a large, white-haired gentleman smoking a cigar.

Lisette didn't hear one word of the following conversation. She felt sick, so cold inside that she doubted she would ever be warm again. Greg's revulsion against Germans was bone deep. The sights he had seen at Dachau had scarred him for life. In Greg's eyes all Germans were Nazis. There were no exceptions. They were all to be abhorred and shunned. The past that she had tried so hard to forget couldn't be forgiven. It was an impossibility.

". . . and he really is the most fantastic photographer," Dinah Warner was saying vivaciously to her. "His photographs of young children are incredible. I'm sure he'd take the most stunning shots of Dominic . . ."

Dominic. Half French, half German. Dominic. The child Greg believed to be his son. The child who was the image of his German father.

"Are you all right?" Dinah Warner was saying anxiously. "You look deathly. I think you'd better sit down for a minute. I'll go and get Greg."

She saw Dinah interrupt his conversation with the New York businessman. She saw Greg's swift frown of concern, saw him excuse himself and begin to thread his way through the crush toward her. She saw the female eyes that turned in his direction, saw the speculation, the heat, that his powerfully built, slim-hipped body aroused. There was an air of negligent sexuality about him that was infinitely disturbing, a masculinity that was palpable.

"Tired, sweetheart?" he asked, his brandy-dark eyes filled with concern.

She nodded, confounded by desire for him, rigid with guilt and shame.

That night, for the first time, she had to feign her response when he made love to her. She wanted him with every nerve of her body, but she was sexually crippled by the enormity of her deceit. It was as if her body were punishing her for her crime. She was frozen with guilt. Frigid with it.

She lay awake in his arms for hour after hour, tears burning the backs of her eyes, praying that she would become pregnant, and be able to give him a child that was truly his. A child would free her of the self-inflicted nightmare she had plunged into.

He was delighted when two months later, she told him she was expecting another baby.

"It will be a Christmas baby," she said, her eyes shining. "Won't it be the most marvelous present in the world?"

He held her tightly against him, his hands sliding up into her hair, his kiss her answer. It was a long time before he released her. When he did, he said, with a slight frown, "What about our trip? I promised you we'd spend the New Year of '47 in France."

He saw longing touch her eyes, and then she gave a Gallic shrug. "I don't mind about the trip. I just want to have this baby and make you happy."

"You don't need to have another baby to make me happy," he said, his white teeth flashing in a grin of amusement. "And I see no reason why we should cancel our plans. We'll have this baby *and* we'll go to France. Are Luke and Annabel still going to be spending the New Year at Valmy?"

She nodded, glad that she no longer felt constraint at the mention of Luke's name. "Yes. Papa is eager to show off the restoration work. Luke was over for a visit a few months ago and apparently told him that he thought it would be another five years before Valmy was habitable once more. Papa wants to prove to him how wrong he was."

"It will be quite a reunion," Greg said, slipping his arms around her waist, feeling desire for her grow and harden. "All three of us back at Valmy again. Just like it was in May '44."

She turned her head away from him quickly, but not before he saw a flare of emotion he did not understand flash across her face. What was it? Pain? Anguish? Was she still entertaining regret for having married him so hastily when she believed Luke to be dead?

"Let's go to bed," he said, sliding his hands up to her breasts. His doubts and jealousy about her feelings for Luke

231

had been dormant for months now. He wasn't going to let one fleeting moment of doubt resurrect them.

She stilled her inner trembling and turned to him, slipping her arms around his neck. For a second, the image of Dieter had been so strong that it had taken her breath away: Dieter in the first week of that now long ago May; racing into the château after his mad dash to Paris; taking her in his arms and telling her that he loved her, that he would always love her, before sprinting from Valmy to face the approaching invasion fleet; Dieter, dying in her arms, his lifeblood sticky on her hands, staining Valmy's ancient cobblestones a dark, hideous crimson.

Gently Greg pulled the pins from her hair, unbuttoned her blouse, and eased her down on the bed. She tried to close her mind to her memories, to respond lovingly to him, but the guilt that had frozen her after the Warners' party still lingered. She couldn't overcome it. She loved him and she needed him, but she could no longer respond to him. And he knew it.

"What's the matter?" he asked urgently, his brows flying together as he stared down at her. "Is it me? Don't you love me, Lisette?"

"Oh, yes," she gasped, wrapping her arms around him tightly, pressing her cheek against his shoulder, her tears scalding his flesh. "I *do* love you, Greg! It's just . . ." She floundered helplessly. The only words that made any sense were the truth: she was frozen with guilt, and to tell him the truth would be to lose him. "It's just that I'm tired . . . ," she said, hating herself for the feebleness of her lie. "It's probably the baby." She hugged him tighter. "I'll be all right in a few months' time, I promise I will."

It was at a party the week before they were due to leave for Europe on the *Normandie* that she met Jacqueline Pleydall. She had not really wanted to go to the party. She was much bigger and far more uncomfortable with this second baby than she had been with Dominic.

"You look fabulous," Greg had said to her, passing his hand caressingly across the full ripeness of her stomach as she faced herself in the mirror, bemoaning her size.

"The only thing I can possibly wear is a tent!"

"Then wear the raspberry tent you wore to Chrissie's birthday dinner," he said in amusement. "You looked stunning in it."

She made a little moue, unconvinced, and he laughed. She was as beautiful, heavy with child, as she had been when svelte. If it hadn't been for the difference the baby had made in their sex life, he would have been quite content for her to have been permanently pregnant. But the baby *had* made a difference. Her tiredness had not abated. He had been forced to the reluctant conclusion that not until the baby was born would things be back to normal between them.

"Once the baby is here, everything will be all right," she had reassured him fiercely. "I know it will be!"

He had told her not to worry, and he had kept a tight rein on his physical desire for her. He had not been at her side throughout her pregnancy with Dominic, and this curtailment of the sexual side of their marriage had taken him by surprise. He would be glad when her pregnancy was over, when the deeply sexual side of her nature once more left him in no doubt as to the depth of her love for him.

The raspberry chiffon dress made her feel graceful and almost slender again. She looped a rope of pearls around her throat, put pearl and diamond studs in her ears, and sprayed herself with perfume.

He dropped a kiss on the nape of her neck. "Ready?" he asked, and she saw the heat at the back of his eyes and knew she had only to reach out and touch him, to say one word of encouragement, and the party would be forgotten.

"Yes," she said, turning away from him, hurting with her own need. How she ached for him, yearned for him. Yet she dare not reach out for fear of the failure, the frigidity, that would surely follow.

Her hand trembled as she picked up her evening purse. In another two months her torment would end. The child she gave Greg would be his. She would be free of her burden of guilt.

She had become accustomed to meeting the same, small, wealthy circle of people at every party and function they attended. In some ways San Francisco was as parochial as Sainte-Marie-des-Ponts. As they were waiting to greet their host and hostess, she became aware of a tall, willowy blond she hadn't seen before.

"Who is the girl over by the window?" she asked Greg curiously. "The one wearing a black dress that looks as if it's a Balenciaga."

233

Greg glanced across the room, and as he did so the woman's gaze met his. Lisette sensed Greg tense, saw the girl turn away from him quickly, a flush of color warming her cheeks.

"Jacqueline Pleydall," he said with unusual terseness. "She's been in New York for the past year. She's a fashion buyer for *Vogue.*"

Lisette felt a stab of shock. Her gaze flew once more in the blonde's direction, but her back was now firmly to them, and she was talking to Frank Warner.

"Were you once engaged to her?" she asked, oddly disconcerted.

"No." His brows flew together. "Whatever gave you that idea?"

"Oh . . . I thought . . . I overheard it somewhere . . ."

"People assume," he said, and there was a tight look around his mouth that she had never seen before. "We were very close once. But we were never engaged."

Lisette dragged her attention away from Jacqueline Pleydall long enough to greet her host and hostess, but as they began to circulate, she found her attention returning again and again to the sleek, golden-haired young woman who had apparently thought that one day she would be Mrs. Greg Dering. Jacqueline was extraordinarily beautiful. Her hair was shoulder length, falling seductively at either side of her face in deep, undulating waves. Her face was fashionably made up: her eyebrows arched, her mouth a glossy red. She looked very American, very self-assured. And yet she had flushed like a schoolgirl when she and Greg had looked at each other. She didn't move from her position at the window, and Greg showed no hurry to make his way across to her, but Lisette knew that the woman was acutely aware of Greg's presence and was hungrily curious about the woman who had won Greg. Lisette fervently wished she had asked him about Jacqueline when she had first heard the gossip aboard the *Liberté*. She should have given him the opportunity then to tell her exactly what his relationship to the woman had been.

"And so they see it as a form of economic imperialism," Frank Warner was saying to her.

Lisette gave an apologetic smile. "I'm sorry, Frank. I wasn't listening. Who sees what as economic imperialism?"

Greg was talking to their host. Jacqueline Pleydall, now that Frank was no longer monopolizing her, was moving easily from group to group, drawing nearer and nearer to him.

"Stalin," Frank said as their champagne glasses were replenished. "He thinks the Marshall Plan for financially propping up war-devastated Europe, Germany included, is devious. He doesn't see it for what it is—a genuine attempt by America to get Europe back on its feet."

Lisette's fingers tightened fractionally around the stem of her glass. She loathed talking about Europe with Greg's friends. They discussed the war and its aftermath so glibly, and they had so little real understanding. German jackboots had not marched through San Franciscan streets. Their museums and art galleries had not been looted of their treasures. The Presidio had not been requisitioned by the German High Command. They thought they knew what Europe had suffered, but they didn't. Only the Americans who had been there and who had fought had any understanding, and even for them it hadn't been the same as it had for the British and French and Russian soldiers and civilians who had seen their lands ravaged, their cities bombed to rubble.

". . . so the Russians see the aid, even the tractors and trucks we are giving, as being politically and militarily motivated . . ."

Greg had turned his head in Jacqueline Pleydall's direction. She was smiling at him, an uncertain, almost nervous smile.

"I must say I'm not sure myself why the aid has to extend to the Germans," Frank continued, helping himself to a lobster *vol-au-vent*. "After all, they were the cause of all the damage, weren't they?"

Lisette tuned him out. Greg had moved away from the circle of people he had been talking to and was now standing with Jacqueline Pleydall. He looked completely at ease, and though she was gazing at him with rapt attention, his own attention seemed to be diverted. He kept glancing away from her, as if searching for someone.

Lisette sighed. Greg was looking for her. The sudden

tightening around her heart vanished. She laid a hand on Frank's tuxedoed arm. "I'm sorry, Frank. Will you excuse me for a moment?" and without waiting for an answer, she slipped away from him and crossed the room to her husband.

"Hello darling, I thought you were lost," he said with a grin, his arm sliding surely and securely around her waist. "I don't think you have met Jacqueline, have you? Jacqueline, Lisette. Lisette, Miss Jacqueline Pleydall."

"I'm very pleased to meet you," Lisette said, feeling large and bulky and very, very pregnant.

"And I you," Jacqueline said, but the flush had returned to her cheeks, and as her eyes met Greg's, Lisette saw undisguised misery in their depths.

"It's been a long time, Greg," she said unsteadily as if Lisette had not joined them. "Five years. Frank tells me that Germany was pretty hideous for you."

"For me and hundreds of thousands of others," Greg agreed dryly.

"I would have liked to have seen you, been able to talk about it . . ."

Greg's arm tightened around Lisette's waist. "We're leaving for Europe in a few days' time, but when we return, you must have dinner with us. Lisette's cooking is becoming the talk of 'Frisco."

Jacqueline bit her bottom lip, and Lisette felt suddenly very sorry for her. Dinner *à trois* was obviously not what she had wanted. She wanted Greg, and he had married someone else.

"Will you excuse us, Jacqueline," Greg was saying with smooth politeness. "We have a lot of people we want to say good-bye to before we leave for France."

"Yes, of course." Her eyes were suspiciously bright. "Have a nice trip, Greg."

Lisette knew that Jacqueline watched intently as they crossed the room to speak to the Warners. She wondered what kind of a letter Greg had written from France telling her of his marriage. Had he written before they were married or after?

"Let's go home," he whispered to her, his hand hot around her waist. "I've had enough socializing for one evening. I want you to myself."

She leaned against him, overcome by desire. Perhaps

tonight it would be different. Perhaps tonight she could forget her guilt. Perhaps it could once more be as glorious between them as it had been in Paris.

In the darkness of the speeding limousine, she put her hand on his. "Were you very much in love with her?" she asked, hoping passionately that the answer would be no.

He had no need to ask to whom she was referring. He flicked the wheel to the right with an easy movement of his hand, speeding up into Pacific Heights.

"I thought I was," he said, taking his eyes briefly from the road ahead and smiling down at her, "until I met you."

She breathed a sigh of relief. "I think," she said, leaning her head on his shoulder, "that she is still very much in love with you, Greg."

"And I," he said, his voice catching and deepening, "am very much in love with you, Mrs. Dering."

They sped up the last spur of the hill, sweeping into the drive of their home. She knew she wouldn't speak of Jacqueline Pleydall again, but she wouldn't forget her. If she continued to fail Greg in the privacy of their bedroom, she knew Jacqueline would be waiting, willing to offer him any comfort he might desire.

Lisette was ecstatic with joy as their ship neared Le Havre.

"Here we are again, back to the rain and the wind," Greg said wryly as the mist rolled back from the approaching cliffs and France loomed ahead of them.

"Oh, but it's beautiful!" Lisette said rapturously, turning her face up to the rain, drinking in the sight of the gray, storm-tossed clouds, the rain-washed light.

Greg shot her a quick, surprised glance. In the year they had been in America, she had never given any indication that she might be homesick. He had assumed she had been as delighted to leave war-torn France as he had been. In his eyes, Normandy was insufferably cold and gray. He found the thickly hedged fields and narrow winding lanes claustrophobic, the high, slate-roofed houses dour. It had not occurred to him that she felt differently, and he realized, with a stab of shock, how insensitive he had been.

"Look," she cried as they neared the coast. "Salt marshes,

Greg! Sand dunes! Oh, is that Sainte-Marie's church spire? And is that Valmy, Greg? Oh, it is! I'm sure it is!"

Henri de Valmy was waiting to greet them on the dockside. "Welcome home, *ma chère*," he said, hugging her close. "Welcome back to France!"

"It's so good to be home, Papa!" She turned swiftly round to where Simonette was standing, a warmly wrapped Dominic in her arms. Joyously she took him from her. "This is France, Dominic! You must take your first footsteps on French soil!"

Dominic, who had already taken many faltering ones on board the *Normandie*, laughed delightedly.

"Walk, Maman," he said, his eyes shining. "Walk!"

"It's so good to have you home," her father was saying, his eyes bright with unshed tears. "Your mother is waiting for us at Valmy. She hasn't been very well lately. She cannot seem to shake a cold she got some time ago."

"Is she staying at Valmy long?" Greg asked as they walked to the waiting Citroën.

"For the Christmas celebrations and New Year. Valmy is now remarkably comfortable. Reconstruction work has been going on nonstop since April. The left wing is completely livable, though the main rooms—the grand dining room, and the salon—are going to take much longer to restore."

"Have Luke and Annabel arrived, Papa?" Lisette asked as they all squeezed into the Citroën.

"Two days ago. His wife is a very nice girl. They came over to visit me shortly after their marriage. I think he would live here if he could. Normandy seems to have seeped into his blood."

Greg asked him how long he thought the reconstruction work would take before it was complete, what he thought of Churchill's view of an iron curtain having descended across Europe, if de Gaulle's popularity was still strong. But as the Citroën roared along the familiar country roads and lanes, Lisette fell silent. She had been away for little more than a year, and now she was back again and nothing had changed. The landscape was still at the mercy of the sea. The trees along the coast still leaned landward, leafless and bent beneath the force of the gales that blew in from the west. The waves still hurled themselves unceasingly at the foot of the cliffs. And Valmy still stood, its golden walls scarred, blackened by smoke, but still wonderful, still superbly magnificent.

They sped past the gatehouse, and she averted her head swiftly. The cherry tree would be bare. Dieter's grave would be stark. She dare not allow herself to think of it with Greg so close beside her, so aware of every shift in her emotions. She would visit it in the morning. Alone. She would plant spring bulbs and take a bouquet of winter aconite. She saw her father's gaze fly to hers in the rearview mirror. She saw all his unspoken questions about herself and Greg—about Dominic, about the coming baby. She smiled at him and saw him visibly relax. She would not burden him with her unhappiness during the past months. It was nearly at an end now. The baby would be born while they were in France. No one would ever know the price she had paid for her deceit.

The ancient Citroën rattled past the last of the linden trees rounding the huge circle of grass that fronted the château. The winter sun sparkled on the tall, narrow windows. The slate-roofed turret pierced the sky line. The great oak door opened, and her mother ran out from the hall toward the still-moving car, Luke and a tall, fair-haired girl walking swiftly in her wake.

"Welcome home, *chérie!*" her mother cried, and before the Citroën had even shuddered to a halt, a heavily pregnant Lisette had flung open the car door and was running, hurtling into her mother's outstretched arms.

17

It was so good to be home that Lisette wept for joy. Valmy's walls enfolded her. The château's gutted heart had been lovingly rebuilt. The grand dining room and the main salon had yet to be completed, but Valmy still stood, was lived in again.

"It's wonderful, Papa!" she said, gazing round at the new

plasterwork, the new woodwork. "I can't believe so much has been done in only a year!"

"I had nothing else to do with my time but harass the workmen, *ma chère*," Henri said, his pleasure at her approval obvious.

Luke leaned against one of the newly plastered walls and watched her. Her greeting had been warm and spontaneous and completely asexual. She had hugged him tight. Hugged Annabel. And he had had to clench his hands into fists to prevent himself from seizing hold of her and taking her where she stood. God, but she was beautiful. He had forgotten how much. He had forgotten how unknowingly provocative she was, how innocently sensual.

Gone were the heavy stockings and sturdy shoes that he remembered, the serviceable wool sweaters and tweed skirts. In their place were gossamer sheer stockings and exquisite gray suede shoes and a dress of pale mauve that fell softly from her shoulders, the skirt rustling caressingly against her legs as she walked. Her hair no longer tumbled freely down her back. It was caught up in a glossy chignon, and he wanted to hold her against him—to pull the pins from her hair and to watch as it cascaded down over her shoulders, her breasts; to wind his fingers in it; bury his face in it.

"Papa says that you never believed Valmy would be habitable by Christmas," she was saying to him, her voice warm with affection.

They were all in the room that had been her father's study and was now a living room. The chairs and deep cushioned sofas were covered in rose-pink chintz. A log fire was burning pungently in the grate. Henri de Valmy was pouring a sherry for Annabel. Greg and her mother were discussing the changes that were taking place in Paris.

He didn't want to talk about Valmy. He didn't want to utter meaningless platitudes. Polite, social conversation was for other people—not for them.

"Let's go where we can talk," he said, his voice low and urgent, his blue eyes hot.

Her gaze flew to Greg, but he was still talking to her mother. Annabel was listening intently to something Henri was saying. No one had overheard him.

"Not now," she said. She had hoped Luke would meet her

as a friend, that his marriage to Annabel would have put an end to his desire for her.

A lock of straight black hair fell low across his forehead. His lean, olive-toned face was tense. "To hell with later," he said fiercely. "I want to talk to you now!"

". . . de Gaulle's resignation as provisional president of France is a tragedy," her father was saying gravely. He turned toward them. "You saw it coming, didn't you, Luke?"

Luke's nostrils flared with impatience. Everyone's attention was now drawn toward him. Escape with Lisette was impossible. "He was heading a coalition government," he said tersely. "It was obvious there would be severe disagreements within the Assembly about the scope of his power, and it was equally obvious that he wouldn't concede an inch on any issue."

"But to resign!" Annabel said, aghast. "I can't believe it. I remember seeing him on the newsreels when Paris was liberated—striding down the Champs-Elysées, so proud and so sad, a tidal wave of people surging in his wake. He was like a giant! Head and shoulders above all those around him. The newscaster said it was obvious that he was the man destined to govern France."

"And so he will, my dear," Henri said with quiet confidence. "Eventually."

Héloïse picked up her embroidery, turning away from Luke and asking Annabel if there were still food shortages in London. Henri rose to his feet, poking the fire and throwing another log on to burn. Luke's hand shot out, encircling Lisette's wrist tightly. "Now!" he whispered savagely.

"I should offer you the commiserations of the victor, Luke," Greg said suddenly, rising from the chair and crossing to the drinks cabinet.

Luke released Lisette's wrist abruptly. "What the devil do you mean?"

Greg shrugged, pouring himself a calvados. "The Chemico account," he said easily. "I won, you lost."

Some of the tenseness left Luke's body. "Oh, that," he said, struggling for self-control. "I'd forgotten."

Greg swirled his drink round in the glass. "An account that size takes a lot of forgetting," he said with a slight quirk of his brow. "What else have you on your mind, Luke?"

The atmosphere in the room had changed subtly. Annabel looked from Greg to her husband, perplexed. There was an undercurrent of tension between them that she didn't understand. Luke had been furious when Dering Advertising had picked up the Chemico account, but she hadn't thought it had made any difference in his relationship with Greg. She knew they had met in the days immediately after the Allied landing, and she knew that those days had affected Luke profoundly. In the year since the war had ended, he had returned twice to Normandy to visit Henri de Valmy, and she knew that he had been looking forward eagerly to this reunion with the Derings.

"Nothing," Luke snapped tersely, and then, seeing the puzzled expression on his wife's face, aware that both Henri and Héloïse were looking at him curiously, he forced a grin. "Just don't do it too often. I want to make it onto the board at Thomson's, and I won't be able to do so if I keep losing accounts to Dering."

The conversation turned from advertising to speculation as to how long it would be before de Gaulle came out of his self-imposed retirement and assumed power again. Luke raged inwardly, knowing that further conversation was impossible between himself and Lisette while Greg was in the room. He had not realized how hard seeing her again would be, how impossible it would be to hide his feelings. The silk dress hung gently from her shoulders, swirling about her knees, disguising but not concealing her pregnancy. A spasm of jealousy knifed through him. He had never been to bed with her. Never made love to her.

Ever since he had spoken to her, she had kept her violet-dark eyes carefully averted from his. Now, as the conversation turned to America's plan for aid for Europe, she ran her forefinger thoughtfully round the rim of her sherry glass. She had beautiful hands, long and narrow with pearl-lacquered, almond-shaped nails. He imagined them moving languorously over his body. Caressing. Arousing.

"Greg says we should visit Paris for a day while we are here," Annabel was saying to him. "That would be nice, darling, wouldn't it?"

He had almost forgotten Annabel's existence. Unwillingly, he dragged his thoughts away from Lisette and turned his attention to his wife.

"I haven't escaped from London to plunge almost immediately into another capital city," he said tersely. "If you want to do a day's sight-seeing, and if Greg is going, perhaps you could go with him."

Greg's eyes narrowed. It was obvious that Lisette would not be going on any trip to Paris. Luke was not being very subtle.

"I'd love to escort Annabel and Lisette around Paris," he said easily, "but it would be too tiring for Lisette. We shall be staying at Valmy until the baby is born."

Annabel looked disappointed. "We're here for two weeks, darling," she said persuasively, reaching to take hold of his hand. "Surely one day in Paris wouldn't spoil the holiday for you."

It would be one day less with Lisette—one day of not seeing her, not hearing her voice.

Annabel's eyes were pleading. She was his wife. She adored him. It wasn't her fault that he didn't love her.

"Just one day," he said, and then, making an enormous effort at normality, "But no shopping, Annabel. I haven't come to France to be financially ruined by Parisian couturiers!"

They all laughed, and the atmosphere lightened, becoming once more carefree. Héloïse de Valmy was delighted to be reunited with her daughter. Henri was relieved to find that Lisette's marriage to Greg was apparently a happy one. Annabel was pleased to have at last met Lisette, who had saved Luke's life, and Greg, who had shared the horrors of D day with him. Lisette, reassured by Luke's response to Annabel's request, was smiling at a remark of her father's.

Both Greg and Luke stared at Lisette. Her head was tilted slightly to one side—the thick sweep of her lashes soft against her cheeks, the delicately etched line of her cheekbones and jaw heartbreakingly pure.

Luke's heart banged against his ribs. America had not changed her. She was still exquisitely French—effortlessly graceful, vibrantly sensual.

Rage and longing soared through his veins: rage at having lost her; at seeing her with Greg's ring on her finger, Greg's baby in her womb. He wondered if she had told him yet about Dieter Meyer, or if he still believed Dominic to be his son. If she had, and the marriage had survived, then he knew there was little hope for the future he was dreaming of. But if she hadn't, then there was still a chance. He still had the power to wreck Greg Dering's life, to destroy his marriage.

He barely gave a thought to his own marriage. He had known Annabel for over ten years. She was in love with him. She had money. She was pretty and charming and intelligent. She was a superb hostess, and she was good in bed. She was, all in all, a very satisfactory wife. But he wasn't in love with her, and he knew he never would be in love with her. He was in love with Lisette. Now that he had seen her again, he realized it was ridiculous for him to envision a life without her. Determination tightened within him. The first thing he had to do was talk to her. He had to find out how much Greg Dering knew.

Greg was marveling at his ability to present a cool facade to the world. Inside he was furious with Luke. Luke's pretty new wife hadn't heard the urgency in Luke's voice when he had asked Lisette to meet him in private, but Greg had. If it hadn't been for Annabel and the de Valmys' presence, he would have slammed his fist into Luke's jaw there and then. From the minute they had arrived at Valmy, he had been aware of every word, every look, that had passed between Lisette and Luke. So far he had seen no sign that Luke's still-burning passion was reciprocated. Lisette had greeted him warmly, but nothing in her manner or voice had indicated that she was meeting again a man she had loved or still loved. Watching her now, as they all sat in the same room, Greg knew he had no need for jealousy. But he was angry. Luke risked distressing Lisette by his behavior. Not only that. He was going to make his new wife very unhappy.

He shot her a quick glance. She was a pretty girl, slightly plump, her fair hair worn in a fashionable shoulder-length bob. As he watched her, she stretched out her hand, setting her sherry glass on the coffee table, and he saw with shock that she wasn't plump at all. She was pregnant. Fury licked through him. What the devil was Luke playing at? He'd been married for only six months. His wife obviously adored him. He was about to become a father. And he was risking it all for a woman who was no longer in love with him—a woman who had never been in love with him.

"Shall we go in to dinner?" Héloïse de Valmy asked, rising.

Greg stood up and crossed the room to Lisette. As he approached her chair, she looked up at him, all the love she felt for him shining in her eyes. His breath caught in his throat. Luke Brandon could go to hell for all he cared. He wouldn't destroy their marriage. Nothing on earth would do that.

Lisette slept very little that night. It was strange to be sleeping beneath Valmy's roofs again. Memories crowded in on her, thick and fast, and she made no attempt to stifle them. In a room far above her, the tiny turret room, Dominic had been conceived. She remembered the way the lamplight had flickered against the tapestried walls, the sound of the distant sea as it had surged up onto the shingles. It all seemed so long ago, so far away. She realized that, for the first time, she was remembering Dieter without pain. Greg stirred slightly in his sleep, his arms still around her. She remembered how unfaithful she had felt when she had first entered his arms on the night of their marriage, as if she had been about to commit an infidelity. His hand was around her waist, and she covered his strong fingers with her own. As she did so, past and present seemed to dovetail together. She had loved Dieter, and because of her love for him, she was better able to love Greg. And Dieter would have approved of Greg Dering. He was the kind of man he would have admired.

It was early dawn when she slipped quietly from the château, gathering a bouquet of winter aconites and purple irises. The rose gardens were stark and bare as she hurried through them, the dew wet on the grass beyond.

She entered the small churchyard with its tumbledown walls, walking swiftly past the graves of long dead de Valmys to the two graves that rested without headstones in the far corner. She saw with a spring of gratitude that her father had carefully tended both graves, Dieter's as well as Paul's. Winter jasmine had been planted, and hyacinths and Chinese witch hazel.

She laid a cluster of winter aconite and irises on Paul's grave, then walked the few yards to where the cherry tree leaned protectively over the green mound that covered Dieter. She stood there for a long time, the December sun slowly rising, touching the bare branches with golden light.

She folded her hands across her swollen stomach. The baby would be born within a few weeks. The guilt that was marring her life with Greg would soon be lifted. The future stretched out before her. Greg and Dominic and the new baby. "It's going to be all right, Dieter," she said softly. "Everything is going to be all right for me. I know it is." She felt closer to him now, secure in her love for Greg, than she had done since the day he had died. She laid her bouquet of flowers tenderly on his grave and walked back toward the château, certain that the shifting pattern of her life had changed for the last time.

Luke was waiting for her in the rose garden. "Does Greg know of this early morning visit?" he asked tersely, white lines etching his mouth, his brilliant blue eyes hard with the jealousy he could not conceal.

It was an encounter she had known she would have to face sometime. His manner the previous day had made it obvious that there were questions he was going to ask about Greg and Dominic, questions to which she had no satisfactory answers.

"No," she said, wishing he would put an end to his torment and to hers. "Greg still doesn't know about Dieter, or Dominic. That's what you want to ask, Luke, isn't it?"

He stepped toward her, seizing her wrists. "For God's sake, can't you see what a mistake you made?" he rasped, his eyes blazing. "He wouldn't stay with you if he knew! You're building your marriage on a sham, Lisette!"

She tried to wrench her hands free of his grasp. "I'm building it on love!" she cried, her voice anguished. "Let me go, Luke! Nothing can be achieved by talking like this. Nothing!"

"Who else can you talk to about it?" he asked savagely. "Your mother doesn't know! No one knows! Only I know."

"My father knows," she said, her eyes bright with pain, "and he doesn't make me suffer over it as you do, Luke!"

"Your father wants to believe it never happened," Luke snapped cruelly. "But it *did* happen, Lisette. I *know* it happened. Dear God in heaven, I killed Meyer! He spoke his dying words to me! I have every right to talk about it with you!"

"You have no right to cause me anguish! I made my decision and I'm living by it. If you're a friend, then you will

246

support me, not try to destroy me!" The agony in her voice was naked.

He groaned, folding her in his arms, burying his head in her hair. "I'm sorry, my love," he whispered hoarsely. "I don't want to hurt you. I just want you to understand what a mistake you made." He lifted his head from hers, his lean, dark face tortured. "I want you to love me, Lisette, not Greg, not the memory of Dieter Meyer, but me. That's all I've ever wanted."

She took his hand and pressed it against her cheek. "I do love you, Luke. I love you as a friend. And I don't want to lose you as a friend. Don't drive me away from you, please."

He turned away from her defeatedly. "It's been a year," he said, his voice bleak. "I thought by now there would be a chance, that you would have discovered it was impossible to live with Greg and not tell him."

She thought of the misery of the last few months, of the shame and suffering she endured every time Greg proudly referred to Dominic as his son—every time Isabelle Dering rhapsodized over her grandson.

"No," she lied. "I haven't. I love Greg and I'm happy."

Luke stood silent for a long moment, his back to her, his hands thrust deep into his pockets, then he shrugged. "Then there's no more to say," he said at last, turning toward her with the lopsided grin she remembered so well. "As Greg said yesterday. He won. I lost."

"Rubbish," she said, relieved that they were back on the old familiar footing of friendship, and taking his arm. "You haven't lost at all, Luke. You have Annabel, and she's far, far too good for you."

Luke laughed. "I won't argue with that," he said as they began to walk back together toward the château. "She's expecting a baby at Easter, did you know?"

"No, I didn't, but it's wonderful news, Luke. I'm so happy for you."

"I wish I could be generous hearted and say that I was happy for you," he said, his eyes darkening. "But I can't. Don't ask it of me."

"I won't," she said gently. "But you'll feel differently soon, Luke. I know you will."

Her fierce optimism sustained her all through Christmas and the New Year. They were staying in Normandy until the baby was born. When they returned to America, it would be as a happy, united family.

"How do you think Dominic will react to his new sister or brother?" Greg asked her as they walked along the cliff tops and he carried a warmly wrapped and rosy-cheeked Dominic high on his shoulders.

"He will be very pleased, won't you darling?" Lisette said, raising her face to Dominic's and blowing him a kiss.

In the second week of January, Luke and Annabel returned to London. "Promise me you'll let me know as soon as the baby is born," Luke said to her as he helped Annabel into their waiting car.

"I will," she promised, her hand in Greg's. "We want you to be godfather, remember?"

"I will be. London is only six hours away." He remembered when Dominic had been born, when they had been so close he had thought nothing could separate them. "Good-bye Lisette," he said, his voice thick with emotion. "Take care."

Together she and Greg waved as the car sped down the drive, and then turned and walked, hand in hand, into the château.

The next two weeks were the most emotionally peaceful Lisette had ever known. She was certain of the future, confident of recapturing the happiness she and Greg had known in Paris, and looking forward to the birth of their child.

"It's a pity Auge has retired to Nice," her father said to her as they shared a predinner drink. "He would have liked to have delivered this baby. Your coming back to Normandy for the birth would have pleased him."

"It is sufficient for me that you are pleased," she said, squeezing his hand, knowing how happy he was that his grandchild was to be born in France.

The baby was born in Bayeux's maternity hospital five days later. Greg had driven her there in the Citroën, terrified that the baby would put in as speedy an appearance as Dominic had. It didn't. He had to wait a grueling fifteen hours before the nurse came and told him he had a daughter.

When at last he was allowed to see Lisette, he was shocked by the blue shadows beneath her eyes, her obvious exhaustion.

"I thought it was going to be so easy for you," he said, his voice choked as he took her hand.

"So did I," she said, a wry smile touching her lips. "It will teach me never to assume."

He leaned forward and kissed her. "Thank God it's over," he said hoarsely. "I couldn't bear it if anything happened to you. It would destroy me."

She touched his strong-boned face tenderly with her fingertips. "Nothing is going to happen to me," she said gently, loving him so much that it hurt. Her fingers tightened in his, her eyes beginning to sparkle with amusement. "After all the trouble I've gone through, providing you with a daughter, aren't you going to say hello to her?"

He grinned. In his concern for her, he had forgotten all about the baby. "Yes," he said, "after I have kissed you again."

The baby lay in his arms, tightly swaddled, her eyes closed, her face red. "She's fantastic," he said delightedly. "Does she look like Dominic did?"

"A little."

Their daughter did not look at all like Dominic. Dominic's hair had been corn gold. Their daughter's hair was dark and thick, already beginning to curl.

"She's wonderful," Greg said again, holding his daughter with exquisite tenderness. "Absolutely marvelous!"

Lisette lay back against her pillows, content. This was the moment she had waited for, the moment when Greg held his child in his arms.

"Dominic is going to be thrilled with her," he said. "I've promised him he can visit you tomorrow and have a peep at her."

The tiniest shadow touched her eyes. She had been confident she would no longer experience a stab of conscience when Greg spoke Dominic's name, his voice full of pride and love. Yet a spasm of pain had come so automatically, she had been unable to suppress it.

"What name are we going to give her?" she asked, determined it would not do so again.

"The name we agreed on," he said, laying his daughter gently back in her cradle. "Lucy."

* * *

249

The christening was held in the same small church they had married in. Madame Pichon was in attendance, as was Madame Chamot and old Bleriot. Luke had traveled from London to act as godfather. Annabel had apologized for not accompanying him, saying that pregnancy and channel crossings were not compatible. She had sent her love, and a cobweb-fine christening shawl she had made herself.

Dominic stood on sturdy legs, holding his grandfather's hand, his eyes curious as Father Laffort sprinkled water on the baby's head. Lisette looked across at him, her eyes full of love. It was nearly two years to the day since he had been born. The February sunlight streamed in through the stained glass windows above the altar. Two years—and now she had another child, a daughter. They were a family, and in three days' time, they would be returning home.

Lisette leaned on the deck rail as the ship eased away from its berth, staring out at the coast of France until it merged into the horizon and could be seen no more. She wondered how long it would be before they returned, until she could smell the fresh, clean fragrance of the apple orchards again, hear the sea birds calling above the surging waves of the Channel. The chill sea wind struck through her coat, and she turned away, feeling very French, very conscious of her love for her country as she left it for the second time. She refused to panic when, six weeks after Lucy's birth, she and Greg began to make love again and her body continued to fail her.

"What's the matter, Lisette?" he asked, staring down at her as she lay beneath him in their brass-headed bed. "Why are you so tense? It's as if you're afraid."

She forced a smile, sliding her arms up around his neck. "Silly," she said, her voice a trifle unsteady. "What could I possibly be afraid of? It's just too soon after the baby's birth, that's all."

A month later she consulted a gynecologist. "There are minor lesions at the neck of the womb," the gynecologist told her. "Nothing serious, but it would be advisable to delay another pregnancy for a year or so."

"Would they be responsible for a . . . a change in my attitude?" she asked, the color rising in her cheeks.

The gynecologist frowned. "I'm afraid I don't understand your question, Mrs. Dering."

Lisette's hands tightened in her lap. "My responses—in bed—no longer seem to be the same as they once were. Could the lesions you spoke of be responsible?"

He shook his head. "No, but please don't worry. Having a baby is a major emotional trauma. It can take a little time before marital intimacy returns to normal."

She thanked him, asked him to send his bill, and took Dominic on a promised trip to the zoo.

"Smile, Maman," Dominic said to her as he threw nuts for the monkeys. "Please smile."

She smiled and hugged him tight, fighting down the fear that gripped her. She was panicking unnecessarily. Lucy's birth had been difficult. She was still only two months old. She needed time, that was all. She wasn't suffering from guilt anymore, just the aftereffects of an arduous birth.

"Daddy! Daddy!" Dominic called, running to find him the instant they returned home. "We went to the zoo! There were lions and tigers and an *enormous* ephelant!"

"Elephant," Greg corrected him with a grin, bending down and opening his arms wide for Dominic to run into them.

"*And* there were monkeys!" Dominic added with a giggle. "We gave them nuts to eat and they were funny and made me laugh!"

Greg swung him high in his arms and looked at Lisette, his eyebrows quirking. "Was it fun? You look tired."

She gave him a bright, quick smile. "Of course I'm not tired," she said, and he knew she was lying. "It was a lovely day. We enjoyed ourselves immensely."

There were shadows beneath her eyes. Slowly he lowered Dominic to the floor. "Go and say hello to Lucy," he said gently to the boy. "She's with Simonette in the nursery."

"What's the matter?" he asked when Dominic had run from the room. "Something is wrong between us, Lisette. I want to know what it is."

"Nothing is wrong," she said sharply, turning away from him and taking off her jacket, laying it over the back of a chair.

He made no attempt to touch her. He leaned against the open door leading into their bedroom and watched her, his gold-flecked eyes deeply troubled. "You're lying to me," he said quietly. "You've been lying to me for months. I want to know why."

251

She spun to face him, terrified that he had guessed the truth, that she was on the verge of losing him. "I don't know what you mean!" she cried, her eyes wide and dark, her fear naked in her voice.

His brows flew together. He crossed the room swiftly, seizing hold of her shoulders. "What the devil is the matter, Lisette? What are you afraid of?"

Her hands were against his chest. She could feel his heart beating, feel his strength. She swayed slightly, knowing how easy it would be to bury her fears and hurts in his arms, knowing how deeply she would hurt him if she did so.

"Nothing," she whispered. "There is nothing wrong, Greg. Please believe me."

For a moment he had thought she was going to confide in him, to trust him enough to tell him what was marring their happiness. He hooked a finger under her chin and tilted her face to his. "I'm thirty-two years old, Lisette," he said, and his voice had a hard quality in it she had never heard before. "I like women. I know women. And I know damn well when one is lying to me in bed."

The thickly carpeted floor shelved away from her, the precipice she had skirted for so long opening wide at her feet. "You're wrong," she gasped, her heart slamming against her breastbone, the blood thundering in her ears. "I love you! I love you more than anything else in the world!"

"Then show me," he demanded, his eyes dark, his hands sliding down her thighs, lifting her skirt, moving caressingly upward.

She sobbed, confounded by desire for him, terrified that she would be unable to give rein to it.

He held her close, lowering her to the floor, his mouth hot and hard on hers, his hands insistent. She gasped, her arms tightening around him, loving him so much she was dying by inches. He took her fiercely, savagely, without restraint, and she cried out beneath him, her eyes closed, her hair tumbling from its chignon, damp with sweat.

In the seconds before he reached his own shattering climax, he looked down at her, breathing harshly, but there was no triumph in his eyes—only an agony of suspicion that had not been stilled.

18

"Luke and Annabel have a daughter!" Lisette said, walking into the sun-filled breakfast room that looked out over the bay, a letter in her hand. "Isn't that lovely news, Greg? They have named her Melanie."

"I can't quite see Luke as a fond father," Greg said dryly, helping himself to a warm croissant. He had forgotten what an American breakfast was. Lisette still cooked and baked as if she were in France.

"Why not, *chéri?*" she asked, pausing as she passed his chair to drop a kiss on his cheek. "I think Luke will make a very fine father. He will be very English, very correct."

Greg laughed, his pinprick of irritation at hearing Luke's name on her lips, dying. "Yes, it would have been Eton, Oxford, and the Guards if Melanie had been a boy. I'm not sure what the set pattern will be for a girl."

Lisette sat down, her hair falling softly onto her shoulders, her rose-pink chiffon negligee cascading in flounces around her. "I must send Annabel a gift for the christening. Perhaps if I shopped this morning, we could meet for lunch?"

He was having lunch with Nick Elliot of Clayton Advertising, but he knew immediately that he would cancel it. He would see Nick later in the week. He couldn't resist the prospect of meeting an effervescent Lisette for lunch.

"I'll meet you at one o'clock at the Atlantis," he said, reluctantly pushing his chair away from the table and rising. "I have to go now, sweetheart. I have a meeting with the board at nine. If you want to send something really special to Annabel, why don't you pay a visit to Tiffany's?"

Her eyes widened. "But that would be horrendously expensive, *chéri!*"

He grinned down at her. "It's never stopped you from shopping there before. Why let it stop you now?" He cupped her chin in his hand, tilting the perfection of her heart-shaped face to his, silencing her mock-outraged rebuke with a kiss.

She was laughing as he left her. The mornings were always the best times between them. She could express her love for him freely, secure in the knowledge that the kisses, the touches, would not end in bed. It was only in bed that the panic came, that the guilt she tried so hard not to think about threatened to crush her.

She stared out through the vast windows, down the lushly foliaged hillside to the city and the sparkling blue water beyond. She had been so confident that her guilt would trouble her no more once Lucy was born, and she had been so sadly wrong.

Her eyes clouded. She no longer knew if Greg was aware of the constraint that paralyzed her when she was in his bed. Since the day she had taken Dominic on his trip to the zoo, neither one of them had ever brought up the subject of their physical relationship. It was as if they both knew that to mention it again would be to plunge them down a precipice from which there would be no recovery.

She wasn't sure, but she thought he no longer made love to her as often as he had once done. And when he did, she tried so hard to be responsive that there were times when she nearly convinced herself that everything between them was once more as it had been in the early days of their marriage—the days before they had come to America, before she had seen Isabelle Dering's face light with joy at holding the child she thought was her grandson, at hearing the pride in Greg's voice as he introduced Dominic to his family and friends.

She rose from the table, her eyes dark. *Did* she convince Greg? She had no way of knowing. She could only pray that he was convinced of her love for him—that he did not doubt her, that he would continue to love her—for without his love, there would be no joy in her life, no happiness at all.

She went into the children's rooms, kissing them good morning, telling Dominic that she would be out until the afternoon, and asking him to be good for Simonette.

She enjoyed her mornings in the city. Greg had brought her a midnight-blue Lincoln Zephyr convertible, and she loved driving it herself, taking the swooping, switchbacked hills with a steady hand and eye. She bought an antique silver christening mug, and had Melanie's name and the date of her birth engraved on it, then she browsed through an art gallery on Grant Avenue before driving to meet Greg at the Atlantis.

It was a new restaurant, small and exclusive, catering to a select clientele. Greg saw the maître d'hôtel snap instantly to attention as Lisette entered—saw heads turn in her direction—saw the looks of undisguised admiration from the men and the envy from the women, as she walked with effortless grace down the center of the crowded room. She had never made any effort to look American. She was as French now as she had been the day he had met her. Everything she wore was starkly simple and exquisitely chic.

Her burnished black hair was swept high on her head in a perfectly plain knot. There were pearls at her ears and throat. Her dress was of ivory silk, the neckline softly cowled, the skirt swirling around her knees in a river of tiny, impeccably executed pleats. Her stockings were sheer, her ivory kid pumps teeteringly high, and over her arm was a short, chocolate-mink jacket that he had bought her after Lucy's birth.

There was unfettered pleasure in his eyes as she sat down opposite him. "You look ravishing," he said as he smelled the clean, sweet fragrance of her hair and the underlying note of her French perfume. He reached out, taking her hand in his. "Let's not bother with lunch," he said, his voice thickening. "Let's drive home and make love."

She dropped her eyes from his immediately, and he cursed himself for a fool. For months now, he had kept his passion on a tight rein, fearful that by giving full vent to it he would drive her away from him. The intoxicating pleasure he had felt when she had entered the restaurant shriveled and died. He felt cold and sick inside, certain that she didn't love him, that she had never loved him. He forced an easy grin.

"Perhaps not," he said, leaning back against the banquette and picking up the leather-bound menu. "It would make a dreadful mess of your hair."

She laughed, and beneath her laughter he heard her relief, and the cold, hard knot deep in his belly tightened. She had married him in haste, and she was too warm-hearted, too generous by nature, to tell him so. He had suspected it for months, ever since she had been pregnant with Lucy. Now he was sure of it.

"A Caesar salad, escargots, and two Tournedos Rossini," he said tersely to the waiter who hovered at his side. "And a bottle of burgundy."

He was angry. Angry with her. Angry with himself. What God-almighty ego had persuaded him he had only to tell her she would learn to love him for it to become the truth? Beneath the immaculate cut of his lightweight business suit, the lean, tanned contours of his body tensed. He could confront her with it, as he had nearly confronted her once before. And if she admitted it, what then? Was he prepared to say good-bye to her, to allow her to return to France with Dominic and Lucy, to pretend that their marriage had never existed?

He drained the whiskey he had been drinking and ordered another. He couldn't do it. He had fallen in love with her within minutes of meeting her, and he still loved her. He loved her so much he would happily die for her, and under no circumstances would he do anything, *anything*, that would drive her from him. His hand tightened around his glass. He knew what the first thing was he had to do. He had to stop driving her farther and farther away from him with his physical demands. He had to settle for what she gave freely—her friendship, her affection.

"What did you buy for Melanie's christening present?" he asked, forcing his voice to be negligent, to betray none of his inner torment.

"An antique silver mug," she said, her eyes flying to his, uncertain as to whether or not he was disappointed that she had not returned home with him.

"Did you have it engraved?" he asked, aware that his knuckles were white. God in heaven, as if he cared what she had bought for the Brandons! Luke's face burned in his memory: Luke at the château, telling him that he intended marrying Lisette. Luke, who had lived with her for months at Valmy while he had been fighting his way through the hell of the Ardennes. Luke, who had been with her when Dominic was born, who had loved her then and who loved her still. He fought the memories down. To dwell on thoughts of Luke Brandon was to go mad.

"Let's go up to Lake Tahoe for the weekend," he said, pushing his barely touched plate of escargots away from him. "We haven't been there for months, and Dominic enjoys it."

Her eyes shone. "That would be lovely, Greg. The woods around the lake remind me of the beech woods at Valmy."

Despite his pain, Greg laughed. "There's not the remotest similarity between the redwood forests north and west of Tahoe, and the chocolate box beech woods at Valmy, sweetheart. Normandy itself could be dropped into the forests up there and quite easily be lost."

"Big is not always best," she said with husky laughter, glad that the moment of awkwardness between them had faded. "Just because the Tahoe and Eldorado forests *remind* me of Valmy's beech woods, does not mean that they are as *beautiful* as Valmy's beech woods!"

They had gone to Lake Tahoe, and in the succeeding months they visited the Napa Valley, Salt Lake City, La Jolla, and Mexico. The agency continued to flourish. When Greg went on business trips to New York, Lisette accompanied him. They employed another nanny to help Simonette. They entertained on an even bigger and grander scale. The success of Dering Advertising made them newsworthy. Greg was a millionaire. He was young, handsome. Their photographs appeared with increasing frequency in newspapers and magazines. They were a stunning couple: Greg with his tousled shock of sun-bleached hair, his powerful shoulders, his easy manner; Lisette, with her dark vibrancy, her captivating French accent, her exquisite grace. They were a couple who had everything—a couple who were envied wherever they went.

"I can only help you if you trust me, Mrs. Dering," Dr. Helen Rossman said, leaning back in her leather swivel chair and surveying Lisette with interest.

"I do trust you," Lisette said, the roof of her mouth dry. She hadn't known what to expect from a psychiatrist. It had taken months for her to pluck up the courage to make an appointment, and now that she had, she knew she was on the defensive. She didn't want to tell this stranger about her intimate life with Greg. "I'm sorry," she said, rising. "I've

257

made a mistake. I shouldn't have come. Forgive me for taking up your time, Dr. Rossman."

"Not at all," Dr. Rossman said, unperturbed. "But as you are paying for the hour of my time that you have booked, it seems a shame to waste it. Why not sit in silence for a little while. Silence is so very hard to come by, isn't it?"

Lisette looked at her doubtfully but sat back in her very comfortable chair. It was impossible to guess how old Helen Rossman was. She could have been anywhere from thirty-five to fifty. She wore no makeup—made no concessions to femininity at all. Her hair was dust-colored, pulled tightly away from her face in an unbecoming bun.

The silence began to grate on Lisette's nerves. "It isn't a psychiatrist I need at all," she said suddenly. "I'm not mad. I don't need to find out what is wrong with me, I already know. I really am wasting your time, Dr. Rossman." She began once again to rise.

Dr. Rossman smiled. "Please tell me," she said. "I'm very interested."

Lisette closed her eyes for a moment and then said, "I love my husband. I love him desperately. But I freeze when he touches me. I can't give him the physical love he deserves or receive the physical love that I need."

"Were you once able to do so?" Dr. Rossman asked, picking up a pencil and surveying the tip thoughtfully before laying it down again.

"Yes. At first. When we were in Paris."

"You said that you knew what was wrong with you, Mrs. Dering. Does that mean you know why your responses have changed?"

Lisette's heart-shaped face was taut. Her hands tightened in her lap. Apart from her father and Luke, she had never spoken of Dieter to anyone. She was not sure she could do so now. She took a deep, steadying breath. "I am a French-woman, Dr. Rossman. I met my husband when he landed with the Allies on D day. We were married six weeks later." She paused. The room remained silent. Dr. Rossman seemed to be intently studying the pattern on the floor-to-ceiling curtains. "A few hours after we were married, he returned to his battalion, and I did not see him again for ten months." She passed a hand unsteadily across her eyes. "When he returned,

I had a three-month-old baby. My husband was thrilled, delighted. He said his sister had been a seven-month baby. He didn't give me the chance to explain . . ."

The silence this time was longer. Dr. Rossman waited. Her interest seemed to have shifted from the curtains to the pattern on the carpet.

"The baby wasn't his. I had meant to tell him. I intended to tell him . . ."

Again there was silence. "But you never did," Dr. Rossman prompted at last.

Lisette shook her head. "My baby's father was a German. My husband was among the first to liberate Dachau. He would never have understood. If I had told him, I would have lost him."

"I see," Dr. Rossman said, doodling idly on a sheet of paper. "When did you begin to feel the weight of your deception?"

"When I came to America. When I saw my mother-in-law's joy at believing herself to be a grandmother. When I heard my husband introducing Dominic as his son." She leaned forward, her eyes burning. "I understand *why* I feel guilty, Dr. Rossman! But why should it affect me in this way? Why should it sexually freeze me?"

Helen Rossman's eyes were compassionate. "Because you are afraid," she said gently. "You are afraid of the moment of orgasm, afraid of losing control. To lose control would be to render yourself powerless against your driving need to tell your husband the truth. In the moment of orgasm, there is no control. There is an emotional and physical explosion, a loss of identity and sense of separate being—a momentary disintegration of self. It is then that your subconscious knows you would be vulnerable, then that you would break down and tell him the truth. And to prevent that happening, your subconscious mind is protecting you. It is not allowing such a moment to occur. It is, as you so accurately describe it, freezing you— removing you from danger."

Lisette stared at her, appalled. "Then there is nothing I can do?"

Dr. Rossman continued to doodle lightly on her notepad. "Many women have the same problem, or a similar problem, Mrs. Dering. A woman does not always know who the father of her child is. She has an affair. There are sexual relations between herself and her lover. Between herself and her husband. She becomes pregnant. In those circumstances, most women, if they have decided to carry the child, have one of two decisions to make: to continue the marriage, or to terminate it and begin a new life with their lover. Either way, they have to convince themselves that the child they are carrying is the child of the man they have chosen to stay with. And they do so. They have, after all, a fifty-fifty chance of being right."

Lisette's eyes flew wide. "But that is terrible!"

"Perhaps, but it is reality. It is a way of maintaining sanity, of coping. The human mind is very flexible, Mrs. Dering. We believe what we want to believe, and, in believing it, it becomes the truth."

"But I *know!*" Lisette protested, rising abruptly to her feet. "There is no fifty-fifty chance that Dominic is Greg's child! He isn't. He's Dieter's son! I can't lie to myself like that! It isn't possible!"

"Then you must tell your husband the truth. I cannot remove the guilt you feel. Only you can do that. But I would advise you not to free yourself of your burden until you are quite sure you are strong enough to live with the possible consequences."

Lisette drove south of the city, parking the car at the side of the freeway, walking for hour after hour on a deserted stretch of beach, the sea wind tugging at her hair. Her visit to Dr. Rossman had resolved nothing. She understood her frigidity a little better, but that was all. She could not free herself of it. It was the prison she had entered of her own volition on that far distant day when Greg had stood magnificently naked in the room above the stables and had first held Dominic in his arms.

Greg knew that most men would have sought satisfaction elsewhere. There were times when the temptation came, but he ruthlessly suppressed it. He loved Lisette. He was damned if he was going to cheapen that love by squandering it elsewhere.

In the years after Lucy's birth, he had steeled himself to approach Lisette sexually less and less. The effort had nearly killed him. Only the knowledge that the less frequently he made demands on her, the more relaxed she became, gave him the strength to continue.

He had known that he stood no hope of success unless they slept separately. Even now, years later, he could remember the raw agony he had felt when he had suggested that they have separate bedrooms. He had wanted to see shock on her face. Horror. He had wanted her to say immediately that such an arrangement was unthinkable. She hadn't. She had stood very still, sand clinging to her sandals from one of her long walks on the beach, her hair windblown, her eyes so dark he could read no expression in them.

"You said you had been sleeping badly, and I thought . . ."

"Yes," she had said quickly. Too quickly. "I understand."

She had been wearing a sweater of rich cornflower blue over a pair of white slacks. The desire to touch her, to hold her, had been almost more than he could bear. "It was just a thought, Lisette. We don't have to. Not if you don't want to." He had stepped toward her, intending to crush her against him, to tell her that it was the last thing in the world he wanted.

She had turned away from him swiftly. "I think it's a good idea," she had said, her eyes avoiding his. "I don't sleep well, and I know how it must disturb you. I'll move your things for you tomorrow."

All his doubts had crystallized into certainty. He had spun on his heel, striding quickly from the room, not trusting himself to remain.

"Papa is not very well," Lisette said, her brows puckering into a frown as she read the latest letter from France. "Mama says it's a slight stroke. She wants him to move to Paris for good, not just for the winter months, but he's refusing. He says no power on earth will remove him from Valmy."

Greg looked across at her. They were sitting on the patio, watching as Dominic and his friends did spring dives into the pool. Whenever a letter came from Valmy, Lisette was pensive, and he knew no matter how hard she tried to hide it, she was longing for rain-washed skies and apple orchards and deep-shaded, high-hedged country lanes. He frowned. It had been six years since their last visit. Dering Advertising was flourishing and could survive quite well without him for five or six weeks, but Frank Warner was due to appear before the House Un-American Activities Committee, and he had promised to give him all the support that he could.

"Would you like to see him?" he asked as Dominic hurled himself into the pool with a somersault and his friends cheered.

"*Alors!* Of course I would like to see him," she said, her eyes overly bright. "But the agency . . . Dominic's schooling . . ."

"They'll survive," he said, and then, reluctantly, "But we won't be able to leave till the end of next month. Frank Warner has been subpoenaed to appear before the House Un-American Activities Committee."

"*Frank* has?" She stared at him aghast. "*Frank? Mon Dieu!* How could anyone, even a fanatic like McCarthy, suspect *Frank* of being a communist? Why, he's not even political!"

Greg's mouth tightened. He had not intended telling her about Frank's subpoena. McCarthy's witch-hunt for communists and radicals reflected too shamefully on his country.

Lisette was still staring at him with horror. "But I thought you said that House committee was nothing but a backwater for racially prejudiced political has-beens?"

"So it was. Unfortunately, McCarthy has altered all that. He's found a handful of communists in the government, and now panic has set in and he's been given a free hand to subpoena anyone who can be even remotely suspected of being a communist or a radical."

"But, *Frank!* He doesn't hold a hard-line view on anything! Why should they have picked on Frank?"

"Because he mixes socially in government circles. Because he's a chatterbox," Greg said, the white lines around his mouth deepening. The Committee is scrounging for information. They want him to testify on the subject of his acquaintances, past and present."

Lisette stood up, white and trembling. "*Merde!* That is disgusting! I can't believe that such a thing is happening! Not here, in America!" She pushed her hair away from her face, her eyes flashing. "Who will this McCarthy start chasing next? Homosexuals? Jews?"

Greg shook his head. "No, it won't go that far, Lisette. Not now that Eisenhower is president."

She stared down at him. "And Frank? What will he do?"

"He's going to take the Fifth Amendment."

"And what does that mean?" Lisette asked, confused. "Does it mean that he will refuse to testify against his friends?"

Greg nodded.

"And then what will happen to him?"

Greg rose, crossed to the poolside bar, and poured a drink. "It means he could end up being blacklisted," he said heavily. "Financially no one will deal with him any more. His company will be ruined."

"Could he be jailed?" Lisette asked as he passed her a large gin and tonic. "Isn't that what they did to the writer Dashiell Hammett, when he refused to testify?"

Greg nodded. "Yes, but he'll be doing the right thing, Lisette. He'll be taking a stand against them, and God knows, someone is going to have to soon, and in a big way."

There was something in his voice that chilled her. The dark pupils of her eyes dilated.

"*Alors!* Have you been subpoenaed, Greg? Are you going to have to testify to them?"

He grinned. The conversation had brought them suddenly very close together. "No, don't worry about me. But by the time Eisenhower comes to the end of his term of office, I think you'll find me giving the next Democratic candidate a lot of support. I might even run for Congress myself."

A month later Frank appeared before the House committee and took the Fifth Amendment, refusing to testify. He was jailed for contempt, and Greg flew back from Washington alone, his fury white-hot.

"Isn't there anything anyone can do?" Lisette asked despairingly when he had showered and changed.

He shook his head. "Not yet, but McCarthy's days are coming to an end. He's beginning to express open hostility toward Eisenhower, and he's fast losing support in the Senate. When we come back from France, I'm going to put the entire resources of Dering Advertising behind an attempt to show the public just what it is McCarthy stands for."

A shadow touched her eyes. "I received a letter from

263

maman this morning. Our visit is going to coincide with a visit by Luke and Annabel. You don't mind, do you, *chéri?*"

He turned away from her, strong and lithe, his jeans hugging his hips, his shirt open at the throat revealing a pelt of darkly curling hair.

"No," he said, and only the sharpest ear could have detected a note of terseness in his voice. He had long since convinced himself that Luke Brandon was not the cause of the unhappiness that lay, unacknowledged, at the heart of their marriage. He was certainly not going to delay taking Lisette home to Valmy simply because Luke would be there at the same time.

He turned toward her and felt the same rising fervor at the sight of her that he had felt when they had first met.

"Melanie will be company for Lucy," he said, not really caring whether she would be or not. Caring about nothing but his driving need to make love to Lisette, knowing that if he did so, her response would be feigned—a sham that he had not the courage to tell her he had seen through long ago.

"Will *Grand-père* speak only French?" a very American Lucy asked curiously as they stood at the deck rails waiting for their first view of France.

"Nearly," Lisette said with a laugh. "And you must speak French, too, Lucy. Do you remember the nursery rhymes I taught you? '*Sur le pont d'Avignon. Frère Jacques, Frère Jacques?*'"

Lucy's rosy cheeks were like ripe apples, her hair a tumbled mass of curls. "I don't like speaking French, Mummy. It takes me so long to say what I want to say. I can never remember the words like Dominic. My tongue gets fast."

"That's because you're a chatterbox, *ma petite*," Lisette said, hugging her tight. "Look! Can you see the white of the cliffs? That's France, *chérie*. We're nearly home!"

Lucy looked up at her mother curiously. "We've just left home," she said with childlike logic. "We won't be going back for ages and ages. Not until the end of summer."

Lisette leaned eagerly over the deck rail, her eyes shining. "This is my home," she said rapturously. "This is France!"

She was shocked by her father's frailty. He had begun to stoop, and there was a hesitancy about his movements that had never been there before.

"Oh it's so good to be home, Papa," she said, perching on the arm of his chair, her arm lovingly around his shoulders. "Why does San Francisco have to be so very far away?"

He had pressed her hand to his cheek, overjoyed at having her home once more, at having his grandchildren running noisily through the château and gardens.

"Luke and Annabel and Melanie arrived five days ago," he said contentedly. "He looks very much the Englishman when he arrives: always the dark suit, the white shirt, the very correct tie with the tiny, tiny dots." He chuckled with amusement. "And then he unpacks his luggage, and he wears a turtleneck sweater and slacks, and the suit stays in the back of his closet until it is time for him to return to England."

Lisette was looking forward to seeing Luke again. For six years their letters had flown across the Atlantic. His, addressed ostensibly to both herself and Greg. Hers, addressed to both himself and Annabel. Both knew it was a politeness. Neither Greg nor Annabel was really interested in what they had to say to each other. Luke's letters were full of his regular visits to Valmy—of news of Sainte-Marie-des-Ponts, of old Bleriot's health and Madame Pichon's retirement. Lisette's letters were full of Dominic and Lucy, but Dominic was mentioned far more often than Lucy. Not because she loved Dominic more. She didn't. Lucy was just as fiercely precious to her. But because Luke was the only person with whom she could discuss Dominic without restraint. She could tell him how he looked, what he was achieving, without having to suffer the well-meant lies of how very like Greg he was. With Luke, there was no pretense, no lies. He was, as she had said he would be many years before, her very best friend.

Luke felt sick with impatience to see her again. Six years! Christ! How had he endured it? He had no intention of enduring it again. He had recently become chairman of Johnson Matthie Advertising, and as Johnson Matthie had an office in Los Angeles, he was determined that he would find the need to visit the West Coast of America on a regular basis.

He had missed her arrival by minutes, having been asked for the tenth time by Annabel to put the tennis nets up on the courts so that they would be ready for their and the children's use.

"She's gone up to greet her father," Annabel had said soothingly. "Greg is in the library indulging his taste for calvados with Héloïse. Dominic has taken Melanie exploring. Lucy is having a little sleep."

Good manners demanded that he go immediately into the library and renew his acquaintance with Greg. He would not do so. Greg could wait. He had taken the stairs two at a time, walking feverishly up and down the long gallery that ran outside the first floor bedrooms, waiting impatiently for her to emerge from Henri de Valmy's bed-sitting room.

When she did, he knew that his wait, all his waiting, had been worthwhile. She was twenty-seven now, no longer a girl but a woman. Her hair was swept into a perfectly combed knot, accentuating the shape of her tiny ears and her remarkable violet eyes. She was wearing a cream linen suit and a vanilla silk blouse, and her shoes were high and open toed; her perfume, the same elusive fragrance he had remembered for six years.

"I was beginning to think you had drowned in the crossing," he said, striding toward her, seizing hold of her shoulders, drinking in the sight of her.

She laughed, pleased to see him despite his fervor that always disconcerted her. "We're not late, Luke. The ship only docked two hours ago."

"You're six years late," he said grimly, lowering his head to kiss her.

She turned her face swiftly, so that his impassioned kiss earned her cheek, not her lips.

"We're *friends*," she said, catching hold of his hands tightly, her voice fierce. "Friends, Luke. Not lovers. Don't spoil this homecoming for me, please."

His lean dark face was so harsh as he looked down at her that it could have been the face of an Arab, not an Englishman. "Are you happy?" he demanded savagely. "Do you still love him?"

It was easier to answer the second question than it was the first. "Yes, I still love him," she said, her eyes holding his steadily. "I will always love him, Luke."

266

He drew in his breath, his nostrils pinched and white. "And are you happy?" he asked relentlessly. "Does he know yet? Have you told him?"

She shook her head, turning away from him, beginning to walk along the gallery toward the stairs. "I haven't told him. It's been too long, Luke. I can never tell him now."

"And Dominic?" he asked, walking at her side, hating the fact that in another few minutes he would have to share her with her mother, with her children, with Greg. "Don't you want to tell him about Dieter? Don't you want him to know about his father?"

He saw the pain in her eyes, saw her almost physically flinch, and knew his words had found their mark. "He could, if you wanted him to," he continued relentlessly. "He could if you weren't so scared of Greg leaving you!"

She wheeled round to face him, suddenly angry. "But I *am* scared of Greg leaving me! I love him! I don't want to live without him for an instant, Luke! Do you understand me? No matter what the cost, it will be worth it if only Greg continues to love me!"

There was such passion in her voice that he knew he had lost his battle for her, even before it had begun. "Then there's nothing more to say," he said, spinning on his heel, walking away from her. She ran after him, catching hold of his arm.

"Don't be foolish, Luke! I've looked forward so much to being with you again, to seeing Melanie and Lucy play together, to be back at Valmy. Please don't fight with me!"

He looked down at her, a lock of his dark, straight hair falling low across his brow, his eyes bleak with the fury of his defeat. From downstairs they could hear the faint sound of childish voices.

"Please, Luke," she repeated, her eyes pleading with him for understanding.

There was a long, taut moment, and then he shrugged, smiling ruefully. "Okay. You win. Let's face the troops together, *ma brave.*"

She laughed, slipping her arm through his, walking happily with him down the staircase to where the children and Annabel and Greg and her mother waited.

* * *

267

"I'm only going to speak French now that I am in France," Dominic was saying with eight-year-old importance.

"I want to speak French, too," Melanie said, gazing up at him adoringly. "Please can I speak French, Mummy? What is French? Is it nice? Can Lucy speak it?"

"I'm sure Lucy can speak a little French," Annabel said indulgently. "Now why don't you come with me to the bathroom and wash all those grass stains off your hands and knees? Wherever have you been?"

"I've been exploring with Dominic. We've found lots of nice places and—"

"Excuse me," Annabel said apologetically to Lisette and Héloïse. "I must take her to the bathroom. I can't imagine how she got so dirty. She's only been out of my sight for a few minutes."

Greg grinned as a concerned Annabel led a reluctant Melanie in the direction of soap and water. "Annabel is going to have to learn that Melanie is going to be permanently covered with scratches and grazes and grass stains if Dominic has adopted her as an acolyte. They were attempting to climb onto the stable roof when I called them in. I thought it best Annabel didn't know."

Luke gave him a lopsided grin, his hands deep in his trouser pockets. "Your judgment was correct," he said good-naturedly. "Melanie only goes out with her mother or a nanny when we're at home. These weeks at Valmy are going to open up a whole new world for her."

As they all strolled into the grand salon for tea and scones and thick creamy slices of local cheese, Luke reflected again on how curious it was that, despite all his jealousy, he should be unable to harbor dislike for Greg. If it hadn't been for Lisette, he would have liked to have thought of him as a good friend.

"I see you scooped both Alloys International and Quay Med last month," he said to Greg as Héloïse de Valmy, still regally beautiful in silver-gray silk, began to pour tea.

"You pitched for Quay Med as well, didn't you?" Greg said, allowing the conversation to flow along the safe, uncontroversial channels of their mutual profession.

He knew damn well where Luke had been only minutes ago. Waylaying Lisette, no doubt propositioning her—his wife and child only rooms away. The anger Luke always aroused in him flared through him, and he controlled it with difficulty. Luke's long-standing obsession with Lisette was something he had long ago learned to live with. He glanced at Lisette as Luke began to tell him about his agency's Quay Med campaign. She was sitting on the chintz covered sofa, her long, slim legs crossed at the ankles, her head tilted slightly to one side as she listened to her mother recounting details of her father's illness. He could well understand why Brandon was still obsessed with her. So was he. And he was no nearer a total possession of her than Brandon was. The physical barrier that had come down between them so many years ago had never been lifted. There were times when he thought he must have dreamed the night of their marriage—the long, hot, passion-filled nights in Paris. Her sexuality then had been deep, freely given—a glorious expression of her love for him and of her need of him. Now it was so suppressed it was hard to believe it had existed at all. He wondered when she had realized the mistake she had made. Had it been when she first had to leave France? Had that been the turning point that had ripped the heart out of their marriage?

"I'll be making a trip to our Los Angeles office toward the end of the year," Luke was saying. "Is it okay if I pay a flying visit to San Francisco? It will seem strange seeing you on home ground and not in France."

"I think 'Frisco is big enough for both of us," Greg said with the easy manner that always disconcerted Luke. He was never sure of Greg—never sure how much he knew or suspected, never sure what his inner feelings were. He was a man whose outward negligence covered a driving ambition that had made Dering Advertising one of the top American agencies—a man who had made lieutenant colonel by the age of twenty-seven, a man it would be very dangerous ever to underestimate.

Héloïse de Valmy had suggested a walk through the rose gardens before they retired to their rooms to change for dinner, much to Greg's bemusement. "Does your mother really expect me to don a tuxedo for dinner, sweetheart?" he asked as he closed the door of their room behind them.

Lisette sank wearily onto the bed, kicking off her shoes and stretching out full length on the blue silk counterpane. "I'm afraid so, *chéri*."

Greg stepped into the adjoining bathroom and turned on the shower. "Luke says he never changes out of denims the whole time he's here."

A smile touched the corners of Lisette's mouth. "That's when he's here alone with papa, and maman is in Paris. When maman is in residence, denim is definitely not for the dining table!"

Greg had pulled off his shirt, his socks. Through the open doorway she watched him as he unzipped his trousers, stepped out of them, and tossed them to one side. Her throat tightened as he stepped into the shower. In San Francisco, they now had separate bedrooms. It meant she had little opportunity to enjoy the pleasure of seeing him naked. She had died inside when he had suggested they sleep apart. She had wanted to hurl herself into his arms and tell him she never, ever, wanted to sleep apart from him. But she had not done so. She had been too frightened.

The newspapers were full of stories of deserted war brides. Their husbands had married in haste in the heat of war and had brought them home to America: French, Dutch, and English wives had found themselves in a strange country, a strange culture, without family or friends, and the marriages had all too often suffered accordingly. When Greg's ardor had cooled toward her, Lisette had been terrified that he, too, was beginning to realize how impetuously he had married and was, perhaps, beginning to regret it.

The jets of water were turned off. She watched as he toweled himself dry, as he wrapped the towel around his waist and walked back into the bedroom.

"It looks as if Lucy is not going to see much of Melanie these holidays," he said, opening the armoire and taking a shirt from the hanger, a dark pair of trousers, a tuxedo. "She's been following Dominic about all day like a little shadow."

Lisette raised herself up on one arm. If she reached out, her fingertips would just skim his golden-honey skin. She curled them tightly in her palm, knowing where such a gesture would lead, longing for it and dreading the wave of frigidity it would bring in its wake.

He laid the clothes over a chair and sat down beside her on the edge of the bed, strapping on his wristwatch. She could see the pearls of water clinging to the curling mass of his hair—

the smooth, bronzed flesh of his shoulders; the long, strong ripple of his spine. She closed her eyes, dizzy with desire. Why, in God's name, didn't her guilt stifle desire as well as response? Why was she left with the agony of one without the relief of the other?

"Do you want a drink before you shower?" he asked her, turning his head, his eyes meeting hers.

His movement had been too quick, too sudden. He had surprised the hunger in her eyes. The physical longing. His own desire ignited immediately. "Lisette!" His voice was choked. He twisted round on the bed, pulling her toward him. She could feel the dampness of his skin, smell the lingering fragrance of shampoo and soap. She gave a small, inarticulate cry, her arms going around his neck as his mouth closed hard and sweet on hers.

For a few dizzying moments it was as though the restraint that had built up between them had never been. The towel around his waist slid to the floor. His body imprisoned hers, her fingers curled in his hair. His lips were on her neck, the base of her throat. He unbuttoned the ivory silk blouse with speed, glorying in the sight of her breasts as he eased them free of her lace-edged brassiere.

"Oh God, Lisette, I love you . . . Love you . . ." His voice throbbed. He didn't wait for her to slip free of her skirt. He pushed it high, his hands sliding down to her hips, pressing her in toward him. She gasped aloud, pushing herself up to meet him, desire running through her like liquid gold—burning and consuming. He groaned above her, his body entering hers, and then she arched her back, not in passion but in a rictus of frigidity. This man who loved her so much, who had given her so much, was being deceived by her in the most monstrous, shameful way possible. If he knew, he would leave her. He would look at her with loathing and disgust and wish he had never seen her—never touched her.

"What's the matter, Lisette?" His voice was harsh, almost a shout. He had seen the flare of panic in her eyes. The emotional and physical drawing back. For years he had tried to pretend it didn't exist. Now he could pretend no longer. *"Don't you want me?"* he demanded, his gold-flecked eyes blazing, his face savage. *"Don't you love me?"*

"Yes," she sobbed. "Please believe me . . ."

He didn't believe her, and his fingers tightened on her shoulders till she cried out with pain. He took her with the ferocity of frustration, uncaring of her hands pushing against his chest, her cries of protest.

"*What the hell is the matter with you?*" he yelled down at her. "*Why the devil do you freeze when I touch you? . . . turn away from me when I reach out for you?*"

Her skirt was still around her waist, her hair tumbled from its sleek knot. "I don't know!" Tears were pouring down her face. "But I love you, Greg! I love you more than anything else in the world!"

"*I don't believe you!*" He sprang from the bed, hardly able to contain his rage and pain. Dear God in heaven, where had the scene now taking place sprung from? In three quick strides he was in the bathroom, pulling on his discarded clothes.

"Where are you going?" she asked, pulling herself to her knees, her clothes in disarray, her hair tumbling wildly around her shoulders.

"*I don't know!*" His face was bone-white, his eyes brilliant with pain. "*Somewhere where I can forget the travesty of our marriage!*" and he spun on his heel and strode from the room. The door rocked on its hinges as he slammed it behind him.

19

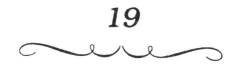

She didn't cry. She was beyond tears. She sat huddled on the edge of the bed, her arms folded tight around her, her breathing harsh and erratic. He had gone. She didn't know where. She didn't know when he would return, and when he did return, she didn't know what she could possibly say to him. He had accused her of not loving him, and she had denied it. But if she had accused him similarly, would he have been able to deny it with the same vehemence? She didn't think so.

She rose from the bed and crossed to the window, leaning her aching head against the cool pane. It was odd that here, where it had all begun between them, it was all coming to a hideous end. He had married her knowing little more about her than her name. She wondered when he had begun to regret his haste. Had it been when he had seen Jacqueline Pleydall again? When he had suggested that they no longer share the same bed? She didn't go down for dinner. She asked her mother to make her apologies on her behalf, pleading a headache. If Greg, too, failed to appear at the table there would be anxious speculation as to why, but she was too weary to care. She wanted, with all her heart, to be able to slide her arms around Greg's waist and to lean her head against the reassuring strength of his chest, secure in the knowledge that he loved her. And she could do so no longer.

Greg had stormed out of the château, striding white-faced through the gardens and out across the open land that led to the headland. The heat of the day had faded, the wind was blowing in from the Channel strongly and mare's tails scudded across a leaden sky. He began to run, wishing to God he could drive the pain and fury away. Why, in the name of all that was holy had he allowed himself to bring to the surface the hurt that had smoldered for so long? There could be no going back now to the easy camaraderie that had been so carefully nurtured between them. He had destroyed it all by his need of her—his rage at meeting again that total withdrawal of herself that cheated him of possession of her.

The waves hurled themselves remorselessly at the cliff face, clawing deep into the chalk, surging and ebbing over a shingle of water-smoothed pebbles. He panted to a halt. It was a coastline he loathed. Even now he had only to close his eyes a fraction, and he could see the ships as they had approached the shore, see the running figures of his comrades as they were mowed down by the hundreds. A pillbox still stood, gaunt and bleak, staring out over the heaving gray waters. How Lisette could retain affection for such a glacial, inhospitable sea he had never been able to understand. He had thought she would be captivated by the dazzling blue shimmer of the Pacific, but she had not been. She had never said so, but he knew that blue sea and pristine white surf were no compensation to her for windswept beaches and the cold, inhospitable waters that pounded her native shoreline.

He stood, his hands dug deep in his trouser pockets, his brows pulled together until they met as he stared out over the heaving waves. What would her reaction be if he suggested that they end their marriage? If he told her there was no need for her to return to America with him? That she could stay in Normandy forever and never leave it? He spun swiftly on his heel, facing Valmy and the beech woods and the distant spire of the church he had been married in. He couldn't do it. He couldn't envisage life without her. If she left him, it would have to be of her own volition.

He began to walk back across the marram grass toward the château. There was nothing for it but to return. To exercise the iron-strong control that had so shatteringly and suddenly just let him down. He swore savagely beneath his breath. There would be Luke to endure. The chatter of the children. The anxious curiosity in his father-in-law's eyes if it became obvious that he and Lisette were at odds with each other. The facade of a happy marriage would have to be maintained at least for the length of their stay. And afterward? His hands clenched. He would think of afterward later. For the moment, he had dinner with his in-laws and the Brandons to survive.

"Lisette has a headache," Héloïse said, disguising her surprise at his arrival at the dinner table in casual slacks and sweater, and at his apparent ignorance of Lisette's condition.

"The trip over was rougher than we had anticipated," Greg said in an effort to explain Lisette's indisposition, aware of a flare of curiosity in Luke's sharp blue eyes. "The *Ile de France* is not half so steady as we had been led to believe."

Henri, who had never ventured on a boat in his life, laughed. It was a long time since he had dined downstairs, and though he was disappointed Lisette had not been able to join them, he was enjoying himself.

"Better the *Ile de France* than the little tubs Luke and Annabel crossed from England in," he said as his wife lit the candles in the ornate candelabra, and shadows danced softly over crisp white table linen and silver.

Dinner seemed endless. Greg wanted to excuse himself and go to Lisette. He wanted, somehow, to put right all that had gone wrong between them.

"What do you think of *Time* magazine's choice of the German Chancellor as 'Man of the Year'?" Henri asked him as homemade vichyssoise was followed by trout in almonds and *Mange-tout*. "A bit of a surprise, don't you think?"

Greg shrugged. "Not really. Adenauer is in favor at the moment. He's seen as being responsible. Cautious."

"Responsible and cautious my foot," Luke said disparagingly. "He's a wily old devil who wants to make quite sure that America will defend West Germany for him in the event of a Russian invasion."

Greg didn't reply. Luke's nearness, only feet away from him, was almost unbearable. For years he had fooled himself into thinking that Luke had meant nothing to Lisette. Now he was no longer sure.

"He's a brilliant politican," Henri said grudgingly, "and his anti-Nazi record is faultless."

"Wasn't he mayor of Cologne before the Nazis came to power?" Annabel asked.

Greg didn't listen to Henri's reply. He was thinking of Lisette, of his need for her—his love for her.

"Would you like some cheese, Greg?" Héloïse repeated, her eyes concerned and curious. It was the third time she had asked him.

"No, thank you, Héloïse." He forced a smile, making a superhuman effort at civility, doing his best to ignore the hungry speculation in Luke's eyes as with painful slowness raspberry sorbet followed the local cheese; coffee the sorbet.

"How about a glass of good French brandy?" Henri said to him as the meal at last drew to a close. "I'm not allowed to drink as much of it as I would like, these days, but a small glass won't do me any harm."

"Not tonight, Henri," Greg said, trying to keep the strain he was feeling from showing in his voice. "Lisette may be wanting a warm drink or some more aspirin. I'll join you in a brandy tomorrow night."

"*Je comprends*," Henri said, knowing that he would still be able to enjoy a glass of brandy with Luke. "Good-night, *mon fils*."

Greg escaped from the room with relief. Pretense came hard to him, which was why the hideous scene between him and Lisette had taken place. He had been unable to sustain the pretense that everything was all right between them any longer. They had to find a new basis for their marriage, one that was founded on truth.

She was asleep when he returned to their room. It was a sign of how distressed she had been that her suit and silk blouse lay carelessly over the back of a chair and had not been put away. He undressed quietly and slid into bed beside her, lying on his back, his hands behind his head, staring up at the darkened ceiling, wondering where all the happiness they had known, all the laughter, had gone.

When he awoke she was sitting at the dressing table, dressed in dark gray slacks and a black sweater, brushing her hair away from her face. Through the mirror her eyes flew to his. Neither of them spoke. At last he said, "You were asleep when I came to bed. I hope I didn't disturb you."

"No."

She didn't turn to face him, every line of her body was tense, almost as if she expected a physical blow. "Where did you go?"

He pushed himself up against the pillow. "To the head-land."

There was another silence, and then she said, her fingers twisting around the filigree handle of the hairbrush, "Do you want a divorce?"

Shock reverberated through him. He felt as if he had been kicked in the chest. "No!" he said explosively, swinging his legs from the bed, his eyes holding hers through the mirror. She was deathly pale, her accent heavy as it always was when she was distressed.

"But I thought . . ."

"No divorce." His voice was hard.

She turned slowly on the dressing-table stool until she was facing him. "Are you sure?" she asked, her eyes huge in the whitened mask of her face.

"I'm quite sure," he replied tersely. "We've been married for eight years. I would like us to stay married."

"Yes." Her hands were trembling slightly, and she curled her fingers over the edge of the stool. Of course he didn't want a divorce. A divorce would distress his mother, devastate the children. He was a mere three feet away from her. He was naked, the morning sunlight bronzing his powerful chest and shoulder muscles—his hips lean, his legs strong. His arms were resting on his knees, clasped lightly. She could see the dark curling mass of his pubic hair, the full, luscious weight of his sex, and quickly averted her eyes, confounded by desire—Desire that guilt would not allow her to assuage.

She rose to her feet unsteadily. "I promised I would take the children shrimping this morning."

"Yes." His eyes held hers, their gold-flecked depths revealing nothing of his inner agony. "About last night, Lisette. The sex. It won't happen again. I promise."

"Yes," she said, her voice strangled, and escaped from the room before he could see the anguished tears scalding her eyes.

She took the children shrimping in the rock pools at Vierville, and by the time they returned for lunch, she was able to present a facade of normality. In the afternoon, they all piled into Henri's ancient Citroën and visited Falaise where William the Conqueror had been born.

"Who was William the Conqueror?" Dominic asked as they climbed up the hill toward the castle.

Melanies eyes widened. "Don't you know about William the Conqueror?" she asked, astonished. She had thought Dominic knew everything. "William the Conqueror conquered England."

Dominic shrugged dismissively. "That's *English* history," he said contemptuously. "Why should I know about *English* history?"

Melanie was nonplussed. She thought everyone knew about English history. She struggled to keep pace with him as he strode on ahead of their parents and Lucy. "Because he was a Frenchman," she said at last.

Dominic grinned at her. She was the first girl he had ever liked. "He was a Norman, you silly," he said affectionately. "Let's run on and see if there are any murder holes. Do you know what a murder hole is, Mel?"

"No," Melanie panted, red in the face with effort as she struggled to keep pace with him. "But I'd like to learn, Dominic. Will you show me?"

"My goodness, why did they always have to build everything on a hill?" Annabel gasped with a laugh. "I'm suddenly not as interested in medieval architecture as I thought I was. I think I'll stay down here and browse around the village square."

"I'll stay with you," Lisette said considerately.

Annabel shook her head. "No, don't do that, Lisette. I'm depending on you to be able to tell Melanie the history of the castle. I'll meet you all back at the car. Who knows, if I'm lucky, I may be able to get an ice-cool Pernod at the café."

With an amiable smile, she waved them on ahead of her and set off back in search of shade and a cooling drink.

"What *is* the history of the castle?" Luke asked, indifferent to his wife's retreat.

"In 1027 Robert, duke of Normandy, returning to this castle, fell in love with a young girl who was doing her wash in the street," Lisette explained, aware of how near to her Greg was, of how his hand had not once reached out for hers as it would normally have done. "Her name was Arlette, and he fell in love with her, and it was here, at Falaise, that their son, William, was born."

"How come the duke was so sure that the child was his?" Luke asked conversationally, his gaze on the great keep rearing above them.

Lisette stumbled, and Greg's hand shot out to steady her and then, almost immediately, released her.

"I suppose because . . . because he trusted her," Lisette said, her heart slamming against her chest.

Luke turned to her, his smile dazzling. "Of course," he said. "That's all men can ever do, isn't it? Trust that the children they rear are their children by blood. If Robert was deceived, he wouldn't be the first poor devil to be so, would he?"

The sun was brilliant. It bounced off the white stone of the castle walls, searing the eyes. Lisette paused, her black sweater emphasizing the paleness of her face and the haunted depths of her eyes. "I think perhaps Annabel was right," she said unsteadily. "It would be far more sensible to sit in the shade with a Pernod than struggle around castle ruins in this heat."

"Nonsense," Luke said remorselessly. "Melanie is dying to hear the story of the duke and Arlette. You can't turn back now."

Greg had been walking slightly ahead of them. He stopped suddenly, shielding his eyes against the glare of the sun. "Where are Dominic and Melanie?" he asked sharply. "I can't see them anywhere."

They halted, staring around them. Lucy was placidly picking wild flowers, but there was no sign of Dominic or Melanie.

"Is the inside of the castle safe?" Greg asked, wheeling around to her.

"I don't know. I should think so. I haven't been here for years and—"

"There they are!" Luke said. "How the devil did they get up there?"

Greg swore under his breath. A nonchalant Dominic was executing a perilous circuit around the top of the castle walls, a triumphant and perspiring Melanie in his wake. He broke into a run. He wasn't worried about Dominic's safety. His son was surefooted and agile, but he doubted that Melanie was as nimble.

Luke made no effort to follow him. He turned his back on the castle, on his daughter and Greg, and said abruptly, "What the devil's the matter?"

"Nothing," she said, trying to walk past him.

He caught her arm, spinning her around to face him. "Don't lie to me, Lisette! I know you too well. Now what the hell is wrong?"

There was concern as well as curiosity in his eyes. She said bleakly, "Greg doesn't love me, Luke. He hasn't done so for a long time."

Luke stared at her in incredulity. "What do you mean, he doesn't love you? Of course he loves you! He's crazy about you!"

She shook her head, every line of her body tired and defeated. "Things aren't what they seem, Luke. At home we have separate bedrooms. We rarely make love and when we do—" She couldn't continue. She shrugged her shoulders expressively. "If you wished me to be unhappy with Greg, you've had your wish granted, Luke."

It was what he had wished, what he had prayed for. But now that it had happened, now that she was standing before him, her eyes pools of misery, he knew that he wasn't glad. He said gently, "I'm sorry, Lisette. Truly I am."

"Thank you." She put her hand in his, a sad smile

touching her mouth. "Things never are what you expect them to be, are they?"

In the distance he could see Annabel sitting outside a café, sipping Pernod beneath the shade of a large, striped sunshade. "No," he said ruefully. "They aren't."

They stood together for a moment, not speaking, and Lisette was filled with a rare sense of closeness. Luke understood her. There was a verbal shorthand between them that she shared with no one else. She knew he knew she was thinking of Dieter, of the plans they had made to live in Switzerland. And she knew he was thinking of his wartime return to Valmy—of his confidence she would accept his proposal of marriage, of his certainty they would live their lives together.

"Greg has reached the children," she said, looking past him and up to the castle. "Isn't it strange that it is Dominic and Melanie who are inseparable and not Melanie and Lucy?"

"Melanie is like Dominic, an adventurous spirit," Luke said, aware that Greg could now see them clearly. He dropped her hand, turning and continuing to walk toward the castle's entrance. "Lucy is far more timid, not at all like Dominic. Isn't it ever commented on?"

"No," she said, aware of sheer relief at being able to talk honestly. "Everyone says how very alike they are, even though it is patently obvious they aren't."

"And Greg?"

He saw the pain touch her eyes, then she said quietly, "I don't think it has occurred to him to look for similarities between them. He simply loves them as they are. And they love him."

As they neared the castle entrance, they could see Greg waiting for them, an animated Dominic holding on to one hand as he begged to be allowed to climb to the top of the thirteenth-century tower, Melanie clasping the other. Luke felt a flare of jealousy. Melanie never held his hand with such adoration. He wondered what it was about Greg that drew people to him so unerringly, and he wondered if Lisette could possibly be right in her belief that he no longer loved her. It seemed incredible, but if it *were* true, then surely it meant she would, in time, turn for love elsewhere? Feeling more optimistic than he had for a long time, he grinned broadly at

Greg as he strode up the last few yards of the path and stepped into the castle's shade.

"Right," he said buoyantly. "What happened to Duke Robert and his beggarmaid? Did they live happily ever after, or did she leave him for another?"

"After the birth of William, Robert married her off to a Norman aristocrat, and she had two more sons," Lisette said, avoiding his eyes.

"That's sad," Melanie said, disappointed. "She should have lived with the duke for ever and ever and then the story would have had a happy ending."

"It did have a happy ending," Luke said, and as he began to walk toward the massive keep he was smiling, ". . . for the aristocrat."

The days took on pattern and regularity. In the mornings the children played in and around Valmy. In the afternoons they set out with a picnic and, with Greg at the wheel of the Citroën, visited abbeys and castles and market towns. Annabel had no interest in history or architecture, but she was like a contented cat, happy to accompany them and to sit in the shade sipping a cooling drink while they went sightseeing with the children. They visited Château Gaillard, which had been the fortress of Richard Cœur de Lion, and they visited the market place in Rouen where Joan of Arc had been burned at the stake. They walked through the beech woods and visited Madame Pichon and Madame Chamot. They stood long and silently in the American war cemetery above Omaha, and the British war cemetery at Bayeux.

"Is there a German cemetery?" Dominic had asked with interest. His mother had taken in a sharp little breath, and his father had said steadily, "Yes, there is, Dominic, but there is no need for us to visit it."

They spent several days sailing in a yacht Greg had hired at Trouville. They ate *Tripes à la mode de Caen* and laughingly assured Annabel she was eating mushrooms. They picnicked with bottles of ice-cold calvados and muscadet and bought bread at roadside *boulangeries*, eating it with thick, creamy slices of Pont-l'Evêque and Camembert and slabs of local paté. They swam in the chilly sea at Deauville and joined the locals in a game of *boules* at Brionne. Through the day everything was outwardly normal. No one, apart from Luke, guessed at their estrangement. At night Lisette lay sleepless, conscious of Greg's body beside hers, so near and yet so very far from her.

He had been true to his word. Since the evening he had slammed so furiously out of their room, he had not once approached her sexually. She missed the comfort of his nearness, the reassuring weight of his arm around her shoulders, his hand on her waist. Sometimes, in hungry need of physical contact, she feigned sleep and turned toward him, resting her head lightly on his chest. His arm would cradle her near, but his lips did not move to her hair, his hand did not seek her breast, and she knew that his gesture was without desire. He no longer needed her. He had told her so quite plainly. She had no need for pretense now, and the knowledge brought her no relief, only a misery that was absolute.

"I don't want to go home, mummy!" Melanie wailed as the Brandons' luggage was carried out to the waiting taxicab. "I want to stay here with Dominic!"

"Hush, darling." Annabel said soothingly. "Dominic isn't staying here, my pet. He has to go home too."

"Then I want to go home with Dominic," Melanie persisted tearfully. "Please can I, mummy? I'll be ever so good, I promise!"

"No, darling," Annabel said distractedly. "Dominic lives in America, a long, long way away."

Melanie stared at her, appalled. "You mean I won't ever see Dominic again? Not ever?"

"Of course you will. Some day. Now kiss Aunt Héloïse good-bye and get into the taxicab."

Melanie ignored the elegant figure of Aunt Héloïse and raced toward Dominic. "I don't want to go, Dominic! Please say I can stay with you! Please!"

Dominic shrugged miserably. "I'm sorry, Mel," he said, his hands dug deep in his pockets, his gray eyes bleak. "You have to go back to London. But I'll see you again. I promise I will."

Melanie turned to her mother, her small face pinched and white. If Dominic said she had to go, then she had to go. She wondered if she would die from loneliness. Obediently, she said good-bye to Aunt Héloïse and Uncle Henri, and Aunt

Lisette and Uncle Greg and Lucy, and climbed into the rear of the taxicab. She wouldn't cry. Dominic would think her a baby if she cried.

Her father was kissing Aunt Lisette good-bye and a funny little muscle was twitching at Uncle Greg's jawline. She liked Uncle Greg. She liked France. If Dominic lived in America, then she was sure she would like America too. She didn't want to go home to London. Not ever. Her father stepped into the cab and slammed the door behind him. Everyone was waving good-bye, everyone but Dominic. He was standing apart from his parents and grandparents, his hands still deep in his pockets, his eyes suspiciously bright.

"Good-bye, Dominic," she whispered, raising her hand against the glass and waving until she could no longer see him, until the taxicab turned left at the end of the long, linden-flanked drive and plunged down the steep hill toward Sainte-Marie-des-Ponts.

Lisette had always enjoyed the five-day crossing from Le Havre to New York. It was as if France stayed with her until the moment she disembarked. The menus were in French, the food was French. The cabin staff spoke French. Their fellow passengers were often French. It was only when she stepped ashore that she felt the spasm of alienation she had felt so many years before. Here, she was no longer Madame Dering, but Mrs. Dering; no longer a Frenchwoman in France, but a stranger in a country she had never succeeded in making her own. She let out a long sigh. Before, it had not mattered. Greg had loved her, and she had wanted passionately to make him happy. Now he loved her no longer. He would not tell her so. He was too kind for that. But she had known, the day he had suggested they sleep apart, the luster of their marriage was fading for him.

Greg canceled the booking he had made at the Plaza. He had intended that they spend a week in New York before traveling home, but he was no longer in the mood for an extended holiday. He wanted the whole debacle to come to a swift end. He had stood on the walls of Falaise castle and seen her spontaneously put her hand into Luke Brandon's, seen the misery on her face as she had looked up at him—misery occasioned, no doubt, by the fact that all physical contact

283

between them was restricted to the moments when he, Greg, was out of sight. He had known he should have asked her for a divorce. He had tried to make her happy and he had failed. There was an ease between herself and Brandon that he knew was not there in his own relationship with her. She seemed visibly to relax in Brandon's company, to shed whatever inner burden she carried.

He had not asked her for a divorce. He could not. He knew he had lost her as a lover, but he clung hungrily to the shreds that remained. She was still at his side. He could see her, hear her. Outwardly their family unit was secure. And as long as he made no physical demands on her, there was every chance that it would remain secure. His eyes darkened. He wasn't a eunuch. If he didn't share her bed, there would have to be other beds. He didn't for one moment think she would mind. But he had to be sure.

They were alone in their compartment; Chicago was behind them, the prairies ahead.

"Our marriage underwent quite a change while we were in France," he said abruptly. "I have to know that you're happy with it, Lisette."

She dropped the book she had been trying to read, and he was aware again of the air of frailty that clung to her—that had no doubt clung to her when she had braved bombs and mortar shells to save Luke Brandon's life—that had clung to her through the long days and nights when she had worked tirelessly in the makeshift operating theater. It was the kind of frailty that invited outrage—a sexual frailty that had instantly aroused him and still aroused him. He moved abruptly to the window, knowing that if he weakened, if he reached out for her, there would be a hideous reenactment of the scene that had taken place between them at Valmy.

"Do you mean, am I happy that you no longer make love to me?" she asked uncertainly. She was wearing a high-necked dress of raspberry crushed wool. Her hair fell softly to her shoulders, and she looked heartbreakingly young, far too young to be the mother of two children, one of them a boy of eight.

"No, that speaks for itself." His voice was savage and she flinched. He didn't look at her. He stared out over the flashing panorama of endless wheat, his eyes narrow, his mouth a tight, thin line.

She remembered the laughing soldier who had swung her around in his arms on his return to Valmy—the laughter of their days in Paris, the laughter that had sustained them even when the physical side of their marriage was degenerating, and that sustained them no longer.

"Then I'm sorry," she said. "I don't understand."

He swung to face her. "We've agreed there'll be no divorce. The problems are too great. You would want to return to France, and I couldn't possibly let you take the children." He saw her shudder and hated himself for the threat that had been implicit in his words. She would never leave him if it meant leaving Dominic and Lucy as well. "But if I'm no longer sleeping in your bed," he continued brutally, "then I'll have to sleep in other beds."

For a moment she did not understand what he meant, and then understanding came and she gasped for breath as if she had been physically struck.

"Can you think of another alternative?" His eyes burned hers. She could, but it was one she was in no position to suggest. She had failed him miserably in bed, and now he no longer desired her there. Was he suggesting she return to France, leaving the children behind her? She felt as if she were drowning, as if her lungs were incapable of taking in air. "No," she said stiffly, her voice that of a stranger. "I can think of no other alternative, Greg."

She saw the bitter disappointment flare through his eyes before he turned his head away from her, and knew that he had wanted her to say that a divorce was possible, that she would allow him custody of the children. In a polite, tight voice, she excused herself, stepping out of the compartment and stumbling along the corridor, blinded by her tears.

It was a week later that she saw him with Jacqueline Pleydall. Dominic and Lucy had returned to school. She had survived the days since Greg's shattering announcement that he no longer intended to be faithful to her by clinging steadfastly to the routine of their lives. She continued to breakfast with him before he left for the agency. They spoke of Dominic's near fluency in French, of the agency's pitch for a pharmaceutical account, of the opening of a local art gallery. It was the conversation of near strangers.

Chrissie had telephoned her, eager to regale her with gossip after her two-month absence, and they had arranged to meet for lunch and to browse around the shops together afterward.

Lisette had parked the car outside the restaurant and was just about to step out onto the sidewalk when she saw Greg. He was head and shoulders above the other pedestrians, the cut of his dark business suit immaculate, his thick shock of curly hair burnished bronze by the sun. She saw him grin and her heart missed a beat. Not since before their trip to France had she seen his eyes crinkle at the corners, his teeth flash in one of his brilliant smiles. She smiled back, fumbling eagerly with the catch on the Lincoln's door, and then she saw that he was not smiling at her, that he had not even seen her. His gaze had gone beyond her to the tall, slender blond crossing the road to meet him. She sank back against the Lincoln's pale blue leather upholstery, watching as the blond ran up to him, as his arms closed round her, as they entered the restaurant hand in hand.

She had thought she had long since become immune to shock, that nothing had the power to devastate her, as Dieter's death had devastated her. She had been wrong. She was shaking uncontrollably. He had told her, warned her. Yet in the deepest recess of her mind, she had not believed him. She slammed the car into gear, screaming out into the mainstream of traffic without even looking to see if her way was clear. She forgot all about Chrissie. She was overcome with the need to escape, to put as many miles as possible between herself and the crucifying reality of Greg, his arm circling Jacqueline Pleydall's waist.

She swerved onto Marina Boulevard, speeding past the Presidio military base with scant regard for other traffic. He didn't want a divorce. He had told her he didn't want a divorce. She clung to the knowledge like a drowning man to a piece of driftwood. A reconciliation then? Yet what reconciliation could there be when her frigidity had ensured that their bed was not a haven but a battleground? She swerved to a halt, knowing that Greg had not betrayed her, but that she had betrayed him. Crossing her arms on the steering wheel, she lowered her head to her hands and wept unrestrainedly.

In some strange way things were better between them after she knew Jacqueline Pleydall had eased her way back into his life. She never told him she had seen them together. She was too fearful of where such a conversation would lead. But she now had much more to think about and dwell upon than her guilt over his belief that Dominic was his son. She had loved him for a long time, but in the months after she had seen him with Jacqueline, she knew that she was as fiercely in love with him as a young girl is with the first love of her life. She saw him not as her husband, kind and caring, but as other women did—as Jacqueline Pleydall no doubt saw him: an indecently handsome man, tall and toughly built, carrying the glamour of his wealth and his position as head of one of the world's most successful advertising agencies with nonchalant ease.

Their bedrooms remained separate, but something of their old camaraderie returned. There were family breakfasts on the patio, family excursions to the beach and to the mountains. She was grateful for any physical contact at all—his fingers brushing hers as they both reached for a picnic basket at the same time, his hand steadying her as they walked with the children up through the woods around Lake Tahoe.

With bitter irony she knew that now he no longer needed her body; her body was at last free of the shackles that had constrained it for so long. If he turned to her now, she would be able to respond with all the passion she had always felt for him. But he didn't turn to her. He was affectionate and considerate—and he made no sexual overtures to her whatsoever.

She discovered painfully what Luke and Greg had sensed about her from the first—that she was a woman of deep sexual needs. Her frigidity had stifled those needs, hidden them from her, but now they could be hidden no longer. She was confounded by desire for a man who no longer made any attempt to share her bed—a man to whom she could only show her love by her care for his child and for the child he believed was his. When Luke telephoned her from Los Angeles saying he was attending Johnson Matthie's annual general meeting and asking her to meet him, she knew that she dare not agree.

287

"What do you mean you can't meet me?" he asked incredulously. "Of course you can meet me!"

"No!" There was an underlying panic in her voice, and his eyes sharpened—his hand tightening around the telephone. "I can't meet you, Luke. I've arranged to take the children to Carmel."

"You're lying," he said smoothly. "The children are at school. I know. I spoke to Greg on the phone only five minutes ago."

"Oh . . ." She closed her eyes. He was her friend, her best friend, and she wanted to see him more than anything in the world. She opened her eyes. She was not in love with him. She was not going to go to bed with him. She was panicking unnecessarily.

"It will take you about five hours to drive up here. I'll meet you outside the Presidio. And then we'll go for lunch."

"Good," he rasped. "*Tu m'as manquée.* I missed you."

"I missed you too," she said, and as she put the receiver back on its rest, her hand was trembling.

20

The house was empty. The children were at school. It was her housekeeper's day off. She walked quickly up the wide sweep of the stairs, refusing to think any further than that she was getting ready to meet a friend for lunch. If Greg had been home, no doubt they would have gone to meet Luke together. But Greg hadn't been home, and he wouldn't be home until late. He would be with Jacqueline Pleydall. She stepped into her bathroom, turning on the shower with a sharp twist of her hand. She mustn't think about it. To think about it would be to go mad. She undressed quickly, then stepped beneath the steaming spray of water, turning her face upward, closing her mind to everything but the feel of the water on her skin, the fragrance of the soap, refusing to acknowledge the abyss yawning wide at her feet.

She dressed as if she were going to meet Greg: a cream silk dress she had bought in France, a long strand of pearls dipping to precisely the right length on the softly draped neckline, sheer stockings, high ivory kid pumps. She swept her hair off her neck, piercing the neat twist she created with long, tortoiseshell pins, spraying *Je Reviens* on her throat and wrists. She paused as she left the room, looking at herself in her full-length mirror. She looked very French, very chic—not at all American. It was how Greg liked her to look. A spasm of pain crossed her face. She picked up a small clutch bag that matched her dress, closed the door behind her, and ran lightly down the stairs. She mustn't think of Greg. To think of Greg was to think of Jacqueline Pleydall—of Jacqueline Pleydall enjoying his kisses, his love-making.

She slid behind the wheel of her Lincoln Zephyr, turning on the ignition, forcing herself to think instead of where she would take Luke for lunch. She should have booked a table at the Atlantis. She accelerated, moving smoothly from first gear to second to third. Below her, in the bay, a large freighter was slowly gliding beneath the Golden Gate Bridge, the sun dazzling on the line of foam in its wake. It would be pleasant to eat down by the water. Perhaps they could go to one of the Italian restaurants on the wharf or to Pier 39.

For three hours she browsed around the shops, buying a sweater for Lucy, a leather belt for Dominic, and then, refusing to acknowledge her rising tension, she drove toward the Presidio. She glanced at her watch, knowing she was early, that Luke would still be on the freeway. As she eased to a halt, the door of a blue Cadillac parked a little way ahead of her flew open and Luke catapulted out onto the sidewalk, sprinting toward her.

She was only halfway out of the car when he grabbed hold of her, his hand closing around her wrist, pulling her out of the driving seat and upright against him.

"You must have driven like a bat out of hell," she began, laughing, and then her laughter faded. His body was hard and strong against hers. She could hear his heart slamming, see the hunger in his eyes.

"God, but I've missed you," he said fiercely, and uncaring of the curious stares of passing pedestrians, he tightened his arms around her, and his mouth came down unhesitatingly on hers.

She knew then what she had known and refused to acknowledge ever since the moment she had agreed to meet him. She was no longer going to spurn his advances. He loved her, and her body was desperate for love. With a low moan of capitulation, she pressed herself feverishly against him, her arms flying around his neck, her mouth parting willingly beneath his.

A tremor ran through him. She sensed his astonishment, his incredulity. He pushed her away from him, holding her savagely by the arms, his eyes burning questioningly into hers. At what he saw there, he whipped open the Lincoln's passenger seat door, bundled her inside, strode around to the driver's seat, and slid swiftly behind the wheel.

"Where to?" he asked tersely, gunning the car into life.

"I don't know—" Her voice was hoarse. "Anywhere—"

He shot out into the main stream of traffic, heading south, and she knew there would be no lunch, that it was not a restaurant he was searching for. She didn't even notice the name of the motel. It was as if all the pent-up sexual longings of years were screaming for fulfillment. She clung to his arm as he veered into the parking lot, thrusting open her car door the instant he screamed to a halt, running with him across the tarmac to the reception desk. Luke made no pretense of decency. He didn't explain their lack of luggage. He didn't refer to her as his wife. He simply booked a double room, snatched the key from the bellboy's hand, then strode along thickly carpeted corridors toward the room as if his life depended on the speed with which he reached it.

He didn't ask her anything, didn't speak to her. The door slammed shut behind him, and he seized her, crushing her against him, his mouth savaging hers.

She knew what she was doing. She knew she wasn't in love with him—that she never would be in love with him, that what was taking place was an act of lust, not love. Her lips ground passionately beneath his. It was lust that she craved. She burned with the need to give vent to the sexuality she had suppressed for so long. Luke knew her. He knew things about her no one but her father knew. He knew, and he didn't care. It was the only aphrodisiac she needed.

They fell together on the bed, tearing with animal-like ferocity at each other's clothes. His shirt was open to the waist, but he didn't remove it. To remove it would have meant releasing his hold on her, and now that his hands were at last on her naked flesh, he wouldn't release his hold for a second. The exquisite French dress had been ripped from her shoulders, baring her breasts, the skirt pushed high, the silk lying in a tumbled swathe around her waist. Neither of them had consideration for the other. There was no gentleness, no tenderness. He spread-eagled her beneath him, unzipping his fly, crushing her breasts in both his hands as he plunged into her with the pent-up longing of years.

Her nails gouged his shoulders. She bit him, tasting blood, arching her spine, her head back, eyes closed as spasm after spasm rocked through her. But it was not Luke's name she cried out as her body gave itself to the pleasure so long denied by guilt. It was Greg's.

He couldn't get enough of her. He was blind and deaf, lost in a world that held only Lisette. Lisette, crying out beneath him, Lisette, her mouth and tongue avid for his; Lisette, surrendering utterly—her legs around him, her nails scoring his flesh—as hungry for him as he had been, for years, for her. He felt himself spurt into her, heard himself shout with triumph, and then, his heart crashing against his ribs, he collapsed, spent, on top of her.

For a long time neither of them moved. Motes of dust danced in the slatted light of the blinds. In a distant room music played. The pillows were on the floor, the sheets rucked around them. He lifted himself up on his arms, staring down at her. "Why?" he asked. "After all these years, Lisette. Why now?"

Slowly she opened her eyes, and he saw pain and defeat in their violet-dark depths. "Because you know me," she said at last, her voice bleak. "Because you love me as I am."

"And Greg doesn't?"

She rolled away from him, standing and pulling her dress up on her shoulders, walking to the window. "No," she said, gazing through the blinds at a minuscule lawn and a scattering of trees. "Greg doesn't know me at all. I made myself a stranger to him when I allowed him to think that Dominic was his son. I thought by that lie, I would keep him. Instead, I lost him."

"And you still love him?"

She turned to face him. Between them there had never been any lies. "Yes," she said, "but apart from the early days when we were in Paris, I have never been able to show him how much. And now he no longer cares."

Luke lay on the bed, raised up on one elbow. It was pointless to ask if she loved him. He knew she didn't. But now that they had become lovers, he knew they would remain lovers. He said brusquely, "Unpin your hair."

His body was less powerful than Greg's—leaner and darker. The tight black curls on his chest grew low, skimming his taut stomach, merging with the thick tangle of his pubic hair. His body wasn't the body she wanted. He wasn't the man she loved. But with him she experienced a sense of freedom she knew she would experience with no one else. There were no secrets between them, no pretense.

Slowly she lifted her arms and eased the tortoiseshell pins free. The thick, glossy cloud of her hair tumbled to her shoulders, swinging forward at either side of her face. Luke's eyes gleamed. That was how he had first seen her, not sleek and sophisticated, but with her face flushed with exertion and danger, her eyes bright, her hair loose and free.

"Come back to bed," he said huskily. "The afternoon is only just beginning."

She stood, framed by the light seeping through the shutters, then slowly she slipped her dress from her shoulders, easing it down over her hips, stepping free of it. As she moved toward the bed, she was overcome by a feeling of inevitability. This was the moment they had both been traveling toward for so long, the moment Luke had always known they would reach. She knelt on the bed, the slatted sunlight falling in golden bars on her nakedness. "I don't love you," she said as he cupped her breasts. "Whatever happens between us, there can be no lies, Luke." She shivered as his fingers brushed her nipples, as he drew her close against him. "I'm so very weary of lies," she whispered, and then he slid her beneath him, his mouth covering hers, and the only sound to fill the room were the urgent, hoarse cries of their lovemaking.

It was dusk by the time they walked back across the motel's parking lot to her car. "I fly back to London in two days' time," he said as he opened her door for her. "I won't be able to see you again before I leave, but I'll be back soon. Within the month." He slid behind the wheel and eased the Lincoln out onto the freeway. "And no more motel rooms. The ex-creative director of Johnson Matthie's Los Angeles office is in London for a year. He's offered me his beach house at Carmel any time I'm over here long enough to make use of it. And from now on, I'm going to be here quite a lot."

"And Annabel?" she asked, a shadow touching her eyes. "Won't she want to come with you?"

"No," he said unequivocally. "We don't have that kind of marriage. Annabel hates to leave London. Her friends are there. Her social life continues quite happily whether I'm at her side or not. Coffee with women friends at Fortnum's. Afternoons at the Royal Academy. First nights at Covent Garden. Our affair will take nothing away from Annabel. She has my respect. She'll always have that, but she's never had my love."

Lisette looked across at his hawklike silhouette. "Not ever?" she asked, suddenly chilled.

He turned his head toward her, amused. "No," he said. "How could she? All the love I'm capable of has been yours and you know it."

"Poor Annabel."

"Annabel is perfectly happy. She has a beautiful home in Knightsbridge, a delightful daughter, a husband who rarely refuses any of her requests. If you need to feel sorry for anyone, feel sorry for me. How the hell am I going to survive with the width of America and the Atlantic between us?"

"You'll find a way," she replied, knowing that she must not think of Annabel.

He grinned, swerving out of the mainstream of traffic, drawing to a halt behind the dark blue Cadillac he had driven from Los Angeles. "I'll telephone you," he said. He switched off the ignition and turned toward her, his face fierce. "And when I do I'll give you the address of the cottage in Carmel." He pulled her close, his hand sliding up into her hair, holding her fast as his mouth bruised hers. Seconds later he was gone, slamming the Lincoln's door behind him, striding swiftly to his rented Cadillac.

She slid across into the Lincoln's driver's seat, watching as he gunned the Cadillac into life and deftly eased it out into the busy stream of traffic heading south. She waited until she could no longer see him, and then she turned the key in the Lincoln's ignition, knowing that Greg would already be home, that he would ask her courteously how she had spent her afternoon, that once again she would be caught up in the familiar pattern of deceit.

"Did Lisette leave a message as to where she was going?" Greg asked Simonette as she supervised the children's supper.

Simonette shook her head. "No, Mr. Dering. I had a dental appointment this morning, and when I got back after lunch, her car had gone but there was no message."

"Perhaps mummy has gone to Auntie Chrissie's," Lucy suggested helpfully. "Did you know that Aunt Chrissie is going to get married and that I'm going to be a bridesmaid? I'm to have a pink satin dress with rosebuds on the sleeves and all around the hem, and—"

Dominic snorted derisively and Lucy glared at him. "Dominic is jealous because he thinks he'll look silly if he's a page boy and so he isn't going to be anything at all."

"Thank goodness," Dominic said with heartfelt relief. "Aunt Chrissie wanted me to wear a white satin shirt and white satin trousers." He grinned at his father. "I told her I was too old to be dressed like that, that I'd just look stupid, and she's asked her boyfriend's nephew to be a page boy instead."

Lucy began to say that Auntie Chrissie's boyfriend's nephew would make a much better page boy than Dominic, and Greg, knowing how long the argument would continue, ruffled Dominic's hair and left them to it.

It was nearly eight o'clock. Although Lisette often drove quite considerable distances in her search for solitude, she was nearly always back in time for dinner. He poured himself a scotch, then walked out onto the patio, staring reflectively down the hillside toward the bay. It was too early yet to worry about her whereabouts, and in a way, he was relieved by her absence. He needed to be alone to think about the letter

Jacqueline had written him and that he had received at the agency that morning.

He had known from the very beginning of their renewed relationship that he was being unfair to her. She had believed his marriage was disastrous and that it would only be a matter of time before he freed himself of it. His hand tightened around his whiskey glass. She was damned right about his marriage being a disaster, but he had never intended to free himself of it, and he didn't intend to now. He had not brought the letter home with him. He had not needed to. It had been quite short, pathetically dignified.

". . . if I accept the offer to become fashion editor for *Femme*, it will mean becoming a permanent resident in Paris. I doubt I shall ever receive another such offer. The magazine has a vast circulation, and the position as fashion editor is a prestigious one. But if I accept, it will mean the end of everything there is between us. Please, please, my darling, tell me it is a step I must not take, that there is a future for us. The years of waiting for you to return when you were fighting in Europe were so long. And when you did return, it was with a girl you scarcely knew, as your bride. You know now what a mistake you made. Why, oh why, won't you admit it? I love you so much, and yet, even now, I am not sure that my love is returned. I'm leaving for New York this evening, for I know if I see you again, no matter what your answer is, I shall not have the strength to say good-bye to you. I shall be at the Plaza. Please, my darling, please tell me I can turn down *Femme's* offer, that I can return to San Francisco, knowing you do truly love me and that we will soon be married . . ."

He had crumpled the letter in his fist, despising himself for the hurt he had caused her and that he was about to cause her again. He drained his whiskey glass, knowing what he had to do, wondering if he were mad. Jacqueline idolized him. She had been faithful for four long years while he had been away in Europe fighting the Germans. She had loved him then and she loved him now. And he was going to sever their relationship

295

for a woman he no longer slept with—a woman who no longer made any gesture of physical love toward him, a woman who so obsessed him that anything was preferable to being separated from her. Grim-faced, he turned on his heel and walked back into the house, picking up the nearest telephone, asking to be connected to the Plaza Hotel, New York.

Lisette heard the click of the telephone receiver being replaced as she hurried past the closed door of the living room and up the stairs to her bedroom. It was eight-thirty. She wondered if Greg had eaten alone or if he had waited for her. She gazed, appalled, at her reflection in the mirror. Her hair was disheveled, her face bereft of makeup. Swiftly she unzipped her crumpled dress, tossing it to one side, taking a turquoise silk Balmain from a padded hanger and laying it on the bed. She powdered her face quickly, applied lipstick and mascara, and swept her hair high into a simple knot. Without changing her shoes or stockings, she stepped into the Balmain, smoothing the skirt, dabbed perfume on her throat and wrists, and left the room without even pausing to check her reflection in the mirror.

For a split second, as she entered the living room, she thought he had been in an accident, or that he had received bad news. The flesh was drawn tight across his cheekbones, the lines running from nose to mouth gouged deep.

"What is it?" she asked anxiously, remembering the telephone call, thinking immediately of the children. "Is anything wrong?"

His mouth quirked in a humorless smile. "No, I was just wishing an acquaintance success in a new job in Paris."

"Oh," she said awkwardly, sensing that something, possibly at work, had disturbed him. "Have you eaten?"

"Not yet. Would you like a drink?"

"Yes, please. A Scotch."

He raised one eyebrow slightly. She rarely drank anything other than wine. "I take it it's been a bad day," he said, pouring two fingers of Scotch into a glass and topping off his own.

"No." Her voice was unsteady. She wondered how she had ever imagined that this new deceit would be bearable. He handed her her glass, and she took it, her eyes avoiding his, turning away from him and walking over to the windows.

"Luke rang me this morning from Los Angeles," Greg said, watching her, his eyes curious. "He said he might try and visit here before he flies back to London. Did he ring you?"

"No. Yes." Her hand tightened nervously on her glass. "Yes, he rang me, but no, he isn't going to have time to visit us. He's flying back to London almost immediately."

"That's a pity," Greg said neutrally. "I would have liked to have seen him away from Valmy. I can't imagine him anywhere else. Certainly not here."

Lisette stared out over the bay. Luke and Valmy. Luke shooting Dieter in the black and white flagstoned hall. Luke asking her to marry him. It would have been better if she had done so. She hadn't loved him then, and she didn't love him now, but if they had married, no one else would have been hurt. Not Greg. Not Annabel. With Luke, there would have been no need for deceit. She would not have turned into a person she abhorred.

"Let's eat," she said, knowing that Simonette would have left a cold meal ready for them. The first deceit had been so very long ago—deceiving her father over her work for the Resistance. Then she had fallen in love with Dieter, and deceit had become a way of life. There had been a short time when she had been free of it, after she had married Greg and before Luke had told her of the enormous mistake she had made in thinking Greg knew, and did not care, about her love for Dieter. She could scarcely remember what it had felt like. From the moment Greg had taken Dominic in his arms, believing him to be his son, deceit had become her permanent companion. Now, willfully, she was adding to it.

"You must have been disappointed at not seeing Luke while he's over here," Greg was saying as he sat opposite her at their rosewood dining table.

"Yes," she said, her voice tight in her throat, the last shreds of her self-respect shriveling and dying.

21

There were times, through that first long, hot summer of their affair, when she wondered if she would ever be happy again. She had the sexual release she had craved for so long, but she had neither joy nor peace of mind. Her unfaithfulness had made the division between herself and Greg complete. They were like two people standing on opposite sides of a river bank, exchanging polite courtesies and very little else. They met at the breakfast table, they met in the evening, but the endearments, the gestures of affection that had once been part of their life together were now gone. She could no longer call him *chéri*, not when she knew that a mere telephone call would take her again to Luke's bed. There were times when she could barely remember the hope she had felt in the early days of their marriage—the warm, encompassing security of knowing that he loved her, the joy and delight as her affection for him had deepened into a love transcending even the love she had felt for Dieter. It had all seemed so wonderful once. And it had all come to nothing.

Once a month, sometime twice, she drove south out of San Francisco and down to Carmel. She never stayed the night, not even on the occasions when Greg was away on business trips in New York or London. Staying away from home at night would mean lying to Dominic and Lucy about her whereabouts, and there had been enough lies already, a multitude of them. She had no intention of beginning to tell them to her children.

The cottage in Carmel was set back from the beach, surrounded by a windbreak of trees. There were times, at dusk, when she could imagine herself in Normandy again, but then she would feel the warmth in the evening air and the illusion would vanish, and the old desolation would creep around her heart as she longed for a very different sea, a very different coast.

"I would take you back there," Luke had said to her, striding across the beach to where she stood, her hands deep in the pockets of her jeans, the sea wind tugging at her hair.

She had not needed to ask where he was talking about. Luke had always had the ability to read her thoughts. She had not turned to him as he came up behind her, his hands cupping her shoulders, his head bending forward, his mouth brushing her hairline—the curve of her cheek—the corner of her mouth.

She had stared out over the inexorably rolling waves and had allowed temptation to surge over her. Normandy, with its salt marshes and sand dunes, and its cold, clear light. Normandy and Valmy. Home.

Her nails bit deep into her palms. It wasn't Dominic and Melanie's home. Their home was with Greg. He would not allow them to be taken away from him.

"No," she said bleakly. "I shall not be going back to Normandy again, Luke. Not ever."

He shrugged, turning her around to face him, confident that she would one day return, and that when she did, he would be at her side.

"Let's make love one more time before you drive back to 'Frisco," he said, holding her close as he began to walk back with her toward the cottage. "It will be another three weeks, maybe four, before I see you again."

She leaned against him, her arm around his waist. The vast distance between San Francisco and London was treated by Luke as if it were a mere twenty-minute drive. Sometimes they had only the one afternoon together. She had told him he was mad, flying so far and at such expense, for little more than a lunch date. He had grinned, telling her he would be the judge of whether his journey was worth it or not. The trips had continued. To Luke, determined to continue seeing her at any cost, the Atlantic Ocean was as easily traversable as the English Channel.

They stepped into the cottage, closing the door behind them. It was autumn now and driftwood was piled high in the open fireplace. A copy of Zola's *Thérèse Raquin* in French lay open on a low table. There were more books in French on the shelves. A silver-framed photograph of her mother and father stood on an old English desk, a photograph of Valmy beside it. The room bore witness to both their personalities. The flowers in pretty porcelain bowls were arranged with a flair that was exquisitely French. The modern paintings on the walls were unmistakably Luke's choice, collected by him on his many trips to the Los Angeles art galleries.

As they climbed the burnished wood stairs to the little yellow bedroom above, Lisette wondered for the thousandth time why she was able to give to Luke freely and without inhibition that which she longed to give Greg. She paused in the doorway of the room, suddenly loath to enter. The ferociousness of their lovemaking had never abated. There were times when it shocked, even frightened her. There was no gentleness in their couplings, little tenderness. Luke's need of her and hers of him were violent and deep, a thirst that had constantly to be slaked, but it wasn't love.

She hugged her arms around herself, remembering the lamplit turret room, the sound of the waves running up the shingle. There had been love there. There had been love in the tiny room beneath the eaves of Madame Chamot's cottage on the night of her marriage. But in this room she came to so often of her own volition, there was only Luke's obsession to possess her and her own, crushing loneliness.

Luke pulled off his shirt, threw it over a velvet-upholstered, button-backed chair, and kicked off his shoes. "What's the matter?" he asked, his eyebrows quirking as she remained in the doorway, making no move toward the large, patchwork-quilted bed.

"It's late," she said with a small, apologetic gesture of her hands. "I can't stay any longer, Luke. I'm sorry."

His brows flew together as his shirt followed his tie. He had traveled thousands of miles to see her, to hold her, and she was anxious about returning to San Francisco late. Late for what?

"What's the hurry?" he asked, jealousy raging through him as he strode toward her. "Greg won't be waiting for you. He'll be out with his ladyfriend!"

She winced and he grabbed her, wanting to hurt her as much as she hurt him. "For Christ's sake, forget him!" he said savagely, his fingers digging deep into her flesh as he pulled her against the hard nakedness of his chest. "He doesn't want you! Doesn't love you! He's a rich man's son who thought it amusing to bring a French bride home as a trophy of war! The amusement's worn off, Lisette. He should have married a nice American girl—a girl with no past, a girl with no country to be homesick for, a girl who would never have had cause to lie to him!"

"But he didn't," she flared passionately. "He married me and I'm *glad* he married me, Luke! Even if he no longer loves me, I'm glad he loved me once! . . . that he wanted me for his wife!"

He tilted her face to his, his eyes burning into hers, knowing that he was on the verge of losing her once again. "He loves you no longer," he said fiercely. "*I* love you, and in every possible way I'm going to show you just how much!"

Greg sat back in his chrome and leather chair and viewed the latest Dering three-minute commercial with narrowed eyes. It was good. The client was one of the largest candy manufacturers in the country, and the campaign to launch a new chocolate bar with the line "Can't resist them," linking television and magazine and billboard advertising, had worked well. He flicked the control button off and walked over to the well-stocked bar to pour himself a Scotch. It was nine-thirty at night and the luxurious conference room was empty. Nick Burnett, his creative director, had wanted to stay behind and discuss the strategy for the new cosmetic account they had lured from a rival agency, but Greg had told him there was no hurry, that they could discuss it in the morning.

Nick had shrugged and been disappointed, but had not argued. Greg's mouth tightened as he swirled ice cubes around in his glass. Over the last six months he had become a man very few people chose to argue with. His easygoing affability was a thing of the past. Now he rarely smiled. Unhappiness had made him curt and unapproachable. He drained his glass and walked over to the windows, staring out over the darkened streets to where the bay gleamed silkily in the distance. He was thirty-six. He was rich, successful, attractive to women— and as miserable as hell. Jacqueline's letter lay open on his desk:

301

. . . so I am going to marry him. I have no illusion
that my letter will devastate you, that you will
immediately realize what a mistake you made in
encouraging me to leave for Paris. You didn't love
me, and to be fair to you, you never pretended`you
did, not after you had married. But what kind of a
marriage is it? I still don't know and still don't
understand. I loved you very much, Greg. I doubt
that I will ever love my Frenchman as much, but I
will try. Good-bye, my darling . . .

She was right in supposing her letter had not devastated
him. He had felt only relief. Her unhappiness had weighed on
his conscience, and now, at last, he felt free of it. She would
make a good wife and mother. No doubt, in time, she would
come to love her Frenchman far more than she had ever loved
him. He hoped so.

Nevertheless, her letter *had* unsettled him. She had
asked, in writing, the question he had been asking himself for
months. Just what kind of a marriage did he have? Ever since
their return from France nearly a year ago, there had been no
sexual relationship between him and Lisette. She had retreated from him not only physically but mentally as well. He
no longer knew what she was thinking or feeling. She ran his
home superbly. She was a marvelous hostess, a perfect mother.
She turned heads in the most crowded and star-filled of rooms.
And she was as far removed from him as the moon.

He turned away from the window and poured himself
another drink. She wasn't happy, he could see that by her eyes,
by the desolation that filled them when she thought herself
unobserved . . . His own eyes hardened. There had been a
time when he had believed he would do anything in the world
to make her happy. Now he knew it wasn't so. It was their
marriage that was causing her misery, and he did not have the
strength to free her from it. The Scotch burned the back of his
throat. Jesus God. Why couldn't things be as they had been
when they were living in Paris? What the hell had happened to
turn them into the polite strangers who now shared the same
house but not the same bed, who appeared together in public
and avoided each other's company in private? No wonder
Jacqueline had been unable to understand. He himself didn't

understand. He only knew he had still not reached the point where living without her would be preferable to the raw hurt he suffered by continuing to live with her.

When he arrived home, he found her sitting at her desk in the small downstairs room she had turned into a study for herself. She was writing, the soft light of the desk lamp casting a halo around the dark sheen of her hair as it fell forward, curtaining her face.

"I phoned home at lunchtime but you weren't here. Had you gone to Chrissie's?" he asked, stepping into the room.

She looked up, startled, and almost immediately he could see the shutters coming down behind her eyes.

"No . . . I went for a drive . . . And a walk." Her voice was stilted, and he felt like an inquisitor.

"North or south?" he asked, forcing a smile, wanting to prolong the conversation, and knowing very well that she regarded his presence in her room as an invasion of her privacy.

"I . . . South. To Carmel." She had turned her head away from him, and he could no longer see her face. He saw she had been writing to her father when he had disturbed her. The blue airmail letter still rested, half finished, beneath her hand.

"I would have thought Carmel too touristy for you," he said with surprise.

"No, I like the beach. It reminds me of home."

She sounded as if she had been crying. Home. She had lived with him in San Francisco for all these years and Normandy was still home to her. He moved toward her, resting his hand lightly on her shoulder. It was the first physical contact there had been between them for months. He felt her tremble beneath his touch and said gently, "I didn't know you were still so homesick, sweetheart. We could go back again if you wished."

She gave a small gasp, and he knew he had been right, that she had been crying. "If you are so unhappy, perhaps it would help if you talked to me," he said compassionately, raising his hand from her shoulder and stroking the silky fall of her hair. It had been a long time since he had run his fingers through the long, shining strands and felt the soft sweep of it brush against his chest.

She turned then, looking up at him, her eyes resolute. "Yes," she said, her voice tight in her throat, her hands trembling as she laid them in her lap. "I've wanted to talk to you for a long time, Greg. Let me talk to you now."

He knew that if he lowered his head to hers, if he kissed her, she would not turn away from him. The breath was so tight in his chest that he could hardly breathe. The moment had come out of nowhere, and he was determined not to let it go.

"Then let's talk," he said huskily, cupping the perfection of her face in his hand as his mouth closed over hers.

The fountain pen she had been holding dropped from her fingers. It had been so long since he had called her sweetheart that at first she had thought her hearing was deceiving her. His mouth moved on hers, warm and sweet, infinitely tender. She knew she dare not think of Luke, of the savage lovemaking that had taken place only hours ago in the cottage at Carmel. She dare think of nothing that would freeze her as Greg drew her slowly to her feet, fitting her body snugly against his, letting her feel the hardness of him, the raging desire.

"I love you, Lisette," he said, his voice raw with need. "I've always loved you. I've never stopped loving you."

Her skin burned where his lips touched it. She wanted to ask a thousand things. If he still also loved Jacqueline Pleydall. If he would move back into her bedroom again. Her fingers curled in his hair, her body pressed against his, and she knew that the time for questions was later. Much later. She could allow nothing, no memory or guilt, to sabotage this moment of reconciliation. This time she would not fail him. This time she would show him how very, very much she loved him—how wonderful things could still be between them.

The telephone bell shattered the silence. His mouth didn't move from hers as she reached out for the receiver, lifting it and letting it fall unanswered on the leather top of her desk.

". . . I'm phoning from the airport." The faint, precise English tones were unmistakable. "Annabel phoned me an hour or so ago, just before I left Carmel. She wants to know if Melanie can come and visit you for a couple of weeks . . ."

Slowly Greg raised his head from hers and looked down at her, his face white.

". . . she can stay in the cottage at Carmel of course, if I'm over at the same time . . ."

"My God—" Greg whispered disbelievingly, releasing his hold on her so abruptly that she nearly fell. "So that's whom you were with this afternoon!"

". . . For goodness sake, Lisette. Yes or no?" Luke continued impatiently. "My flight is already boarding."

"He was over here on business." Her lips were so dry she could hardly speak. "Naturally I drove down to say hello to him. I was going to tell you, but—"

"No!" His face looked as if it had been carved from stone. "You wouldn't have told me, Lisette. You would have kept it to yourself as you keep everything to yourself. God only knows how often he flies over here, how often you see him." His nostrils flared. There were thin white lines around his mouth. "Don't let me encroach on your time any longer," he said savagely. "You obviously have better things to do with it," and he turned away from her, striding from the room, not trusting himself to remain a moment longer.

"Lisette, for God's sake, what's the matter? Are you there?" Luke demanded querulously.

Blindly she groped for the desk and the telephone. "Yes," she said unsteadily, "I'm here."

Another five minutes and his telephone call wouldn't have mattered. She would have told Greg everything that she had kept secret for so long. She would have told him about Dieter. About Dominic. Even about Luke. No matter what his reaction, she would have been free of her burden. Now it weighed on her heavier than ever, crushing the life out of her.

"What do I tell Annabel? Can Melanie come over and stay with you?"

She sat on the edge of the desk, pushing her hair away from her face, her voice weary. "Yes," she said, knowing there was no way she could refuse. Annabel would be offended if she did; Melanie hurt. Dominic, if he got to know of the refused request, would be outraged.

"Good. Melanie will fly out to you next weekend. I'll let you know the estimated time of arrival of her flight. I'll see you myself a couple of weeks later. *Au revoir.*"

"*Luke!*"

He had been in the act of replacing the receiver. "Yes?" he

305

said, arrested by the urgency in her voice. "What is it? If I don't board now I'm going to miss my flight."

"I won't be seeing you in two weeks' time. Not while Melanie is staying here. It isn't possible."

"Don't be so ridiculous! Of course you'll see me. What difference does Melanie make?"

"I can't look after her in my home and then leave her to commit adultery with her father," she said, hysteria rising in her throat.

"You're being oversensitive," Luke retorted crisply. "Of course you'll see me. *Au revoir* for now. I must go."

"*I won't be seeing you!*" she cried fiercely, but it was too late. The connection had been severed.

Slowly she replaced the receiver knowing she would never see him again, not as a lover. Whatever had existed between them was over. Greg had told her that he loved her, and he had never lied to her. It might be weeks, months even, before the moment of trust that had flared between them could be recaptured, but when it was, she was going to ensure there would be no Luke to shatter and destroy it.

The next morning, when he had finished discussing the strategy for the newly acquired cosmetic account, Greg said casually to Nick Burnett, "Have you any idea how often Johnson Matthie's London chairman, Luke Brandon, comes over here?"

Nick picked up an armful of storyboards from Greg's desk and rubbed his nose reflectively. "Enough to make his counterpart in L.A. nervous. Rumor has it that he's renting Steve Bernbach's place in Carmel."

"Is that the cottage Johnson Matthie used for the 'Nostalgia' shoot last year?"

"Yup. All oak beams and roses around the door. Very picturesque. It should suit Brandon down to the ground."

Greg forced a dismissive grin. "Okay, Nick. Thanks. Let me have the new outline as soon as possible."

Nick left the room and Greg wrote the words "Bernbach" and "Carmel" down on his notepad and circled them, staring at them for a long time, his face hard.

* * *

"You mean that Melanie is coming here? To San Francisco? Today?" Dominic asked disbelievingly. "But why didn't you tell me? How long have you known? How long is she going to stay?"

"I knew a week ago," Lisette said unperturbedly, pouring milk for Lucy and passing it across the breakfast table to her. "I didn't tell you because I knew you would think and talk of nothing else."

A faint flush touched Dominic's cheeks. "That's not true," he said, feigning an indifference he was far from feeling. "I'm just interested, that's all." The slight shrug of his shoulders was so like Lisette's Gallic, dismissive shrugs that for the first time in days a smile tugged at the corners of Greg's mouth.

"I expect you will be too busy to spend much time with her," he said, knowing very well that the instant Melanie arrived they would be inseparable.

Dominic grinned. His father was teasing him, but he didn't mind. He'd much rather he teased him than look forbidding and unapproachable. His grin faded, and the anxiety he felt with increasing frequency returned. There had been a time when his father had never been unapproachable, a time when he had always been laughing. He looked at his parents, wondering why they so rarely smiled at each other, talked to each other. It was the first time in a month they had all breakfasted together. He said, "Can we go camping while Mel is here? We haven't been for ages and ages. We could go up to Lake Tahoe and teach Mel how to fish."

Greg hesitated, wondering if the seven-year-old Melanie would be less tomboyish than the six-year-old Melanie had been, and if Dominic was about to be disappointed. "We can go if Melanie wants to go," he said guardedly, "but she might prefer to stay in town with your mother and Lucy."

Dominic stared at him. "I meant for us *all* to go to Lake Tahoe," he said, looking suddenly very small and hunched.

The tension across the table, with its gay checkered cloth and pristine white china was palpable. Lucy looked up from spreading honey on her croissant, regarding her parents curiously.

"I don't think your mother would like—" Greg began, rising abruptly and picking up his jacket.

"I'd like to go to Tahoe very much," Lisette said before he could finish.

Their eyes met and held. She could feel her heart beating fast and light. It was another chance. The only chance there had been since the night of Luke's disastrous telephone call. "I've missed our weekends in the mountains," she said, willing him to understand, to reach her halfway. "It's two years since we last went. It's time we went again."

The plea in her soft, smoky voice was unmistakable. He halted in the act of putting on his jacket, his muscles tense, a dark eyebrow rising slightly. Since the night he had discovered she had been secretly meeting Luke, he had cut her out of his heart and mind as if with a surgeon's knife. The New York model who had been his mistress ever since Jacqueline had left for France had been rapturous at discovering he was contemplating divorce, and disbelieving when he had told her he had absolutely no intention of marrying her.

"I think you would find the lake inhospitable at this time of the year," he said, his voice so oddly abrupt that Dominic stared at him in astonishment.

"Oh!" She turned her head quickly away from him, wiping Lucy's mouth with a napkin, not wanting him to see her hurt. They had lived as strangers for so long that he had become a stranger—a tall, powerfully built stranger with thick brown curly hair and brandy-colored eyes; a stranger whose masculinity confounded her; a stranger she was desperately and hopelessly in love with.

He shrugged on his jacket and picked up his briefcase, eyeing her curiously. She was wearing a raspberry-pink sweater and a white exquisitely tailored skirt. Her hair had fallen forward at either side of her face, and he resisted the urge to reach out and touch it, to tilt her face to his and to kiss her ruby red mouth.

He wondered if she had suggested accompanying him to Lake Tahoe in order that Melanie would feel part of a secure family unit, or to please Dominic. A frown furrowed his brown. Certainly Dominic was beginning to notice their estrangement and to suffer because of it. A wave of love, fierce and protective, swept over him. No matter what happened, he would be damned to hell before he saw either of his children hurt. He looked at Dominic's pinched white face and said tersely, "If you really want to come with us to Tahoe, Lisette, you'd better buy yourself a new parka and buy one for Melanie as well. I doubt if she'll be bringing one with her from London."

Her eyes flashed up to his, but he wasn't looking at her any longer. He was ruffling Dominic's hair, wiping Lucy's sticky kiss from his cheek, promising them he would be home early to greet Melanie.

As his silver-blue Cadillac limousine swept away down the drive, she stood at the window watching. His days were now as much a mystery to her as hers were to him. The gossip columns told her more about his life than he did—how he had staunchly supported Eisenhower in his successful bid for the White House, how it was rumored that he, himself, was thinking of running for Congress.

The Cadillac disappeared from view, and she wondered if he would be seeing Jacqueline Pleydall at lunchtime—if he really would come home early that evening; if she would ever, ever have the courage to talk to him as she knew she must.

Early morning fog hung thick and heavy across the bay, and she shivered, hoping that it would clear before Melanie's flight was due, turning away as the slow hoot of fog horns echoed over the invisible water.

"Can I come with you to meet Melanie?" Dominic asked as Lucy excused herself from the table and began to gather up her school books.

"No, *chéri*, you must go to school."

Dominic stared at her, appalled. "That isn't fair! She'll be expecting me to be there when she lands! Please, Maman."

His use of his baby name for her was an indication of how distressed he was by her refusal. She hugged him tight. "*Alors!* Is it so important, *mon petit?*"

Dominic's eyes, gray and black-lashed, held hers. "Yes, Maman. We're friends," he explained.

She ruffled his dark gold hair. "Then you must come with me," she said with a catch in her throat. "I'll tell Simonette that only Lucy is going to school today."

"*Merci, Maman,*" he said, his eyes shining.

As she checked that Lucy had all her school books with her, Lisette wondered why Dominic should so happily speak to her in her own language when Lucy never did. In three years' time he would be offered the choice of taking German or Spanish in school. She wondered which he would choose. It would be strange to hear him speaking his father's language. Her eyes were pensive as she kissed Lucy good-bye. The German language was his birthright. She hoped passionately that it would be his choice but knew she would say nothing to influence his decision, for she was quite sure Greg would be as appalled if he chose it, as she would be pleased.

"Can we take Mel to Chinatown and to the zoo?" Dominic asked eagerly as they waited at the airport.

"We shall take Melanie wherever she wants to go," Lisette promised, wondering what Dieter would have said to the friendship between his son and Luke Brandon's daughter. She had begun to think of him more and more, trying to imagine what his advice to her would have been. He had been a man who had hated deceit, a man who had valued courage. As a flight attendant approached, a shining-eyed Melanie holding onto the woman's hand, she knew very well what his advice to her would have been: to tell Greg the truth and to live with the consequences. The worst thing that could happen was that he would leave her, but in every way that mattered, he had left her already.

"*Auntie Lisette! Dominic!*" Melanie cried, tearing herself free of the flight attendant's restraining hand and hurtling to meet them.

As her arms opened wide and she hugged Melanie tight, Lisette knew that her decision was made and that she would not go back on it. She would do nothing while Melanie was with them. The risk of Melanie overhearing when she confessed to her affair with Luke was too great. But the instant Melanie returned to London, she would drive down to Carmel and remove her possessions from the cottage. She would end the affair she should never have started in the first place. And she would tell Greg the truth.

"I was on the airplane for ages and ages," Melanie said rapturously to Dominic as they climbed into the Lincoln. "I had breakfast and lunch and dinner on the plane, and I never fell asleep once, even though daddy said I would!"

"Well, don't fall asleep now," Dominic said, grinning. "We've going to show you the Golden Gate Bridge."

"Gosh!" Melanie said, leaning forward to look out the windows as they swept out onto the freeway. "What a huge road! I'm going to enjoy America, Dominic. I know I am!"

* * *

Dering Advertising soared five floors above street level. Greg strode through his deeply carpeted private entrance, bypassing the glamorously dramatic reception area with its wall of bronze-tinted mirrors and twenty-foot semicircular desk. His elevator sped upward. The top floor was his private domain. It was there that the wheeling and dealing took place, there that all major decisions were made. He ran a mental eye over the appointments ahead of him that day.

A meeting with Nick to see the first visuals for the "Cosmetics *à la carte*" campaign. A nine-thirty meeting with Hal Green to make final the details of Dering's takeover of Hal's agency. A meeting with his chief accountant. An eleven o'clock meeting with Nick, the media, and board directors; lunch with the chairman of United Oil. Then to Acapulco to meet with the chairman of Wainwright to discuss a possible merger. He had intended piloting himself to the Acapulco meeting and maybe staying over a day. If he did so, he would be unable to keep his promise to Dominic.

He strode out of the elevator. The decor was all white, beige and gray; the walls, covered in oatmeal cream linen. "Cancel the Acapulco meeting," he said to his secretary, pulling down the knot of his tie and undoing the top button of his shirt as he slid his briefcase onto the massive surface of his white oak desk. "Reschedule it for Monday. Tell Russell I want to see Mr. Fox of United Airlines for ten minutes before he takes him into their meeting, and tell Grant that the position of our Chrysler ad in this morning's *New York Times* was bad and that the client was right. The Chrysler logo needs to be bigger."

"Yes, Mr. Dering," she said, swiftly reading down his page of appointments. She would have laid down and died for him if he had asked her. Her predecessor had warned her not to fall in love with him, but it had been easier said than done. Greg Dering reminded her of a riverboat gambler with his rumpled hair and easy assurance. There were rumors he was squiring one of New York's top models whenever business took him to the East Coast, which was two or three times a month. She didn't know if the rumors were true or not. The silver-framed photograph of his French wife still stood on his desk.

"Is everything ready for the eleven o'clock meeting?" he

311

asked, taking off his jacket and sliding it around the back of his chrome and leather chair.

"Yes, Mr. Dering," she said, going mentally over the check list for the conference room. Ashtrays, pencils, carafes of ice water, the thick, white notepads that Mr. Dering doodled on whenever a strategy meeting was in progress.

"Good." He settled back in his chair and reached for the phone. As she left the room she was sure the number he asked for was a New York number.

By nine-fifteen Greg knew his usual concentration had deserted him. He couldn't keep his mind on Nick's layout for the "Cosmetics *à la carte*" campaign, and he couldn't care less about the Hal Green takeover bid. He kept thinking of the way Lisette had spoken to him across the breakfast table—the naked plea in her low, husky voice; the feeling he had had that she was trying to reach out to him, trying to narrow the distance between them.

"The main decision we have to make is whether we are going to go for purity or sophistication," Nick was saying, laying a half-dozen glossy photographs on Greg's desk. "This girl has enomous vitality. She'd look great on the posters, but there's a lack of sophistication about her that worries me. 'Cosmetics *à la carte*' is an up-market product. We need a girl with the kind of sensuality that other women will want to emulate. Someone with style and panache and inner warmth."

"Then forget this little lot," Greg said, sifting dismissively through the photographs Nick had laid on his desk. "All you have here is veneer—surface glamour with no depth. We want a flesh-and-blood woman to promote 'Cosmetics *à la carte*,' someone with the kind of femininity that is timeless." His gaze fell on his photograph of Lisette. It had been taken on a sunny day, in the beech woods at Valmy. She was laughing, her head tilted slightly to one side, her hair falling in a long, smooth wave to her shoulders, a scarf knotted with careless elegance at her throat. "Someone whose face will stay in the memory for a lifetime," he said, a pulse throbbing at the corner of his jaw.

"Jeez," Nick said expressively, scooping up the photographs. "Where am I going to find a woman like that?"

Greg didn't tell him. He was no longer listening to him. Twenty-four hours ago, he had been contemplating divorce. Now he was no longer so sure.

312

"Mr. Green is waiting to see you," his secretary was saying.

Greg continued to stare at the photograph. She had said that she wanted to talk to him, and he had denied her the opportunity. Had she guessed he was contemplating a final break between them? Was she distressed at the prospect? Indifferent?

He rose abruptly. "Cancel the eleven o'clock conference," he said, swinging his jacket over his shoulder. "Tell Green I'll see him tomorrow."

"But Mr. Dering . . . ," his secretary gasped, running after him as he strode from the room. "Mr. Green has flown all the way from Houston for this morning's meeting!"

"Reschedule it. If he doesn't like it, tell him the deal is off."

"But Mr. Dering—"

The elevator doors closed behind him. She turned wide-eyed to Nick. "The Hal Green takeover is worth hundreds of thousands of dollars! What's come up that's more important?"

Nick shrugged. "God knows," he said, staring dismally at the rejected photographs in his hand. "I don't."

Greg slammed the Cadillac into first gear, speeding up the ramp of the underground garage and out into the brilliant winter sunlight that had followed hard on the heels of the morning fog. He felt exactly as he had on that far-off day in Normandy, when he had driven from the carnage of St. Lô, hurtling back through the high-hedged lanes to Valmy, knowing he had to see her again, if only for a moment.

He careened out into the main street, glancing down at his watch. Ten o'clock. She would be at the airport, meeting Melanie. He overtook a trailer, showing scant regard for the municipal speed limit. The first sight anyone wanted to see when he arrived in 'Frisco was the bridge, and the best place to view the bridge was from the "Top of the Mark" on Nob Hill.

He sped up to the forecourt of the Mark Hopkins Hotel, slewing in behind half a dozen parked cars, seeing with relief the unmistakable midnight-blue of Lisette's Lincoln convertible. He swung in behind it, his sense of *déjà vu* stronger than

313

ever. He had returned from St. Lô to Valmy on gut instinct, and he was following that instinct now. He sprang out of the car, slamming the door behind him, shielding his eyes against the sun. He could see easily the rich cornflower blue of her sweater and the pristine white of her slacks. She was standing fifty or sixty yards away, pointing something out to Melanie, her hair no longer falling unrestrainedly to her shoulders but tied at the nape of her neck with a ribbon, as it had been when she had first entered his arms, so many years ago.

He made no move toward her. He leaned against the Cadillac's door, his hands in his pockets, his stance as negligent and confident as it had been when he had waited for her against the gateway that led from Valmy's drive into the sun-warmed courtyard.

Dominic was talking to Melanie now, pointing out a ship that was making its way into the bay. Lisette stood straight, turning round to check on the Lincoln, freezing into immobility as their eyes met.

For a long moment neither of them moved. Behind her, the bridge spanned the bay, Marin County barely visible in the distance, and then, just as he had known she would, she began to walk toward him, slowly at first, and then with increasing speed. He grinned, opening his arms wide, and the intervening years went whistling down the wind as she began to run, her smile as dazzling as it had been on that long-ago afternoon when he had returned to Valmy and asked her to marry him.

22

As she pressed herself fervently against him, Greg felt again the certainty he had felt at Valmy—the certainty that he loved her, that she would one day love him; the certainty that he wanted to spend the rest of his life with her. His arms tightened around her. She had not entered them of her own volition since the hideous night when he had walked out of their bedroom at Valmy. For the first time in all the long, tortured months he had endured since then, he wondered if she had been as lonely as he had been.

He tilted her face up to his, tracing the delicate line of her cheekbone and jaw with his fingertip. "It's been a long time," he said huskily, wondering how he could ever have contemplated a divorce—ever have contemplated a life of acting as escort to glamorously beautiful women who were not Lisette, who had not an eighth of her radiant sensuality.

"Too long," she whispered, feeling his heart slam against hers, feeling again the sensation of safety and security that he had always engendered in her, the feeling of being encompassed by his love.

For a long moment his eyes held hers. He wanted to ask why, after all this time, she was returning to him. He wanted to ask about her meeting with Luke—to ask what it was that had gone wrong between them in the months and years following Lucy's birth. Instead he said, "I love you, Lisette. I've always loved you," and as the children ran laughingly up to them, he lowered his head to hers, kissing her with a passion that left no room for doubt.

"Daddy! Daddy! Are you going to spend all day with us?" Dominic asked, his eyes shining.

Slowly, regretfully, Greg lifted his head from Lisette's. "I think spending the day together would be a very good idea," he said, amused at their predicament: lovers, who had not made love for months, prevented from doing so by the presence of their child.

At the incongruity of their situation, answering laughter bubbled up in her. There would be time, later, for lovemaking. And time now for all the gestures of affection she had so missed between them. Her hand slid into his, their fingers interlocking tightly.

"I think we should take Melanie down to the bay for a late breakfast, and then, if she isn't too tired, perhaps we could go to the zoo," she said, knowing that the happiness now suffusing her would remain until it was time for Melanie to leave them—until it was time for them, at last, to talk.

"Oh, I'd *love* to go to the zoo!" Melanie said, her rosy-cheeked face ecstatic, "and I'm not a bit tired!"

"We'll go in the Cadillac, I'll have the Lincoln picked up later," Greg said, wondering what Hal Green and the chairmen of United Oil and Wainwright would say if they knew that instead of keeping his appointments with them, he was strolling like a tourist around the vast acres of the city's zoo.

They breakfasted down by the wharf, enjoying Melanie's delight as she tasted blueberry jam and bagels for the first time, and then they drove out to the Zoological Gardens, feeding seals and koala bears, watching the big cats prowl their enclosures. Lisette had done some hasty shopping down by the wharf, and they picnicked on paté and French bread and Brie, sitting on the grass while Dominic and Melanie ran off to see if the elephants here were as big as the elephants in the London Zoo. As Greg leaned on one arm at her side, it seemed to Lisette as if this was how they had always been—happy and in love—a family like so many other families strolling in the zoo gardens.

"You said you wanted to talk to me," he said, and the illusion vanished.

"Yes." She had been lying at his side, her head resting against his chest. She sat up, hugging her legs with her arms, knowing that she had to distance herself from him before she could continue. After a moment she said, "I've wanted to talk to you for years, Greg. Ever since you returned to Valmy when the war was over. Ever since we began our life together."

He continued to lie at her side, resting his weight on his arm. "Then why didn't you?" he asked, forcing his voice to be casual, almost indifferent.

There was a long silence. He saw her knuckles whiten as she hugged her legs tighter, her eyes fixed unseeingly ahead of her, resolutely avoiding his. "Because I was afraid," she said at last.

"Are are you still afraid?" he asked quietly, his brows flying together, small white lines etching his mouth.

She turned her head and looked at him. "No," she said, and there was surprise in her voice. "The worst that could happen, happened anyway. You stopped loving me."

He sat bolt upright. *"That's not true!"* He seized her shoulders, swinging her around to face him, his eyes blazing.

"You asked if I would mind if we slept apart." There was no accusation in her voice, only remembered hurt. "You renewed your affair with Jacqueline Pleydall."

316

His fingers dug savagely into her shoulders. "I asked if you minded if we slept apart because I wanted you to say no! I wanted you to realize where your unresponsiveness to me was leading!"

She stared at him. "And Jacqueline Pleydall?" she asked, stunned.

The lines around his mouth deepened. "I renewed my affair with Jacqueline because I was devastated by what was happening to us. She offered solace and comfort, and I was selfish enough to take it."

Her mouth was suddenly dry, her throat tight. "And does she still offer solace and comfort?" she asked, not able to tear her eyes away from his, seeing again the gold flecks in the amber-dark depths, seeing incomprehension and then incredulity.

"My God! You don't think I'm still having an affair with her, do you?" The expression on her face was his answer. He ran his hand through the thick tumble of his hair, searching for the right words, knowing that even as he told her that his affair with Jacqueline was over, he would have to admit to other, possibly more hurtful affairs. "Jacqueline wanted from me what she had always wanted from me—marriage. I told her it was impossible. She left America for France months ago, and I haven't seen her since. Apart from one letter, in which she told me she was to marry a Frenchman, we haven't corresponded."

He saw Lisette's relief and, before she could express it, continued ruthlessly, "I hurt Jacqueline unforgivably, and I determined I would never hurt anyone else in the same way, but that doesn't mean there haven't been other women, Lisette. There have. Women better suited than Jacqueline was to an affair with a man who has no intention of marrying them."

"Is there someone now?" She had twisted onto her knees, her gaze holding his, knowing the answer.

He gave a slight, almost indiscernible shrug of his shoulders. "Yes. There is a woman in New York."

She knew from the tone of his voice that the woman in New York was unimportant.

He was watching her curiously, waiting, she knew, not for her reaction to his disclosures, but for what she had still to tell him.

"What I have to say isn't quite so easy," she said, a catch in

317

her voice as she saw Dominic and Melanie walking over the grass toward them. "It concerns Luke . . . and I don't want to talk about Luke while Melanie is with us."

Greg turned his head, watching the children as they approached. "No," he said, certain of what it was she was going to tell him, and as unhappy to hear it as she was to tell it. "Let's leave all revelations concerning Luke until Melanie returns to England."

"And other revelations?" she asked quietly as he rose to his feet.

She saw shock flare through his eyes, then he said tightly, "Are there other revelations?"

She nodded, her face set and pale.

The white lines etching his mouth grew more pronounced. "They've waited all these years," he said decisively, stretching out his hand to her and drawing her to her feet. "They can wait two weeks longer."

She felt weak with relief. It was a reprieve—no matter what happened when Melanie left for England and she told him at last about Dominic's paternity, about her affair with Luke. There were two weeks in which she could make some sort of recompense, in which she could show him how very much she loved him.

That night, when the children were asleep, they made love. It was nothing like her lovemaking with Luke, nothing like the tortured, anguished lovemaking they had endured in the years following Lucy's birth. It was as if they were once more beneath the eaves of Madame Chamot's cottage, once more touching for the first time, surrendering with wonder and passion to their overwhelming physical need of each other.

"I love you . . . love you . . . love you . . . ," she whispered as he cradled her beneath him, his hands caressing the soft, gentle curve of her thighs, his lips moving hotly from her mouth to her throat to the rose-pink upthrust of her nipples. His head moved lower, and she cried out in pleasure, her hips moving up to meet him, her fingers tightening in his hair as his hot, stabbing tongue searched and found.

She moaned rapturously, overcome by the sense of completeness, the sense of rightness that his lovemaking gave her. It was like flying, like the sensation in dreams of having wings and soaring high above the earth. With a deep groan of need, he entered her and she gasped, her arms tightening around him, knowing that this time frigidity would not cripple her—that the climax they reached would be as perfect, as cataclysmic, as the climax they had reached together on that long-ago night in Sainte-Marie-des-Ponts.

"I love you, Lisette . . . love you . . . ," he uttered hoarsely as they moved together, ascending a summit so high, so terrible in its beauty, that he doubted he would survive it. He heard her cry his name, felt his very heart jar and move, and then hot gold shot through him, and he knew, as the most intense orgasm of his life convulsed him, that they had conceived another child.

Lisette felt as she had felt with Dieter in the turret room at Valmy, that she had stepped out of time, that the days that followed had no relation to anything that had gone before, or that would come after. She savored every moment, every second, storing them away in her memory so that nothing would ever be able to rob her of them.

"I don't want Melanie to go back to London," Dominic said to her as the first magic-filled week ended, and the second week began.

She had hugged him, not letting him see the agony that flashed through her eyes. "No, *mon petit*," she had said, her voice even huskier than usual. "Neither do I."

As he walked disconsolately away from her, she wondered, with terror, if Greg would no longer wish to act as a father to him when he knew the truth, if she was putting not only her own happiness at risk, but his also. Her nails dug deep into her palms. If she was, it was the terrible price she would have to pay. She could only pray that not only would Greg forgive her, but that in time Dominic would forgive her too.

"I won't be able to come with you to the airport to see Melanie off," Greg said the day before Melanie was due to leave. "United Oil is coming in to discuss next year's campaign."

"That's all right, *chéri*," she said, her smile brilliant, refusing to think of the moment when Melanie left, thinking only of the day stretching out before them, the day he had promised to spend entirely with her.

He stood behind her, sliding his arms around her waist. "How about a few days in Texas next week? Now that the Hal Green deal has gone through without a hitch, I'd like to fly down there and personally cast my eye over the new agency."

"Texas would be lovely," she said, her voice faltering slightly. By next week he would probably not want to go anywhere with her, might not even still be living with her.

"That's good," he said, sliding his hands up toward her breasts. "And now, if Simonette has taken all those incredibly inquisitive children bowling, let's take advantage of our privacy and go to bed."

It was only ten o'clock in the morning, and they returned to bed as hungrily and as eagerly as two healthy animals in heat. At lunchtime he took her to the most exclusive restaurant in San Francisco and ordered lobster and champagne.

"If this is what it's like staying home and not working, I might just retire," he said grinning, clasping her hands lightly in his.

"*Alors!* And miss all the wheeling and dealing that you love so much?" she said, her mouth curving into a deep smile. "I think you would get very bored, very quickly, *mon amour.*"

He laughed. "I doubt it. The wheeling and dealing is pretty fraught with tension at the moment. Del-Air Airlines has appointed a new marketing director, and he's unhappy with the campaign we produced that was reviewed and approved by his predecessor."

"Is there any real chance of him moving the account?" she asked, realizing how little he had talked to her of business in the past, how far she had distanced herself from all that was important to him.

"He will if we don't produce an outstanding advertising campaign," he said, topping off her glass of champagne, only the hardening of his jawline indicating how serious such a loss would be.

"Then perhaps you should be at the agency now and not here with me," she said anxiously.

He squeezed her hand reassuringly. "Don't worry about it, sweetheart. Nick's working on the new campaign now. If there's a problem, he'll be on the telephone to me within minutes. I told him where I was lunching. Now stop worrying."

"Did you also tell him where you could be contacted at ten o'clock this morning?" she asked mischievously.

His eyes gleamed. "No, you saucy wench, I didn't. Nor have I told him where he would be able to contact me at three o'clock this afternoon, but I have a shrewd suspicion it will be in the same place!"

"Excuse me, Mr. Dering," the maître d'hôtel said deferentially. "There is a telephone call for you."

"Damn and blast," Greg said explosively, throwing his napkin on the table, excusing himself from her and striding over toward the telephone.

She knew by the grim expression on his face as he spoke to Nick that their last, idyllic day had come to an end.

"I'm sorry, my love," he said when he returned. "It's action stations. I won't even be able to take you back home. I'll phone for a cab for you."

"Will you be able to finish lunch?" she asked, fighting down a wave of panic, trying not to let her distress show.

He shook his head. "No, I'm leaving now. It could be a long session, so don't worry if I'm not home until the wee hours. We'll make up for everything next week in Texas."

"Yes," she said, her eyes brilliant, her kiss warm, her heart breaking. "Next week."

He left her with the same speed with which Dieter had left her on the morning of the invasion. A telephone call. Departure. She shivered, overcome by a sense of time and events repeating themselves.

"Would Madame like dessert?" the waiter asked.

"No, thank you." She picked up her purse and stood. She was being foolish. Dieter had left her to face death in battle. Greg had left her for no other reason than a boardroom skirmish.

The maître d'hôtel deferentially slipped her full-length mink around her shoulders. She thanked him, feeling chilled. Dieter had returned to her only to die in her arms. Greg would return to her and she, herself, would say the words that would destroy his love for her.

"A taxicab is waiting, Madame," the maître d'hôtel said,

wondering why such a beautiful woman, with a rich, handsome husband who obviously adored her, was looking so sad.

"Thank you," she said again, and he was touched by the sweetness in her voice. He wondered how old she was. Twenty-five? Twenty-six? Perhaps even older. There was a timelessness about her that would never date. She was a woman who would be beautiful, even when old.

"Good-bye, Madame," he said again, wishing he could offer her some comfort. "*Au revoir.*"

She waited for him that evening, sitting alone on the patio looking out over the silky blackness of the bay. The hills beyond were veiled in mist, the distant lights of Marin sparkling like diamonds in the dusk. He didn't return. At nine he telephoned, his tone apologetic. "This is going to be an all-night session, sweetheart. I won't be back before Melanie leaves. Say good-bye to her for me and pack your bags. I've arranged for us to fly down to Houston tomorrow night."

"That'll be nice, *chéri.*" There was an underlying tremble in her voice that belied her words. He frowned. He had nearly forgotten the confession she had waited so long to make to him.

"If you're worrying about the talk we still have to have, please don't," he said, signaling to Nick, who was waiting to go into the conference room, that he was about to join him.

"But I am worried," she said, wishing that he was in the room with her, that she could reach out and touch him, bury herself in his arms. "I have left it so long . . . and there is so much to say."

"About Luke?" His deep-dark voice was understanding.

"*Oui, chéri.* About Luke, and about Dominic."

"The reply to your telex has just come in, Mr. Dering," his secretary interrupted. He took it from her and glanced over the list of figures.

"Good-bye, *chéri,*" Lisette was saying. "*Je t'adore.*"

He was just about to ask her why she should want to talk about Dominic in the same breath as Luke, but the line had gone dead.

"Everyone is waiting for you, Mr. Dering," his secretary prompted as he seemed about to redial.

"Yes." He jettisoned all thoughts of Luke Brandon. They

would talk about Luke when the marathon meeting he was about to enter was over, when they were on their way to Houston. "Make sure there's plenty of coffee on hand," he said, "and bring the strategy file in with you."

"I don't want to go home *at all!*" Melanie said emphatically the next morning when her suitcases were brought down from her room and stowed in the Lincoln's trunk.

"You will be able to come again, *ma petite*," Lisette said comfortingly, wondering if Luke would allow her to visit again when their affair was over.

"I think it's rotten," Dominic said, his face pale, his eyes fierce. "Mel living in London and me living in San Francisco and never being able to see each other."

"We will when we grow older," Melanie said optimistically. "Daddy lives in London and yet he flies to Los Angeles every month, sometimes twice a month. Mummy doesn't like it. She says she doesn't know why he doesn't live here permanently!"

"Is that true, Maman?" Dominic asked with interest. "Why doesn't Uncle Luke come here and stay with us?"

"Because he is far too busy," Lisette said, turning quickly away from their questioning faces, an anguished flush staining her cheeks.

"And why can't I go to the airport?" Dominic continued relentlessly. "I'd much rather go to the airport with Mel than go to school."

"School is very important, Dominic," Lisette said, knowing that that was not the real reason she had been so firm about his not accompanying them. It was because she knew that later in the morning Greg would return from his all-night meeting with Del-Air, and it was then that she had to talk to him. There could be no further equivocation, no further postponement.

Lisette walked up to the observation deck, waiting until the plane had taxied down the runway and then winged upward, the sun silver on its wings. In fourteen hours' time Melanie would be back in London with Annabel and possibly with Luke.

She walked quickly out of the observation deck and headed toward the parking lot. Within days, Luke would be in

323

Carmel, demanding to see her. She opened the car door and slid behind the wheel. She still hadn't told him that their affair was over. She still hadn't removed her possessions from the cottage they had shared. She swung left onto the freeway, knowing she must do so immediately, that by the time she spoke to Greg, every link with Luke had to be severed. She pressed her foot down hard on the accelerator, ignoring the turnoff that would lead her toward home, continuing south toward Carmel.

Greg emerged from his conference room at nine-thirty, tired and disheveled, but with the Del-Air promotion ready to present. He glanced down at his watch. Melanie's flight was at ten. With luck he would still be in time to wave good-bye to her. He dismissed his chauffeur. Easing the Cadillac limousine out of the underground garage, he was satisfied with the strategy they had hammered out, looking forward to the next few days in Texas with Lisette. No matter what she told him about Luke, it would not come as a shock to him. He had long ago accepted that her relationship with Luke, before he himself had met her, was one that still had to be exorcised. He ran his hand over the early morning stubble on his jaw. Hopefully, at last, that exorcism was about to take place.

Traffic was heavy, and it was five past ten by the time he sped down the turnoff toward the airport. Melanie's flight would have left, but with luck Lisette would still be on her way from the observation deck to her parked car. As he entered the short-term parking lot, he saw the unmistakable gleam of her midnight-blue Lincoln speeding toward a distant exit. He slewed around in pursuit, pressing his hand hard down on the Cadillac's horn to attract her attention. He saw her slow down at the gates and then, ignoring his efforts to halt her, saw her turn left, quickly picking up speed.

"Damn," he said beneath his breath, keeping her in sight, settling down to the task of trailing her all the way back to Pacific Heights.

Lisette took the coast road, driving south through Half Moon Bay and Davenport, mentally checking how long it would be before she was back home again. Two hours for the drive down, half an hour to collect her belongings, fifteen minutes for the telephone call she had to put through to Luke at his London number, and then a two-hour drive back home again. The speedometer flicked from sixty-five to seventy. She had never been so eager to arrive in Carmel, never more determined that she would never visit it again.

Greg grinned to himself as he overtook a red Ford convertible, keeping her well in sight. She would have the shock of her life when she looked through her driving mirror and saw who it was hard on her heels. As she increased speed, not slowing down for the turnoff he had expected her to take, he frowned, puzzled. She'd known that he would be arriving home at this time, that he wanted them to leave for Texas as quickly as possible, and he couldn't for the life of him imagine where it was she was going.

Five minutes later he knew only too well. They were on U.S. 101, heading toward Los Angeles on the route that retraced the route of the old Camino Real, the Royal Road the Spanish had built over two hundred years before—the route that would take her to Carmel.

For a moment he had been unable to believe it. He had checked the road signs, checked the Lincoln Zephyr and then, knowing there was no mistake, that she was speeding as fast as she could to a reunion with Luke, he had dropped back, no longer eager that she should see him, his face gaunt, his eyes burning, as he followed her to her rendezvous.

The Santa Cruz Mountains soared magnificently skyward on her left, but she paid them not the slightest attention. It would be the early hours of the morning in London. With luck, Luke would be spending the night alone at his penthouse flat. If she was unlucky, he would be at home in Kent with Annabel. Monterey Bay gleamed glossily on her right-hand side, sailboats skimming the azure-blue water. She bit the corner of her lip anxiously. The telephone call would wake him, would wake Annabel. She drove into Del Monte and out of it again, flashing on to Pacific Grove, and on toward Carmel.

Waking Annabel was a risk she would have to take. She couldn't end her affair with Luke by a letter. Their lives had been too closely woven for too long for her to treat him in such a cavalier fashion. She had to speak with him, if not face to face then over the telephone. She slowed down, driving through Carmel's main, tourist-thronged street, and out onto the beach road that led to the cottage. There was a hint of fog rolling in from the sea, and the wind-contorted trees hiding the cottage from view were reminiscent of the trees that shielded Valmy from the sea.

She drew to a halt, turning off the Lincoln's engine, stepping out into the salt-laden air. She had told Luke she would never return to Valmy, but she knew now that she had meant she would never return to Valmy without Greg. The homesickness that never quite left her flooded over her. The beach stretching away at her feet for endless miles was alabaster white, far more perfect, far more aesthetically beautiful than the beach below the cliffs at Valmy. No men had died here, no blood had been spilled, and yet it failed to move her. She knew no matter how often or how long she walked here, she would not gain the comfort she gained when walking the beaches of France.

The wind was strong, lifting her hair away from her face, stinging her cheeks. She gave a last look seaward, then turned, took out her door key, and entered the cottage for what she knew would be the last time.

Greg's knuckles whitened on the wheel as he followed her through the small villages strung out like jewels along the coastline. He couldn't believe what she was doing, couldn't believe she was capable of such an outrage. As they entered Carmel, he allowed her to drive on, knowing very well where she was going, and knowing he need no longer keep her in sight. He had been to the cottage Luke was renting from Steve Bernbach when Bernbach had given a party before departing for his new job as creative director of Johnson Matthie's London office. He knew very well where it was, how secluded it was, how perfect for the kind of trysts he now knew Lisette was keeping with Luke Brandon. The road was bumpy, covered with drifts of sand, and he drove slowly, not wanting his journey to come to an end, not wanting to be brought face-to-face with her faithlessness.

Lisette looked quickly around the small living room. Her copy of *Thérèse Raquin* still lay open on the low coffee table. There were other books of hers on the shelves. Books and photographs and French cigarettes. She ran quickly up the stairs to the bedroom, appalled at how many things had been accumulated during the months of their affair.

Hurriedly she opened the closet doors, pulling dresses out and piling them on the bed behind her. She had been crazy driving straight down without returning home for a suitcase. She would have to throw everything into the Lincoln's trunk, and it would take her three, possibly four trips, to carry everything downstairs. Within minutes her side of the closet was empty. Luke's clothes hung alone. She turned quickly away from them to the dressing table, scooping up an armful of toiletries and then froze, her eyes widening in horror.

Downstairs a door had opened and closed. Male footsteps crossed the living room, ascended the stairs.

She wheeled around, certain that it was a burglar, then the bedroom door opened, and she said unbelievingly, "Luke!"

"Whom else did you expect?" he said with a grin.

"But I thought you were in London!"

"I flew back last night. I've just taken my car into Carmel to be serviced and walked back along the beach."

He saw the dresses on the bed, the toiletries in her arms, and his grin vanished. "What the devil are you doing?" he demanded savagely. He strode over to her and grabbed her arms, uncaring of the bottles and jars that tumbled to the floor. "Why are you here if you thought I was in London? Where the hell are you taking your clothes?"

"I'm taking them away with me, Luke," she said, hating herself for the pain she knew she was causing him. "I'm not coming here again. Our affair is over—"

"*Like hell it is!*" He swept the remaining toiletries from her grasp, pulling her to him, his face convulsed with rage.

"Please be reasonable, Luke! It should never have started . . . It could never lead anywhere . . . Never come to anything . . ."

"*It didn't have to lead anywhere!*" he shouted, his eyes blazing. "*All it had to do was continue!*"

She tried to free herself from his grasp, but he was holding her with ferocious strength. "Oh, no, you don't, Lisette! You're not going anywhere! You're staying here, with me! And when you leave, you're going to leave with me! You're not going back to San Francisco. We've playacted long enough! From now on our affair is going to come out into the open!

327

We're going to live together! Stay together! Die together, if necessary."

"You're talking like a lunatic, Luke! We have no *right* to be together! Annabel loves you. She's waiting for you now, right at this very moment."

"I don't give a damn about Annabel!" he snarled, pushing her back onto the bed, pinioning her beneath him. "It isn't Annabel who obsesses me! It isn't Annabel whom I fly thousands of miles to see! It's you, and by God, you're not going to walk out on me now! Not after all that we've been to each other!"

"No, Luke! Please," she cried as he imprisoned her hands high above her head with one hand and wrenched open the buttons on her blouse with the other. His fingers dug deep into the flesh of her breast, his mouth coming down hard on her rose-pink nipple, sucking and biting as his knee forced her legs open. "For God's sake, stop it!" she pleaded, twisting fruitlessly beneath him, held as fast as if she had been in a vise, and then, desperately, "I don't love you, Luke!"

He raised his head, his dark, lean face rapacious. "I don't care," he yelled back at her, pushing her skirt high, tearing ruthlessly at her panties, silencing her protests with his mouth as he plunged savagely into her.

Greg had parked the Cadillac beneath the trees, the blood pounding in his ears, the pain behind his eyes murderous. He had seen Luke approach from the beach, had seen him enter the cottage, and had known that it was not only in battle that he was capable of killing a man. He had closed the Cadillac's door quietly behind him, a nerve jumping violently at the corner of his jaw, his fists bunched as he unhesitatingly followed.

The living room was nothing like he remembered. Bernbach had had the walls covered with stills from successful campaigns. They had all been removed. Works of modern art hung in their place, marrying oddly with the conventional, classic red leather sofas and high-winged chairs. There was an open book on a coffee table. He picked it up. It was a copy of *Thérèse Raquin* in French. There were other books in French on the shelves, a copy of *Le Monde* in a magazine rack. He picked it up and noted the date. It was a month old.

His gaze flicked around the rest of the room, noting the photograph of Henri and Héloïse, the photograph of Valmy. The cottage hadn't been a casual meeting place, it had been a regular retreat, somewhere she had come to often and over a long period. He wondered how he ever could have imagined that her meetings with Luke had consisted of lunch and dinner dates. Why he had not realized it was not unfulfilled love for Luke she had been about to confess to, but adultery—adultery that was long-standing and that she had no intention of forsaking.

From above came the unmistakable creak of a bed, the shout of a male voice at the height of orgasm. Slowly, surely, his face an unrecognizable mask of rage and jealousy and bitter, blinding hurt, he began to climb the stairs.

23

Midday sunlight streamed into the bedroom. The walls were yellow, the floor, polished oak, covered with gaily colored Mexican scatter rugs. Neither of them gave any sign of having heard Greg's approach. Luke's body pinioned Lisette's beneath him, his hands on her breasts, his mouth devouring hers. Neither of them had had the patience to wait to remove their clothes. Lisette's blouse was open wide, the straps of her brassiere pulled down, the lush weight of her breasts exposed. He noticed how dark Luke's hands looked against the creamy white flesh, how dark the hairs on his knuckles were.

Every detail of the room and the figures on the bed were imprinted in his mind as if it were a photograph: the bowl of winter roses on a bedside table; the blue-black sheen of her hair as it spread across the pillows; Luke's shirt, pulled from the band of his trousers—the undone belt, the shoes kicked hastily to the floor. Greg was engulfed by horror, drowning in it. Lisette's scarlet cotton skirt was pushed high to her waist, looking like a swathe of blood against the white lace counterpane. Her hands were pushed hard against Luke's chest, shoving him away as if she sensed the presence of an intruder, as if she, at least, had heard his approach.

"*Bastard!*" he yelled, his voice contorted in his throat. He sprang forward and seized Luke by the shoulders, pulling him away from her, clenching his fist and propelling it into his jaw. The force of the blow lifted Luke from the bed, sending him sprawling to the far side of the room. He was aware of the flash of surprise in Luke's eyes, of Lisette's agonized scream, of her scrambling to her knees on the bed, and then Luke was hurtling toward him, fists clenched, eyes murderous.

Bone smacked against bone. Blood spurted. The bowl of winter roses smashed to the floor. Luke had no intention of fighting like a gentleman; his fists hit low, doubling Greg up in agony. With a savage expletive, Greg hit back, landing a cruel, short-arm jab at Luke's throat. Luke spun backward, tottering, and Greg was on him, his face highlighted by sweat, blood running down his cheek from a cut on his temple, his breath rasping, short and hard. His hands were on Luke's throat, and then Luke's knee came up high and they were apart again, gasping for breath as they picked themselves up from the floor, facing each other with heads low and fists swinging.

"*Arrête!*" Lisette screamed. "*Stop it! For God's sake, stop it!*" Luke rushed bull-like at Greg, and Greg sidestepped but not quickly enough. Luke's fist caught him high above the heart, and they were locked again in a hideous, swaying, battering fight with no holds barred. Blood spurted from Luke's nose, spattering the walls, the floor. Greg's shirt was dark with sweat, clinging to his back, outlining the bulge and strain of his muscles as he slammed into Luke, sending him backward, leaping on top of him as he crashed down on the spilled water and the broken shards of the rose bowl.

"Bastard! Bastard! Bastard!" he yelled, straddling Luke, his hands once more closing tightly on his throat.

"*Stop it! You'll kill him!*" Lisette screamed, catapulting to his side, her hands grabbing hold of his arm, tugging with all her strength to break his grip.

"*I should have killed him years ago!*"

Luke's fingers clawed futilely on Greg's hands, his tongue protruding between his teeth, his eyes bulging.

"*Stop it! For God's sake!*" Greg's arm was like an iron bar as Lisette tried to pry it away. She saw Luke's face begin to turn blue, heard a hideous gurgle in his throat, then Greg's hands slackened and slipped. Luke twisted free of him, rolling clear, vomiting on the polished oak floor.

Panting, Greg rose to his feet, looking contemptuously down at Luke and then at Lisette, distraught and disheveled, her eyes black pits of horror in the chalk-white triangle of her face.

"He's still alive," he spat at her savagely. "And he's all yours! That's all you've ever wanted, isn't it? Well, now you have him and I wish you joy of him!"

He spun on his heel, striding toward the stairs, and she rushed after him, seizing hold of his arm.

"*No, Greg!*" She gasped desperately. "*You don't understand! Please listen to me!*"

"*I understand perfectly!*" he shouted, shaking himself free of her. "*I've understood for a long time, Lisette! Longer than you could possibly imagine!*"

He threw her away from him, and she fell against the wall. "*No!*" She choked. "*You haven't understood, Greg! You don't understand now!*"

He sprinted down the stairs, and she hurled herself after him, her hair spilling around her shoulders, her breasts sheened with sweat. "*Please wait, Greg!*" she cried, tears running down her face. "*Please wait!*"

Blood still streamed from the cut on his face. He charged across the open ground to the trees, yanking open the Cadillac's door, not even bothering to look at her. "*It's over,*" he said brutally, twisting his key in the ignition. "*Nothing can explain what I saw in that room!*"

She ran frantically after him. "*No, Greg! Don't go! Listen to me, please!*"

He swore viciously, gunning the engine into life. She called his name again, her fingers touching the Cadillac's fender, and he surged away from her, sending her sprawling to the ground. She stumbled to her feet, calling his name, beginning to run after him, but it was too late. The Cadillac was a hundred yards away, speeding down the beach road, a cloud of dust and sand swirling in its wake.

He was shaking, shuddering from head to toe. Jesus God.

It had been worse than anything he had ever remotely imagined. He swung the wheel hard left, surging off the unmade beach road onto the road leading into Carmel. He had known they had been meeting each other. He had known about the cottage, but even then he had not truly believed they were lovers. He took a curve with a scream of tires. How long had it been going on? Months? Years? He slammed his foot down harder on the accelerator. No wonder she had needed to talk to him. No wonder the prospect of such a talk had terrified her.

He overtook a Ford and a van, streaming down the middle of the road, his knuckles white on the wheel, the veins at his temples bulging and knotting. Luke and Dominic. She had wanted to talk to him about Luke and Dominic. He swerved out of the path of an oncoming truck. Why Dominic? What possible connection could there be between Luke Brandon and their son? The answer roared at him, pain jackknifing up his arm, blasting into his chest. Brandon had loved her before he, Greg, had even met her, Brandon had intended to marry her. The pain was crucifying, crushing the air out of his lungs. He had wanted to marry her in order to legitimize their coming child—the child that had been born only eight months after D day, only seven months after he, himself, had married her.

As his chest seemed to implode and the Cadillac veered toward the stream of oncoming traffic, he knew that somewhere, deep in his subconscious, he had always known it: Dominic was not his son. The child he loved, the child he had reared, was not his. The pain was insupportable. He fell across the wheel, no longer able to breathe, his last conscious thought as the Cadillac rocketed off the road: Dominic must not know. Dominic must never know.

She stood on the sand-blown track—the dust, gouged by the wheels of his car, heavy in the air. There would be no trip to Texas now, no bright new future. Her courage to talk to him had come too late. It was over. He himself had said so. The salt-laden air stung the tears on her cheeks. She raised her hands, wiping them away. There would be time enough for tears in the future, no doubt all the time in the world. For now, she had to finish what she had set out to do, and then she would return home, to whatever awaited her there.

Luke was sitting in the bathroom, his head in his hands. He looked up as she entered, and she saw the ugly weals around his throat, the purple bruising of thumb marks on his larynx.

"Let's go," he said curtly, rising to his feet and crossing to the sink. He splashed cold water on his face. "There's a London flight at four this afternoon. We should be able to get tickets for it easily enough." He picked up a towel and wiped water away.

"I'm not going with you, Luke," she said quietly. "I'm not ever going to see you again."

He flung the towel away, saying remorselessly, "Of course you are. You're going to divorce Greg. I'm going to divorce Annabel. We're going to get married just as we should have years ago." He took her arm, walking her out of the bathroom and into the bedroom. "We can be packed and out of here in fifteen minutes. There'll be no need for us ever to return. We'll live in London . . ."

Gently she removed his hand from her arm. "I'm not going with you, Luke," she repeated. "I'm going back to San Francisco."

He stared at her incredulously. "But why, for Christ's sake? There's no future for you there! Your future is in London, with me!"

She scooped up an armful of her clothes. "No," she said steadily. "My future has never been with you, Luke. All we have is a shared past. It's never been enough, and it isn't enough now." She stood for a moment, looking at him, remembering the first time she had seen him, remembering Valmy. "Good-bye, Luke," she said, and turned and walked down the stairs, putting him out of her life forever.

She knew the instant she arrived home something was terribly wrong. Simonette's station wagon was parked at an odd angle, the door wide open as if she had hurtled herself from it and into the house. She slewed her car to a halt behind it, and even as she was still stepping from the car, Simonette had flung the front door open and was running toward her, her face stricken.

"Oh, thank God you're back, Madame! I've tried to get in touch with you everywhere, but no one knew where you were and—"

Lisette broke into a run. "*What is it?*" she demanded, grabbing her. "*Is it the children? Where are Lucy and Dominic?*"

"They're still at school. I thought it best they stay there. I—"

"*What's happened?*"

"Mr. Dering . . . He's had a heart attack at the wheel of his car—"

"*No!*" It was a howl of protest. She swayed on her feet, her face ashen. "*Where is he?*" she cried, turning and running toward the car.

"San Francisco General," Simonette said, sprinting after her. "But you can't drive yourself there, Madame! You're too shocked! Madame—"

The Lincoln's door slammed. Lisette's hands were shaking as she switched on the ignition. A heart attack. He could be dead. Dying. Tires screamed as she reversed out of the drive, as she slammed into first gear, then second. She had to reach him, had to be with him. "Oh God!" she prayed as she careened out into the mainstream of traffic. "Don't let Greg die! Do anything, anything, but don't let him die!"

"He's in the operating room," a nurse said, guiding Lisette competently toward a chair. "He'll probably be there for several hours. Is there anyone you would like to contact to come and sit with you while you wait?"

Lisette shook her head. She didn't want anyone. There was no one who would be able to understand her anguish, no one she could tell of the way they had parted—the savage recriminations, the crucifying hurt. And if he died? She had a duty toward his parents, toward Chrissie. "Yes, there is someone," she said. "His mother and father. His sister."

"I'll contact them for you," the nurse said compassionately. "A doctor will be with you the instant there is any news."

It was the longest wait of her life. At six o'clock a gowned and masked surgeon walked wearily from the operating room and told her that Greg was on his way to intensive care. He had a broken arm and pelvis. Damage to the lower vertebrae. But he was alive and he was going to stay alive.

"Can I see him?" she asked as her mother-in-law lowered her head to her hands and wept with relief.

"A nurse will take you up as soon as he's been settled. But you won't be able to stay. Intensive care is no place for visitors and he won't be conscious for six or seven hours yet."

"I understand." She tried to smile her thanks, then she saw the deep frown puckering his brow and she said fearfully, "What is it? What is it that you haven't told me?"

He took off his surgical skull cap, running his fingers through thick, grizzled hair. "The nerve damage to the lower vertebrae was severe, Mrs. Dering," he said reluctantly. "You must be prepared for the fact that your husband may never walk again."

She spent the night at the hospital, refusing to leave, drinking endless cups of black coffee. The doctor had told her that the heart attack could have happened at any time, but she remembered the fist slamming hard above his heart, the raw agony on his face when he had told her that their marriage was over, and she knew that she was responsible.

"What level of stress can my husband cope with?" she asked the young intern who came to her in the early hours of the morning to tell her that Greg was on the verge of recovering consciousness and that she could return to his side.

He stared at her. "I'm sorry, Mrs. Dering. I don't understand. Your husband has just suffered a heart attack and undergone major surgery. He's not able to cope with stress of any kind. Why do you ask?"

She pushed a dark fall of hair away from her face and he was shocked by the suffering in her eyes. "My husband and I quarreled very badly shortly before his accident," she said unsteadily. "He may not want to see me."

He regarded her compassionately, understanding now the reason for the depth of her distress. "I think he will want to see you," he said gently. "But if he doesn't, then the nursing staff will know, and you will be asked to leave."

"Thank you."

Her voice had a husky quality and the faint trace of an accent. He remembered from his case notes that she was French and wondered how he could have forgotten. Even though she had slept in the white silk blouse and scarlet cotton skirt that she had been wearing when she had first rushed into the emergency room, she still looked chic, with that curious edge of elegance that was so peculiarly European. As she began to walk away from him, he said hesitantly, "Mrs. Dering . . . Excuse me . . . Are you perhaps worrying that it was your quarrel that triggered your husband's heart attack? That you, in fact, are responsible for it?"

She turned toward him and he read his answer in her anguished eyes. "Yes," she said simply. "I know I am."

Her hair skimmed her cheekbones, falling softly to her shoulders, making her look ridiculously young. He wished suddenly she were not married, that her husband were not lying only minutes away in intensive care. He said, his voice thickening, "I doubt that very much, Mrs. Dering. Heart attacks are organic in origin. A marital quarrel would not be enough to induce one in an otherwise healthy man. However, there must be no more quarrels, no more emotional disturbances. Not for a long time."

Her eyes held his, wide and dark. "How long is a long time, doctor?" she asked, suddenly very still.

He frowned, his voice grave. "Not until your husband has recuperated fully, and even then, there must be no violent shocks. It would be too foolish a risk."

She sat by the bed, wanting to hold his hand and not daring to. The intravenous needle was inserted just above the wrist, and she was terrified that when he opened his eyes, when he saw her, he would try to free himself from her touch and dislodge it.

He looked curiously relaxed, his handsome face almost boyish. The lines of rage and pain that had ravaged his face when he had slammed out of the cottage were now smoothed away. Only the laugh lines remained, creasing the corners of his eyes, etching his mouth. She stretched out her fingers, touching his with butterfly lightness, loving him with all her heart and knowing she could never again expect that love to be returned.

"He should recover consciousness at any moment, Mrs. Dering," a nurse said to her quietly. She paused to look at his chart, then walked back to the bank of monitors that reported the vital signs of the patients in her care.

Lisette felt fear squeezing her heart. What would she see in his eyes when he looked at her? Would he remember?

Would she have to leave him almost immediately and perhaps be asked not to return? Slowly, surely, his fingertips moved against hers.

"Oh, *chéri*," she whispered. "Please let me stay with you. Please don't send me away!"

His eyelashes fluttered once and were still, then moved again and lifted.

"*Bonjour, chéri*," she said softly.

His fingers tightened on hers. "Hello, sweetheart," he whispered, and she knew he had not remembered, he would not remember for hours. Once again, she had been given a reprieve.

"I love you, *mon amour*," she said huskily. "I love you more than you will ever know."

He tried to smile. "I love you too," he said hoarsely, then the nurse was bending over him saying, "Everything is all right, Mr. Dering. Please don't try to talk any more. Not for a little while."

"Okay," he said, his voice befuddled, his eyes closing as he drifted back into drugged sleep. "Anything you say . . ."

Lisette knew, as she left the ward, that those few precious moments had given her the courage she needed to face the future. She had been told that it would be seven or eight hours before she would be able to see him again, long enough for her to return home, to shower and change, and to catch a little sleep.

Simonette was waiting for her, and as she sank gratefully into the Lincoln's passenger seat and allowed Simonette to drive, she felt almost calm. He would not want to see her when his memory returned. He would demand a divorce. There would not be one. She was going to remain at his side no matter what he said or did. She knew now that he had continued to love her all through the years she had believed he was regretting their marriage, that he had loved her right until the moment he had walked into the small bedroom at Carmel and had had all his illusions about her smashed to smithereens. Her hands clenched in her lap. There could be no explanations now. The doctor's words had been explicit: no stress. The truth about Dominic had been a secret for nine years; it would have to remain a secret. She could give Greg no reason for the way she had withdrawn from him and turned, in misery and guilt, to Luke. But she would stay with him. If he refused to accept her as his wife, then she would be his nurse. She would be anything at all, just as long as she remained in his life.

Her hopes that it would be days before his memory returned were dashed the instant she returned to his bedside.

"You'll want a divorce in order to marry Luke," he said, his voice raspy, his eyes burning, his face ashen beneath the bronzing of wind and sun, far paler than it had been when he had first gotten out of surgery.

"No." Her voice was calm. She wondered if he remembered the words of love he had spoken to her in his drugged haze only hours earlier. "My affair with Luke is over."

"Why?" he demanded savagely. "Because of this?" His hand moved violently over the sheet, indicating the tubes and drips, the swathes of bandages.

"I'm sorry, Mrs. Dering," a nurse said, walking quickly over to them. "But if Mr. Dering is going to become distressed, I must ask you to leave."

"Mrs. Dering is leaving," Greg said, his voice hard, his eyes merciless.

She left, because she had no alternative. Over the next few days she sat on a hard, straight-backed chair outside his room as his mother and father, as Chrissie and Nick, visited him. She suffered their puzzlement with dignity and without offering any explanation.

"Will my husband see me now?" she asked the nursing staff time and time again, and always the answer was no.

The surgeon who had operated on him talked to her for over an hour, showing her X rays, explaining the damage that had been done to Greg's vertebrae. The nerves were injured but were not dead. There was no reason why he shouldn't walk again, but at the moment the nerves and muscles were not responding to treatment. When he was discharged from the hospital it would be in a wheelchair. There would have to be months of physiotherapy, perhaps years.

She knew the surgeon had also spoken to Greg, that he was facing the news alone.

Nick visited regularly, carrying in the armfuls of files and correspondence that Greg insisted on seeing.

"Has he told you what he intends to do about the agency?" Lisette asked him one evening when he came away from Greg's private room with a sheaf of memos.

Nick flushed. He found the sight of Lisette, sitting with exquisite dignity and patience as she waited for Greg to agree to see her, acutely embarrassing. God alone knew what had happened between them. No one seemed to know—not his family, not the hospital staff. But whatever it was, he was sure it was distress over it that was delaying Greg's recovery.

"He says there are going to be no changes, Mrs. Dering. He's going to recuperate, and then he's going to continue running it."

"I see, Nick. Thank you." There were blue shadows beneath her eyes, and her skin was so pale it was almost translucent. He wondered how long it had been since she had slept properly, or since she had eaten.

"Mrs. Dering," he said awkwardly, "I know it's none of my affair . . . , but whatever has gone wrong between you and Mr. Dering . . . I'm sorry."

A small smile touched her mouth. "Thank you," she said again, her eyes so sad that his heart ached.

Unhappily he turned away, wondering if there was any truth in the rumors about the woman in New York, if Greg really was contemplating a divorce. He shook his head uncomprehendingly. He would have staked his life on the fact that the Derings had been meant for each other, that they were crazy about each other. He stepped out onto the sidewalk and hailed a cab, baffled by their obvious estrangement.

When Nick had gone, Lisette walked the few yards to the door of Greg's room and paused uncertainly. She didn't blame him for not wanting to see her. In his eyes, she had gone straight from his arms to Luke's. He would not believe her if she told him it was rape, not when he had seen the evidence of the long-standing nature of their affair. She closed her eyes, wondering how she could have brought so much misery to the lives of those she loved, so much misery to herself. Then, resolutely, she pushed open the door and entered the room.

His gaze flew to hers, his face immediately tightening. "We have nothing to say to each other," he said as she moved toward the bed.

"I have something to say to you, *chéri*," she said huskily, and he was shocked by the suffering etched on her face, the deep circles carved beneath her eyes. "It is that I love you. That I want to stay with you. That I want to remain a part of your life."

He had rehearsed, several times, what he would say to her. She had betrayed and deceived him on the deepest level possible for a man to be betrayed and deceived. She had allowed him to think that another man's child was his son. She had continued, probably for years, to be lovers with the child's father. He winced with physical pain as he remembered their holidays at Valmy, the times he had seen her with Luke and been absolutely sure of her faithfulness. They had probably been lovers then, had probably been lovers ever since Luke's wartime return, weeks before Dominic was born.

He had lain awake for hours, his uninjured hand clenched into a fist, wondering how she could have borne seeing Dominic and Melanie playing together, how she could possibly have agreed to Melanie staying with them. It was an act beyond comprehension.

He had thought also of Dominic, of the child he loved and who thought of him as his father. He had expected his feelings to undergo a change and had been staggered to discover that the knowledge made not the slightest bit of difference to the love he felt for him. In every way that mattered, he *was* Dominic's father. He was the one Dominic came to for advice, for hugs, for companionship. There was far more to fatherhood than mere genetics. It had been an astonishing revelation and hard on its heels had come another.

If he told Lisette he knew the truth, there would be nothing at all to prevent her from joining Luke in London and taking Dominic with her. He would be forfeiting the fatherhood he cherished, losing the child who, for all intents and purposes, was his son.

She stood at the foot of his bed, a black wool dress clinging softly to the firm upthrust of her breasts, skimming her hips, and he wondered how he ever could have imagined that he was, at last, free of her. Her hair was swept into a knot, emphasizing her delicate bone structure, the enormous dark eyes, the gently curving mouth. It was a face that had haunted him all through the months of fighting in France and Germany, a face he had known he would never forget. He felt something like despair. He still loved her. It wasn't possible for him *not* to love her. And now, because of her guilt, she was telling him her affair with Luke was over, that she wanted to remain his wife.

None of the things he had been going to say were said. Instead he said tersely, "Sit down. You look ill."

He saw something very like hope spring to her eyes as she moved to his side and wondered for a moment if he had been wrong about her motives.

"They told me about your legs, *chéri,*" she said, a catch in her voice. "I'm sorry. So very sorry."

His eyes hardened. He had known she would feel responsible—responsible for his heart attack, for the subsequent crash, for the injuries he had received. And because she felt responsible, she was staying with him, not because she loved him—he didn't believe that for a moment—but because her own peculiar brand of honor demanded it. And if he rejected her, what would happen then? There would be a custody battle for the children. He would lose perhaps not only Dominic, but Lucy as well. And there would be no more hope of recapturing the happiness they had once known together. His eyes smoldered. He was too weak to face such a future. The charade of their marriage, for Dominic's sake, for Lucy's sake, would have to continue.

24

When Greg was discharged from the hospital, he went to Mexico to recuperate, but he did not take Lisette with him. There was no way they could go back to the relationship they had enjoyed during the two weeks of Melanie's visit: she was in love with Luke; she had always been in love with Luke. He would be damned to hell before he would accept embraces that were motivated by pity.

It was while he was in Mexico that she lost the baby that had been conceived in such rapture. He knew she grieved, but it was a grief she locked deep inside her, refusing to talk about it, unable to accept any comfort.

In May she received a letter from her father telling her that Luke and Annabel were divorcing, and that Luke was giving up his life in London and was buying a farm on the outskirts of Bayeux. Greg watched her read it, knowing very well the news it contained.

It was common knowledge that Johnson Matthie was looking for a new chairman, and the advertising grapevine had quickly passed the word along that not only was Luke Brandon leaving Johnson Matthie, but that he was not moving to another agency. He was abandoning his business career entirely and moving, minus his wife and child, to a farm he had bought in the Normandy countryside. There were rumors the girl he had been in love with had died; that in his grief, he was fast becoming a recluse.

He studied Lisette as she slipped the letter into her desk. Her face betrayed no hint of what she was feeling. He had no doubt that for Luke, Lisette was as good as dead. He knew there had been no correspondence between them, that she had kept her word to him and that the affair was over.

"What does your father have to say?" he asked, propelling his wheelchair smoothly forward toward her.

She raised her shoulder in a slight, dismissive shrug, her eyes carefully avoiding his. "Maman is not going to visit Valmy at all this year. They will spend two weeks together in Nice in June, and then maman will return to Paris and papa and his nurse to Valmy."

It was a hot day, and she was wearing a pale mauve silk shirt and a brilliant turquoise skirt, her legs bare, her feet in delicate sandals, her hair swept up in an elegant figure eight.

"Any other news?" he asked with forced indifference.

There was a brief, almost imperceptible pause, then she said, with a too bright smile, "No, *chéri*. Madame Bridet's arthritis is worse, Madame Chamot is visiting her daughter in Toulouse, and life in Sante-Marie-des-Ponts is continuing as usual."

His lips tightened. Some devil inside him wanted to hear Luke's name on her lips, wanting to hear the inflection in her voice, see the expression in her eyes when she uttered it. Jealousy rocked through him. He had come to terms with his disability. He had come to terms with the fact that Dominic was not his son. But he could not come to terms with the fact that her love was given elsewhere.

"I'm flying to Washington in the morning," he said, expertly spinning the wheelchair around and away from her. "I want to close the United Motels deal personally."

Her too bright smile faded, and the immeasurable sadness that filled her eyes whenever she thought herself unobserved returned.

"Would you like me to come with you, *chéri?*" she asked tentatively, knowing what his answer would be.

"No." The wheelchair did not stop in its smooth passage to the door. "It's going to be all work. I would have no time to keep you company."

"Will your secretary be going with you?" she asked, trying to keep her voice light.

The wheelchair halted and he turned around, regarding her steadily with brandy-dark eyes. "Yes," he said. "She always travels with me." And then his wheelchair shot out into the hallway and she was once more alone.

Although he had made no sexual overture to her since his accident, she knew it was not because he was incapable of lovemaking. He was. He was also physically just as attractive as he had ever been. He had returned from Mexico determined the wheelchair would make as little difference to his life as possible, and he had succeeded admirably.

He exercised fiercely every day, his arm and back muscles rippling with vigor. He still drove himself, his wheelchair in the trunk of his adapted Cadillac limousine. He continued to fly to Washington, to New York, to Houston, to Acapulco. He attended dinners and banquets and film premiers, and by sheer force of will and personality was still regarded as one of the most sexually attractive men in whatever gathering he found himself.

People who had heard of his accident and had not met him since expected to feel pity and repulsion, and perhaps even curiosity, when they met him again. None of them did so. He was an object for no one's pity; he was a big, handsome,

343

powerful man, as much in demand socially as he had ever been.

Lisette had met his blond, Swedish secretary only on a few occasions, but they had been enough to convince her that the girl was in love with him. She rose from her desk, her heart hurting, wondering if they slept together, and if, when he made his frequent trips to New York, he still met the woman he had admitted to having had an affair with. Her nails pressed deep into her palms as she walked toward the French windows that led out onto the patio.

She had been as loving toward him, as physically demonstrative as it was possible to be when meeting with no encouragement. As the weeks had turned into months and his attitude toward her had not altered, she had been filled with growing despair. There were scores of men who would have been only too happy to offer her comfort, but she had frozen any overture the instant it had been made. She didn't want another affair. She didn't simply want sex. She wanted love and sex with Greg.

She stepped out into the early summer heat. In a few weeks' time she would be thirty. If Dieter had lived, he would have been forty-four. A tide of grief swept over her, ripping wide the dusty years and sending them scattering. Dieter had loved and understood her. There had been no lies between them, no deceit. In that moment, on the patio of her San Francisco home, her pain at his loss was as raw as it had been on the morning of his death.

"What am I to do?" she whispered. "Oh, Dieter, my love, what am I to *do*?"

"Why couldn't Mel visit us at Easter?" Dominic asked when Lisette came into his room that night to check that he had finished his homework.

He turned down the volume on his record player, subduing the raucous tones of a young white singer who sounded black. "She wanted to come."

"Who is the singer?" she asked, wondering what she could say to him to soften his disappointment.

He shrugged impatiently. "A guy called Presley." He took out a crumpled blue air-mail letter from his school bag. "She says she had to go to her grandmother's for three weeks because her mother went on a trip to Italy with friends. She says her grandmother finds her a nuisance and she didn't like it there. She wants to know if she can come here for the summer holidays instead."

Lisette hugged him. "It's a very long way, *mon petit*. And Melanie's mother will probably have made other plans."

"But we could *ask*," Dominic persisted. "*Please*, Maman."

Lisette wondered what Greg's reaction would be to the prospect of having Melanie once more beneath his roof. He had liked her enormously, and his generous nature wasn't one that was likely to bear resentment toward a child, no matter what his feelings for her father.

She spoke to him the evening he returned from Washington. ". . . and so Dominic would like Melanie to come over for the summer holidays. They get on so well together, *chéri*, and if Annabel is agreeable . . ."

He stared at her as if she had taken leave of her senses. "Have Brandon's *daughter!* Dominic's s—" He broke off sharply. "Have her *here?* After all that has happened? Sweet Christ, you must be mad!"

She had been writing a letter to her father. Her gaze flew to his, the blood draining from her face as she saw the depth of his fury. His eyes were like live coals, his knuckles white on the arms of his wheelchair.

"I'm sorry," she stammered, thinking of his heart, terrified that he was going to have another attack. "Truly I am. I won't mention it ever again—"

The expression in his eyes made her gasp. There was such bitter, burning contempt in them she could hardly breathe. "Greg, please . . ." She rose dizzily to her feet but he shot the wheelchair around, not even pausing to look behind him as she swayed against her desk, her face ravaged.

The whole hideous scene had been for nothing. A week later she received a terse, typewritten letter from Annabel in which she said she had discovered that Dominic and Melanie were corresponding. She had forbidden Melanie to continue the correspondence and wished Lisette to instruct Dominic likewise. Luke was in Normandy. There was to be a divorce on the grounds of his desertion. He had, however, told her the truth—that he had never loved her, that it was Lisette he loved and had always loved. He had told her of their affair, that he had no intention of ever living with her and Melanie again. Lisette would understand there could be no further communication between them, or between their children. Their friendship, so grossly betrayed, was at an end.

Dominic had been uncomprehending. "But *why* can't I write to Mel any more?" he asked in bewilderment. "Why won't Aunt Annabel let her write to me?"

"Because she and Uncle Luke no longer live together," Lisette said, hating herself for being the cause of his hurt, hating Luke for his unnecessary callousness to Annabel.

"But I still don't understand—"

"Aunt Annabel has been badly hurt, Dominic. She doesn't want to be reminded of the past, and we are part of her past. And so she has asked us not to communicate with her, or with Melanie."

"That's silly, and I shall still write!" Dominic said savagely, pulling away from her, not allowing her to comfort him.

Lisette never knew how long Dominic persisted in writing to Melanie, but no letters came back in reply. Her father wrote that Annabel and Melanie never visited Normandy and that Luke rarely spoke of them. Luke had bought a fifteen-hundred-acre farm about ten miles from Valmy, and was a regular visitor.

Lisette was scrupulous in making no reference to Luke in her answering letters, but her father continued to document Luke's visits, happily unsuspecting that his information wasn't welcome. In 1959 he wrote, jubilant about de Gaulle's return to power, *At long last the man destined to govern France is governing her. I can't tell you how happy I am to see* mon chèr gènèral *once again in the Elysée palace. As for Luke, he is to marry a young schoolteacher from Caen. Her name is Ginette Duboscq, and she has been several times to Valmy. She is very pretty and many years Luke's junior.*

Lisette put the letter carefully away and hoped that Luke would be happy. She knew now she never would be. Nothing had changed in her relationship with Greg. There was an unseen barrier between them that was never either scaled or broken down. The memory of the happiness they had known when Melanie had visited them was no longer a comfort to her but a torment. Her sexual feelings had always been strong. She knew now it was her own sexuality that had precipitated her affair with Dieter, that had given her the rashness to enter into marriage with a man she barely knew. And that sexuality now had no outlet. She was thirty-four. She was still beautiful, still desirable, but her emotional life was a desert, her inner loneliness absolute.

Very occasionally she received news of Annabel and Melanie. Annabel had continued to keep in sporadic touch with Héloïse. Christmas cards were exchanged, postcards sent. A year after Luke had remarried, Annabel had followed suit. Her second husband was a peer of the realm, a widower, and extremely wealthy. Melanie was fourteen and attending Benenden Girls' School in the depths of the Kent countryside. Lisette's impression was that Melanie was an encumbrance whom Annabel's new husband was quite happy to do without.

Dominic no longer asked about her. He was sixteen, happy in his schoolwork and with a large circle of friends. Despite Greg's disability, his camping trips with Dominic continued. One summer they went as far north as Alaska, another as far south as Oaxaca. There was never any suggestion from Greg that she should accompany them. Those days were over.

"I wish we could go and visit *Grand-mère* and *Grand-père* this summer," Lucy said one afternoon as they sat around the pool. "We haven't been back to Valmy for years and years and years, and yet daddy is always flying to Europe on business trips."

From a portable transistor radio, Connie Francis bemoaned the fact that her lover had lipstick on his collar.

"Yes, why can't we?" Dominic asked, rolling over onto his stomach, putting down the book he had been reading. "We've all got loads of free time in the summer, and *Grand-mère* and *Grand-père* would love to see us."

Lisette was grateful for the dark glasses hiding her eyes. "*On verra*," she said with a slight shrug. "We'll see."

"Does daddy visit Valmy when he's in Europe?" Lucy asked interestedly, looking across to the far side of the pool where Greg was asleep.

"I imagine so," Lisette said, knowing very well he did not. Luke's presence so near to Valmy ensured that Greg never paid any visits.

347

Connie Francis was replaced by a warbling Neil Sedaka.

"Then it's high time we all went," Lucy said, stretching her arms high above her head. "A lovely, long, lazy summer in Normandy. It will be delicious."

"But probably not possible," Lisette said lightly, trying to keep the strain she was feeling from being revealed in her voice. "*Grand-mère* and *Grand-père* go away to Biarritz in the summer."

Dominic looked at her curiously. "But you haven't seen them since we were tiny, Maman. Don't you miss them?"

She flashed him a quick, brilliant smile. "*Alors!* Of course I miss them, but we exchange letters nearly every week, and photographs . . ."

"*Grand-père* sent me some photographs last week," Lucy said, delving into the tote bag at her side. "I forgot all about them. Look, here is one of *Grand-mère* in the rose garden, and here's another of her with Uncle Luke."

Luke stood with his arm lightly around her mother's shoulders. He was as tall, as dark as ever. He was wearing a turtleneck sweater and jeans, smiling into the camera, an attractive droop of unaffected self-deprecation twisting the corners of his mouth. She put the photograph down quickly and Dominic picked it up.

"Here's another one," Lucy was saying. "This is of Uncle Luke's new wife. Doesn't she look pretty? I can't remember what Aunt Annabel looked like. Oh, look, here's a dear one of *Grand-mère*'s two spaniels. Aren't they sweet?"

The photographs were thrust into her hand. Luke's wife, Ginette Duboscq, was petite and slender, with dark hair curling softly around her face and a wide, curving smile.

"Does Mel ever visit Valmy?" Dominic asked, his brows pulling together in a frown so reminiscent of Dieter that Lisette's heart jerked in her chest.

"I don't think so," she said unsteadily, and then, as his eyes sharpened with concern at the tone of her voice, added with a smile and a laugh, "But, *on ne sait jamais, mon chèr.* One never knows."

Lucy began to chatter about school and girlfriends and the photographs were put away. Lisette felt inexpressible relief. There were times when she wondered if Luke's move to Normandy had been done with the same callousness that had prompted him to tell Annabel not only that he no longer loved her, but that he had never loved her. While he was a regular visitor to Valmy, visits by her were impossible. He had ensured, either intentionally or unintentionally, that she could not return home.

A maid came out to inform Lucy that there was a caller for her. "Oh, gosh, that'll be Rod," she said, scrambling to her feet. "We're going to the movies, to see Charlton Heston in *Ben Hur*. Bye, Mom. See you later." She gave Lisette a hurried kiss and dashed into the house.

"My siesta is over as well," Dominic said, rising. "I promised Alex I'd play baseball this afternoon."

"Will you be in for dinner, *chéri?*" Lisette asked, looking at him with pride as he picked up his book. At sixteen, he was already six feet tall, with broad shoulders and the same air of utter assurance that his father had possessed.

"Maybe. I'll give you a call later this afternoon." He grinned down at her as he passed her lounge chair. He adored her and had never considered it a threat to his masculinity to show how much. He squeezed her shoulder affectionately, and then he was gone and Greg said quietly, "You won't, of course, allow them to go."

She had known he had overheard, that he had simply been waiting for Dominic and Lucy to leave before speaking.

"To Valmy?" she said with the cool lack of expression that had become a habit over the years. "No, of course not."

He looked across at her, his eyes narrow, the lines of his face harsh. A moment ago Lucy had unwittingly shown Dominic photographs of his father, and Lisette had watched her do so and had not even flinched. He wondered what her feelings had been, and he wondered if Henri had sent other photographs of Luke, photographs that had never been shown.

"If Lucy and Dominic want to visit Héloïse and Henri, it might be possible for them to do so," he said, watching her carefully. "Not at Valmy, of course, but perhaps they could join Héloïse and Henri in Biarritz."

She was wearing a one-piece swimming suit of kingfisher blue, the sun golden on her skin, her hair falling softly to her shoulders. It was impossible to imagine she had a son of sixteen. In the merciless afternoon sunlight, she didn't look a day over twenty-five.

Her eyes widened, the irises almost purple, the thick sweep of her lashes lustrous. "But that would be a wonderful idea, Greg!"

He knew if he suggested that she accompany them, she could quite easily see Luke. Biarritz was only a day's hard drive from Bayeux. He could see the homesickness in her eyes, hear it in her voice.

"Why don't you go with them?" he said, hating to see her unhappiness, knowing that a reunion between her and Luke was a risk he must take.

Her eyes shone and she sprang instinctively to her feet, crossing to his side as if about to give him a kiss of thanks. He moved swiftly, picking up the portable telephone at the side of his lounge chair, stopping her spontaneous gesture almost the instant it was made.

"I want a Toronto number," he said tersely to the operator.

She halted a few feet away from him, and he knew he only had to raise his eyes to hers and she would step forward again. He didn't do so. Only by freezing all his desire for her could he continue to live with her in the travesty of their marriage. His sexual energies were expended elsewhere, with women he knew were not motivated by pity—women who had no guilt to purge, or a sense of duty to fulfill.

"Thank you, *chéri*," she said hesitantly, and then, as he continued with his telephone call, she turned on her heel and walked disconsolately away.

For two consecutive years, she spent July and August in Biarritz in the company of her children and her parents. She spoke nothing but French from the moment she set foot on French soil to the moment she left, much to the exasperation of Lucy who spoke hardly a word. Dominic loved Biarritz because he could surf to his heart's delight. Lisette loved it because, if she closed her eyes, she could imagine herself on the beach below Valmy, imagine she was home again.

The Kennedys were in the White House, and on her visits to France Lisette felt proud of both the country of her birth and America. Ever since the presidential visit to Paris in 1961, France had taken Jacqueline Kennedy to its heart.

"She is marvelous," her father said to her as they strolled together on the promenade, "so dark-haired and pretty and chic. Just like you." She laughed and told him not to be silly, but she, too, admired Jacqueline Kennedy enormously, and when she went back to America she involved herself more and more in Democratic fund-raising activities.

In 1963, Lisette's father wrote to her saying they would not be vacationing in Biarritz that year. He had suffered ill health all through the winter, and Héloïse was taking the unprecedented step of closing her apartment in Paris and joining him at Valmy. He hoped she and the children would join them there for the summer.

"No," Greg said tightly when she showed him the letter. "Under no circumstances."

She had not argued with him, but she was aware of an increasing sense of bewilderment. It had been nine years since that hideous day at the cottage in Carmel. She had neither seen nor corresponded with Luke since. Greg's nature was not a vindictive one. He was a generous man, a compassionate man. Yet there was an almost frightening glitter in his eyes whenever Valmy was mentioned, and she knew it was because he was thinking of Luke—of Luke's nearness to Valmy, of his biweekly visits there.

"If we're not going to Biarritz, can I go with the Morgans to Hawaii?" Lucy asked, applying amethyst-blue shadow to her eyelids and studying the result with interest.

"I imagine so," Lisette said equably, watching as Lucy applied more eye shadow, knowing that interference would be unwelcome.

"Dominic is going backpacking in Europe. He's going to travel through Belgium and into Germany, and then go down into Italy. He says he may even cross over into Africa."

"I thought he wanted to go through France and into Spain," Lisette said as generous applications of eyeliner and mascara completed Lucy's toilette.

"He's changed his mind. He wants to practice his German, and he wants to see the Alps and drink Chianti in the Tuscan hills." She surveyed her handiwork in the mirror, then looked up at her mother, a slight frown puckering her brows. "Why are you looking so pensive, Mom? Are you envying him Rome and Venice and Florence?"

Lisette gave her a quick smile. "Yes," she lied. "Of course I am." But she wasn't. She was thinking of him visiting his

351

father's country. She was remembering Dieter telling her about his childhood—about walks in the Tiergarten, iced lemonade at the Hotel Adlon, chocolate cake at Sacher's. For days there had been no escaping thoughts of Berlin. The newspapers had been full of accounts of President Kennedy's visit there. He had stood, looking out over the wall that divided the city, and proclaimed *Ich bin ein Berliner!*—"I am a Berliner." Lisette had felt the tears burn the backs of her eyes. Dieter would not have resented John F. Kennedy's presence in Berlin, and he would have applauded his words.

"Why don't you make a trip to Italy this summer, Mom?" Lucy asked her, swinging around on her dressing-table stool, her honey-brown eyes so like Greg's, concerned. "You're going to be very lonely in San Francisco this summer. Daddy is going to London to receive treatment from this new neurosurgeon he has found. Dominic will be in Europe. I shall be in Hawaii. What on earth will you do with yourself until we return?"

"I shall be very busy," Lisette said firmly. "I'm on so many charity and Democratic fund-raising committees that I've lost count. I have a series of talks to give to women's groups on French art and literature. I have the French classes I give to deprived children. My diary is exceptionally full, and I doubt if I will have time to miss any of you."

Lucy grinned. "Of course you'll miss us," she said, rising and picking up her purse. "See you later, Mom. I'll be in by ten. Bye."

"*Au revoir, chérie*," Lisette said, her smile fading as her daughter whirled from the room. She stared at her reflection in Lucy's dressing-table mirror. She would be busy as she always was, and she would be lonely. In all her years in America, she had made no real friends of her own. The friends that she lunched with and played bridge with, the friends she visited the theater and the art galleries with, were Greg's friends as well as hers. There was no one else she could talk to, no one with whom she could be herself: Lisette de Valmy, unhappily married to a man she loved too much to leave.

She put the top back on one of Lucy's lipsticks, tidying the disarray Lucy had left behind her. It would be a long summer. The London neurosurgeon, who was optimistic that he could restore movement to Greg's legs, had told him to expect a stay in London of at least three months. Perhaps Lucy was right. Perhaps she should take a trip somewhere by herself, but where? The only place she really wanted to go was London, with Greg, but he had already said he intended making the trip alone.

"Write me every day, *mon chèr*, even if it is only one line on a postcard," Lisette said as she accompanied Dominic to his flight gate. "I want to know where you are, and I shall plot your progress through Europe on a map, just as if I were a French general."

Dominic laughed, kissing her cheek. "I will." He looked down at her tenderly. "Take care," he said, and then he was gone, striding through the gate, tall and broad shouldered, moving with an athlete's muscular coordination and grace, drawing admiring feminine glances in his wake.

There was no good-bye at the flight gate when Greg left for London. Airports were one place he felt self-conscious about his disability. This time he was leaving with the fierce hope it would be the last time he would ever have to do so in a wheelchair, that when he returned, it would be on his own two feet. Dr. Muir, the London neurosurgeon who was to treat him, had achieved brilliant results with other cases similar to Greg's. Healthy tissue was to be grafted onto damaged tissue. Movement would be brought to limbs that had been previously thought permanently immobile. His own prognosis was good. There was no reason for him not to anticipate one hundred percent success.

"You have enough money in your current account for the entire time I will be gone," he said to Lisette as his chauffeur carried his bags to the car. "If you do need more, call the bank and they'll transfer it."

She didn't want to talk about money. She wanted to talk about the surgery that lay ahead of him, the possibility he would be able to walk again. She wanted to hug him, and kiss him good-bye, and tell him how very much she loved him. She said instead, "Thank you, *chéri*. Perhaps, if I take the trip to Italy, I could stay in London for a few days on my way home . . ."

"No!" His eyes had darkened. The strain of the three months ahead of him would be bad enough without the added strain of enduring, lovelessly, Lisette's presence. He had already come to terms with the fact that if and when he ever walked again, she would very probably leave him. There would be nothing further to keep her. Her duty to him would have been discharged. He said tersely, "Don't worry about me. Everything is going to be fine. I'll telephone you from the clinic. Good-bye, Lisette."

"Good-bye," she said sadly, glad that he turned away from her quickly, that he couldn't see the tears in her eyes.

Dominic's first postcard home was from Brussels.

"I'm sitting in a café on the Grand Place, and you'll never guess who is with me. Mel! She's vacationing with an aunt. From here they're going to Cologne and then down the Rhine as far as Heidelberg. The travel books say that if one sits in a café on the Grand Place for long enough, the whole world will eventually walk by, but who would have believed I would have met Mel after so many years! The incredible thing is, she hasn't changed a bit! I was sitting enjoying a beer, and then I heard this *very* English accent complaining that a pigeon had messed up her hair and when I turned around it was Mel! Must dash now. Much love, D."

Lisette read and reread the postcard. Melanie. She wondered if she was as pretty and as ebullient now as she had been as a little girl. It seemed strange to think that after all Annabel's attempts to sever the friendship that had existed between Dominic and Melanie as children, it should be renewed so eagerly after a chance meeting in a Belgian square. Fate, she decided bemusedly, and thought no more about it till Dominic's next two postcards arrived from Koblenz and Mannheim.

"Mel isn't going back home with her aunt when we reach Heidelberg. She's going to continue with me into Italy. Southern Germany is fabulous. The most beautiful countryside I've ever seen. Much love, D."

She stared down at his bold, confident handwriting, appalled. Melanie was so young. She could not imagine for a moment that Annabel's permission had been sought. If it had been, she knew it would never have been given. Dominic was the last person in the world Annabel would want consorting with her daughter. The very mention of Dominic's name would bring back memories of Luke's faithlessness. She would hate the thought of any further links between their two families almost as much as Greg would.

She wrote to him, *poste restante*, praying that her letter would reach Heidelberg before they left for Italy. She insisted that Melanie return home and that they not even consider spending the summer together. She pointed out that Melanie was very young, and that her suddenly going off with a boy she hadn't seen for years and scarcely knew,' would cause her mother untold distress. She demanded, in the strongest terms, that he telephone home immediately.

She received no reply and no telephone call. The next postcards were from Austria. The aunt had returned to England. The Alps were magnificent. The swimming in the mountain lakes breathtakingly cold. By the beginning of the following week they hoped to be in Italy.

There had been nothing she could do. She had dialed international information and had asked the operator for Annabel's telephone number, but the number was not listed. She had been ashamed of her relief. By the end of July, postcards were coming from Italy—from Pisa and Florence. They were in love with Florence. They thought they might never leave. Lisette had felt faint and wondered why there was no reaction from Annabel. By the beginning of August, she was convinced that neither the aunt nor Melanie had told Annabel who was accompanying her daughter on her extended holiday.

She had other worries too. Greg had undergone surgery four times, and though some movement had been restored to his legs, there was still doubt whether success would be one hundred percent: whether he would be able to walk again, unaided.

In the last week of August, Dominic's postcard was from Geneva. They were on their way back, and he was returning to

355

England with Mel. He was going to visit his father in London. It had been a fantastic summer. He had a brilliant piece of news and couldn't wait to tell her it.

Lisette had put the postcard down weakly, filled with a sense of foreboding stronger than any she had ever known.

25

Greg leaned on the parallel bars in the physiotherapy room, sweating from every pore. He had walked three yards. It had been the equivalent of climbing Everest. Three yards, and tomorrow it would be six yards, and the day after it would be twelve. The miracle he had waited nine years for had at last taken place.

It had always been a possibility. The spinal nerves had not been severed. There had always been hope, and now that hope had become reality. He hauled himself back into his wheelchair. It was too soon to tell anyone. There would be many weeks of physiotherapy before he could walk for long periods unaided, but when he returned to America, it would be on his own two feet. The years of physical handicap would be over.

"There's a visitor to see you, Mr. Dering," a nurse said, walking into the physiotherapy room with a smile. "I told him you were nearly through in here and that you would be back in your room in about ten minutes."

Greg frowned. He wasn't expecting any visitors. No one, apart from his immediate family and Nick, knew where he was. He hadn't wanted to face pity if the surgery he had undergone had been unsuccessful.

"Did he give a name?" he asked, accepting the hand towel she offered him, wiping the sweat from his face and neck.

"The young Mr. Dering," the nurse said, her smile

dimpling her cheeks. "He's carrying the largest knapsack I've ever seen in my life. If the head nurse sees him, she'll have him thrown out before you've even had the chance to say hello."

"Then she had better not see him," Greg said with an answering grin, thrusting the towel into her waiting hand and propelling his wheelchair swiftly out into the corridor and toward the elevator.

Minutes later he catapulted into his private room and Dominic, in faded jeans and T-shirt, sprang toward him, hugging him tightly. "It's great to see you, Dad! How is everything?" His gray eyes were urgent. "Has the surgery been a success?"

"Give it another month," Greg said with a grin, "and you'll be able to see for yourself exactly what kind of a success it's been."

Dominic's whoop was ecstatic. "You mean you're going to be able to walk again? That's fantastic! Does Mom know yet? Does Lucy?"

"No, I didn't intend to tell anyone until I could also give a physical demonstration. You took me by surprise, that's all."

"That makes us even. I have some news for you that no one else knows yet. I'm engaged. We want to be married just as soon as Mel can get permission."

Greg's brow quirked quizzically. "Don't you think you're just a little bit young to be diving into marriage? And who is Mel? The last girl you were dating was Jodie Brooks."

"Jodie Brooks? Who is Jodie Brooks?" Dominic asked, laughing. "And yes, of course you know her. I'm going to marry Mel. Mel Brandon."

Every vestige of color fled from Greg's face. He tried to speak and couldn't. Tried again and choked.

"What is it?" Dominic asked in concern, his smile vanishing. "Do you want a drink of water? Shall I call for a nurse?"

Greg shook his head violently. "No! Nothing." He fought for control of speech. "You can't marry Melanie Brandon," he rasped out at last. "You can't even think of it!"

"But why not?" Dominic demanded. "I know we're both young, but we've spent the whole summer together and—"

"My God!"

357

"What is it, Dad? Are you sure I shouldn't ring for a nurse?"

"No!" As Dominic reached out to touch the bell, the wheelchair shot across the room, his father's hand clamping viselike on his wrist. "Listen to me, Dominic! You can't marry Mel! It's out of the question. Is that understood?"

"No." The bewilderment he felt was giving way to anger. He hadn't expected his father to be ecstatic at the prospect of his marrying young, but he had never envisioned such a violent response. "I love Mel. I've always loved her. And I'm going to marry her."

There was steely defiance in his voice. Greg could feel sweat breaking out on his forehead, trickling down his spine. "Are you lovers?" he demanded harshly.

A spasm of shock flared across Dominic's face. "No," he said angrily, color mounting his cheeks. "You think she's pregnant, don't you? You think that's why we're so eager to get married! It isn't like that. We're in love and we want to get married, but we're not lovers! Not yet!"

"*Thank Christ!*" Greg passed a hand across his eyes. He was in a nightmare from which there was no waking. There was no way, without giving him a reason, that Dominic would cease seeing Melanie. No way he could prevent their relationship from deepening into one of incest.

"You can't marry Melanie," he repeated, his voice raw. "Please take my word for it, Dominic. Please trust me."

"No!" It was the first ugly quarrel they had ever had, and he didn't understand why they were having it. He picked up his rucksack, his face white. "I'm sorry, Dad, but I'm going to marry Mel."

Greg's face was haggard. It was the most terrible moment of his life, and there was no avoiding it. If he didn't speak now, more sins would be innocently heaped upon the multitude of sins that had gone before. "You can't marry Melanie," he said brokenly, and then, at last, despairingly, "She's your half-sister."

Dominic stared at him and then gave an awkward laugh. "You're not well, Dad. You're hallucinating." He walked up to Greg and put his hand on his shoulder, giving it a reassuring squeeze. "I guess they've been pumping you full of drugs. You need a rest. I'll come back and see you later."

Greg seized the hand on his shoulder, his eyes glittering, the line of his mouth merciless. "I'm not drugged! Nothing on God's earth would have induced me to tell you the truth if it wasn't for the thought of the two of you marrying! Now listen to me, Dominic! Luke Brandon is your father. You were conceived before I even met your mother. When we married, she thought Brandon was dead. Now do you understand?" His eyes were like burning coals. "*You can never marry Melanie!*"

Dominic backed away from him. "You're lying," he whispered. "She isn't my sister . . . She can't be my sister . . . It's too horrible. Too monstrous . . ." He blundered into the door. "Oh Jesus! You're lying! Please tell me you're lying!"

Greg sped his wheelchair over to him and grabbed hold of his hands. "I'm not lying, Dominic! It's the truth, and it has to be lived with!"

"Oh Jesus *God!*" Dominic wrenched his hands from Greg's hold. "How could you not tell me . . . All these years . . ." Tears poured down his cheeks. "I thought you were my father . . . I thought—" He crashed dizzily across to the handbasin and vomited.

"Dominic! Please!" Greg's voice was agonized. "In every way that matters, I *am* your father! I love you . . . care for you . . . am proud of you."

"*No!*" Dominic raised his tortured face from the basin. "Brandon is my father! Oh Jesus! *Brandon!*" He stumbled over to the door. "I'll never forgive you! I'll never forgive any of you! Not my mother! Not Brandon! I never want to see you again! Not for as long as I live!"

"*Dominic!*"

The door rocketed shut, and by the time Greg had wrenched it open, Dominic was at the far end of the hospital corridor, running, weaving out of the way of astonished visitors and medical staff, heading for the nearest flight of stairs.

"*DOMINIC!*" he roared again, but it was too late. His son was gone.

Dominic stumbled out into the street and knew he was going to be ill again. He vomited into the gutter, staggered forward a couple of paces, and vomited again. People looked at him with contempt, walking around him, keeping their

distance. He was uncaring—blind and deaf and dumb with
pain. He had never envisioned there could be such agony. It
ripped through him, tearing him apart until he felt he was
bleeding to death from the wounds his father's words had
inflicted. No. Not his father. Luke Brandon was his father. A
slick, smooth-talking Englishman whom he had never liked,
even as a child. He gasped for breath. It wasn't possible to live
with such pain. It wasn't possible to bear it. And Melanie.
Dear God in heaven! *Melanie!*

He lurched out into the traffic, buses and taxicabs
swerving violently to miss him. Horns blared. People shouted.
Melanie. How could he tell Melanie? How could he possibly
go through life without Melanie?

He was supposed to have met her outside the National
Gallery in Trafalgar Square at one o'clock. He couldn't have
found his way there if he had tried. He didn't know where he
was, or where he was going. A policeman stopped him and
asked him politely if he needed any assistance. He had said
that he didn't, tears streaming down his face. He staggered
through a maze of smart streets that brought him eventually to
the hurtling thoroughfare of Oxford Street. There was a small,
tree-lined square beyond it. He collapsed onto one of the
benches, burying his head in his hands, sobbing like a child.

She was still waiting for him, five hours later, when a
taxicab unloaded him outside the National Gallery's front
entrance.

She ran toward him, dark curls bouncing. "Dominic!
What's happened? What's wrong?" Her pretty face, usually so
rosy and merry, was pinched with anxiety. "Is it your father? Is
he . . . ?"

"Dad's fine." He wondered how he could possibly say the
word. Greg wasn't his father. Luke Brandon was his father.
Luke Brandon. Melanie's father. Their father. He felt as if he
were in a Bosch painting, as if hell were all around him—
pressing in on him, burying him alive.

"But you're so late . . ." She tucked her hand into his.
"You look ghastly, Dom. What is it? What's happened?"

He tried to remove her hand from his arm but couldn't.
His limbs were leaden, weighed down with grief. "I've been
walking . . . thinking . . ." His voice was unrecognizable,
even to himself. He knew what it was he had to do. He knew

what he had to say to her. He couldn't tell her the truth. He couldn't fill her life with the horror his own would always be filled with. He thought of their nights together in Italy—of their closeness as they had lain together in the shelter of their small tent, of her softness, her warmth, his mouth on the unblemished beauty of her skin, his hands on her small, round breasts. He said, "We've been too rash, Mel. It was a good vacation, a super trip. But it's over now. We're idiots to try and make more of it than there is."

"*Dom!*" Her hand fell away from his arm, her eyes widening, incredulous. "I don't understand . . ."

"You're too young, Mel. It's crazy to think of becoming engaged at our ages."

"We don't have to be engaged if you don't want to be. All we have to do is be together."

"No." He couldn't look at her. There was a statue of a British king standing a yard or so away from them, and he stared at it fixedly. "It was a good trip, Mel. I won't forget it. But I'm not going with you to Kent. I'm flying back home tonight."

"*Dom!*" Her cry was anguished. "Dom, you can't mean it! Please tell me you don't mean it!" Her pretty face, always so happy, so vital, was white and devastated. "Dom—"

She reached out again for him, and he knew he couldn't endure another second. "I love you, Mel," he gasped, then spun away from her, charging through the tourists thronging the pavement, running out into the square, his arm high, flinging himself into the first taxicab to swerve to a halt for him.

"*Dom!*" He could hear her frantic cry above the roar of the surrounding traffic. "*Dom!*"

He didn't look around. It was over. He no longer had a family. He no longer had Mel.

"Where to?" the cab driver asked.

"Heathrow Airport."

He had his credit cards. He had the clothes in his knapsack. And before he faced a life in which his mother, and Greg and Lucy, and Mel had no part, there was one thing he had to do. He had to speak to the man who had fathered him. He had to go to Normandy and tell Luke Brandon that he knew he was his son.

* * *

361

"There's a telephone call for you from America, Mr. Dering," a nurse said, popping her head around the door, handing him the telephone receiver.

Greg was still panting, his fingers locked on the arms of his wheelchair, his face ashen. Her smile vanished. "Are you all right, Mr. Dering?"

"Yes, perfectly." The last thing he wanted were questions and well-meaning interference.

The nurse frowned, certain that he was lying.

"Thank you, nurse." His voice was abrupt. Her brows rose slightly. In the three months he had been in her care, she had never met with anything but civility from him. She left the room, vaguely perturbed, wondering if she should mention Mr. Dering's change of temper to the head nurse to pass along to his doctor.

Greg closed his eyes for a moment, struggling for composure. A call from America. It would be from Nick. Agency business. He looked at his watch. Twelve-thirty. Four-thirty A.M. in California. It was obviously something important. His fingers closed around the telephone receiver.

"Hi, Nick. What's the trouble?"

"It isn't Nick," Lisette said, her voice faint, her accent thick as it always was when she was distressed. "Papa is dead—" She broke off and he knew that she was crying. "I'm flying to Paris tonight. The funeral is Thursday—"

Christ! That was all he needed. A family funeral. Dominic unreachable. Brandon at Valmy. Lisette unaware that her son knew the truth of his parentage and the way she had deceived him.

"I'll be there," he said harshly.

"But your treatment, *chéri*—"

A spasm of pain crossed his face. He couldn't hear her use the careless endearment without remembering when it had been used in passion. "*Je t'adore, chéri. Je t'aime, chéri.*"

"I've recovered from the surgery," he said abruptly. "The physiotherapy won't suffer from a few days' interruption." He wondered how he would be able to bear seeing her again. She had destroyed not only his life but Dominic's as well. They would never be a family again. Dominic was lost to both of them.

362

Her voice was warm with gratitude. "*Merci, chéri. Au revoir.*"

His hand was trembling as he replaced the receiver. He would have to tell her. It seemed curiously fitting that when he did so, they would be at Valmy. He rang for the nurse. He needed a bag packed, a flight booked.

Lisette landed at Orly Airport the next morning and hired a chauffeur-driven car to take her and Lucy to Valmy. It had been a long, tiring flight, and she was emotionally drained. This was not how she had wanted to return home. Her eyes were dark with grief as their car sped through the French countryside.

"You loved *Grand-père* very much, didn't you?" Lucy asked, slipping her hand comfortingly into her mother's.

"Yes, *chérie*. He was always patient. Always kind." Her eyes were full of shadow as she looked back down the years, remembering. "He understood me and knew more about me than anyone knew."

"More than Dad?" Lucy asked with surprise.

"Yes," Lisette replied, looking out the car window at the passing countryside, her voice so sad that Lucy fell silent.

They drove through Evreux and Bernay, on into the heart of Normandy. The September sun was hot; the fields of ripened wheat, golden. White wisteria and even whiter roses were thick on the walls of the frame houses with their carved facades and high, slate roofs.

"I couldn't live here," Lucy said suddenly as they plunged down a high-hedged lane flanked by lush pastureland. "It's so quiet and tidy and . . . un-American."

Lisette said nothing. She was wondering how she would ever find the strength to leave.

"Isn't Uncle Luke's farm near here?" Lucy asked as Bayeux was left behind them and they sped on toward the coast.

"Yes," Lisette said, her voice dying in her throat. "Somewhere near here."

Luke. He would be at the funeral. He would probably even be at Valmy. There would be his new wife to meet. There would be the strain of all of them being together under the same roof: Luke, Greg, herself. The car window was open, and she could smell the salt tang of the sea. They were nearly there. The beech woods closed around them, the sunlight amber as it streamed through the leaves, the bracken already turning to autumn gold. They surged up the last incline; the trees fell away, and Valmy stood before them in all its ancient splendor. Nothing had changed. It was still beautiful, still perfect—its windows catching the sunlight, its turret piercing the skyline like a castle in a children's fairytale.

As they swept around the circle of grass fronting the entrance, the heavy, brass-studded door opened, and her mother stepped out to greet them.

"Welcome home, *ma chère*," she said, her voice thick with tears as Lisette flung herself from the car, running toward her, her arms outstretched.

The tears that Lisette had fought back during the long journey could be checked no longer. As her arms closed around the fragile figure of her mother, they flowed down her cheeks unrestrainedly. Until that moment, she had not truly been able to believe in the fact of her father's death—not until her mother had stepped forward to greet her, alone.

"There is tea waiting for you in the salon," Héloïse said at last, the skin like parchment across her still superb cheekbones, her eyes blue-shadowed with grief. "Dominic arrived here two hours ago. Greg landed some thirty minutes ago. He telephoned from the airport and should be with us shortly."

"Dominic?" Lisette asked incredulously. "But how did he know? Who told him?"

"No one had told him, *ma chère*," Héloïse said as they entered the salon. "He was very deeply shocked and distressed."

"But where is he? I thought he was in London . . ."

"He paid his respects to his grandfather's body and then said he wanted to visit Luke. He wasn't sure just where the farm was and so I told him. He borrowed the gardener's bicycle and left about an hour ago."

Lisette stared at her. "*Dominic* has gone to visit Luke? But he doesn't know Luke! They haven't met since Dominic was eight or nine years old!" She remembered Melanie and sat down weakly. "Oh, no!" she whispered. "Not now . . . Of all times . . ."

Héloïse began to pour tea from an elegant silver teapot.

"There is no reason why Dominic should not visit Luke, *chérie*. Without Luke, I don't know how your father would have managed these last years. He called in on him every day. If he had been his son, he couldn't have been kinder to him."

Kind. It was not a quality Lisette had ever associated with Luke. And now Dominic was, in all probability, going to tell him he was in love with Melanie, that they had spent the summer together.

"I don't think I want any tea, Maman," she said, rising unsteadily. "I think I'd like some fresh air. A walk . . ."

"Do you want me to come with you?" Lucy asked, concerned.

"No, thank you, *chérie*." She didn't want anyone. She wanted to be alone. To think. She wanted to know what she was going to say to Greg when he arrived, and she had to tell him about Dominic's and Melanie's love affair. What would she say to Dominic if Luke had been callous enough to tell him the reason for their two families becoming estranged?

With her head aching, she stepped out of the salon and into the flagstoned hall where Dieter had died, walking past the now rarely opened doors of the restored grand dining room, through the kitchen and the courtyard beyond. She could hardly breathe for memories. Dieter. Elise. Her father. Rommel, sweeping down on Valmy flanked by outriders. Greg in his jeep, a helmet crammed on his curly brown hair, his eyes crinkling at the corners, his teeth flashing in a broad, irresistible smile.

She walked past the stables and down toward the rose gardens. There was still a mass of bloom: the Gloire de Dijon her father had so loved; pale-flushed Ophelias. She wondered where the years had gone to, and knew, if they had been filled with love given and love received, she would not be regretting them. But only a few short months had been spent in loving. The rest had been arid years of guilt and deceit—lonely, wasted years, gone beyond recall.

26

Dominic skimmed down the high-hedged Norman lanes, his handsome young face hard, his jaw clenched. In the past twenty-four hours he had lost everything that was dear to him: his respect for his mother, his belief that Greg was his father, the prospect of a future with Mel as his wife. And now his grandfather was dead.

He was dazed by grief, numb with it. How could Greg and his mother have continued a friendship with Luke after their marriage? It made no sense at all. How could Luke, being his father, have shown no sign of the fact? As hard as Dominic tried, he could remember no act of partiality shown to him by Luke. He had always been indifferent to him. A nerve throbbed at the corner of his jaw. But then Luke had always been indifferent toward Melanie as well. Children bored him, and he had never made any pretense of liking them.

A signpost with the farm name on it swung gently in the breeze at the roadside. Dominic veered down a cart track, cycling between rich cornfields and apple orchards, surprised to find the farm was a working one and that the sign was not just a pretentious and empty title. The building itself was manorial: large and sprawling, with a slate roof and leaded windows. In espousing the country life, Luke Brandon had done so in style and comfort. Dominic's heart began to slam as he skidded to a halt. Surely the knowledge that Luke was his father should make him feel differently about him. Surely he should not still feel the innate distaste for him that he had always felt.

The front door was made of heavy oak and was surrounded by baskets and tubs of flowers. He dropped the

366

knocker hard against the wood with a spurt of anger. This was the man who had taken advantage of his mother when she was only eighteen years old, who had, from what Greg had told him, led his mother to believe that he was dead. Rage flooded through him, and as he reached out for the door knocker again, the door swung suddenly open.

She was so young that he stared at her with amazement. Her hair was dark, looped back softly over her ears, gathered in a ribbon at the nape of her neck. She looked so much like his mother that all he could do was stare.

"Can I help you?" she asked curiously.

He struggled to recover his equilibrium. "Yes. I would like to speak to Luke Brandon. My name is Dominic Dering."

Her eyes lit with recognition, and her mouth curved into a welcoming smile. "Dominic! How nice. I've heard so much about you from Melanie. Please come in."

It was not what he had expected. He stared at her again, took a deep breath, and followed her into a wide quarry-tiled hallway.

"Luke, *chéri!* We have a visitor!" she called from the foot of the broad sweep of highly polished wood stairs.

"Coming!" From somewhere above them a door slammed, footsteps were heard approaching the head of the stairs. Dominic's throat tightened. His father. It was incredible. Unbelievable.

Luke began to descend the stairs, adjusting the sleeves of a turtleneck sweater, running his hand through his hair. The door was still open, sunlight streaming into the hall below him. He could see Lisette. Petite, slender, her dark hair pulled madonnalike away from her face, her strongly marked brows heightening the delicacy of her cheekbones and jaw. And he could see Dieter. Strong, powerful, every line of his body tense, his blond hair tousled, his harsh, hard-boned face raw with pain. He stumbled, his hand shooting out to the banister to steady himself. It wasn't Lisette. It was his wife. And it wasn't Dieter.

"Who the hell—?" he began fiercely.

"It's Dominic," his wife said cheerily. "Isn't it a nice surprise?"

Luke gasped for breath, his face ashen. Dominic. His likeness to Dieter was so strong, so marked, that even now he found it hard to believe he wasn't once more at Valmy, standing at the head of the stairs, raising his pistol, taking aim, firing. "My God!" he whispered and then, abruptly, "Melanie isn't here. She isn't arriving until this evening."

It was Dominic's turn to be disoriented. "I don't understand—"

Luke descended the remaining stairs swiftly. "Melanie," he said curtly. "That's why you've come, isn't it? She said you'd had a row. She asked if she could stay for a few days before returning to school. Her ferry docks at Le Havre just after six."

Dominic's head felt as if it were splitting apart. He said hoarsely, "I didn't come here to see Mel. I came here to see you."

"Would you like a coffee?" Luke's wife asked. "An aperitif?"

"Why?" Luke asked, as they both ignored her.

"I want to talk to you."

Luke's eyes narrowed sharply. "About what?" The boy looked ill, almost deranged.

"About the war. About Valmy."

Luke's mouth tightened. So the boy knew about his father, about his father's death. He wondered who had told him. "Then let's talk outside," he said, glancing quickly at Dominic's pockets, at his belt, satisfied that the boy wasn't armed and hadn't come with a half-baked idea of revenge.

"But surely some coffee . . . ," Ginette said bewilderedly.

"Later." He dropped a swift kiss to her temple. "And some cognac as well, I think."

"But it's only two in the afternoon . . ."

Luke whistled a large, ungainly labrador to his heels and said to Dominic, "Come on, let's walk."

They stepped out onto the gravel, the dog bounding joyously ahead of them. Neither of them spoke. Luke led the way, away from the farmhouse and toward a thicket of trees. The fields on either side of them were well tended. He took a pipe out of his pocket, thumbing the tobacco down and lighting it. "Right," he said at last, when they were a good half mile from the house. "What is it you want to know?"

Dominic stopped walking, waiting until Luke also stopped and turned around to face him. "I want to know," he said, his jaw clenched, his eyes burning, "Why you have never told me that I'm your son?"

Luke took the pipe out of his mouth and blew a wreath of blue smoke skyward. It was not what he had expected, and his relief was intense. "Would you care to repeat that question?" he asked with interest. "I don't think I can have heard it right."

"You smarmy bastard!" Dominic yelled, his self-control deserting him, tears terrifyingly near to the surface. "I know damn well that you're my father! That you and my mother were lovers! That she only married Greg because she thought you were dead!"

Luke eyed him with amazement. "And just who filled your head with that nonsense?" he asked laconically.

"*Bastard!*" Dominic shouted again, his fist shooting out to Luke's jaw. Luke sidestepped swiftly, deflecting the blow with ease.

"Oh no, you don't!" he said, seizing Dominic's wrist and wrenching it halfway up his back. "Now who the hell told you that I was your father?"

"Greg!" Dominic gasped, wincing with pain.

Luke's brows shot upward and then he began to laugh. "That's funny," he said, releasing his hold of him. "My God, I wish I'd known years ago that was what he believed!"

Dominic stared at him. "Then it's not true? You're not my father?"

Luke shook his head in mock regret. "No, Dominic, I am afraid the honor is not mine."

"Then who?" Dominic began, and he suddenly remembered Melanie and he didn't care. "Oh Christ!" he gasped ecstatically, staggering with relief. "Then I can marry Melanie. *I can marry Melanie!*"

"You can if you can get her mother's permission," Luke said dryly.

"What about your permission?" Dominic asked bluntly.

Luke shrugged, his voice indifferent. "If you want to marry when you're both scarcely out of the schoolroom, I shall not exert any effort to prevent you." A smile twitched at the corner of his mouth. He wondered how long Greg had known that Dominic was not his son. How long he had believed that he, Luke, was Dominic's father. How long he had suffered. The dog circled around them, impatient for the walk to continue. "As I am not your father, don't you want to know who is?" he asked curiously.

Dominic was suddenly very still. "Do you know?"

Luke's lean, olive-toned face was amused. "Oh, yes," he said, a smile touching the corners of his mouth. "I know. I've always known."

"Then tell me."

Luke shook his head, picking up a stick and throwing it for his dog. "No," he said with infuriating complacence. "It isn't for me to tell you. It's for your mother. She'll be at Valmy by now. Héloïse said their flight landed at noon."

Dominic glanced at his watch. It was two-thirty. He had nearly four hours before meeting Melanie at the ferry. "I will ask," he said grimly, spinning on his heel and breaking into a run.

She was in the rose garden. He crashed the bicycle to the ground, then ran across the terrace and down the moss-covered steps. Her gaze flew upward, and he saw that she had been crying.

He remembered his grandfather's death and was ashamed that, in his relief over Melanie, he had forgotten it.

"Dominic!" She rose to her feet, smiling through her tears, her happiness at seeing him piercing him to the heart. She was his mother. He loved her, and whoever his father was, he knew now that it would make no difference to that love.

"Hello, Maman," he said, walking swiftly toward her, hugging her tight.

She scarcely reached his shoulder. She was wearing a black woolen dress, exquisitely cut, and sheer black stockings and black suede, open-toed shoes. Her hair was loose, falling softly about her shoulders, smelling fragrant and clean.

"I missed you, *mon chèr*," she said, smiling up at him, tears still trembling on her thick, lustrous lashes. There were pearls at her ears, a heavy rope of pearls about her neck. She looked no older than the girl Luke Brandon had married.

"I need to talk to you, Maman," Dominic said, taking her hand, beginning to walk with her down one of the petal-strewn pathways. "I need to know about my father."

"Your father?" Of all the things she had expected him to say to her, she had not expected it to be about Greg. "But he's well. The surgeon is optimistic that the last operation was a success and—"

"Not Greg, Maman," he said steadily. "My father."

She froze, the blood draining from her face.

"I'm sorry, Maman," he said compassionately, "but I have to know the truth."

"But who told you?" she whispered. "How did you know?"

Her face was so white, it looked like carved ivory.

"Dad told me. Whoever my father is, I guess Greg will always be dad to me. He told me so himself, but I didn't believe him. I didn't understand what he meant. I do now."

"Greg told you—" She swayed.

"He thought Luke was my father. He told me that you and Luke had been lovers before he met you, that you thought Luke was dead when you married."

Her cry was the cry of a small, wounded animal.

"Why doesn't he know the truth, Maman? Why did you never tell him?"

"Because—" Her voice was choked in her throat. "Because I thought he would leave me—that he would be so shocked by the truth that he would never want to see me again—"

Dominic took hold of her shoulders gently. "He loves you, Maman. There is nothing in this world you could do that would shock him so much that he would leave you."

"I killed that love many years ago," she said, her eyes wide and dark and anguished.

He shook his head, feeling suddenly older than her and wiser. "There is no way you could kill his love for you, Maman. Not ever. Now I want to know. Who is my father?"

She closed her eyes for a second, and when she opened them, the tears sparkling on her eyelashes were no longer for Henri. "Come with me, *mon chèr*," she said, taking his hand, her fingers interlocking tightly with his. "Let me show you." She led him out of the rose garden and into the meadow beyond, the meadow that led to the tiny church and the overgrown graveyard and the cherry tree leaning over a blossom-covered grave.

"His name was Dieter Meyer," she said, her voice thick with relief and love, "and he came to Valmy in the spring of 1944—"

She told him everything. She told him about her fateful bicycle ride, about her agony at falling in love with a German. She told him about Rommel, and Elise, and their efforts to pass information to the Allies. She told him about Paul Gilles and André Caldron, and the way they had died. She told him about Black Orchestra. She told him about their meetings in the small turret room, about their plans to be married, of their delight when they had known they were to have a child.

She told him about D day, and about Dieter's death, and the only thing she did not tell him was the identity of the soldier who had fired the fatal shots. She told him about the tortured, grief-stricken days that had followed, of how she thought she had lost the baby, of her decision to marry Greg. And she told him of Greg's return in 1945, of his part in the liberation of Dachau, and of her conviction that he would leave her if he ever learned that she had loved a German.

"You were wrong, Maman," Dominic said at last, gently. "He believed and lived with something far worse than the truth." He plucked a wild rose and laid it on his father's grave, and then he said, "I'm going to meet Melanie, Maman. I'm going to bring her back to Valmy."

When her mother died, Valmy would be hers. She would never live in it again, but she knew that Dominic would, that he would live in it with Melanie, that his children would run freely through the rooms his father had entered as an invader.

He left her, and she stood for a long time thinking about the past, about the pain Greg had endured, about the depth of his love for her. The sun began to lose its mid-afternoon heat, and she still stood, looking down at Dieter's grave, knowing that ever since his death she had lived in a Gethsemane of her own making. Love had been within her grasp all along. Greg had known that Dominic was not his son, and it had made no difference to the love he had given her. She knew now that if she had told him about Dieter, it, too, would have made no difference to the love he felt for her. She had grossly underestimated the man she had married, and because she had done so, because she had been a coward when she should have been brave, they had known years of unhappiness.

She heard the familiar chink of wheelchair wheels and spun around. The shadows were long on the grass, the sun flushed with rose, low in the sky.

He halted a yard or so away from her. He was wearing jeans and an open-necked linen shirt, his muscles beneath the fine fabric hard and strong. There were no lines of pain on his face. He looked bronze and healthy, and she wanted him so much that she felt physically weak.

"Dominic told me where to find you," he said, and there was an expression in his eyes she had never seen there before Love and relief and compassion inextricably mixed. "He told me why you were here."

"And you understand?" She could hardly breathe.

"Yes," he said gently. "Now I do."

"Oh, *chéri!*" She stepped toward him, her hands outstretched. "Please forgive me!"

A smile tugged at the corners of his mouth. "I forgave you a long time ago, sweetheart," he said, and then, as she gasped with disbelief, he rose to his feet and closed the distance between them with sure, firm steps.

"*Greg!*" Her face was radiant as his arms closed around her. "Why didn't you tell me? Why didn't you telephone?"

He smiled down at her. "Because I wanted to show you," he said huskily, "and now I want you to show me something," and very gently he led her toward the cherry tree and the grassy mound that lay beneath it.

For a long time they stood silently, hands clasped, and then he said compassionately, "Did you love him very much, sweetheart?"

"Yes." Her voice was thick with memories. "With all my heart." She raised her face to his, the silk-dark fall of her hair soft against her cheeks. "And that is how I love you, *chéri.* Always and forever."

He turned her around to face him, and above the slope of his shoulder she could see Valmy, its walls blue-spangled in the early evening light. For eighteen years she had been homesick for it, pining for Norman fields and high-hedged lanes and the chill, gray sea of the Channel. She knew, as his arm tightened around her, that she would never be homesick for it again, that the years of pain and loneliness were at an end.

373

"You are my life, Lisette," he whispered, and as his mouth came down on hers, hot and sweet, the shadows of the cherry tree reached out, touching them gently, before merging softly into the deepening dusk.